D1639193

Great Russian Stories

To a great roommate —
Christmas 1967.

Bob Powers

Great
RUSSIAN
Stories

✠
✠ ✠ ✠
✠ ✠
✠ ✠ ✠
✠

Selected by Isai Kamen

VINTAGE BOOKS
A DIVISION OF RANDOM HOUSE
New York

Acknowledgments:

Lermontov's "Taman," from *A Hero of Our Time,* is a revised version of an edition published by Alfred A. Knopf, Inc.; Copyright, 1924, by Alfred A. Knopf, Inc.

Turgenev's "The Singers," from *A Sportsman's Notebook,* is reprinted by arrangement with The Cresset Press Ltd.

Dostoevsky's "The Peasant Marey" and "The Dream of a Ridiculous Man," translated by David Magarshack, are published by arrangement with John Lehmann Ltd.

Dostoevsky's "The Crocodile," translated by Constance Garnett, is used with the permission of The Macmillan Company.

Chekhov's "Gooseberries" is from *The Portable Chekhov* edited by Avrahm Yarmolinsky; Copyright 1947 by The Viking Press, Inc., N.Y., and reprinted by their permission.

VINTAGE BOOKS
are published by ALFRED A. KNOPF, INC.
and RANDOM HOUSE, INC.

Contents

✠

Alexander Pushkin

The Queen of Spades

✠

The Queen of Spades signifies secret ill will,
NEW FORTUNETELLER

I

When bleak was the weather,
The friends came together
To play.
The stakes, they were doubled;
The sly ones, untroubled,
Were gay.
They all had their innings,
And chalked up their winnings,
And so
They kept busy together
Throughout the bleak weather,
Oho!

There was a card party at the rooms of Narumov of the Horse Guards. The long winter night passed away imperceptibly, and it was five o'clock in the morning before the company sat down to supper. Those who had won, ate with a good appetite; the others sat staring absently at their empty plates. When the champagne appeared, however, the conversation became more animated, and all took a part in it.

"And how did you fare, Surin?" asked the host.

"Oh, I lost, as usual. I must confess that I am unlucky: I never raise the original stakes, I always keep cool, I never allow anything to put me out, and yet I always lose!"

"And you have never been tempted? You have never staked on several cards in succession? . . . Your firmness astonishes me."

"But what do you think of Herman?" said one of the guests,
pointing to a young engineer. "He has never had a card in his
hand in his life, he has never in his life doubled the stake, and
yet he sits here till five o'clock in the morning watching our
play."

"Play interests me very much," said Herman: "but I am
not in the position to sacrifice the necessary in the hope of
winning the superfluous."

"Herman is a German: he is prudent—that is all!" observed
Tomski. "But if there is one person that I cannot understand,
it is my grandmother, the Countess Anna Fedotovna."

"How? What?" cried the guests.

"I cannot understand," continued Tomski, "how it is that
my grandmother does not punt."

"What is there remarkable about an old lady of eighty not
gambling?" said Narumov.

"Then you know nothing about her?"

"No, really; haven't the faintest idea."

"Oh! then listen. You must know that, about sixty years
ago, my grandmother went to Paris, where she created quite
a sensation. People used to run after her to catch a glimpse of
'la Vénus moscovite.' Richelieu courted her, and my grandmother maintains that he almost blew out his brains in consequence of her cruelty. At that time ladies used to play faro.
On one occasion at the Court, she lost a very considerable
sum to the Duke of Orleans. On returning home, my grandmother removed the patches from her face, took off her hoops,
informed my grandfather of her loss at the gaming table, and
ordered him to pay the money. My deceased grandfather, as
far as I remember, was a sort of butler to my grandmother. He
dreaded her like fire; but, on hearing of such a heavy loss, he
almost went out of his mind; he calculated the various sums
she had lost, and pointed out to her that in six months she had
spent half a million, that neither their Moscow nor Saratov
estates were near Paris, and finally refused point-blank to pay
the debt. My grandmother slapped his face and slept by herself as a sign of her displeasure. The next day she sent for
her husband, hoping that this domestic punishment had produced an effect upon him, but she found him inflexible. For
the first time in her life, she condescended to offer reasons and
explanations. She thought she could convince him by pointing
out to him that there are debts and debts, and that there is a
great difference between a Prince and a coachmaker. But it

was all in vain, grandfather was in revolt. He said 'no,' and that was all. My grandmother did not know what to do. She was on friendly terms with a very remarkable man. You have heard of Count St. Germain, about whom so many marvelous stories are told. You know that he represented himself as the Wandering Jew, as the discover of the elixir of life, of the philosopher's stone, and so forth. Some laughed at him as a charlatan; but Casanova, in his memoirs, says that he was a spy. But be that as it may, St. Germain, in spite of the mystery surrounding him, was a man of decent appearance and had an amiable manner in company. Even to this day my grandmother is in love with him, and becomes quite angry if anyone speaks disrespectfully of him. My grandmother knew that St. Germain had large sums of money at his disposal. She resolved to have recourse to him, and she wrote a letter to him asking him to come to her without delay. The queer old man immediately waited upon her and found her overwhelmed with grief. She described to him in the blackest colors the barbarity of her husband, and ended by declaring that she placed all her hopes in his friendship and graciousness.

"St. Germain reflected.

" 'I could advance you the sum you want,' said he; 'but I know that you would not rest easy until you had paid me back, and I should not like to bring fresh troubles upon you. But there is another way of getting out of your difficulty: you can win back your money.'

" 'But, my dear Count,' replied my grandmother, 'I tell you that we haven't any money left.'

" 'Money is not necessary,' replied St. Germain. 'Be pleased to listen to me.'

"Then he revealed to her a secret, for which each of us would give a good deal . . ."

The young gamblers listened with increased attention. Tomski lit his pipe, pulled at it, and continued:

"That same evening my grandmother went to Versailles *au jeu de la Reine.* The Duke of Orleans kept the bank; my grandmother excused herself in an offhanded manner for not having yet paid her debt, by inventing some little story, and then began to play against him. She chose three cards and played them one after the other: all three won at the start and my grandmother recovered all that she had lost."

"Mere chance!" said one of the guests.

"A fairy tale!" observed Herman.

"Perhaps they were marked cards!" said a third.

"I do not think so," replied Tomski gravely.

"What!" said Narumov. "You have a grandmother who knows how to hit upon three lucky cards in succession, and you have never yet succeeded in getting the secret of it out of her?"

"That's the deuce of it!" replied Tomski. "She had four sons, one of whom was my father; all four are desperate gamblers, and yet not to one of them did she ever reveal her secret, although it would not have been a bad thing either for them or for me. But this is what I heard from my uncle, Count Ivan Ilyich, and he assured me, on his honor, that it was true. The late Chaplitski—the same who died in poverty after having squandered millions—once lost, in his youth, about three hundred thousand rubles—to Zorich, if I remember rightly. He was in despair. My grandmother, who was always very hard on extravagant young men, took pity, however, upon Chaplitski. She mentioned to him three cards, telling him to play them one after the other, at the same time exacting from him a solemn promise that he would never play cards again as long as he lived. Chaplitski then went to his victorious opponent, and they began a fresh game. On the first card he staked fifty thousand rubles and won at once; he doubled the stake and won again, doubled it again, and won, not only all he had lost, but something over and above that. . . .

"But it is time to go to bed: it is a quarter to six already."

And indeed it was already beginning to dawn; the young men emptied their glasses and then took leave of one another.

II

*—Il paraît que monsieur est
décidément pour les suivantes.
—Que voulez-vous, madame? Elles
sont plus fraîches.*

SOCIETY TALK

The old Countess X. was seated in her dressing room in front of her looking glass. Three maids stood around her. One held a small pot of rouge, another a box of hairpins, and the third a tall cap with bright red ribbons. The Countess had no longer the slightest pretensions to beauty—hers had faded long ago—but she still preserved all the habits of her youth, dressed in strict accordance with the fashion of the seventies, and made as long and as careful a toilette as she would have done sixty years previously. Near the window, at an embroidery frame, sat a young lady, her ward.

"Good morning, *Grand'maman*," said a young officer, entering the room. "*Bonjour, Mademoiselle Lise. Grand'maman*, I have a favor to ask of you."

"What is it, Paul?"

"I want you to let me introduce one of my friends to you, and to allow me to bring him to the ball on Friday."

"Bring him direct to the ball and introduce him to me there. Were you at N.'s yesterday?"

"Yes; everything went off very pleasantly, and dancing kept up until five o'clock. How beautiful Mme. Yeletskaya was!"

"But, my dear, what is there beautiful about her? You should have seen her grandmother, Princess Darya Petrovna! By the way, she must have aged very much, Princess Darya Petrovna."

"How do you mean, aged?" cried Tomski thoughtlessly. "She died seven years ago."

The young lady raised her head and made a sign to the young man. He then remembered that the old Countess was never to be informed of the death of any of her contemporaries, and he bit his lip. But the Countess heard the news with the greatest indifference.

"Died!" said she. "And I did not know it. We were appointed maids of honor at the same time, and when we were being presented, the Empress . . ."

And the Countess for the hundredth time related the anecdote to her grandson.

"Come, Paul," said she, when she had finished her story, "help me to get up. Lizanka, where is my snuffbox?"

And the Countess with her three maids went behind a screen to finish her toilette. Tomski was left alone with the young lady.

"Who is the gentleman you wish to introduce to the Countess?" asked Lizaveta Ivanovna in a whisper.

"Narumov. Do you know him?"

"No. Is he in the army or is he a civilian?"

"In the army."

"Is he in the Engineers?"

"No, in the Cavalry. What made you think that he was in the Engineers?"

The young lady smiled, but made no reply.

"Paul," cried the Countess, from behind the screen, "send me some new novel, only, pray, not the kind they write nowadays."

"What do you mean, *Grand'maman?*"

"That is, a novel, in which the hero strangles neither his father nor his mother, and in which there are no drowned bodies. I have a great horror of them."

"There are no such novels nowadays. Would you like a Russian one?"

"Are there any Russian novels? Send me one, my dear, please send me one!"

"Good-by, *Grand'maman:* I am in a hurry. . . . Good-by, Lizaveta Ivanovna. What, then, made you think that Narumov was in the Engineers?"

And Tomski withdrew from the dressing room.

Lizaveta Ivanovna was left alone: she laid aside her work and began to look out of the window. A few moments afterwards, from behind a corner house on the other side of the street, a young officer appeared. A deep blush covered her cheeks; she took up her work again and bent her head over the frame. At the same moment the Countess returned, completely dressed.

"Order the carriage, Lizaveta," said she; "we will go out for a drive."

Lizaveta arose from the frame and began to put away her work.

"What is the matter with you, my dear, are you deaf?" cried the Countess. "Order the carriage to be got ready at once."

"I will do so this moment," replied the young lady, and ran into the anteroom.

A servant entered and gave the Countess some books from Prince Pavel Alexandrovich.

"Tell him that I am much obliged to him," said the Countess. "Lizaveta! Lizaveta! Where are you running to?"

"I am going to dress."

"There is plenty of time, my dear. Sit down here. Open the first volume and read aloud to me."

Her companion took the book and read a few lines.

"Louder," said the Countess. "What is the matter with you,

my dear? Have you lost your voice? Wait—give me that foot-stool—a little nearer—that will do!"

Lizaveta read two more pages. The Countess yawned.

"Put the book down," said she. "What a lot of nonsense! Send it back to Prince Pavel with my thanks. . . . But where is the carriage?"

"The carriage is ready," said Lizaveta, looking out into the street.

"How is it that you are not dressed?" said the Countess. "I must always wait for you. It is intolerable, my dear!"

Liza hastened to her room. She had not been there two minutes, before the Countess began to ring with all her might. The three maids came running in at one door and the valet at another.

"How is it that you don't come when I ring for you?" said the Countess. "Tell Lizaveta Ivanovna that I am waiting for her."

Lizaveta returned with her hat and cloak on.

"At last you are here!" said the Countess. "But why such an elaborate toilette? Whom do you intend to captivate? What sort of weather is it? It seems rather windy."

"No, Your Ladyship, it is very calm," replied the valet.

"You always speak thoughtlessly. Open the window. So it is: windy and bitterly cold. Unharness the horses. Lizaveta, we won't go out—there was no need for you to deck yourself out like that."

"And that's my life!" thought Lizaveta Ivanovna.

And, in truth, Lizaveta Ivanovna was a very unfortunate creature. "It is bitter to eat the bread of another," says Dante, "and hard to climb his stair." But who can know what the bitterness of dependence is so well as the poor companion of an old lady of quality? The Countess X. had by no means a bad heart, but she was capricious, like a woman who had been spoiled by the world, as well as avaricious and sunk in cold egoism, like all old people who are no longer capable of affection, and whose thoughts are with the past and not the present. She participated in all the vanities of the great world, went to balls, where she sat in a corner, painted and dressed in old-fashioned style, like an ugly but indispensable ornament of the ballroom; the guests on entering approached her and bowed profoundly, as if in accordance with a set ceremony, but after that nobody took any further notice of her. She received the whole town at her house, and observed the strictest

etiquette, although she could no longer recognize people. Her
numerous domestics, growing fat and old in her antechamber
and servants' hall, did just as they liked, and vied with each
other in robbing the moribund old woman. Lizaveta Ivanovna
was the martyr of the household. She poured tea, and was
reprimanded for using too much sugar; she read novels aloud
to the Countess, and the faults of the author were visited upon
her head; she accompanied the Countess in her walks, and
was held answerable for the weather or the state of the pavement. A salary was attached to the post, but she very rarely
received it, although she was expected to dress like everybody
else, that is to say, like very few indeed. In society she played
the most pitiable role. Everybody knew her, and nobody paid
her any attention. At balls she danced only when a partner was
wanted, and ladies would only take hold of her arm when it
was necessary to lead her out of the room to attend to their
dresses. She had a great deal of *amour propre,* and felt her
position keenly, and she looked about her with impatience for
a deliverer to come to her rescue; but the young men, calculating in their giddiness, did not condescend to pay her any
attention, although Lizaveta Ivanovna was a hundred times
prettier than the bare-faced and cold-hearted marriageable
girls around whom they hovered. Many a time did she quietly
slink away from the dull and elegant drawing room, to go and
cry in her own poor little room, in which stood a screen, a
chest of drawers, a looking glass and a painted bedstead, and
where a tallow candle burned feebly in a copper candlestick.

One morning—this was about two days after the card party
described at the beginning of this story, and a week previous
to the scene at which we have just assisted—Lizaveta Ivanovna
was seated near the window at her embroidery frame, when,
happening to look out into the street, she caught sight of a
young officer of the Engineers, standing motionless with his
eyes fixed upon her window. She lowered her head and went
on again with her work. About five minutes afterwards she
looked out again—the young officer was still standing in the
same place. Not being in the habit of coquetting with passing
officers, she did not continue to gaze out into the street, but
went on sewing for a couple of hours, without raising her head.
Dinner was announced. She rose up and began to put her
embroidery away, but glancing casually out the window, she
perceived the officer again. This seemed to her very strange.
After dinner she went to the window with a certain feeling

of uneasiness, but the officer was no longer there—and she thought no more about him.

A couple of days afterwards, just as she was stepping into the carriage with the Countess, she saw him again. He was standing close to the entrance, with his face half concealed by his beaver collar, his black eyes flashing beneath his hat. Lizaveta felt alarmed, though she knew not why, and she trembled as she seated herself in the carriage.

On returning home, she hastened to the window—the officer was standing in his accustomed place, with his eyes fixed upon her. She drew back, a prey to curiosity and agitated by a feeling which was quite new to her.

From that time on not a day passed without the young officer making his appearance under the window at the customary hour. A spontaneous relationship was established between them. Sitting in her place at work, she would feel his approach; and raising her head, she would look at him longer and longer each day. The young man seemed to be very grateful to her for it: she saw with the sharp eye of youth, how a sudden flush covered his pale cheeks each time that their glances met. By the end of the week she smiled at him. . . .

When Tomski asked permission of his grandmother the Countess to present one of his friends to her, the young girl's heart beat violently. But hearing that Narumov was not an engineer, but in the Horse Guards, she regretted that by her indiscreet question, she had betrayed her secret to the volatile Tomski.

Herman was the son of a Russified German, from whom he had inherited a small fortune. Being firmly convinced of the necessity of insuring his independence, Herman did not touch even the interest on his capital, but lived on his pay, without allowing himself the slightest luxury. Moreover, he was reserved and ambitious, and his companions rarely had an opportunity of making merry at the expense of his excessive parsimony. He had strong passions and an ardent imagination, but his firmness of disposition preserved him from the ordinary errors of youth. Thus, though a gambler at heart, he never touched a card, for he considered his position did not allow him—as he said—"to risk the necessary in the hope of winning the superfluous," yet he would sit for nights together at the card table and follow with feverish excitement the various turns of the game.

The story of the three cards had produced a powerful impression upon his imagination, and all night long he could think of nothing else. "If only," he thought to himself the following evening, as he wandered through St. Petersburg, "if only the old Countess would reveal her secret to me! If she would only tell me the names of the three winning cards! Why should I not try my fortune? I must get introduced to her and win her favor—perhaps become her lover. . . . But all that will take time, and she is eighty-seven years old: she might be dead in a week, in a couple of days even! . . . And the story itself: is it credible? . . . No! Prudence, moderation and work: those are my three winning cards; that is what will increase my capital threefold, sevenfold, and procure for me ease and independence."

Musing in this manner, he walked on until he found himself in one of the principal streets of St. Petersburg, in front of a house of old-fashioned architecture. The street was blocked with carriages; one after the other they rolled up in front of the illuminated entrance. Every minute there emerged from the coaches the shapely foot of a young beauty, a spurred boot, a striped stocking above a diplomatic shoe. Fur coats and cloaks whisked past the majestic porter.

Herman stopped. "Whose house is this?" he asked the watchman at the corner.

"The Countess X.'s," replied the watchman.

Herman trembled. The strange story of the three cards again presented itself to his imagination. He began walking up and down before the house, thinking of its owner and her marvelous gift. Returning late to his modest lodging, he could not go to sleep for a long time, and when at last he did doze off, he could dream of nothing but cards, green tables, piles of banknotes and heaps of gold coins. He played card after card, firmly turning down the corners, and won uninterruptedly, raking in the gold and filling his pockets with the notes. Waking up late the next morning, he sighed over the loss of his imaginary wealth, then went out again to wander about the streets, and found himself once more in front of the Countess' house. Some unknown power seemed to draw him thither. He stopped and began to stare at the windows. In one of these he saw the head of a black-haired woman, which was bent probably over some book or handwork. The head was raised. Herman saw a fresh-cheeked face and a pair of black eyes. That moment decided his fate.

III

Vous m'écrivez, mon ange, des lettres de
quatre pages plus vite que je ne puis les lire.

A CORRESPONDENCE

Lizaveta Ivanovna had scarcely taken off her hat and cloak, when the Countess sent for her and again ordered the carriage. The vehicle drew up before the door, and they prepared to take their seats. Just at the moment when two footmen were assisting the old lady into the carriage, Lizaveta saw her engineer close beside the wheel; he grasped her hand; alarm caused her to lose her presence of mind, and the young man disappeared—but not before leaving a letter in her hand. She concealed it in her glove, and during the whole of the drive she neither saw nor heard anything. It was the custom of the Countess, when out for an airing in her carriage to be constantly asking such questions as: "Who was that person that met us just now? What is the name of this bridge? What is written on that signboard?" On this occasion, however, Lizaveta returned such vague and absurd answers, that the Countess became angry with her.

"What is the matter with you, my dear?" she exclaimed. "Have you taken leave of your senses, or what is it? Do you not hear me or understand what I say? . . . Heaven be thanked, I am still in my right mind and speak plainly enough!"

Lizaveta Ivanovna did not hear her. On returning home she ran to her room, and drew the letter out of her glove: it was not sealed. Lizaveta read it. The letter contained a declaration of love; it was tender, respectful, and copied word for word from a German novel. But Lizaveta did not not know anything of the German language, and she was quite delighted with the letter.

For all that, it troubled her exceedingly. For the first time in her life she was entering into secret and intimate relations with a young man. His boldness horrified her. She reproached herself for her imprudent behavior, and knew not what to do. Should she cease to sit at the window and, by assuming an appearance of indifference toward him, put a check upon the young officer's desire to pursue her further? Should she send his letter back to him, or should she answer him in a cold and resolute manner? There was nobody to whom she could turn in her perplexity, for she had neither female friend nor adviser. . . . At length she resolved to reply to him.

She sat down at her little writing table, took pen and paper, and began to think. Several times she began her letter, and then tore it up: the way she had expressed herself seemed to her either too indulgent or too severe. At last she succeeded in writing a few lines with which she felt satisfied.

"I am convinced," she wrote, "that your intentions are honorable, and that you do not wish to offend me by any imprudent action, but our acquaintance should not have begun in such a manner. I return you your letter, and I hope that I shall never have any cause to complain of undeserved disrespect."

The next day, as soon as Herman made his appearance, Lizaveta rose from her embroidery, went into the drawing room, opened the wicket and threw the letter into the street, trusting to the young officer's alertness.

Herman hastened forward, picked it up and then repaired to a confectioner's shop. Breaking the seal of the envelope, he found inside it his own letter and Lizaveta's reply. He had expected this, and he returned home, very much taken up with his intrigue.

Three days afterward, a bright-eyed young girl from a milliner's establishment brought Lizaveta a letter. Lizaveta opened it with great uneasiness, fearing that it was a demand for money, when suddenly she recognized Herman's handwriting.

"You have made a mistake, my dear," said she; "this letter is not for me."

"Oh, yes, it is for you," replied the pert girl, without concealing a sly smile. "Have the goodness to read it."

Lizaveta glanced at the letter. Herman requested an interview.

"It cannot be," said Lizaveta Ivanovna, alarmed both at the haste with which he had made his request, and the manner in which it had been transmitted. "This letter is certainly not for me."

And she tore it into fragments.

"If the letter was not for you, why have you torn it up?" said the girl. "I should have given it back to the person who sent it."

"Be good enough, my dear," said Lizaveta, disconcerted by this remark, "not to bring me any more letters in future, and tell the person who sent you that he ought to be ashamed. . . ."

But Herman was not the man to be thus put off. Every day Lizaveta received from him a letter, sent now in this way, now in that. They were no longer translated from the German. Herman wrote them under the inspiration of passion, and spoke in his own language, and they bore full testimony to the inflexibility of his desire and the disordered condition of his uncontrollable imagination. Lizaveta no longer thought of sending them back to him: she became intoxicated with them and began to reply to them, and little by little her answers became longer and more affectionate. At last she threw out of the window to him the following letter:

"This evening there is going to be a ball at the X. Embassy. The Countess will be there. We shall remain until two o'clock. This is your opportunity of seeing me alone. As soon as the Countess is gone, the servants will very probably go out, and there will be nobody left but the porter, but he, too, usually retires to his lodge. Come at half past eleven. Walk straight upstairs. If you meet anybody in the anteroom, ask if the Countess is at home. If you are told she is not, there will be nothing left for you to do but to go away and return another time. But it is most probable that you will meet nobody. The maidservants all sit together in one room. On leaving the anteroom, turn to the left, and walk straight on until you reach the Countess' bedroom. In the bedroom, behind a screen, you will find two small doors: the one on the right leads to a study, which the Countess never enters; the one on the left leads to a corridor, at the end of which is a narrow winding staircase; this leads to my room."

Herman quivered like a tiger, as he waited for the appointed time. At ten o'clock in the evening he was already in front of the Countess' house. The weather was terrible; the wind was howling; the sleety snow fell in large flakes; the lamps emitted a feeble light, the streets were deserted; from time to time a sledge, drawn by a sorry-looking hack, passed by, the driver on the lookout for a belated fare. Herman stood there wearing nothing but his jacket, yet he felt neither the wind nor the snow.

At last the Countess' carriage drew up. Herman saw two footmen carry out in their arms the bent form of the old lady, wrapped in sables, and immediately behind her, clad in a light mantle, and with a wreath of fresh flowers on her head,

followed Lizaveta. The door was closed. The carriage rolled
away heavily through the yielding snow. The porter shut the
street door; the windows became dark.

Herman began walking up and down near the deserted
house; at length he stopped under a lamp, and glanced at
his watch: it was twenty minutes past eleven. He remained
standing under the lamp, his eyes fixed upon the watch, impatiently waiting for the remaining minutes to pass. At half
past eleven precisely, Herman ascended the steps of the house,
and made his way into the brightly illuminated vestibule. The
porter was not there. Herman ran up the stairs, opened the
door of the anteroom and saw a footman sitting asleep in an
antique soiled armchair, under a lamp. With a light firm step
Herman walked past him. The reception room and the drawing
room were in semidarkness. They were lit feebly by a lamp
in the anteroom.

Herman entered the bedroom. Before an icon case, filled
with ancient icons, a golden sanctuary lamp was burning.
Armchairs, upholstered in faded brocade, and sofas, the gild-
ing of which was worn off and which were piled with down
cushions, stood in melancholy symmetry around the room,
the walls of which were hung with China silk. On the wall
hung two portraits painted in Paris by Madame Lebrun. One
of them represented a plump, pink-cheeked man of about
forty in a light green uniform and with a star on his breast;
the other—a beautiful young woman, with an aquiline nose,
curls at her temples, and a rose in her powdered hair. In all the
corners stood porcelain shepherds and shepherdesses, clocks
from the workshop of the celebrated Leroy, boxes, roulettes,
fans, and the various gewgaws for ladies that were invented at
the end of the last century, together with Montgolfier's balloon
and Mesmer's magnetism. Herman stepped behind the screen.
Behind it stood a little iron bed; on the right was the door
which led to the study; on the left—the other which led to
the corridor. He opened the latter, and saw the little winding
staircase which led to the room of the poor ward. . . . But he
retraced his steps and entered the dark study.

The time passed slowly. All was still. The clock in the
drawing room struck twelve; in all the rooms, one clock after
another marked the hour, and everything was quiet again.
Herman stood leaning against the cold stove. He was calm;
his heart beat regularly, like that of a man resolved upon a

dangerous but inevitable undertaking. The clock struck one, then two; and he heard the distant rumbling of carriage wheels. In spite of himself, excitement seized him. The carriage drew near and stopped. He heard the sound of the carriage step being let down. All was bustle within the house. The servants were running hither and thither, voices were heard, and the house was lit up. Three antiquated chambermaids entered the bedroom, and they were shortly afterwards followed by the Countess who, more dead than alive, sank into an armchair. Herman peeped through a chink. Lizaveta Ivanovna passed close by him, and he heard her hurried steps as she hurried up her staircase. For a moment his heart was assailed by something like remorse, but the emotion was only transitory. He stood petrified.

The Countess began to undress before her looking glass. Her cap, decorated with roses, was unpinned, and then her powdered wig was removed from off her white and closely cropped head. Hairpins fell in showers around her. Her yellow satin dress, embroidered with silver, fell down at her swollen feet.

Herman witnessed the repulsive mysteries of her toilette; at last the Countess was in her nightcap and nightgown, and in this costume, more suitable to her age, she appeared less hideous and terrifying.

Like all old people in general, the Countess suffered from sleeplessness. Having undressed, she seated herself at the window in an armchair and dismissed her maids. The candles were taken away, and once more the room was lit only by the sanctuary lamp. The Countess sat there looking quite yellow, moving her flaccid lips and swaying from side to side. Her dull eyes expressed complete vacancy of mind, and, looking at her, one would have thought that the rocking of her body was not voluntary, but was produced by the action of some concealed galvanic mechanism.

Suddenly the deathlike face changed incredibly. The lips ceased to move, the eyes became animated: before the Countess stood a stranger.

"Do not be alarmed, for Heaven's sake, do not be alarmed!" said he in a low but distinct voice. "I have no intention of doing you any harm, I have only come to ask a favor of you."

The old woman looked at him in silence, as if she had not heard what he had said. Herman thought that she was deaf, and, bending down toward her ear, he repeated what he had said. The old woman remained silent as before.

"You can insure the happiness of my life," continued Herman, "and it will cost you nothing. I know that you can name three cards in succession—"

Herman stopped. The Countess appeared now to understand what was asked of her; she seemed to be seeking words with which to reply.

"It was a joke," she replied at last. "I swear it was only a joke."

"This is no joking matter," replied Herman angrily. "Remember Chaplitski, whom you helped to win back what he had lost."

The Countess became visibly uneasy. Her features expressed strong emotion, but she soon lapsed into her former insensibility.

"Can you not name me these three winning cards?" continued Herman.

The Countess remained silent; Herman continued: "For whom are you preserving your secret? For your grandsons? They are rich enough without it; they do not know the worth of money. Your cards would be of no use to a spendthrift. He who cannot preserve his paternal inheritance, will die in want, even though he had a demon at his service. I am not a man of that sort; I know the value of money. Your three cards will not be wasted on me. Come!"

He paused and tremblingly awaited her reply. The Countess remained silent; Herman fell upon his knees.

"If your heart has ever known the feeling of love," said he, "if you remember its rapture, if you have ever smiled at the cry of your newborn child, if your breast has ever throbbed with any human feeling, I entreat you by the feelings of a wife, a lover, a mother, by all that is most sacred in life, not to reject my plea. Reveal to me your secret. Of what use is it to you? . . . Maybe it is connected with some terrible sin, the loss of eternal bliss, some bargain with the devil. . . . Consider—you are old; you have not long to live—I am ready to take your sins upon my soul. Only reveal to me your secret. Remember that the happiness of a man is in your hands, that not only I, but my children, grandchildren, and great-grandchildren, will bless your memory and reverence it as something sacred. . . ."

The old woman answered not a word.

Herman rose to his feet.

"You old witch!" he exclaimed, clenching his teeth. "Then I will make you answer!"

With these words he drew a pistol from his pocket.

At the sight of the pistol, the Countess for the second time exhibited strong emotion. She shook her head and raised her hands as if to protect herself from the shot . . . then she fell backward and remained motionless.

"Come, an end to this childish nonsense!" said Herman, taking hold of her hand. "I ask you for the last time: will you tell me the names of your three cards, or will you not?"

The Countess made no reply. Herman perceived that she was dead!

IV

7 mai, 18 – –
Homme sans moeurs et sans religion!
A CORRESPONDENCE

Lizaveta Ivanovna was sitting in her room, still in her ball dress, lost in deep thought. On returning home, she had hastily dismissed the sleepy maid, who reluctantly came forward to assist her, saying that she would undress herself, and with a trembling heart had gone up to her own room, hoping to find Herman there, but yet desiring not to find him. At the first glance she convinced herself that he was not there, and she thanked her fate for the obstacle which had prevented their meeting. She sat down without undressing, and began to recall to mind all the circumstances which in so short a time had carried her so far. It was not three weeks since the time when she had first seen the young man from the window —and she already was in correspondence with him, and he had succeeded in inducing her to grant him a nocturnal tryst! She knew his name only through his having written it at the bottom of some of his letters; she had never spoken to him, had never heard his voice, and had never heard anything of him until that evening. But, strange to say, that very evening at the ball, Tomski, being piqued with the young Princess Pauline N., who, contrary to her usual custom, did not flirt with him, wished to revenge himself by assuming an air of indifference: he therefore engaged Lizaveta Ivanovna and danced an endless mazurka with her. All the time he kept teasing her about her partiality for officers in the Engineers; he assured her that he knew far more than she could have supposed, and some of his jests were so happily aimed, that Lizaveta thought several times that her secret was known to him.

"From whom have you learned all this?" she asked, smiling.

"From a friend of a person very well known to you," replied Tomski, "from a very remarkable man."

"And who is this remarkable man?"

"His name is Herman."

Lizaveta made no reply; but her hands and feet turned to ice.

"This Herman," continued Tomski, "is a truly romantic character. He has the profile of a Napoleon, and the soul of a Mephistopheles. I believe that he has at least three crimes upon his conscience. . . . How pale you are!"

"I have a headache. . . . But what did this Herman—or whatever his name is—tell you?"

"Herman is very much dissatisfied with his friend: he says that in his place he would act very differently. . . . I even think that Herman himself has designs upon you; at least, he listens not indifferently to his friend's enamored exclamations."

"But where has he seen me?"

"In church, perhaps; or promenading—God alone knows where. It may have been in your room, while you were asleep, for he is capable of it."

Three ladies approaching him with the question: "*Oubli ou regret?*" interrupted the conversation, which had become so tantalizingly interesting to Lizaveta.

The lady chosen by Tomski was the Princess Pauline herself. She succeeded in effecting a reconciliation with him by making an extra turn in the dance and managing to delay resuming her seat. On returning to his place, Tomski thought no more either of Herman or Lizaveta. She longed to renew the interrupted conversation, but the mazurka came to an end, and shortly afterward the old Countess took her departure.

Tomski's words were nothing more than the small talk of the mazurka, but they sank deep into the soul of the young dreamer. The portrait, sketched by Tomski, agreed with the picture she had formed in her own mind, and that image, rendered commonplace by current novels, terrified and fascinated her imagination. She was now sitting with her bare arms crossed and her head, still adorned with flowers, was bowed over her half-uncovered breast. Suddenly the door opened and Herman entered. She shuddered.

"Where have you been?" she asked in a frightened whisper.

"In the old Countess' bedroom," replied Herman. "I have just left her. The Countess is dead."

"My God! What are you saying?"

"And I am afraid," added Herman, "that I am the cause of her death."

Lizaveta looked at him, and Tomski's words found an echo in her soul: "This man has at least three crimes upon his conscience!" Herman sat down by the window near her, and related all that had happened.

Lizaveta listened to him in terror. So all those passionate letters, those ardent demands, this bold obstinate pursuit—all this was not love! Money—that was what his soul yearned for! She could not satisfy his desire and make him happy! The poor girl had been nothing but the blind accomplice of a robber, of the murderer of her aged benefactress! . . . She wept bitter tears of belated, agonized repentance. Herman gazed at her in silence: his heart, too, was tormented, but neither the tears of the poor girl, nor the wonderful charm of her beauty, enhanced by her grief, could produce any impression upon his hardened soul. He felt no pricking of conscience at the thought of the dead old woman. One thing only horrified him: the irreparable loss of the secret which he had expected would bring him wealth.

"You are a monster!" said Lizaveta at last.

"I did not wish her death," replied Herman: "my pistol is not loaded."

Both grew silent.

The day began to dawn. Lizaveta extinguished her candle: a pale light illumined her room. She wiped her tear-stained eyes and raised them toward Herman: he was sitting on the window sill, with his arms folded and frowning fiercely. In this attitude he bore a striking resemblance to the portrait of Napoleon. This resemblance struck even Lizaveta Ivanovna.

"How shall I get you out of the house?" said she at last. "I thought of conducting you down the secret staircase, but in that case it would be necessary to go through the Countess' bedroom, and I am afraid."

"Tell me how to find this secret staircase—I will go alone."

Lizaveta arose, took from her drawer a key, handed it to Herman and gave him the necessary instructions. Herman

pressed her cold, unresponsive hand, kissed her bowed head,
and left the room.

He descended the winding staircase, and once more entered the Countess' bedroom. The dead old woman sat as if
petrified; her face expressed profound tranquillity. Herman
stopped before her, and gazed long and earnestly at her, as
if he wished to convince himself of the terrible reality; at
last he entered the study, felt behind the tapestry for the
door, and then began to descend the dark staircase, agitated
by strange emotions. "At this very hour," thought he, "some
sixty years ago, a young gallant, who has long been molder-
ing in his grave, may have stolen down this very staircase,
perhaps coming from the very same bedroom, wearing an
embroidered caftan, with his hair dressed *à l'oiseau royal* and
pressing to his heart his three-cornered hat, and the heart
of his aged mistress has only today ceased to beat. . . ."

At the bottom of the staircase Herman found a door,
which he opened with the same key, and found himself in a
corridor which led him into the street.

V

*That night the deceased Baroness von W. appeared to me.
She was clad all in white and said to me: "How are you, Mr.
Councilor?"*
                                                    SWEDENBORG

Three days after the fatal night, at nine o'clock in the morning,
Herman repaired to the Convent of ———, where the burial
service for the deceased Countess was to be held. Although
feeling no remorse, he could not altogether stifle the voice of
conscience, which kept repeating to him: "You are the murderer of the old woman!" While he had little true faith, he
was very superstitious; and believing that the dead Countess
might exercise an evil influence on his life, he resolved to be
present at her funeral in order to ask her pardon.

The church was full. It was with difficulty that Herman
made his way through the crowd. The coffin stood on a
sumptuous catafalque under a velvet baldachin. The deceased
lay within it, her hands crossed upon her breast, and wearing
a lace cap and a white satin gown. Around the catafalque
stood the members of her household: the servants in black
caftans, with armorial ribbons upon their shoulders, and candles in their hands; the relatives—children, grandchildren,
and great-grandchildren—in deep mourning.

Nobody wept; tears would have been *une affectation*. The Countess was so old that her death could have surprised nobody, and her relatives had long looked upon her as not among the living. A famous preacher delivered the funeral oration. In simple and touching words he described the peaceful passing away of the saintly woman whose long life had been a serene, moving preparation for a Christian end. "The angel of death found her," said the preacher, "engaged in pious meditation and waiting for the midnight bridegroom."

The service was concluded in an atmosphere of melancholy decorum. The relatives went forward first to bid farewell to the deceased. Then followed the numerous acquaintances, who had come to render the last homage to her who for so many years had participated in their frivolous amusements. After these followed the members of the Countess' household. The last of these was the old housekeeper who was of the same age as the deceased. Two young women led her forward, supporting her by the arms. She had not strength enough to bow down to the ground—she was the only one to shed a few tears and kiss the cold hand of her mistress.

Herman now resolved to approach the coffin. He bowed down to the ground and for several minutes lay on the cold floor, which was strewn with fir boughs; at last he arose, as pale as the deceased Countess herself, ascended the steps of the catafalque and bent over the corpse. . . . At that moment it seemed to him that the dead woman darted a mocking look at him and winked with one eye. Herman started back, took a false step and fell to the ground. He was lifted up. At the same moment Lizaveta Ivanovna was carried into the vestibule of the church in a faint. This episode disturbed for some minutes the solemnity of the gloomy ceremony. Among the congregation arose a muffled murmur, and the lean chamberlain, a near relative of the deceased, whispered in the ear of an Englishman who was standing near him, that the young officer was a natural son of the Countess, to which the Englishman coldly replied: "Oh!"

During the whole of that day, Herman was exceedingly perturbed. Dining in an out-of-the-way restaurant, he drank a great deal of wine, contrary to his usual custom, in the hope of allaying his inward agitation. But the wine only served to excite his imagination still more. On returning home, he threw himself upon his bed without undressing, and fell into a deep sleep.

When he woke up it was already night, and the moon was shining into the room. He looked at his watch: it was a quarter to three. Sleep had left him; he sat down upon his bed and thought of the funeral of the old Countess.

At that moment somebody in the street looked in at his window, and immediately passed on again. Herman paid no attention to this incident. A few moments afterward he heard the door of the anteroom open. Herman thought that it was his orderly, drunk as usual, returning from some nocturnal expedition, but presently he heard footsteps that were unknown to him: somebody was shuffling softly across the floor in slippers. The door opened, and a woman, dressed in white, entered the room. Herman mistook her for his old nurse, and wondered what could bring her there at that hour of the night. But the white woman glided rapidly across the room and stood before him—and Herman recognized the Countess!

"I have come to you against my will," she said in a firm voice: "but I have been ordered to grant your request. Three, seven, ace will win for you if played in succession, but only on these conditions: that you do not play more than one card in twenty-four hours, and that you never play again during the rest of your life. I forgive you my death, on condition that you marry my ward, Lizaveta Ivanovna."

With these words she turned round very quietly, walked with a shuffling gait toward the door and disappeared. Herman heard the street door bang, and he saw someone look in at him through the window again.

For a long time Herman could not recover himself. Then he went into the next room. His orderly was asleep upon the floor, and he had much difficulty in waking him. The orderly was drunk as usual, and nothing could be got out of him. The street door was locked. Herman returned to his room, lit his candle, and set down an account of his vision.

VI

"Attendez!"
"How dare you say attendez *to me?"*
"Your Excellency, I said: 'Attendez, sir.' "

Two fixed ideas can no more exist together in the moral world than two bodies can occupy one and the same place in the physical world. "Three, seven, ace" soon drove out of Herman's mind the thought of the dead Countess. "Three, seven, ace" were perpetually running through his head and continually on his lips. If he saw a young girl, he would say: "How slender she is! Quite like the three of hearts." If anybody asked: "What is the time?" he would reply: "Five minutes to seven." Every stout man that he saw reminded him of the ace. "Three, seven, ace" haunted him in his sleep, and assumed all possible shapes. The three bloomed before him in the form of a magnificent flower, the seven was represented by a Gothic portal, and the ace became transformed into a gigantic spider. One thought alone occupied his whole mind—to make use of the secret which he had purchased so dearly. He thought of applying for a furlough so as to travel abroad. He wanted to go to Paris and force fortune to yield a treasure to him in the public gambling houses there. Chance spared him all this trouble.

There was in Moscow a society of wealthy gamblers, presided over by the celebrated Chekalinski, who had passed all his life at the card table and had amassed millions, accepting bills of exchange for his winnings and paying his losses in ready money. His long experience secured for him the confidence of his companions, and his open house, his famous cook, and his agreeable and cheerful manner gained for him the respect of the public. He came to St. Petersburg. The young men of the capital flocked to his rooms, forgetting balls for cards, and preferring the temptations of faro to the seductions of flirting. Narumov conducted Herman to Chekalinski's residence.

They passed through a suite of magnificent rooms, filled with courteous attendants. Several generals and privy counselors were playing whist; young men were lolling carelessly upon the velvet-covered sofas, eating ices and smoking pipes. In the drawing room, at the head of a long table, around which crowded about a score of players, sat the master of the house keeping the bank. He was a man of about sixty years of age, of a very dignified appearance; his head was covered with silvery white hair; his full, florid countenance expressed good nature, and his eyes twinkled with a perpetual smile. Narumov introduced Herman to him. Chekalinski shook him by the hand in a friendly manner, requested him not to stand on ceremony, and then went on dealing.

The game lasted a long time. On the table lay more than thirty cards. Chekalinski paused after each throw, in order to give the players time to arrange their cards and note down their losses, listened politely to their requests, and more po-

litely still, straightened out the corners of cards that some
absent-minded player's hand had turned down. At last the
game was finished. Chekalinski shuffled the cards and prepared to deal again.

"Allow me to play a card," said Herman, stretching out
his hand from behind a stout gentleman who was punting.

Chekalinski smiled and bowed silently, as a sign of acqui-
escence. Narumov laughingly congratulated Herman on ending his long abstention from cards, and wished him a lucky
beginning.

"Here goes!" said Herman, writing the figure with chalk
on the back of his card.

"How much, sir?" asked the banker, screwing up his eyes.
"Excuse me, I cannot see quite clearly."

"Forty-seven thousand," replied Herman.

At these words every head in the room turned suddenly
round, and all eyes were fixed upon Herman.

"He has taken leave of his senses!" thought Narumov.

"Allow me to observe," said Chekalinski, with his eternal
smile, "that that is a very high stake; nobody here has ever
staked more than two hundred and seventy-five rubles at a
time."

"Well," retorted Herman, "do you accept my card or not?"

Chekalinski bowed with the same look of humble acqui-
escence.

"I only wish to inform you," said he, "that enjoying the
full confidence of my partners, I can only play for ready
money. For my own part, I am, of course, quite convinced
that your word is sufficient, but for the sake of order, and because of the accounts, I must ask you to put the money on
your card."

Herman drew from his pocket a banknote and handed it
to Chekalinski, who, after examining it in a cursory manner,
placed it on Herman's card.

He began to deal. On the right a nine turned up, and on
the left a three.

"I win!" said Herman, showing his card.

A murmur of astonishment arose among the players. Chekalinski frowned, but the smile quickly returned to his face.

"Do you wish me to settle with you?" he said to Herman.

"If you please," replied the latter.

Chekalinski drew from his pocket a number of banknotes
and paid up at once. Herman took his money and left the

table. Narumov could not recover from his astonishment. Herman drank a glass of lemonade and went home.

The next evening he again appeared at Chekalinski's. The host was dealing. Herman walked up to the table; the punters immediately made room for him. Chekalinski greeted him with a gracious bow.

Herman waited for the next game, took a card and placed upon it his forty-seven thousand rubles, together with his winnings of the previous evening.

Chekalinski began to deal. A knave turned up on the right, a seven on the left.

Herman showed his seven.

There was a general exclamation. Chekalinski was obviously disturbed, but he counted out the ninety-four thousand rubles and handed them over to Herman, who pocketed them in the coolest manner possible and immediately left the house.

The next evening Herman appeared again at the table. Everyone was expecting him. The generals and privy counselors left their whist in order to watch such extraordinary play. The young officers jumped up from their sofas, and even the servants crowded into the room. All pressed around Herman. The other players left off punting, impatient to see how it would end. Herman stood at the table and prepared to play alone against the pale but still smiling Chekalinski. Each opened a new pack of cards. Chekalinski shuffled. Herman took a card and covered it with a pile of banknotes. It was like a duel. Deep silence reigned.

Chekalinski began to deal; his hands trembled. On the right a queen turned up, and on the left an ace.

"Ace wins!" cried Herman, showing his card.

"Your queen has lost," said Chekalinski sweetly.

Herman started; instead of an ace, there lay before him the queen of spades! He could not believe his eyes, nor could he understand how he had made such a mistake.

At that moment it seemed to him that the queen of spades screwed up her eyes and sneered. He was struck by the remarkable resemblance. . . .

"The old woman!" he exclaimed, in terror.

Chekalinski gathered up his winnings. For some time Herman remained perfectly motionless. When at last he left the table, the room buzzed with loud talk.

"Splendidly punted!" said the players. Chekalinski shuffled the cards afresh, and the game went on as usual.

CONCLUSION

Herman went out of his mind. He is now confined in room
Number 17 of the Obukhov Hospital. He never answers any
questions, but he constantly mutters with unusual rapidity:
"Three, seven, ace! Three, seven, queen!"

Lizaveta Ivanovna has married a very amiable young man,
a son of the former steward of the old Countess. He is a civil
servant, and has a considerable fortune. Lizaveta is bringing
up a poor relative.

Tomski has been promoted to the rank of captain, and is
marrying Princess Pauline.

Nikolay Gogol

The
Cloak

✠

In the department of ——, but it is better not to mention the department. The touchiest things in the world are departments, regiments, courts of justice, in a word, all branches of public service. Each individual nowadays thinks all society insulted in his person. Quite recently, a complaint was received from a district chief of police in which he plainly demonstrated that all the imperial institutions were going to the dogs, and that the Tzar's sacred name was being taken in vain; and in proof he appended to the complaint a romance, in which the district chief of police is made to appear about once in every ten pages, and sometimes in a downright drunken condition. Therefore, in order to avoid all unpleasantness, it will be better to designate the department in question, as a certain department.

So, in a certain department there was a certain official—not a very notable one, it must be allowed—short of stature, somewhat pock-marked, red-haired, and mole-eyed, with a bald forehead, wrinkled cheeks, and a complexion of the kind known as sanguine. The St. Petersburg climate was responsible for this. As for his official rank—with us Russians the rank comes first—he was what is called a perpetual titular councillor, over which, as is well known, some writers make merry and crack their jokes, obeying the praiseworthy custom of attacking those who cannot bite back.

His family name was Bashmachkin. This name is evidently derived from bashmak (shoe); but, when, at what time, and in what manner, is not known. His father and grandfather, and all the Bashmachkins, always wore boots, which were resoled two or three times a year. His name was Akaki Akakiyevich. It may strike the reader as rather singular and far-fetched; but he may rest assured that it was by no means far-fetched, and that the circumstances were such that it would have been impossible to give him any other.

This was how it came about.

Akaki Akakiyevich was born, if my memory fails me not, in the evening on the 23rd of March. His mother, the wife of a Government official, and a very fine woman, made all due arrangements for having the child baptized. She was lying on the bed opposite the door; on her right stood the godfather, Ivan Ivanovich Yeroshkin, a most estimable man, who served as the head clerk of the senate; and the godmother, Arina Semyonovna Byelobrushkova, the wife of an officer of the quarter, and a woman of rare virtues. They offered the mother her choice of three names, Mokiya, Sossiya, or that the child should be called after the martyr Khozdazat. "No," said the good woman, "all those names are poor." In order to please her, they opened the calendar at another place; three more names appeared, Trifily, Dula, and Varakhasi. "This is awful," said the old woman. "What names! I truly never heard the like. I might have put up with Varadat or Varukh, but not Trifily and Varakhasi!" They turned to another page and found Pavsikakhi and Vakhtisi. "Now I see," said the old woman, "that it is plainly fate. And since such is the case, it will be better to name him after his father. His father's name was Akaki, so let his son's name be Akaki too." In this manner he became Akaki Akakiyevich. They christened the child, whereat he wept, and made a grimace, as though he foresaw that he was to be a titular councillor.

In this manner did it all come about. We have mentioned it in order that the reader might see for himself that it was a case of necessity, and that it was utterly impossible to give him any other name.

When and how he entered the department, and who appointed him, no one could remember. However much the directors and chiefs of all kinds were changed, he was always to be seen in the same place, the same attitude, the same occupation—always the letter copying clerk—so that it was afterwards affirmed that he had been born in uniform with a bald head. No respect was shown him in the department. The porter not only did not rise from his seat when he passed, but never even glanced at him, any more than if a fly had flown through the reception room. His superiors treated him in coolly despotic fashion. Some insignificant assistant to the head clerk would thrust a paper under his nose without so much as saying, "Copy," or, "Here's an interesting little case," or anything else agreeable, as is customary amongst well-bred officials. And he took it, looking only at the paper, and not observing who handed it to him, or whether he had the right to do so; simply took it, and set about copying it.

The young officials laughed at and made fun of him, so far as their official wit permitted; told in his presence various stories concocted about him, and about his landlady, an old woman of seventy; declared that she beat him; asked when the wedding was to be; and strewed bits of paper over his head, calling them snow. But Akaki Akakiyevich answered not a word, any more than if there had been no one there besides himself. It even had no effect upon his work. Amid all these annoyances he never made a single mistake in a letter. But if the joking became wholly unbearable, as when they jogged his head, and prevented his attending to his work, he would exclaim:

"Leave me alone! Why do you insult me?"

And there was something strange in the words and the voice in which they were uttered. There was in it something which moved to pity; so much so that one young man, a newcomer, who, taking pattern by the others, had permitted himself to make sport of Akaki, suddenly stopped short, as though all about him had undergone a transformation, and presented itself in a different aspect. Some unseen force repelled him from the comrades whose acquaintance he had made, on the supposition that they were decent, well-bred men. Long afterwards, in his gayest moments, there recurred to his mind the little official with the bald forehead, with his heart-rending words, "Leave me alone! Why do you insult me?" In these moving words, other words resounded—"I am thy brother." And the young man covered his face with his hand; and many a time afterwards, in the course of his life, shuddered at seeing how much inhumanity there is in man, how much savage coarseness is concealed beneath refined, cultured, worldly refinement, and even, O God! in that man whom the world acknowledges as honorable and upright.

It would be difficult to find another man who lived so entirely for his duties. It is not enough to say that Akaki labored with zeal; no, he labored with love. In his copying, he found a varied and agreeable employment. Enjoyment was written on his face; some letters were even favorites with him; and when he encountered these, he smiled, winked, and worked with his lips, till it seemed as though each letter might be read in his face, as his pen traced it. If his pay had been in proportion to his zeal, he would, perhaps, to his great surprise, have been made even a councillor of state. But he worked, as his companions, the wits, put it, like a horse in a mill.

However, it would be untrue to say that no attention was paid to him. One director being a kindly man, and desirous of rewarding him for his long service, ordered him to be given something more important than mere copying. So he was ordered to make a report of an already concluded affair, to another department; the duty consisting simply in changing the heading and altering a few words from the first to the third person. This caused him so much toil, that he broke into a perspiration, rubbed his forehead, and finally said, "No, give me rather something to copy." After that they let him copy on forever.

Outside this copying, it appeared that nothing existed for him. He gave no thought to his clothes. His uniform was not green, but a sort of rusty meal color. The collar was low, so that his neck, in spite of the fact that it was not long, seemed inordinately so as it emerged from it, like the necks of the plaster cats which pedlars carry about on their heads. And something was always sticking to his uniform, either a bit of hay or some trifle. Moreover, he had a peculiar knack, as he walked along the street, of arriving beneath a window just as all sorts of rubbish was being flung out of it; hence he always bore about on his hat scraps of melon rinds, and other such articles. Never once in his life did he give heed to what was going on every day in the street; while it is well known that his young brother officials trained the range of their glances till they could see when any one's trouser straps came undone upon the opposite sidewalk, which always brought a malicious smile to their faces. But Akaki Akakiyevich saw in all things the clean, even strokes of his written lines; and only when a horse thrust his nose, from some unknown quarter, over his shoulder, and sent a whole gust of wind down his neck from his nostrils, did he observe that he was not in the middle of a line, but in the middle of the street.

On reaching home, he sat down at once at the table, sipped his cabbage soup up quickly, and swallowed a bit of beef with onions, never noticing their taste, and gulping down everything with flies and anything else which the Lord happened to send at the moment. When he saw that his stomach was beginning to swell, he rose from the table and copied papers which he had brought home. If there happened to be none, he took copies for himself, for his own gratification, especially if the document was noteworthy, not on account of its style, but of its being addressed to some distinguished person.

Even at the hour when the grey St. Petersburg sky had quite disappeared, and all the official world had eaten or dined, each as he could, in accordance with the salary he received and his own fancy; when all were resting from the department jar of pens, running to and fro, for their own and other people's indispensable occupations, and from all the work that an uneasy man makes willingly for himself, rather than what is necessary; when officials hasten to dedicate to pleasure the time which is left to them, one bolder than the rest going to the theatre; another, into the street looking under the bonnets; another wasting his evening in compliments to some pretty girl, the star of a small official circle; another—and this is the common case of all—visiting his comrades on the third or fourth floor, in two small rooms with an anteroom or kitchen, and some pretensions to fashion, such as a lamp or some other trifle which has cost many a sacrifice of dinner or pleasure trip; in a word, at the hour when all officials disperse among the contracted quarters of their friends, to play whist, as they sip their tea from glasses with a kopek's worth of sugar, smoke long pipes, relate at time some bits of gossip which a Russian man can never, under any circumstances, refrain from, and when there is nothing else to talk of, repeat eternal anecdotes about the commandant to whom they had sent word that the tails of the horses on the Falonet Monument had been cut off; when all strive to divert themselves, Akaki Akakiyevich indulged in no kind of diversion. No one could even say that he had seen him at any kind of evening party. Having written to his heart's content, he lay down to sleep, smiling at the thought of the coming day—of what God might send him to copy on the morrow.

Thus flowed on the peaceful life of the man, who, with a salary of four hundred rubles, understood how to be content with his lot; and thus it would have continued to flow on, perhaps, to extreme old age, were it not that there are various ills strewn along the path of life for titular councillors as well as for private, actual, court, and every other species of councillor, even to those who never give any advice or take any themselves.

There exists in St. Petersburg a powerful foe of all who
receive a salary of four hundred rubles a year, or thereabouts.
This foe is no other than the Northern cold, although it is
said to be very healthy. At nine o'clock in the morning, at the
very hour when the streets are filled with men bound for the
various official departments, it begins to bestow such powerful
and piercing nips on all noses impartially, that the poor officials really do not know what to do with them. At an hour
when the foreheads of even those who occupy exalted positions ache with the cold, and tears start to their eyes, the poor
titular councillors are sometimes quite unprotected. Their only
salvation lies in traversing as quickly as possible, in their thin
little cloaks, five or six streets, and then warming their feet in
the porter's room, and so thawing all their talents and qualifi-
cations for official service, which had become frozen on the
way.

Akaki Akakiyevich had felt for some time that his back and
shoulders were paining with peculiar poignancy, in spite of the
fact that he tried to traverse the distance with all possible
speed. He began finally to wonder whether the fault did not
lie in his cloak. He examined it thoroughly at home, and discovered that in two places, namely, on the back and shoulders,
it had become thin as gauze. The cloth was worn to such a
degree that he could see through it, and the lining had fallen
into pieces. You must know that Akaki Akakiyevich's cloak
served as an object of ridicule to the officials. They even refused it the noble name of cloak, and called it a cape. In fact,
it was of singular make, its collar diminishing year by year to
serve to patch its other parts. The patching did not exhibit
great skill on the part of the tailor, and was, in fact, baggy and
ugly. Seeing how the matter stood, Akaki Akakiyevich decided
that it would be necessary to take the cloak to Petrovich, the
tailor, who lived somewhere on the fourth floor up a dark
staircase, and who, in spite of his having but one eye and
pockmarks all over his face, busied himself with considerable
success in repairing the trousers and coats of officials and
others; that is to say, when he was sober and not nursing some
other scheme in his head.

It is not necessary to say much about this tailor, but as it is
the custom to have the character of each personage in a novel
clearly defined there is no help for it, so here is Petrovich the
tailor. At first he was called only Grigori, and was some
gentleman's serf. He commenced calling himself Petrovich from

the time when he received his free papers, and further began to drink heavily on all holidays, at first on the great ones, and then on all church festivals without discrimination, wherever a cross stood in the calendar. On this point he was faithful to ancestral custom; and when quarrelling with his wife, he called her a low female and a German. As we have mentioned his wife, it will be necessary to say a word or two about her. Unfortunately, little is known of her beyond the fact that Petrovich had a wife, who wore a cap and a dress, but could not lay claim to beauty, at least, no one but the soldiers of the guard even looked under her cap when they met her.

Ascending the staircase which led to Petrovich's room—which staircase was all soaked with dishwater and reeked with the smell of spirits which affects the eyes, and is an inevitable adjunct to all dark stairways in St. Petersburg houses—ascending the stairs, Akaki Akakiyevich pondered how much Petrovich would ask, and mentally resolved not to give more than two rubles. The door was open, for the mistress, in cooking some fish, had raised such a smoke in the kitchen that not even the beetles were visible. Akaki Akakiyevich passed through the kitchen unperceived, even by the housewife, and at length reached a room where he beheld Petrovich seated on a large unpainted table, with his legs tucked under him like a Turkish pasha. His feet were bare, after the fashion of tailors as they sit at work; and the first thing which caught the eye was his thumb, with a deformed nail thick and strong as a turtle's shell. About Petrovich's neck hung a skein of silk and thread, and upon his knees lay some old garment. He had been trying unsuccessfully for three minutes to thread his needle, and was enraged at the darkness and even at the thread, growling in a low voice, "It won't go through, the barbarian! You pricked me, you rascal!"

Akaki Akakiyevich was vexed at arriving at the precise moment when Petrovich was angry. He liked to order something of Petrovich when he was a little downhearted, or, as his wife expressed it, "when he had settled himself with brandy, the one-eyed devil!" Under such circumstances Petrovich generally came down in his price very readily, and even bowed and returned thanks. Afterwards, to be sure, his wife would come, complaining that her husband had been drunk, and so had fixed the price too low; but, if only a ten-kopek piece were added then the matter would be settled. But now it appeared that Petrovich was in a sober condition, and therefore rough, taciturn, and inclined to demand, Satan only knows what price. Akaki Akakiyevich felt this, and would gladly have beat a retreat, but he was in for it. Petrovich screwed up his one eye very intently at him, and Akaki Akakiyevich involuntarily said, "How do you do, Petrovich?"

"I wish you a good morning, sir," said Petrovich squinting at Akaki Akakiyevich's hands, to see what sort of booty he had brought.

"Ah! I—to you, Petrovich, this—" It must be known that Akaki Akakiyevich expressed himself chiefly by prepositions, adverbs, and scraps of phrases which had no meaning whatever. If the matter was a very difficult one, he had a habit of never completing his sentences, so that frequently, having begun a phrase with the words, "This, in fact, is quite—" he forgot to go on, thinking he had already finished it.

"What is it?" asked Petrovich, and with his one eye scanned Akaki Akakiyevich's whole uniform from the collar down to the cuffs, the back, the tails and the buttonholes, all of which were well known to him, since they were his own handiwork. Such is the habit of tailors; it is the first thing they do on meeting one.

"But I, here, this—Petrovich—a cloak, cloth—here you see, everywhere, in different places, it is quite strong—it is a little dusty and looks old, but it is new, only here in one place it is a little—on the back, and here on one of the shoulders, it is a little worn, yes, here on this shoulder it is a little—do you see? That is all. And a little work—"

Petrovich took the cloak, spread it out, to begin with, on the table, looked at it hard, shook his head, reached out his hand to the window sill for his snuffbox, adorned with the portrait of some general, though what general is unknown, for the place where the face should have been had been rubbed through by the finger and a square bit of paper had been pasted over it. Having taken a pinch of snuff, Petrovich held up the cloak, and inspected it against the light, and again shook his head. Then he turned it, lining upwards, and shook his head once more. After which he again lifted the general-adorned lid with its bit of pasted paper, and having stuffed his nose with snuff, closed and put away the snuffbox, and said finally, "No, it is impossible to mend it. It is a wretched garment!"

Akaki Akakiyevich's heart sank at these words.

"Why is it impossible, Petrovich?" he said, almost in the

pleading voice of a child. "All that ails it is, that it is worn on the shoulders. You must have some pieces——"

"Yes, patches could be found, patches are easily found," said Petrovich, "but there's nothing to sew them to. The thing is completely rotten. If you put a needle to it—see, it will give way."

"Let it give way, and you can put on another patch at once."

"But there is nothing to put the patches on to. There's no use in strengthening it. It is too far gone. It's lucky that it's cloth, for, if the wind were to blow, it would fly away."

"Well, strengthen it again. How this, in fact——"

"No," said Petrovich decisively, "there is nothing to be done with it. It's a thoroughly bad job. You'd better, when the cold winter weather comes on, make yourself some gaiters out of it, because stockings are not warm. The Germans invented them in order to make more money." Petrovich loved on all occasions to have a fling at the Germans. "But it is plain you must have a new cloak."

At the word "new" all grew dark before Akaki Akakiyevich's eyes, and everything in the room began to whirl round. The only thing he saw clearly was the general with the paper face on the lid of Petrovich's snuffbox. "A new one?" said he, as if still in a dream. "Why, I have no money for that."

"Yes, a new one," said Petrovich, with barbarous composure.

"Well, if it came to a new one, how—it——"

"You mean how much would it cost?"

"Yes."

"Well, you would have to lay out a hundred and fifty or more," said Petrovich, and pursed up his lips significantly. He liked to produce powerful effects, liked to stun utterly and suddenly, and then to glance sideways to see what face the stunned person would put on the matter.

"A hundred and fifty rubles for a cloak!" shrieked poor Akaki Akakiyevich, perhaps for the first time in his life, for his voice had always been distinguished for softness.

"Yes, sir," said Petrovich, "for any kind of cloak. If you have a marten fur on the collar, or a silk-lined hood, it will mount up to two hundred."

"Petrovich, please," said Akaki Akakiyevich in a beseeching tone, not hearing, and not trying to hear, Petrovich's words, and disregarding all his "effects," "some repairs, in order that it may wear yet a little longer."

"No, it would only be a waste of time and money," said Petrovich. And Akaki Akakiyevich went away after these words, utterly discouraged. But Petrovich stood for some time after his departure, with significantly compressed lips, and without betaking himself to his work, satisfied that he would not be dropped, and an artistic tailor employed.

Akaki Akakiyevich went out into the street as if in a dream. "Such an affair!" he said to himself. "I did not think it had come to—" and then after a pause, he added, "Well, so it is! see what it has come to at last! and I never imagined that it was so!" Then followed a long silence, after which he exclaimed, "Well, so it is! see what already—nothing unexpected that—it would be nothing—what a strange circumstance!" So saying, instead of going home, he went in exactly the opposite direction without suspecting it. On the way, a chimney sweep bumped up against him, and blackened his shoulder, and a whole hatful of rubbish landed on him from the top of a house which was building. He did not notice it, and only when he ran against a watchman, who, having planted his halberd beside him, was shaking some snuff from his box into his horny hand, did he recover himself a little, and that because the watchman said, "Why are you poking yourself into a man's very face? Haven't you the pavement?" This caused him to look about him, and turn towards home.

There only, he finally began to collect his thoughts, and to survey his position in its clear and actual light, and to argue with himself, sensibly and frankly, as with a reasonable friend, with whom one can discuss private and personal matters. "No," said Akaki Akakiyevich, "it is impossible to reason with Petrovich now. He is that—evidently, his wife has been beating him. I'd better go to him on Sunday morning. After Saturday night he will be a little cross-eyed and sleepy, for he will want to get drunk, and his wife won't give him any money, and at such a time, a ten-kopek piece in his hand will—he will become more fit to reason with, and then the cloak and that——" Thus argued Akaki Akakiyevich with himself, regained his courage, and waited until the first Sunday, when, seeing from afar that Petrovich's wife had left the house, he went straight to him.

Petrovich's eye was indeed very much askew after Saturday. His head drooped, and he was very sleepy; but for all that, as soon as he knew what it was a question of, it seemed as though Satan jogged his memory. "Impossible," said he. "Please to order a new one." Thereupon Akaki Akakiyevich handed over the ten-kopek piece. "Thank you, sir. I will drink your good health," said Petrovich. "But as for the cloak, don't trouble yourself about it; it is good for nothing. I will make you a capital new one, so let us settle about it now."

Akaki Akakiyevich was still for mending it, but Petrovich would not hear of it, and said, "I shall certainly have to make you a new one, and you may depend upon it that I shall do my best. It may even be, as the fashion goes, that the collar can be fastened by silver hooks under a flap."

Then Akaki Akakiyevich saw that it was impossible to get along without a new cloak, and his spirit sank utterly. How, in fact, was it to be done? Where was the money to come from? He must have some new trousers, and pay a debt of long standing to the shoemaker for putting new tops to his old boots, and he must order three shirts from the seamstress, and a couple of pieces of linen. In short, all his money must be spent. And even if the director should be so kind as to order him to receive forty-five or even fifty rubles instead of forty, it would be a mere nothing, a mere drop in the ocean towards the funds necessary for a cloak, although he knew that Petrovich was often wrong-headed enough to blurt out some outrageous price, so that even his own wife could not refrain from exclaiming, "Have you lost your senses, you fool?" At one time he would not work at any price, and now it was quite likely that he had named a higher sum than the cloak would cost.

But although he knew that Petrovich would undertake to make a cloak for eighty rubles, still, where was he to get the eighty rubles from? He might possibly manage half. Yes, half might be procured, but where was the other half to come from? But the reader must first be told where the first half came from.

Akaki Akakiyevich had a habit of putting, for every ruble he spent, a groschen into a small box, fastened with lock and key, and with a slit in the top for the reception of money. At the end of every half-year he counted over the heap of coppers, and changed it for silver. This he had done for a long time, and in the course of years, the sum had mounted up to over forty rubles. Thus he had one half on hand. But where was he to find the other half? Where was he to get another forty rubles from? Akaki Akakiyevich thought and thought, and decided that it would be necessary to curtail his ordinary expenses, for the space of one year at least, to dispense with tea in the evening, to burn no candles, and, if there was anything which he must do, to go into his landlady's room, and work by her light. When he went into the street, he must walk as lightly as he could, and as cautiously, upon the stones, almost upon tiptoe, in order not to wear his heels down in too short a time. He must give the laundress as little to wash as possible; and, in order not to wear out his clothes, he must take them off as soon as he got home, and wear only his cotton dressing gown, which had been long and carefully saved.

To tell the truth, it was a little hard for him at first to accustom himself to these deprivations. But he got used to them at length, after a fashion, and all went smoothly. He even got used to being hungry in the evening, but he made up for it by treating himself, so to say, in spirit, by bearing ever in mind the idea of his future cloak. From that time forth, his existence seemed to become, in some way, fuller, as if he were married, or as if some other man lived in him, as if, in fact, he were not alone, and some pleasant friend had consented to travel along life's path with him, the friend being no other than the cloak, with thick wadding and a strong lining incapable of wearing out. He became more lively, and even his character grew firmer, like that of a man who has made up his mind, and set himself a goal. From his face and gait, doubt and indecision, all hesitating and wavering disappeared of themselves. Fire gleamed in his eyes, and occasionally the boldest and most daring ideas flitted through his mind. Why not, for instance, have marten fur on the collar? The thought of this almost made him absent-minded. Once, in copying a letter, he nearly made a mistake, so that he exclaimed almost aloud, "Ugh!" and crossed himself. Once, in the course of every month, he had a conference with Petrovich on the subject of the cloak, where it would be better to buy the cloth, and the colour, and the price. He always returned home satisfied, though troubled, reflecting that the time would come at last when it could all be bought, and then the cloak made.

The affair progressed more briskly than he had expected. For beyond all his hopes, the director awarded neither forty nor forty-five rubles for Akaki Akakiyevich's share, but sixty. Whether he suspected that Akaki Akakiyevich needed a cloak, or whether it was merely chance, at all events, twenty extra rubles were by this means provided. This circumstance hastened matters. Two or three months more of hunger and

Akaki Akakiyevich had accumulated about eighty rubles. His heart, generally so quiet, began to throb. On the first possible day, he went shopping in company with Petrovich. They bought some very good cloth, and at a reasonable rate too, for they had been considering the matter for six months, and rarely let a month pass without their visiting the shops to inquire prices. Petrovich himself said that no better cloth could be had. For lining, they selected a cotton stuff, but so firm and thick, that Petrovich declared it to be better than silk, and even prettier and more glossy. They did not buy the marten fur, because it was, in fact, dear, but in its stead, they picked out the very best of catskin, which could be found in the shop, and which might, indeed, be taken for marten at a distance.

Petrovich worked at the cloak two whole weeks, for there was a great deal of quilting; otherwise it would have been finished sooner. He charged twelve rubles for the job, it could not possibly have been done for less. It was all sewed with silk, in small, double seams, and Petrovich went over each seam afterwards with his own teeth, stamping in various patterns.

It was—it is difficult to say precisely on what day, but probably the most glorious one in Akaki Akakiyevich's life, when Petrovich at length brought home the cloak. He brought it in the morning, before the hour when it was necessary to start for the department. Never did a cloak arrive so exactly in the nick of time, for the severe cold had set in, and it seemed to threaten to increase. Petrovich brought the cloak himself as befits a good tailor. On his countenance was a significant expression, such as Akaki Akakiyevich had never beheld there. He seemed fully sensible that he had done no small deed, and crossed a gulf separating tailors who put in linings, and execute repairs, from those who make new things. He took the cloak out of the pocket handkerchief in which he had brought it. The handkerchief was fresh from the laundress, and he put it in his pocket for use. Taking out the cloak, he gazed proudly at it, held it up with both hands, and flung it skilfully over the shoulders of Akaki Akakiyevich. Then he pulled it and fitted it down behind with his hand, and he draped it around Akaki Akakiyevich without buttoning it. Akaki Akakiyevich, like an experienced man, wished to try the sleeves. Petrovich helped him on with them, and it turned out that the sleeves were satisfactory also. In short, the cloak appeared to be per-

fect, and most seasonable. Petrovich did not neglect to observe that it was only because he lived in a narrow street, and
had no signboard, and had known Akaki Akakiyevich so long,
that he had made it so cheaply; but that if he had been in
business on the Nevski Prospect, he would have charged
seventy-five rubles for the making alone. Akaki Akakiyevich
did not care to argue this point with Petrovich. He paid him,
thanked him, and set out at once in his new cloak for the
department. Petrovich followed him, and pausing in the street,
gazed long at the cloak in the distance, after which he went to
one side expressly to run through a crooked alley, and emerge
again into the street beyond to gaze once more upon the cloak
from another point, namely, directly in front.

Meantime Akaki Akakiyevich went on in holiday mood.
He was conscious every second of the time that he had a new
cloak on his shoulders, and several times he laughed with internal satisfaction. In fact, there were two advantages, one was
its warmth, the other its beauty. He saw nothing of the road,
but suddenly found himself at the department. He took off his
cloak in the anteroom, looked it over carefully, and confided it
to the special care of the attendant. It is impossible to say
precisely how it was that every one in the department knew at
once that Akaki Akakiyevich had a new cloak, and that the
"cape" no longer existed. All rushed at the same moment into
the anteroom to inspect it. They congratulated him, and said
pleasant things to him, so that he began at first to smile and
then to grow ashamed. When all surrounded him, and said
that the new cloak must be "christened," and that he must at
least give them all a party, Akaki Akakiyevich lost his head
completely, and did not know where he stood, what to answer,
or how to get out of it. He stood blushing all over for several
minutes, trying to assure them with great simplicity that it
was not a new cloak, that it was in fact the old "cape."

At length one of the officials, assistant to the head clerk, in
order to show that he was not at all proud, and on good terms
with his inferiors, said:

"So be it, only I will give the party instead of Akaki
Akakiyevich; I invite you all to tea with me tonight. It just
happens to be my nameday too."

The officials naturally at once offered the assistant clerk
their congratulations, and accepted the invitation with pleasure.
Akaki Akakiyevich would have declined; but all declared that
it was discourteous, that it was simply a sin and a shame, and

that he could not possibly refuse. Besides, the notion became pleasant to him when he recollected that he should thereby have a chance of wearing his new cloak in the evening also.

That whole day was truly a most triumphant festival for Akaki Akakiyevich. He returned home in the most happy frame of mind, took off his cloak, and hung it carefully on the wall, admiring afresh the cloth and the lining. Then he brought out his old, worn-out cloak, for comparison. He looked at it, and laughed, so vast was the difference. And long after dinner he laughed again when the condition of the "cape" recurred to his mind. He dined cheerfully, and after dinner wrote nothing, but took his ease for a while on the bed, until it got dark. Then he dressed himself leisurely, put on his cloak, and stepped out into the street.

Where the host lived, unfortunately we cannot say. Our memory begins to fail us badly. The houses and streets in St. Petersburg have become so mixed up in our head that it is very difficult to get anything out of it again in proper form. This much is certain, that the official lived in the best part of the city; and therefore it must have been anything but near to Akaki Akakiyevich's residence. Akaki Akakiyevich was first obliged to traverse a kind of wilderness of deserted, dimly-lighted streets. But in proportion as he approached the official's quarter of the city, the streets became more lively, more populous, and more brilliantly illuminated. Pedestrians began to appear; handsomely dressed ladies were more frequently encountered; the men had otter skin collars to their coats; shabby sleighmen with their wooden, railed sledges stuck over with brass-headed nails, became rarer; whilst on the other hand, more and more drivers in red velvet caps, lacquered sledges and bearskin coats began to appear, and carriages with rich hammer-cloths flew swiftly through the streets, their wheels scrunching the snow.

Akaki Akakiyevich gazed upon all this as upon a novel sight. He had not been in the streets during the evening for years. He halted out of curiosity before a shopwindow, to look at a picture representing a handsome woman, who had thrown off her shoe, thereby baring her whole foot in a very pretty way; whilst behind her the head of a man with whiskers and a handsome mustache peeped through the doorway of another room. Akaki Akakiyevich shook his head, and laughed, and then went on his way. Why did he laugh? Either because he had met with a thing utterly unknown, but for which every one cherishes, nevertheless, some sort of feeling, or else he thought, like many officials, "Well, those French! What is to be said? If they do go in for anything of that sort, why—" But possibly he did not think at all.

Akaki Akakiyevich at length reached the house in which the head clerk's assistant lodged. He lived in fine style. The staircase was lit by a lamp, his apartment being on the second floor. On entering the vestibule, Akaki Akakiyevich beheld a whole row of goloshes on the floor. Among them, in the center of the room, stood a samovar, humming and emitting clouds of steam. On the walls hung all sorts of coats and cloaks, among which there were even some with beaver collars, or velvet facing. Beyond, the buzz of conversation was audible, and became clear and loud, when the servant came out with a trayful of empty glasses, cream jugs and sugar bowls. It was evident that the officials had arrived long before, and had already finished their first glass of tea.

Akaki Akakiyevich, having hung up his own cloak, entered the inner room. Before him all at once appeared lights, officials, pipes, and card tables, and he was bewildered by a sound of rapid conversation rising from all the tables, and the noise of moving chairs. He halted very awkwardly in the middle of the room, wondering what he ought to do. But they had seen him. They received him with a shout, and all thronged at once into the anteroom, and there took another look at his cloak. Akaki Akakiyevich, although somewhat confused, was frank-hearted, and could not refrain from rejoicing when he saw how they praised his cloak. Then, of course, they all dropped him and his cloak, and returned, as was proper, to the tables set out for whist.

All this, the noise, the talk, and the throng of people, was rather overwhelming to Akaki Akakiyevich. He simply did not know where he stood, or where to put his hands, his feet, and his whole body. Finally he sat down by the players, looked at the cards, gazed at the face of one and another, and after a while began to gape, and to feel that it was wearisome, the more so, as the hour was already long past when he usually went to bed. He wanted to take leave of the host, but they would not let him go, saying that he must not fail to drink a glass of champagne, in honor of his new garment. In the course of an hour, supper, consisting of vegetable salad, cold veal, pastry, confectioner's pies, and champagne, was served.

They made Akaki Akakiyevich drink two glasses of champagne, after which he felt things grow livelier.

Still, he could not forget that it was twelve o'clock, and that he should have been at home long ago. In order that the host might not think of some excuse for detaining him, he stole out of the room quickly, sought out, in the anteroom, his cloak, which, to his sorrow, he found lying on the floor, brushed it, picked off every speck upon it, put it on his shoulders, and descended the stairs to the street.

In the street all was still bright. Some petty shops, those permanent clubs of servants and all sorts of folks, were open. Others were shut, but, nevertheless, showed a streak of light the whole length of the door crack, indicating that they were not yet free of company, and that probably some domestics, male and female, were finishing their stories and conversations, while leaving their masters in complete ignorance as to their whereabouts. Akaki Akakiyevich went on in a happy frame of mind. He even started to run, without knowing why, after some lady, who flew past like a flash of lightning. But he stopped short, and went on very quietly as before, wondering why he had quickened his pace. Soon there spread before him those deserted streets which are not cheerful in the daytime, to say nothing of the evening. Now they were even more dim and lonely. The lanterns began to grow rarer, oil, evidently, had been less liberally supplied. Then came wooden houses and fences. Not a soul anywhere; only the snow sparkled in the streets, and mournfully veiled the low-roofed cabins with their closed shutters. He approached the spot where the street crossed a vast square with houses barely visible on its farther side, a square which seemed a fearful desert.

Afar, a tiny spark glimmered from some watchman's box, which seemed to stand on the edge of the world. Akaki Akakiyevich's cheerfulness diminished at this point in a marked degree. He entered the square, not without an involuntary sensation of fear, as though his heart warned him of some evil. He glanced back, and on both sides it was like a sea about him. "No, it is better not to look," he thought, and went on, closing his eyes. When he opened them, to see whether he was near the end of the square, he suddenly beheld, standing just before his very nose, some bearded individuals of precisely what sort, he could not make out. All grew dark before his eyes, and his heart throbbed.

"Of course, the cloak is mine!" said one of them in a loud

voice, seizing hold of his collar. Akaki Akakiyevich was about
to shout "Help!" when the second man thrust a fist, about the
size of an official's head, at his very mouth, muttering, "Just
you dare to scream!"

Akaki Akakiyevich felt them strip off his cloak, and give
him a kick. He fell headlong upon the snow, and felt no more.

In a few minutes he recovered consciousness, and rose to
his feet, but no one was there. He felt that it was cold in the
square, and that his cloak was gone. He began to shout, but
his voice did not appear to reach the outskirts of the square.
In despair, but without ceasing to shout, he started at a run
across the square, straight towards the watchbox, beside which
stood the watchman, leaning on his halberd, and apparently
curious to know what kind of a customer was running towards
him shouting. Akaki Akakiyevich ran up to him, and began
in a sobbing voice to shout that he was asleep, and attended to
nothing, and did not see when a man was robbed. The watchman replied that he had seen two men stop him in the middle
of the square, but supposed that they were friends of his, and
that, instead of scolding vainly, he had better go to the police
on the morrow, so that they might make a search for whoever had stolen the cloak.

Akaki Akakiyevich ran home and arrived in a state of complete disorder, his hair which grew very thinly upon his temples
and the back of his head all tousled, his body, arms and legs,
covered with snow. The old woman, who was mistress of his
lodgings, on hearing a terrible knocking, sprang hastily from
her bed, and, with only one shoe on, ran to open the door,
pressing the sleeve of her chemise to her bosom out of modesty. But when she had opened it, she fell back on beholding
Akaki Akakiyevich in such a condition. When he told her
about the affair, she clasped her hands, and said that he must
go straight to the district chief of police, for his subordinate
would turn up his nose, promise well, and drop the matter
there. The very best thing to do, therefore, would be to go to
the district chief, whom she knew, because Finnish Anna, her
former cook, was now nurse at his house. She often saw him
passing the house, and he was at church every Sunday, pray-
ing, but at the same time gazing cheerfully at everybody; so
that he must be a good man, judging from all appearances.
Having listened to this opinion, Akaki Akakiyevich betook
himself sadly to his room. And how he spent the night there,

any one who can put himself in another's place may readily imagine.

Early in the morning, he presented himself at the district chief's, but was told the official was asleep. He went again at ten and was again informed that he was asleep. At eleven, and they said, "The superintendent is not at home." At dinner time, and the clerks in the anteroom would not admit him on any terms, and insisted upon knowing his business. So that at last, for once in his life, Akaki Akakiyevich felt an inclination to show some spirit, and said curtly that he must see the chief in person, that they ought not to presume to refuse him entrance, that he came from the department of justice, and that when he complained to them, they would see.

The clerks dared make no reply to this, and one of them went to call the chief, who listened to the strange story of the theft of the coat. Instead of directing his attention to the principal points of the matter, he began to question Akaki Akakiyevich. Why was he going home so late? Was he in the habit of doing so, or had he been to some disorderly house? So that Akaki Akakiyevich got thoroughly confused, and left him, without knowing whether the affair of his cloak was in proper train or not.

All that day, for the first time in his life, he never went near the department. The next day he made his appearance, very pale, and in his old cape, which had become even more shabby. The news of the robbery of the cloak touched many, although there were some officials present who never lost an opportunity, even such a one as the present, of ridiculing Akaki Akakiyevich. They decided to make a collection for him on the spot, but the officials had already spent a great deal in subscribing for the director's portrait and for some book, at the suggestion of the head of that division, who was a friend of the author; and so the sum was trifling.

One of them, moved by pity, resolved to help Akaki Akakiyevich with some good advice, at least, and told him that he ought not to go to the police, for although it might happen that a police officer, wishing to win the approval of his superiors, might hunt up the cloak by some means, still, his cloak would remain in the possession of the police if he did not offer legal proof that it belonged to him. The best thing for him, therefore, would be to apply to a certain prominent personage; since this prominent personage, by entering into relation with the proper persons, could greatly expedite the matter.

As there was nothing else to be done, Akaki Akakiyevich decided to go to the prominent personage. What was the exact official position of the prominent personage, remains unknown to this day. The reader must know that the prominent personage had but recently become a prominent personage, having up to that time been only an insignificant person. Moreover, his present position was not considered prominent in comparison with others still more so. But there is always a circle of people to whom what is insignificant in the eyes of others, is important enough. Moreover, he strove to increase his importance by sundry devices. For instance, he managed to have the inferior officials meet him on the staircase when he entered upon his service; no one was to presume to come directly to him, but the strictest etiquette must be observed; the collegiate recorder must make a report to the government secretary, the government secretary to the titular councillor, or whatever other man was proper, and all business must come before him in this manner. In Holy Russia, all is thus contaminated with the love of imitation; every man imitates and copies his superior. They even say that a certain titular councillor, when promoted to the head of some small separate office, immediately partitioned off a private room for himself, called it the audience chamber, and posted at the door, a lackey with red collar and braid, who grasped the handle of the door, and opened to all comers, though the audience chamber would hardly hold an ordinary writing table.

The manners and customs of the prominent personage were grand and imposing, but rather exaggerated. The main foundation of his system was strictness. "Strictness, strictness, and always strictness!" he generally said; and at the last word he looked significantly into the face of the person to whom he spoke. But there was no necessity for this, for the halfscore of subordinates, who formed the entire force of the office, were properly afraid. On catching sight of him afar off, they left their work, and waited, drawn up in line, until he had passed through the room. His ordinary converse with his inferiors smacked of sternness, and consisted chiefly of three phrases: "How dare you?" "Do you know whom you are speaking to?" "Do you realise who is standing before you?"

Otherwise he was a very kindhearted man, good to his comrades, and ready to oblige. But the rank of general threw him completely off his balance. On receiving any one of that rank, he became confused, lost his way, as it were, and never knew what to do. If he chanced to be amongst his equals, he was still a very nice kind of man, a very good fellow in many respects, and not stupid, but the very moment that he found himself in the society of people but one rank lower than himself, he became silent. And his situation aroused sympathy, the more so, as he felt himself that he might have been making an incomparably better use of his time. In his eyes, there was sometimes visible a desire to join some interesting conversation or group, but he was kept back by the thought, "Would it not be a very great condescension on his part? Would it not be familiar? And would he not thereby lose his importance?" And in consequence of such reflections, he always remained in the same dumb state, uttering from time to time a few monosyllabic sounds, and thereby earning the name of the most wearisome of men.

To this prominent personage Akaki Akakiyevich presented himself, and this at the most unfavourable time for himself, though opportune for the prominent personage. The prominent personage was in his cabinet, conversing very gaily with an old acquaintance and companion of his childhood, whom he had not seen for several years, and who had just arrived, when it was announced to him that a person named Bashmachkin had come. He asked abruptly, "Who is he?"—"Some official," he was informed. "Ah, he can wait! This is no time for him to call," said the important man.

It must be remarked here that the important man lied outrageously. He had said all he had to say to his friend long before, and the conversation had been interspersed for some time with very long pauses, during which they merely slapped each other on the leg, and said, "You think so, Ivan Abramovich!" "Just so, Stepan Varlamovich!" Nevertheless, he ordered that the official should be kept waiting, in order to show his friend, a man who had not been in the service for a long time, but had lived at home in the country, how long officials had to wait in his anteroom.

At length, having talked himself completely out, and more than that, having had his fill of pauses, and smoked a cigar in a very comfortable armchair with reclining back, he suddenly seemed to recollect, and said to his secretary, who stood by the door with papers of reports, "So it seems that there is an official waiting to see me. Tell him that he may come in." On perceiving Akaki Akakiyevich's modest mien and his worn uniform, he turned abruptly to him, and said, "What do you want?" in a curt hard voice, which he had practised in his room in private, and before the looking glass, for a whole week before being raised to his present rank.

Akaki Akakiyevich, who was already imbued with a due amount of fear, became somewhat confused, and as well as his tongue would permit, explained, with a rather more frequent addition than usual of the word "that" that his cloak was quite new, and had been stolen in the most inhuman manner; that he had applied to him, in order that he might, in some way, by his intermediation—that he might enter into correspondence with the chief of police, and find the cloak.

For some inexplicable reason, this conduct seemed familiar to the prominent personage.

"What, my dear sir!" he said abruptly, "are you not acquainted with etiquette? To whom have you come? Don't you know how such matters are managed? You should first have presented a petition to the office. It would have gone to the head of the department, then to the chief of the division, then it would have been handed over to the secretary, and the secretary would have given it to me."

"But your excellency," said Akaki Akakiyevich, trying to collect his small handful of wits, and conscious at the same time that he was perspiring terribly, "I, your excellency, presumed to trouble you because secretaries—are an untrustworthy race."

"What, what, what!" said the important personage. "Where did you get such courage? Where did you get such ideas? What impudence towards their chiefs and superiors has spread among the young generation!" The prominent personage apparently had not observed that Akaki Akakiyevich was already in the neighborhood of fifty. If he could be called a young man, it must have been in comparison with some one who was seventy. "Do you know to whom you are speaking? Do you realise who is standing before you? Do you realise it? Do you realise it, I ask you!" Then he stamped his foot, and raised his voice to such a pitch that it would have frightened even a different man from Akaki Akakiyevich.

Akaki Akakiyevich's senses failed him. He staggered, trembled in every limb, and, if the porters had not run in to support him, would have fallen to the floor. They carried him out insensible. But the prominent personage, gratified that the effect should have surpassed his expectations, and quite intoxicated with the thought that his word could even deprive a man of his senses, glanced sideways at his friend in order to see how he looked upon this, and perceived, not without satisfaction, that his friend was in a most uneasy frame of mind, and even beginning on his part, to feel a trifle frightened.

Akaki Akakiyevich could not remember how he descended the stairs, and got into the street. He felt neither his hands nor feet. Never in his life had he been so rated by any high official, let alone a strange one. He went staggering on through the snowstorm, which was blowing in the streets, with his mouth wide open. The wind, in St. Petersburg fashion, darted upon him from all quarters, and down every cross street. In a twinkling it had blown a quinsy into his throat, and he reached home unable to utter a word. His throat was swollen, and he lay down on his bed. So powerful is sometimes a good scolding!

The next day a violent fever developed. Thanks to the generous assistance of the St. Petersburg climate, the malady progressed more rapidly than could have been expected, and when the doctor arrived, he found, on feeling the sick man's pulse, that there was nothing to be done, except to prescribe a poultice, so that the patient might not be left entirely without the beneficent aid of medicine. But at the same time, he predicted his end in thirty-six hours. After this he turned to the landlady, and said, "And as for you, don't waste your time on him. Order his pine coffin now, for an oak one will be too expensive for him."

Did Akaki Akakiyevich hear these fatal words? And if he heard them, did they produce any overwhelming effect upon him? Did he lament the bitterness of his life?—We know not, for he continued in a delirious condition. Visions incessantly appeared to him, each stranger than the other. Now he saw Petrovich, and ordered him to make a cloak, with some traps for robbers, who seemed to him to be always under the bed; and he cried every moment to the landlady to pull one of them from under his coverlet. Then he inquired why his old mantle hung before him when he had a new cloak. Next he fancied that he was standing before the prominent person, listening to a thorough setting-down and saying, "Forgive me, your excellency!" but at last he began to curse, uttering the most horrible words, so that his aged landlady crossed herself, never in her life having heard anything of the kind from him, and more so, as these words followed directly after the words "your excellency." Later on he talked utter nonsense, of which nothing could be made, all that was evident being that these incoherent words and thoughts hovered ever about one thing, his cloak.

At length poor Akaki Akakiyevich breathed his last. They sealed up neither his room nor his effects, because, in the first place, there were no heirs, and, in the second, there was very little to inherit beyond a bundle of goose quills, a quire of white official paper, three pairs of socks, two or three buttons which had burst off his trousers, and the mantle already known to the reader. To whom all this fell, God knows. I confess that the person who told me this tale took no interest in the matter. They carried Akaki Akakiyevich out, and buried him.

And St. Petersburg was left without Akaki Akakiyevich, as though he had never lived there. A being disappeared, who was protected by none, dear to none, interesting to none, and who never even attracted to himself the attention of those students of human nature who omit no opportunity of thrusting a pin through a common fly and examining it under the microscope. A being who bore meekly the jibes of the department, and went to his grave without having done one unusual deed, but to whom, nevertheless, at the close of his life, appeared a bright visitant in the form of a cloak, which momentarily cheered his poor life, and upon him, thereafter, an intolerable misfortune descended, just as it descends upon the heads of the mighty of this world!

Several days after his death, the porter was sent from the department to his lodgings, with an order for him to present himself there immediately, the chief commanding it. But the porter had to return unsuccessful, with the answer that he could not come; and to the question, "Why?" replied, "Well, because he is dead! he was buried four days ago." In this manner did they hear of Akaki Akakiyevich's death at the department. And the next day a new official sat in his place, with a handwriting by no means so upright, but more inclined and slanting.

But who could have imagined that this was not really the end of Akaki Akakiyevich, that he was destined to raise a commotion after death, as if in compensation for his utterly insignificant life? But so it happened, and our poor story unexpectedly gains a fantastic ending.

A rumor suddenly spread through St. Petersburg, that a dead man had taken to appearing on the Kalinkin Bridge, and its vicinity, at night in the form of an official seeking a stolen cloak, and that, under the pretext of its being the stolen cloak, he dragged, without regard to rank or calling, every one's cloak from his shoulders, be it catskin, beaver, fox, bear, sable, in a word, every sort of fur and skin which men adopted for their covering. One of the department officials saw the dead man with his own eyes, and immediately recognised in him Akaki Akakiyevich. This, however, inspired him with such terror, that he ran off with all his might, and therefore did not scan the dead man closely, but only saw how the latter threatened him from afar with his finger. Constant complaints poured in from all quarters, that the backs and shoulders, not only of titular but even of court councillors, were exposed to the danger of a cold, on account of the frequent dragging off of their cloaks.

Arrangements were made by the police to catch the corpse, alive or dead, at any cost, and punish him as an example to others, in the most severe manner. In this they nearly succeeded, for a watchman, on guard in Kiryushkin Lane, caught the corpse by the collar on the very scene of his evil deeds, when attempting to pull off the frieze cloak of a retired musician. Having seized him by the collar, he summoned, with a shout, two of his comrades, whom he enjoined to hold him fast, while he himself felt for a moment in his boot, in order to draw out his snuffbox, and refresh his frozen nose. But the snuff was of a sort which even a corpse could not endure. The watchman having closed his right nostril with his finger, had no sooner succeeded in holding half a handful up to the left, than the corpse sneezed so violently that he completely filled the eyes of all three. While they raised their hands to wipe them, the dead man vanished completely, so that they positively did not know whether they had actually had him in their grip at all. Thereafter the watchmen conceived such a terror of dead men that they were afraid even to seize the living, and only screamed from a distance. "Hey, there! go your way!" So the dead official began to appear even beyond the Kalinkin Bridge causing no little terror to all timid people.

But we have totally neglected that certain prominent personage who may really be considered as the cause of the fantastic turn taken by this true history. First of all, justice compels us to say, that after the departure of poor, annihilated Akaki

Akakiyevich, he felt something like remorse. Suffering was unpleasant to him, for his heart was accessible to many good
impulses, in spite of the fact that his rank often prevented his
showing his true self. As soon as his friend had left his cabinet,
he began to think about poor Akaki Akakiyevich. And from
that day forth, poor Akaki Akakiyevich, who could not bear
up under an official reprimand, recurred to his mind almost
every day. The thought troubled him to such an extent, that
a week later he even resolved to send an official to him, to
learn whether he really could assist him. And when it was
reported to him that Akaki Akakiyevich had died suddenly of
fever, he was startled, hearkened to the reproaches of his
conscience, and was out of sorts for the whole day.

Wishing to divert his mind in some way and drive away
the disagreeable impression, he set out that evening for one
of his friends' houses, where he found quite a large party
assembled. What was better, nearly every one was of the same
rank as himself, so that he need not feel in the least con-
strained. This had a marvellous effect upon his mental state.
He grew expansive, made himself agreeable in conversation,
in short, he passed a delightful evening. After supper he drank
a couple of glasses of champagne—not a bad recipe for cheerfulness, as every one knows. The champagne inclined him to
various adventures, and he determined not to return home, but
to go and see a certain well-known lady, of German extrac-
tion, Karolina Ivanovna, a lady, it appears, with whom he
was on a very friendly footing.

It must be mentioned that the prominent personage was no
longer a young man, but a good husband and respected father
of a family. Two sons, one of whom was already in the service,
and a good-looking, sixteen year old daughter, with a slightly
arched but pretty little nose, came every morning to kiss his
hand and say, *"Bonjour, papa."* His wife, a still fresh and
good-looking woman, first gave him her hand to kiss, and then,
reversing the procedure, kissed his. But the prominent personage, though perfectly satisfied in his domestic relations, considered it stylish to have a friend in another quarter of the city.
This friend was scarcely prettier or younger than his wife; but
there are such puzzles in the world, and it is not our place to
judge them. So the important personage descended the stairs,
stepped into his sledge, said to the coachman, "To Karolina
Ivanovna's," and, wrapping himself luxuriously in his warm
cloak, found himself in that delightful frame of mind than

which a Russian can conceive nothing better, namely, when you think of nothing yourself, yet when the thoughts creep into your mind of their own accord, each more agreeable than the other, giving you no trouble either to drive them away, or seek them. Fully satisfied, he recalled all the gay features of the evening just passed and all the mots which had made the little circle laugh. Many of them he repeated in a low voice, and found them quite as funny as before; so it is not surprising that he should laugh heartily at them. Occasionally, however, he was interrupted by gusts of wind, which, coming suddenly, God knows whence or why, cut his face, drove masses of snow into it, filled out his cloak collar like a sail, or suddenly blew it over his head with supernatural force, and thus caused him constant trouble to disentangle himself.

Suddenly the important personage felt some one clutch him firmly by the collar. Turning around, he perceived a man of short stature, in an old, worn uniform, and recognised, not without terror, Akaki Akakiyevich. The official's face was white as snow, and looked just like a corpse's. But the horror of the important personage transcended all bounds when he saw the dead man's mouth open, and heard it utter the following remarks, while it breathed upon him the terrible odor of the grave: "Ah, here you are at last! I have you, that—by the collar! I need your cloak. You took no trouble about mine, but reprimanded me. So now give up your own."

The pallid prominent personage almost died of fright. Brave as he was in the office and in the presence of inferiors generally, and although, at the sight of his manly form and appearance, every one said, "Ugh! how much character he has!" at this crisis, he, like many possessed of an heroic exterior, experienced such terror, that, not without cause, he began to fear an attack of illness. He flung his cloak hastily from his shoulders and shouted to his coachman in an unnatural voice, "Home at full speed!" The coachman, hearing the tone which is generally employed at critical moments, and even accompanied by something much more tangible, drew his head down between his shoulders in case of an emergency, flourished his whip, and flew on like an arrow. In a little more than six minutes the prominent personage was at the entrance of his own house. Pale, thoroughly scared, and cloakless, he went home instead of to Karolina Ivanovna's, reached his room somehow or other, and passed the night in the direst distress; so that the next morning over their tea, his daughter said,

"You are very pale today, papa." But papa remained silent, and said not a word to any one of what had happened to him, where he had been, or where he had intended to go.

This occurrence made a deep impression upon him. He even began to say, "How dare you? Do you realize who is standing before you?" less frequently to the underofficials, and, if he did utter the words, it was only after first having learned the bearings of the matter. But the most noteworthy point was, that from that day forward the apparition of the dead official ceased to be seen. Evidently the prominent personage's cloak just fitted his shoulders. At all events, no more instances of his dragging cloaks from people's shoulders were heard of. But many active and solicitous persons could by no means reassure themselves, and asserted that the dead official still showed himself in distant parts of the city.

In fact, one watchman in Kolomen saw with his own eyes the apparition come from behind a house. But the watchman was not a strong man, so he was afraid to arrest him, and followed him in the dark, until, at length, the apparition looked around, paused, and inquired, "What do you want?" at the same time showing such a fist as is never seen on living men. The watchman said, "Nothing," and turned back instantly. But the apparition was much too tall, wore huge mustaches, and, directing its steps apparently towards the Obukhov Bridge, disappeared in the darkness of the night.

Mikhail Lermontov

Taman

⚜

Taman is the rottenest of all the coastal villages of Russia. It was there that I narrowly escaped death, first by starvation and then by drowning.

I arrived there late at night by post carriage. The driver stopped the tired troika at the gate of Taman's only stone-built house, which stood at the entrance to the town. The sentry, a Cossack from the Black Sea, awakened by the jingle of our harness bells, called out in his barbarous voice, "Who goes there?" A Cossack sergeant and corporal came out. I explained that I was an officer under orders to report for active duty and demanded official quarters. The corporal conducted me all around the town, but every hut we drove up to we found to be already occupied. The weather was cold; I had not slept for three nights; I was very tired and began to lose my temper.

"Take me somewhere or other, you wretch!" I cried. "Even to the devil himself, so long as he has room to put me up!"

"There is one other lodging," answered the corporal, scratching his head. "Only you won't like it, sir. It is uncanny!"

Failing to grasp the exact point of his last word, I ordered him to go on, and, after a long trip over small muddy roads, at the sides of which I could see nothing but old fences, we drove up to a small cabin, right on the shore of the sea.

The full moon was shining on the little reed-thatched roof and the white walls of my new dwelling. In the yard, which was surrounded by a wall of cobble stone, there stood another hovel, smaller and older than the first and all askew. The shore descended precipitously to the sea, almost from its very walls, and down below, with incessant murmur, plashed the dark blue waves. The moon gazed softly upon the waters, restless but obedient to it, and I was able by its light to distinguish two ships lying at some distance from the shore, their motionless black rigging standing out, like cobwebs, against the pale line of the horizon.

"There are vessels in the harbor," I said to myself. "Tomorrow I will set out for Gelendzhik."

I had with me, in the capacity of orderly, a Cossack of the frontier army. I ordered him to take down the suitcase and dismiss the driver, and I began to call the master of the house. No answer! I knocked. All was silent within! What could it mean? At length a boy of about fourteen crept out from the hovel.

"Where is the master?"

"There isn't one."

"What? No master?"

"None!"

"And the mistress?"

"She has gone to the village."

"Who will open the door for me then?" I said, giving it a kick. The door opened and a breath of moisture-laden air was wafted from the hut. I struck a match and held it to the boy's face. It lit up two white eyes. He was totally blind, obviously so from birth. He stood stockstill before me, and I began to examine his features.

I confess that I have a violent prejudice against all blind, one-eyed, deaf, dumb, legless, armless, hunchbacked, and other such people. I have observed that there is always a certain strange connection between a man's exterior and his soul, as if when the body loses a limb, the soul also loses some power of feeling.

And so I began to examine the blind boy's face. But what can be read on a face from which the eyes are missing? For a long time I gazed at him with involuntary compassion, when suddenly a scarcely perceptible smile flitted across his thin lips, producing, I know not why, a most unpleasant impression upon me. I began to feel that the blind boy was not so blind as he appeared to be. In vain I tried to convince myself that it was impossible to counterfeit blindness—and besides, what reason could there be for doing such a thing? But I could not dispel my suspicions. I am easily swayed by prejudice.

"You are the master's son?" I asked.

"No."

"Who are you then?"

"An orphan—a poor boy."

"Has the mistress any children?"

"No. Her daughter ran away across the sea with a Tartar."

"What sort of a Tartar?"

"The devil only knows! A Crimean Tartar, a boatman from Kerch."

I entered the hut. Its whole furniture consisted of two benches and a table, together with an enormous chest near the stove. There was not a single ikon to be seen on the wall—a bad sign! The sea breeze blew through the broken window-pane. I drew a wax candle end from my suitcase, lit it, and began to unpack my things. My sabre and rifle I placed in a corner; my pistols I laid on the table. I spread my felt cloak out on one bench, and my Cossack orderly his on the other. In ten minutes he was snoring, but I could not fall asleep—the image of the boy with the white eyes kept hovering before me in the dark.

About an hour passed thus. The moon shone through the window and its rays played on the earthen floor of the hut. Suddenly a shadow flitted across the moonlit strip on the floor. I raised myself up a little and looked out the window. Again somebody ran by and disappeared—heaven knows where! It seemed impossible for any one to descend the steep cliff over-hanging the shore, but that was the only thing that could have happened. I got up, threw on my tunic, put on a dagger, and with the utmost quiet went out of the hut. The blind boy was coming towards me. I hid close to the fence, and he passed near me with a sure but cautious step. He was carrying a bundle under his arm. He turned towards the harbor and began to descend a steep and narrow path.

"On that day the dumb will cry out and the blind will see," I said to myself, following him just close enough to keep him in sight.

Meanwhile the moon was becoming hidden by clouds and a mist had risen upon the sea. The lantern at the stern of the closer ship was scarcely visible through the mist. Along the shore there glimmered the foam of the waves, which constantly threatened to submerge it. Descending with difficulty, I stole along the steep cliff. All at once I saw the blind boy stop and then turn sharply to the right. He walked so close to the water's edge that it seemed as if the waves might at any moment seize him and carry him off. But, judging by the confidence with which he stepped from rock to rock and avoided the water channels, this was evidently not the first time he had made that journey. Finally he stopped, as though listening for something, sat down on the ground and laid the bundle beside him. Concealing myself behind a projecting rock on the shore, I kept watch on his movements. After a few minutes a white figure appeared from the opposite direction. It came up to the blind boy and sat down beside him. At times the wind wafted their conversation to me.

"Well?" said a woman's voice. "The storm is violent. Yanko will not be here."

"Yanko is not afraid of the storm!" the other replied.

"The mist is thickening," rejoined the woman's voice, sadness in its tone.

"In the mist it is all the easier to slip past the patrol boats," was the answer.

"And if he is drowned?"

"Well, what then? On Sunday you won't have a new ribbon to wear at church."

An interval of silence followed. One thing, however, struck me: in talking to me the blind boy spoke in the Ukrainian dialect, but now he was expressing himself in pure Russian.

"You see, I am right!" the blind boy went on, clapping his hands. "Yanko is not afraid of sea, the winds, the mist, nor the coast guards! Just listen! That is not the water splashing, you can't deceive me—it is his long oars."

The woman sprang up and began anxiously to peer into the distance.

"You are wrong," she said. "I cannot see anything."

I confess that, much as I tried to make out in the distance something resembling a boat, my efforts were unsuccessful. About ten minutes passed thus, when a black speck suddenly appeared among the mountainous waves! At one moment it grew larger, at another moment smaller. Slowly rising on the crests of the waves and swiftly descending from them, the boat drew near the shore. "He must be a brave sailor," I thought, "to cross fourteen miles of strait on a night like this, and he must have had strong reasons for doing so."

Reflecting thus, I gazed with an uncontrollable throbbing of my heart at the little boat. It dived like a duck, and then, with swinging oars—like wings—it sprang forth from the abyss in the raging foam. "Ah!" I thought, "it will be dashed against the shore and broken to pieces!" But it turned adroitly and leaped unharmed into a little inlet. Out of it stepped a man of medium height, wearing a Tartar sheepskin cap. He waved his hand, and all three set to work to drag something out of the boat. The cargo was so large that, to this day, I cannot understand how it was that the boat did not sink.

Each of them shouldered a bundle, and they set off along the shore. I soon lost sight of them. I had to return to my quarters, but I confess I was so uneasy by all these strange happenings that I found it hard to await the morning.

My Cossack was very much astonished when, on waking up, he saw me fully dressed. I did not, however, tell him the reason. For some time I stood at the window admiring the blue sky studded with wisps of cloud and the distant shore of the Crimea, stretched out in a lilac-colored streak and ending in a cliff on the summit of which the white lighthouse gleamed. Then I betook myself to Fort Fanagoriya to ascertain from the Commandant at what hour I was to leave for Gelendzhik.

But the Commandant, alas, could not give me any definite information. The ships in the harbor were either patrol boats or merchant ships which had not yet even begun to take in cargo.

"Maybe in three or four days' time a mail-boat will come in," said the Commandant, "and then we shall see."

I returned home depressed and annoyed. My Cossack met me at the door with a frightened look. "Things look bad, sir!" he said.

"Yes, my friend. Heaven knows when we shall get away!"

At this he became still more uneasy and bending towards me, said in a whisper: "It is uncanny here! I met a sergeant from the Black Sea today—he's an acquaintance of mine—he was in our detachment last year. When I told him where we were staying, he said, 'That place is uncanny; they're wicked people there!' And, indeed, what sort of a blind boy is that? He goes everywhere alone—to fetch water, to buy bread, to the market. They have become accustomed to that sort of thing here."

"Well, tell me though, has the mistress of the place shown up yet?"

"During your absence today, an old woman and her daughter arrived."

"What daughter? She has no daughter."

"Heaven knows who she is if she isn't her daughter. The old woman is sitting over there in the hut right now."

I entered the hovel. A good fire was burning in the stove, and they were cooking a dinner which struck me as being rather luxurious for poor people. To all my questions the old woman replied that she was deaf and could not hear me. There was nothing to be got out of her. I turned to the blind boy who was sitting in front of the stove, putting twigs into the fire.

"Now, then, you blind little devil," I said, taking him by the ear. "Tell me, where were you going with that bundle last night, eh?"

The blind boy suddenly burst into weeping, shrieking and wailing.

"Where did I go? I did not go anywhere. With a bundle? What bundle?"

This time the old woman heard and she began to mutter: "Listen to them plot! And against a poor crippled boy too! What are you after him for? What has he done to you?"

I had enough of this and went out, firmly resolved to find the key to the riddle.

I wrapped myself in my felt cloak and, sitting down on a rock by the fence, gazed into the distance. Before me stretched the sea, still agitated by the storm of the previous night, and its monotonous roar, like the murmur of a town over which slumber is beginning to creep, recalled bygone years to my mind and transported my thoughts northward to our cold capital. Disturbed by my recollections, I became oblivious of my surroundings.

About an hour passed thus, perhaps even more. Suddenly something resembling a song struck my ear. It *was* a song, and the voice was a woman's, young and fresh—but, where was it coming from? I listened; it was a harmonious melody—now slow and plaintive, now fast and lively. I looked around me—there was nobody to be seen. I listened again—the sounds seemed to be falling from the sky. I raised my eyes. On the roof of my cabin stood a young girl in a striped dress and with her hair hanging loose—a regular water nymph. Shading her eyes from the sun's rays with the palm of her hand, she was gazing intently into the distance. Some of the time she would laugh and talk to herself; some of the time she would strike up her song.

I have retained that song in my memory word for word:

> *At their own free will*
> *They seem to wander*
> *O'er the green sea yonder,*
> *Those ships, as still*
> *They are onward going,*
> *With white sails flowing.*

And among those ships
My eye can mark
My own dear bark:
By two oars guided
(All unprovided
With sails) it slips.

The storm-wind raves:
And the old ships—see!
With wings spread free,
Over the waves
They scatter and flee!

The sea I will hail
With obeisance deep:
"Thou base one, hark!
Thou must not fail
My little bark
From harm to keep!"

For lo! 'tis bearing
Most precious gear,
And brave and daring
The arms that steer
Within the dark
My little bark.

Involuntarily the thought occurred to me that I had heard the same voice the night before. I reflected for a moment, and when I looked up at the roof again there was no one to be seen. Suddenly she darted past me, another song on her lips, and, snapping her fingers, she ran to the old woman. A quarrel arose between them. The old woman grew angry, and the girl laughed loudly. And then I saw my Undine running and skipping again. She came up to where I was, stopped, and gazed fixedly into my face as if surprised at my presence. Then she turned away and went quietly towards the harbor. But this was not all. The whole day she kept hovering around my lodging, singing and skipping without a moment's interruption. Strange creature! There was not the slightest sign of insanity in her face. On the contrary, her eyes, which were continually resting upon me, were bright and piercing; they seemed to be endowed with magnetic power, and each time they looked at me they appeared to be expecting a question.

But I had only to open my lips to speak, and away she would run, with a sly smile.

Never before had I seen a woman like her. She was by no means beautiful, but, as in other matters, I have my own views on the subject of beauty. There was a good deal of breeding in her. Breeding in women, as in horses, is a great thing: a discovery, the credit of which belongs to young France. It—that is to say, breeding, not young France—is chiefly to be detected in the walk, in the hands and feet; the nose, in particular, is of the greatest significance. In Russia a straight nose is rarer than a small foot.

My songstress appeared to be not more than eighteen years of age. The unusual suppleness of her figure, the way she had of inclining her head, her long light brown hair, the golden sheen of her slightly sunburnt neck and shoulders, and especially her straight nose—all these held me fascinated. Although in her sidelong glances I could read a certain wildness and disdain, although in her smile there was a certain vagueness, yet—such is the force of predilections—that straight nose of hers drove me crazy. I fancied that I had found Goethe's Mignon—that strange creature of his German imagination. And, indeed, there was a good deal of similarity between them —the same rapid shifts from utmost restlessness to complete immobility, the same enigmatic speeches, the same gambols, the same strange songs.

Towards evening I stopped her at the door and began the following conversation with her.

"Tell me, my beauty," I asked, "what were you doing on the roof today?"

"I was looking to see from what direction the wind was blowing."

"What did you want to know that for?"

"Whence the wind blows comes happiness."

"So? Were you invoking happiness with your song?"

"Where there is singing there is also happiness."

"But what if your song were to bring sorrow?"

"Well, what then? Where things won't be better, they will be worse; and from bad to good again is not far."

"And who taught you that song?"

"Nobody taught me. It comes into my head and I sing. Whoever is to hear it, he will hear it; and whoever ought not to hear it, he will not understand it."

"What is your name, my songstress?"

"He who baptized me knows."

"And who baptized you?"

"How should I know?"

"What a secretive girl you are! But look here, I have learned something about you"—she neither changed countenance nor moved her lips, as though my discovery was of no concern to her—"I have learned that you went to the shore last night." And, thereupon, I gravely retailed to her all that I had seen, thinking that I would embarrass her. Not a bit! She burst out laughing heartily.

"You have seen much, but know little. What you do know, see that you keep it under lock and key."

"But suppose I was to take it into my head to inform the Commandant?" and here I assumed a very serious, not to say stern, demeanor.

She gave a sudden start, began to sing, and disappeared like a bird frightened out of a thicket. My last words were altogether out of place; I had no suspicion then how significant they were, but afterwards I had occasion to rue them.

As soon as evening fell, I ordered the Cossack to heat the teapot, campaign fashion. I lit a candle and sat down by the table, smoking my pipe. I was just about to finish my second glass of tea when suddenly the door creaked and I heard behind me the sound of footsteps and the light rustle of a dress. I started and turned round.

It was she—my Undine. Softly and without saying a word she sat down opposite me and fixed her eyes upon me. Her glance seemed wondrously tender, I know not why; it reminded me of those glances which, in years gone by, so despotically played with my life. She seemed to be waiting for a question, but I kept silence, filled with an inexplicable sense of embarrassment. Mental agitation was revealed by the dull pallor which overspread her face. Her hand, which I noticed was trembling slightly, moved aimlessly about the table. At one time her breast heaved; at another she seemed to be holding her breath. This little comedy was beginning to pall upon me, and I was about to break the silence in a most prosaic manner (that is, by offering her a glass of tea) when suddenly springing up, she threw her arms around my neck and pressed her moist, fiery lips upon mine. Darkness swept over my eyes; my head began to swim. I embraced her with all the strength of youthful passion, but, like a snake, she slipped from my arms, whispering in my ear: "Tonight, when every one is asleep, go to the shore."

Like an arrow she sprang from the room. In the hall she upset the teapot and a candle that was standing on the floor.

"Little devil!" cried the Cossack, who had settled himself on the straw and had contemplated warming himself with the rest of the tea. It was only then that I recovered my senses.

In about two hours' time, when all had grown silent in the harbor, I awakened my Cossack.

"If I fire a pistol," I said, "rush to the shore."

He stared open-eyed and answered mechanically: "Very well, sir."

I stuffed a pistol in my belt and went out. She was waiting for me at the edge of the cliff. Her attire was more than light, and a small kerchief girded her supple waist.

"Follow me!" she said, taking me by the hand, and we began to descend.

I cannot understand how it was that I did not break my neck. Down below we turned to the right and took the path along which I had followed the blind boy the evening before. The moon had not yet risen, and only two little stars, like two guardian lighthouses, were twinkling in the dark blue vault of heaven. The heavy waves, with measured and even motion, rolled one after the other, scarcely lifting the solitary boat which was moored to the shore.

"Let us get into the boat," said my companion.

I hesitated. I am no lover of sentimental trips on the sea, but this was not the time to draw back. She leaped into the boat, and I after her; I had not time to recover my wits before I observed that we were adrift.

"What is the meaning of this?" I said angrily.

"It means," she answered, making me sit on the bench and throwing her arms around my waist, "it means that I love you!"

Her cheek was pressed close to mine. I felt her burning breath upon my face. Suddenly something fell noisily into the water. I clutched at my belt—my pistol was gone! Ah, now a terrible suspicion crept into my soul, and the blood rushed to my head! I looked round. We were about three hundred feet from the shore, and I could not swim a stroke! I tried to thrust her away from me, but she clung like a cat to my clothes, and suddenly a violent wrench all but threw me into the sea. The boat rocked, but I recovered my balance and a desperate struggle began.

Fury lent me strength, but I soon found that I was no match for my opponent in agility. "What do you want?" I cried, firmly squeezing her little hands.

Her fingers crunched, but her serpentlike nature bore up against the torture and she did not utter a cry.

"You saw us," she answered. "You will tell on us." And, with a supernatural effort, she flung me to the side of the boat; we both hung half overboard; her hair touched the water. The decisive moment had come. I planted my knee against the bottom of the boat, caught her by the tresses with one hand and by the throat with the other; she let go my clothes, and, in an instant I had thrown her into the waves.

It was now rather dark; once or twice her head appeared for an instant amid the sea foam, and then I saw no more of her.

I found half of an old oar at the bottom of the boat, and somehow or other, after lengthy efforts, I returned to the harbor. Making my way along the shore towards my hut, I involuntarily gazed in the direction of the spot where, on the previous night, the blind boy had awaited the nocturnal mariner. The moon was already rolling through the sky, and it seemed to me that somebody in white was sitting on the shore. Spurred by curiosity, I crept up and crouched in the grass on the top of the cliff. By putting my head out a little, I was able to get a good view of everything that was happening down below: I was not very much astonished, but almost rejoiced, when I recognized my water nymph. She was wringing the seafoam from her long hair. Her wet garment outlined her supple figure and her high bosom.

Soon a boat appeared in the distance; it drew near rapidly; and, as on the night before, a man in a Tartar cap stepped out of it, but he now had his hair cropped round in the Cossack fashion, and a large knife was sticking out behind his leather belt.

"Yanko," the girl said, "all is lost!"

Then their conversation continued, but so softly that I could not catch a word of it.

"But where is the blind boy?" said Yanko at last, raising his voice.

"I told him to come," was the reply.

After a few minutes the blind boy appeared, dragging on his back a sack, which they placed in the boat.

"Listen!" said Yanko to the blind boy. "Guard that place!

You know where I mean? There are valuable goods there. Tell"—I could not catch the name—"that I can no longer work for him. Things have gone badly. He will see me no more. It is dangerous now. I will look for work elsewhere. He will never be able to find another daredevil like me. Tell him also that if he had paid me a little better for my labors, I would not have left him. For me there is always a path wherever the wind blows and the sea roars."

After a short silence Yanko continued: "She is coming with me. It is impossible for her to remain here. Tell the old woman that it is time for her to die; she has been here a long time, and the line must be drawn somewhere. As for us, she will never see us any more."

"And I?" said the blind boy in a plaintive voice.

"What use have I for you?" was the answer.

In the meantime my Undine had sprung into the boat. She beckoned to her companion with her hand. He placed something in the blind boy's hand and added: "There, buy yourself some gingerbread."

"Is this all?" said the blind boy.

"Well, here is some more." The money fell and jingled as it struck the rock. The blind boy did not pick it up.

Yanko took his seat in the boat; the wind was blowing from the shore; they hoisted the little sail and sped away. For a long time the white sail gleamed in the moonlight amid the dark waves. Still the blind boy remained seated on the shore, and then I heard something which sounded like sobbing. The blind boy was, in fact, weeping, and for a long, long time his tears flowed. . . . I grew heavy-hearted. For what reason had fate thrown me into the peaceful circle of *honorable smugglers?* Like a stone cast into smooth water, I had disturbed their quietude—and I barely escaped going to the bottom like a stone!

I returned to my quarters. In the hall the burnt-out candle was spluttering on a wooden platter, and my Cossack, contrary to orders, was fast asleep, his rifle held in both hands. I left him at rest, took the candle, and entered the hut. Alas! my money box, my sabre with the silver chasing, my Dagestan dagger—the gift of a friend—all had vanished! It was then that I guessed what articles the cursed blind boy had been dragging along. Roughly shaking the Cossack, I woke him up and scolded him in a bad-tempered rage. But what was there to do? Would it not have been ridiculous to complain to the authorities that I had been robbed by a blind boy and all but drowned by an eighteen-year-old girl?

Thank heaven, an opportunity to get away presented itself in the morning, and I left Taman.

What became of the old woman and the poor blind boy I know not. Besides, what are the joys and sorrows of mankind to me—me, a travelling officer, and one, moreover, on government business with an order for post horses?

✠ ✠
✠

Ivan Turgenev

✠ ✠
✠
✠ ✠

The
Singers

✠

The small village of Kolotovka, which once belonged to a lady known in the neighborhood as Fidget from her bold and spirited ways (her real name is not recorded) but is now owned by some German or other from Petersburg, lies on the slope of a bare hill, cleft from top to bottom by a fearsome ravine, which, yawning like an abyss, winds its hollow, eroded way along the very middle of the village street and, worse than any river (for a river could at least be bridged), divides the unfortunate hamlet into two. A few lean willows droop timidly along its sandy sides; at the bottom, which is dry and copper yellow, lie huge flagstones of shale. A cheerless sight, there's no denying—but nevertheless the road to Kolotovka is well-known to all the people of the neighborhood: they use it frequently and as a matter of course.

Right at the top of the ravine, a few paces off the spot where it begins as a narrow crevice, stands a small square cabin, on its own, apart from the others. It is thatched with straw and has a chimney; a single window, like a watchful eye, looks towards the ravine, and on winter evenings, lit up from within, can be seen from afar through the dull frost haze and, for many a peasant on his way, shines out like a guiding star. Over the door of the cabin is nailed a little blue board; the cabin is a pothouse, and goes by the name of the "Snug Nook." It is a pothouse where in all probability drinks are sold no cheaper than the fixed price, but it is much better attended than any other establishment of the same sort in the neighborhood. The reason for this is the tapster, Nikolay Ivanich.

Nikolay Ivanich was once a lithe, curly-headed, ruddy peasant lad, but is now an extremely stout, already grizzled man, with a face deep in fat, eyes of a sly benevolence, and a greasy forehead crisscrossed with a web of wrinkles. He has lived at Kolotovka for more than twenty years. Nikolay is a man of

sagacity and resource, as most tapsters are. Without any special amiability or talkativeness, he has the knack of attracting
and holding customers, who somehow find it entertaining to
sit in front of his counter, under the calm, hospitable, but
watchful eye of their phlegmatic host. He has plenty of common sense; he is well acquainted with the ways of landowner,
peasant and townsman; in difficult situations he can give
shrewd advice, but, like the cautious egoist that he is, he pre-
fers to stay on the sideline and goes no further than a vague
hint, uttered as if without the least purpose, to guide his clients
—and then only his favorite clients—in the way of truth. He
knows what he is talking about on every subject of importance
or interest to the Russian male: horses and cattle, timber,
bricks, crockery, textiles and leather, singing and dancing.
When he has no custom, he is in the habit of sitting like a sack
on the ground in front of the door of his cabin, his thin legs
tucked up beneath him, swapping pleasantries with every
passer-by. He has seen plenty in his time, has outlived more
than a dozen of the lesser gentry who used to look in on him
for a drop of "distilled," knows everything that happens for
a hundred versts around, never lets on, never shows so much
as in his look that he knows what even the most penetrating
police officer fails to suspect. He simply keeps mum, chuckles,
and busies himself with the glasses. The neighbors respect him
deeply: His Excellency Mr. Shcherepetenko, the leading mag-
nate of the district, bows to him affably every time he passes
his abode. Nikolay Ivanich is a man of influence: he forced a
well-known horse thief to return a horse stolen from someone
of his acquaintance; he made the peasants of a neighboring
village listen to reason when they had refused to accept a new
factor, and so on. Incidentally, it mustn't be supposed that he
did this from love of fair play, from any zeal for his neighbors'
interest; no, he is simply at pains to avert anything that might
in any way disturb his own peace. Nikolay Ivanich is married
and has children. His wife, a brisk, sharp-nosed, quick-eyed
townswoman, has lately put on a good deal of weight, just like
her husband. He relies on her absolutely, and the money is
locked up in her charge. The noisily drunk hold her in awe;
she dislikes them; there is no profit from them, only a lot of
noise; the silent and sullen ones are closer to her heart. Nikolay's children are still small. The first ones all died, but the
survivors resemble their parents; it is a pleasure to look at these
healthy children with their clever little faces.

It was an unbearably sultry July day, when I trudged slowly, accompanied by my dog, up the Kolotovka ravine in the direction of the "Snug Nook" pothouse. The sun was blazing away in the sky with a kind of fury; it was mercilessly, bakingly hot; the air was absolutely saturated with choking dust. Glossy rooks and crows, with gaping beaks, looked piteously at the passer-by, as if to beg his sympathy; only the sparrows were undistressed and, fluffing out their feathers, twittered and scuffled about the fences even more actively than usual, or flew up from the dusty road in a flock, or hovered in grey clouds over the green hemp yards. I was tortured by thirst. There was no water at hand: at Kolotovka, as in many other steppe villages, in the absence of springs and wells, the peasants drink a sort of liquid filth from a pond . . . But who would give the name of water to this repulsive draught? I had it in mind to ask Nikolay Ivanich for a glass of beer or kvass.

It has to be admitted that at no season of the year does Kolotovka present a cheering spectacle; but it arouses a particularly mournful emotion when the blazing sun of July rains its pitiless rays on the tumbledown brown roofs, the deep ravine, the parched, dusty common land, on which some thin, long-legged chickens are roaming despondently, and the shack of grey aspenwood with holes for windows, a remnant of the former manor house, grown over with nettles, weeds and wormwood, and the pond, covered with goose feathers, black, molten looking, fringed with half-dried mud, and the sideways listing dam, near which, on the fine-ground, cinderlike earth, sheep, breathless and sneezing from the heat, crowd lugubriously together and with a dismal patience hang their heads as low as can be, as if waiting for the moment when the unbearable sultriness will finally pass. With exhausted steps I was at last nearing Nikolay Ivanich's place, exciting in children the usual amazement, expressed in intense and inane stares, and in dogs the usual indignation, voiced in such hoarse and savage barking that all their insides seemed to be torn loose, afterwards subsiding into a fit of coughing and choking, when suddenly, on the threshold of the pothouse, there appeared a tall man, capless, in a frieze overcoat held below the waist with a blue belt. He had the look of a house-serf; thick grey hair burst out untidily above his dry wrinkled face. He was calling somebody and making vigorous gestures with his arms, which were clearly swinging out much farther than he intended. It was evident that he had already had a drop.

"Come on, come *on!*" he stuttered, raising his thick eyebrows with an effort. "Come on, Blinker, come on! Why, man, you're simply crawling. It isn't right, man. They're waiting for you, and you're just crawling . . . Come on!"

"All right, all right," came a jarring voice, and, from behind the cabin to the right, a short, stout, lame fellow appeared. He wore quite a neat cloth coat, with only one sleeve on; a high, pointed hat, rammed straight down over his brows, gave his podgy, round face a sly, mocking look. His little yellow eyes fairly darted around; a contained, forced smile never left his thin lips, and his long sharp nose stuck jauntily out ahead like a rudder. "I'm coming, my friend," he went on, limping in the direction of the drinking establishment. "What are you calling me for? . . . Who's waiting for me?"

"What am I calling you for?" rejoined the man in the frieze coat, reproachfully. "You're a strange one, Blinker: you're called to the pothouse, and yet you ask: what for? There's all kind of good folk waiting for you: Yasha the Turk, and Wild Master, and the huckster from Zhizdra. Yasha and the huckster have made a bet: they've wagered a quart of beer to see which wins, that is, sings best . . . d'you see?"

"Yasha's going to sing?" said the man nicknamed Blinker, with animation. "You're not lying, Muddlehead?"

"I'm not," answered Muddlehead with dignity. "It's you that's the liar. Of course he's going to sing, if he's made a bet, you ladybird, you twister, you, Blinker!"

"Well, let's go, you ninny," rejoined Blinker.

"Well, kiss me at least, joy of my heart," stammered Muddlehead, flinging his arms out wide.

"You great milksop," replied Blinker, contemptuously elbowing him aside, and they both stooped and went in through the low doorway. The conversation I'd heard excited my keen curiosity. More than once rumors had reached me of Yasha the Turk, as being the best singer in the neighborhood, and now an opportunity had suddenly presented itself to hear him in competition with another master. I quickened my pace and entered the establishment.

Probably not many of my readers have had occasion to look inside a country pothouse—but we sportsmen, there's nowhere we don't go. The arrangement of these pothouses is remarkably simple. They usually consist of a dark entrance passage and a room divided in two by a partition, behind which none of the customers has the right to go. Cut in the partition, above a broad oak table, is a large longitudinal aperture. On this table or counter the drink is sold. Sealed flasks of different measures stand in a row on shelves immediately opposite the aperture. In the front part of the cabin, the part at the disposal of customers, are benches, two or three empty barrels, and a corner table. Country pothouses are for the most part pretty dark and you hardly ever see on their log walls any of those brightly colored popular prints without which the ordinary peasant's cabin is seldom complete.

When I went into the "Snug Nook" pothouse a fairly numerous company was already assembled there.

Behind the counter, suitably enough, and filling almost the whole width of the aperture, stood Nikolay Ivanich. In a gay cotton shirt, with an indolent smile on his chubby cheeks, he was pouring out two glasses of spirits with his podgy white hand for the two friends, Blinker and Muddlehead, who had just come in; behind him, in the corner near the window, could be seen his sharp-eyed wife. In the middle of the room stood Yasha the Turk, a lean, well-built man of twenty-three, dressed in a long-skirted blue nankeen coat. He had the appearance of a dashing young mechanic and looked as if his health was nothing to boast about. His sunken cheeks, great, restless grey eyes, straight nose with its fine, mobile nostrils, his wide-domed forehead with the pale blond curls thrust back from it, his bold but handsome and expressive lips—his whole face revealed an impressionable, passionate nature. He was in great excitement, blinking, breathing irregularly, his hands trembling as if with the fever—and indeed he had a fever, that sudden trembling fever which is so familiar to all who speak or sing in public. Beside him stood a man of about forty, broad-shouldered, with broad cheekbones, and a low forehead, narrow Tartar eyes, a short flat nose, a square chin, and black, shiny, bristlelike hair. The expression of his face, which was swarthy with a leaden undertone, and especially of his full lips, might almost have been called ferocious if it had not been so calmly reflective. He hardly stirred, just looked slowly around like an ox from below the yoke. He wore a sort of shabby frock coat with smooth copper buttons; an old black silk handkerchief swathed his massive neck. He was nicknamed "Wild Master." Right in front of him, on the bench below the icons, sat Yasha's competitor, the huckster from Zhizdra: a short, sturdy man of about thirty, pock-marked and curly-headed, with a blunt, upturned nose, lively brown eyes and a sparse beard. He was looking briskly round, with his hands tucked up beneath him, carelessly swinging and stamping his feet, which were clad in dandified boots with trimmings. He wore a thin new overcoat of grey cloth with a velvet collar, against which a strip of scarlet shirt, buttoned up tightly round his throat, stood out sharply. At a table in the opposite corner, to the right of the door, sat a peasant in a threadbare, greyish coat with an enormous hole at the shoulder. The sunlight fell in a fine, yellowish stream through the dusty panes of the two small windows and seemed unable to dispel the normal darkness of the room: every object was sparsely and patchily illuminated. Nevertheless, it was almost cool in the room and the feeling of stuffiness and sultriness fell from my shoulders like a burden the moment I crossed the threshold.

My arrival, I could see, at first rather confused Nikolay Ivanich's guests; but, observing that he bowed to me as to an acquaintance, they set their minds at rest and paid me no more attention. I ordered some beer and sat down in the corner next to the peasant in the torn coat.

"Well, then," sang out Muddlehead all of a sudden, after drinking a glass at one gulp, and accompanying his exclamation with those strange gestures of the arms without which he evidently never uttered a word. "What are we waiting for? It's time to begin, eh, Yasha?"

"Time to begin," repeated Nikolay Ivanich with approbation.

"Let's begin, if you like," said the huckster coolly, with a self-confident smile. "I'm ready."

"So am I," pronounced Yasha excitedly.

"Well, begin, lads, begin," squeaked Blinker.

But notwithstanding this unanimously expressed wish, neither of them did begin; the huckster did not even rise from his bench—it was as if everyone was waiting for something to happen.

"Begin," said Wild Master sharply and with displeasure.

Yasha shivered. The huckster got up, tightened his belt and cleared his throat.

"Who's to begin?" he asked, with a slight change of voice, addressing himself to Wild Master, who was still standing motionless in the middle of the room, his thick legs widely planted, his powerful arms thrust almost to the elbow into the pockets of his trousers.

"You, huckster, you," murmured Muddlehead; "you, lad."

Wild Master gave him a sidelong look. Muddlehead squeaked faintly, faltered, looked away at the ceiling, wriggled his shoulders and fell silent.

"Draw for it," pronounced Wild Master with deliberation, "and set the quart out on the counter."

Nikolay stooped, groaned, fetched up a quart jug from the floor and set it on the table.

Wild Master looked at Yasha and said: "Well!"

Yasha rummaged in his pockets, found a two-kopek piece and marked it with his teeth. The huckster brought a new leather purse out from the skirt of his coat, slowly undid the strings, poured out a lot of small change into his hand and chose a new two-kopek piece. Muddlehead held out his battered hat with its loose and crumpled peak: Yasha and the huckster threw their coins into it.

"You choose," said Wild Master to Blinker.

Blinker grinned with self-satisfaction, took the hat in both hands and began to shake it up.

For a moment deep silence reigned; the coins chinked faintly against each other. I looked round attentively: every face expressed strained anticipation; even Wild Master had screwed up his eyes; even my neighbor, the peasant in the torn coat, had stuck out his head inquisitively. Blinker put his hand into the hat and drew out the huckster's coin: there was a general sigh. Yasha flushed, and the huckster passed his hand through his hair.

"I *said* it was you," exclaimed Muddlehead, "I said so."

"Now, now, don't get all of a flutter," observed Wild Master contemptuously. "Begin," he continued, nodding to the huckster.

"What shall I sing?" asked the huckster, with rising excitement.

"Whatever you like, of course," rejoined Nikolay Ivanich, slowly folding his arms on his chest. "We can't tell you what to choose. Sing what you like; only sing it well; and then we'll judge as our conscience tells us."

"That's right—as our conscience tells us," repeated Muddlehead, and he licked the rim of his empty glass.

"Just let me clear my throat," said the huckster, fingering the collar of his coat.

"Now, don't waste time—begin!" said Wild Master decisively, and he looked down.

The huckster thought for a moment, shook his head and set off. Yasha stared at him with all his eyes. . . .

But before I proceed to describe the contest itself, it may be as well to say a few words about each of the personages in my story. The ways of some of them were already known to me when I met them in the "Snug Nook" pothouse; I found out about the rest subsequently.

To begin with Muddlehead. His real name was Yevgraf Ivanov; but no one in the neighborhood ever called him anything but Muddlehead, and he used the nickname in speaking of himself, so well did it fit him. And indeed it could not have been better suited to his insignificant, perpetually worried expression. He was an unmarried, drunken houseserf, whose master had long since despaired of him and who, having no duties and receiving not a farthing's wages, nevertheless found means of making merry every day at someone else's expense. He had many acquaintances who treated him to drinks and to tea, though they couldn't have said why, because, so far from being amusing in company, he fairly disgusted everyone with his witless chatter, his unbearable importunity, his feverish movements and his ceaseless unnatural laughter. He could neither sing nor dance; from birth he had never made a clever remark nor even a sensible one; he just muddled along and told any fib that came into his head—a regular Muddlehead! And, with it all, there wasn't a single drinking party for forty versts around at which his spindle-shanked figure failed to turn up among the guests, so used to him had people become, and so tolerant of his presence, as of an unavoidable mishap. True, they treated him contemptuously, but it was Wild Master alone who could put a curb on his crazy moods.

Blinker never left Muddlehead's side. He too was well-served by his nickname, although he didn't blink more than anyone else; but it is a plain truth that the Russians are past-masters at giving nicknames. In spite of my efforts to trace his past in every detail, I found—and so, probably, did many others—that there were dark passages in his career, places which, to use a bookish expression, were veiled in a thick mist of obscurity. I discovered only that he had once been coachman to an old, childless lady, had run away with the troika entrusted to his care, disappeared for a whole year, then, doubtless convinced by experience of the drawbacks and miseries of the vagrant's life, returned, now lame, thrown himself at his mistress's feet and, having expiated his offence by several years of exemplary conduct, had gradually won his way back into her favor, had eventually earned her full confidence and been promoted to the post of clerk; that on the lady's death he had somehow or other acquired his freedom, registered as a burgess, begun leasing melon gardens from the neighbors, grown rich and now lived in clover. He was a man of experience, with his head well screwed on, neither bad nor good, but calculating, rather; a sly dog who understood people and knew how to make use of them. He was cautious and enterprising at the same time, like a fox; chattered like an old crone, never gave himself away, made everybody else speak their mind. What is more, he never posed as a simpleton, as some of the sly ones of his kind do; indeed, pretence could not have come easily to him. I have never seen more penetrating, shrewder eyes than his tiny, cunning "peepers."[1] They never simply looked, they were always searching and spying. Sometimes Blinker would spend whole weeks reflecting on some apparently simple enterprise, then suddenly resolve on a desperately daring course, and you would think he'd break his neck over it . . . you would look again—and it would have come off perfectly, smooth as a knife through butter. He was lucky, believed in his luck and in omens. In general, he was highly superstitious. He was not liked, because he was not in the least interested in others, but he was respected. His family consisted of one small son, whom he fairly adored, and who, brought up by such a father, would probably go far. "Little Blinker's the spit of his father," the old men were already saying of him in low voices, as they sat on the mounds of earth outside their cabins and gossiped on summer evenings; and they all understood what that meant, and didn't need to say more.

Of Yasha the Turk and the huckster there is not much to be said. Yasha, nicknamed the Turk, because he was indeed the offspring of a captured Turkish woman, was at heart an artist in all senses of the word, but by vocation a dipper in a merchant's paper mill. As for the huckster, whose lot, I confess, remains unknown to me, he struck me as a smart, resourceful townsman. Of Wild Master, however, it is worth speaking in rather greater detail.

The first impression his appearance gave was one of rude, ponderous, irresistible force. He was clumsily built, "piled-on,"

---

[1] The people of Orel call eyes "peepers" in the same way as they call a mouth a "gobbler."—*Author*.

as we say in our part of the country, but he fairly radiated irrepressible vitality, and, strangely enough, his bearish figure was not without a certain individual grace, which proceeded perhaps from a completely serene confidence in his own strength. It was difficult to determine at first glance to what condition of life this Hercules belonged. He resembled neither servant nor townsman, neither the impoverished scrivener living in retirement nor the ruined, horse-fancying, quarrel-picking member of the smaller landowning gentry. He was something absolutely special. No one knew whence he had descended on our district; it was said that he came of freeholding stock and had previously been in Government service somewhere or other, but nothing certain was known of this; and indeed there was no one to learn it from—certainly not from him himself: a more taciturn, surly fellow never existed. No one could say for sure, either, what he lived on; he plied no trade, visited no one, hardly knew anyone, and yet he had money; not much, it is true, but money, all the same. He conducted himself, not indeed with modesty—there was absolutely nothing modest about him—but quietly; he lived as if he noticed no one around him and definitely wanted nothing from anyone. Wild Master (such was his nickname; his real name was Perevlesov) enjoyed an enormous influence in the whole neighborhood; he was obeyed instantly and eagerly, although, so far from having any right to give anyone orders, he never made the slightest claim on the obedience of people with whom he came in contact. He spoke—and was obeyed: power always claims its due. He hardly drank, had no dealings with women, and was a passionate lover of singing. There was much that was puzzling about him; it was as if some immense forces were lying, sullenly inactive, within him, as if they knew that, once aroused, once let loose, they must destroy themselves and everything they touched; and I am sadly mistaken if some such explosion had not already occurred in the man's life, so that, taught by experience, and having just escaped destruction, he was now holding himself under an inexorable, iron control. What specially struck me about him was the mixture of a certain inborn, natural ferocity with an equally inborn nobility—a mixture such as I have met in no one else.

So the huckster stepped forward, half-closed his eyes, and began to sing in a very high falsetto. His voice was quite sweet and agreeable, though somewhat husky; he played with it, twirled it about like a toy, with constant downward trills and modulations and constant returns to the top notes, which he held and prolonged with a special effort; he stopped, then suddenly took up his previous tune again with a certain rollicking, arrogant boldness. His transitions were sometimes daring, sometimes rather comical. They would have given a connoisseur great pleasure; they would have shocked a German deeply. He was a Russian *tenore di grazia* or *ténor léger*. He sang a gay dance tune, whose words, so far as I could catch them among the endless embellishments, extra harmonies and exclamations, were as follows:

> *I'll plough a little ground, my lass,*
> *And sow it with scarlet flowers.*

He sang, and we all listened to him with close attention. He clearly felt that he had to do with experts, and so he fairly climbed out of his skin, as the saying goes. Indeed in our country we are connoisseurs of song, and it is not for nothing that the village of Sergiyevsk, on the Orel highway, is renowned throughout all Russia for its specially sweet and harmonious singing. The huckster sang on for quite a while, without arousing any marked sympathy in hs hearers: he missed the support of a choir. At length, after one particularly successful transition, which made even Wild Master smile, Muddlehead could not contain himself and shouted out his satisfaction. Everybody jumped. Muddlehead and Blinker began taking up the tune, joining in and calling: "Smartly does it! . . . Strike it, rascal! . . . Strike it, hold it, you snake! Hold it, go on! Hotter still, you dog, you Herod's son!" and so on. Nikolay Ivanich, behind the counter, waved his head approvingly to right and left. At length Muddlehead began to stamp and scrape his feet and twitch his shoulder,—Yasha's eyes blazed like coals, he trembled all over like a leaf and smiled confusedly. Only Wild Master kept the same countenance and remained motionless as before; but his gaze, fixed on the huckster, softened a little, though his lips kept their contemptuous expression. Encouraged by the signs of general satisfaction, the huckster fairly whirled along and went off into such flourishes, such tongue clickings and drummings, such wild throat play, that at length, exhausted, pale, bathed in hot sweat, he threw himself back, let out a last dying note—and his wild outburst was answered in unison by the company. Muddlehead threw himself on his neck and began smothering him with his long bony hands; a flush came over Nikolay's greasy face, and he seemed to have grown younger; Yasha shouted like a madman, "Bravo, bravo!"—and even my neighbor, the peasant in the torn coat, could bear it no longer and, striking his fist on the table, exclaimed: "A-ha! good, devil take it—good!" and he spat to one side with determination.

"Well, lad, you've given us a treat!" cried Muddlehead, not letting the fainting huckster out of his embrace. "A treat, and that's the truth! You've won, lad, you've won! Congratulations —the quart is yours! Yasha can't touch you . . . Not by a long chalk, I tell you . . . Believe me!" And he again pressed the huckster to his bosom.

"Let him go: let him go, you leech . . ." said Blinker crossly. "Let him sit down on the bench here; he's tired, see . . . You're a fool, lad, a real fool! Why stick to him like a flypaper?"

"Why, then, let him sit, and I'll drink his health," rejoined Muddlehead, going to the counter; "you're paying, lad," he added, turning to the huckster.

The huckster nodded, sat down on the bench, drew a towel out of his cap and began to wipe his face. Muddlehead drank a glass in thirsty haste, groaned, and took on the sad, preoccupied look of the serious drinker.

"You sing well, lad, so you do," observed Nikolay Ivanich amiably. "Now it's your turn, Yasha: don't be nervous, mind. We'll see who's best, we will . . . But the huckster sings well, by God he does."

"Very well, so he does," observed Nikolay's wife, smiling at Yasha.

"So he does, too!" said my neighbor in a low voice.

"Eh, you Polesyan Thomas!"[2] sang out Muddlehead suddenly and, coming over to the peasant with the hole in the shoulder of his coat, pointed a finger at him, began to jump, and burst into a jarring laugh. "You Polesyan! What are you doing here? Come on! you doubting Thomas!" he shouted through his laughter.

The poor peasant grew embarrassed and was just about to rise and depart hurriedly, when all of a sudden came the metallic voice of Wild Master:

"What's that unbearable animal up to now?" he said, grinding his teeth.

[2] The inhabitants of Polesya have a name for incredulity and suspicion.—*Author*.

"Nothing," muttered Muddlehead, "nothing . . . I just . . ."

"All right then, shut up!" rejoined Wild Master. "Yasha, begin!"

Yasha took his throat in his hand.

"Why, lad, there's something . . . why . . . H'm . . . I don't rightly know . . ."

"Now, that'll do, don't be shy. Shame on you! . . . What's the fuss? . . . Sing, as God tells you to."

And Wild Master looked down and waited.

Yasha said nothing, but glanced round and covered his face with his hand. The whole company stared at him with all their eyes, especially the huckster, whose face showed, through its usual self-confidence and the triumph of his success, a faint, involuntary anxiety. He leant against the wall, again tucked his hands in beneath him, but no longer swung his legs. When at last Yasha uncovered his face, it was as pale as a corpse's; his gleaming eyes hardly showed through their lowered lashes. He breathed deeply and began to sing . . . His first note was faint and uneven, and came, it seemed, not from his chest, but from somewhere far away, as if it had chanced to fly into the room. This trembling, ringing note had a strange effect on us all; we looked at one another, and Nikolay's wife stood bolt upright. This first note was followed by another, firmer and more prolonged, but still perceptibly trembling, like a string, when, after the sudden pluck of a strong finger, it wavers with a last, quickly dying thrill: after the second came a third, and, gradually taking on warmth and breadth, the mournful song flowed on its way. *The paths that lay across the field,* he sang, and we all had the feeling of something sweet and unearthly. Seldom, I confess, have I heard such a voice: it was somewhat worn and had a sort of cracked ring; at first it had even a certain suggestion of the morbid; but it also held a deep, unsimulated passion, and youth, and strength, and sweetness, and a deliciously detached note of melancholy. The truthful, fervent Russian soul rang and breathed in it and fairly caught at your heart, caught straight at your Russian heartstrings. The song developed, went flowing on. Yasha was clearly overcome by ecstasy: his shyness had left him, he had surrendered completely to his happiness; his voice trembled no longer—it quivered, but with the scarcely perceptible inner quivering of passion, which pierces like an arrow into the hearer's soul. His voice grew steadily in strength, firmness and breadth. One

evening, I remember, at low tide, on the flat sandy shore of
the sea, which was roaring away menacingly and dully in the
distance, I saw a great white gull: it was sitting, motionless, its
silky breast turned towards the scarlet radiance of sunset, now
and then slowly stretching its long wings towards the familiar
sea, towards the low, blood red sun; I remembered it as I
listened to Yasha. He sang, completely oblivious of his rival
and of us all, but clearly sustained, as waves lift a strong
swimmer, by our silent passionate attention. He sang, and
with every note there floated out something noble and im-
measurably large, like familiar steppe country unfolding before you, stretching away into the boundless distance. I could
feel tears swelling up in my heart and rising into my eyes;
dull, muffled sobs suddenly fell on my ears . . . I looked
round—the tapster's wife was weeping as she leant her
breast against the window. Yasha threw her a quick glance
and his song flowed on still more sonorously and sweetly than
before. Nikolay Ivanich looked down, Blinker turned away;
Muddlehead, quite overcome by emotion, stood with his mouth
stupidly gaping; the little grey peasant was quietly whimpering
in his corner and shaking his head and muttering away bitterly
to himself; down the iron face of Wild Master, from under his
deep overhanging brows, slowly rolled a heavy tear; the huckster had raised a clenched fist to his brow and never stirred.
. . . I cannot imagine how this general state of heartfelt rapture would have been dispelled if Yasha had not suddenly
ended on a high, extremely thin note—as if his voice had
broken. No one shouted, no one even stirred; everyone seemed
to be waiting in case he would sing on; but he opened his eyes,
as if surprised at our silence, cast a questioning glance round
at us all, and saw that victory was his. . . .

"Yasha," said Wild Master, putting a hand on his shoulder,
and—said nothing more.

We all sat as though benumbed. The huckster got up quietly
and went across to Yasha. "You . . . it's yours . . . you've
won," he brought out at last with difficulty and dashed from
the room. . . .

His swift decisive movement seemed to break the spell:
everyone suddenly started talking loudly, joyfully. Muddlehead
sprang up in the air and began to splutter and wave his arms
like the sails of a windmill; Blinker stumbled over to Yasha
and they began to kiss each other; Nikolay Ivanich stood up
and solemnly announced that he would add another quart of
beer on his own account; Wild Master laughed a good-natured

laugh, such as I had certainly not expected to hear from him; the little grey peasant kept on repeating in his corner, wiping his eyes, cheeks, nose and beard on both sleeves: "Good, by God, it's good, why, take me for a son of a bitch, it's good!" and Nikolay's wife, deeply flushed, stood up quickly and went away. Yasha enjoyed his victory like a child; his whole face was transfigured; in particular his eyes simply radiated happiness. He was dragged across to the counter; he summoned over to it the little grey peasant, who had burst into tears, he sent the host's boy after the huckster, whom, however, he failed to find, and the party began. "You'll sing to us again, you'll sing to us until evening," repeated Muddlehead, raising his arms aloft.

I looked once more at Yasha and went out. I did not want to stay—for fear of spoiling my impression. But the heat was still as unbearable as before. It was as if it hung right over the earth in a thick, heavy film; in the dark blue sky, little flashing lights seemed to be astir behind the fine, almost black dust. Everything was still; there was something hopeless, something oppressive about this deep stillness of enfeebled nature. I made my way to a hayloft and lay down on the newly mown but already almost dried up grass. For a while I could not drowse off; for a while Yasha's irresistible voice rang in my ears . . . but, at length, heat and exhaustion claimed their due, and I fell into a deathlike sleep. When I awoke, it was dark all around; the litter of grass smelt strongly and there was a touch of dampness about it; between the thin rafters of the half open roof, pale stars flickered faintly. I went out. The sunset glow had died away long ago, and had left behind only the faintest pallor on the horizon; in the air, so glowing hot not long before, there was still a sense of heat underneath the freshness of night, and the lungs still thirsted for a breath of cold. There was no wind, no cloud; the sky stood round, clear, darkly translucent, quietly shimmering with countless hardly visible stars. In the village, lights twinkled; from the brightly lit pothouse near by came a discordant and confused hubbub, in the midst of which I thought I recognized Yasha's voice. At times there were bursts of wild laughter. I went across to the window and pressed my face against the pane. I saw a sad, though lively and animated scene: everyone was drunk—everyone, starting with Yasha. He was sitting, bare-chested, on a bench, singing in the huskiest voice some dance song of the streets, and lazily plucking and pinching the strings of a guitar. Clusters of wet hair hung above his livid face. In the middle of the pothouse, Muddlehead, coatless and completely "un-screwed," was dancing and hopping away in front of the little peasant in the grey coat; the peasant, in turn, was laboriously stamping and scraping with his exhausted feet, smiling witlessly through his dishevelled beard, and occasionally waving a hand, as if to say: "Let it rip!" Nothing could have been more ludicrous than his face; however high he lifted his brows, his heavy lids refused to stay up and drooped right down over his hardly visible, bleary eyes, which were nevertheless brimming with sweetness. He was in the endearing condition of the completely tipsy, when every passer-by who looks him in the face is absolutely bound to say: "A fine state, a fine state!" Blinker, red as a lobster, nostrils blown out wide, was laughing sardonically from a corner; only Nikolay Ivanich, as befits a good tapster, had kept his imperturbable sang-froid. Many new faces had collected in the room, but there was no sign of Wild Master.

I turned away and struck off quickly down the hill on which Kolotovka stands. A broad plain spreads out at the foot of this hill; swamped as it was with the misty waves of evening haze, it seemed vaster than ever, and as if merged with the darkened sky. I was walking with great strides along the track beside the ravine, when suddenly, from far away on the plain, came a boy's ringing voice. "Antropka! Antropka-a-a! . . ." it called, in stubborn, tearful desperation, with a long dragging-out of the last syllable.

For a few moments it was silent, then began to call again. The voice carried clearly in the unmoving, lightly sleeping air. Thirty times at least it had called Antropka's name, when suddenly, from the opposite end of the meadow, as if from a different world, came a scarcely audible reply:

"What-a-a-a-at?"

The boy's voice called at once, glad but indignant:

"Come here, you devil!"

"What fo-o-o-r?" answered the other, after a pause.

"Because father wants to be-ee-ee-eat you," called the first voice promptly.

The second voice made no further reply, and the boy again started calling "Antropka." I could still hear his cries, growing rarer and fainter, when it had become completely dark and I was passing the bend in the wood that surrounds my village, four versts away from Kolotovka.

"Antropka-a-a," I still seemed to hear in the air, which was full of the shadows of night.

✛ ✛
✛

Fyodor Dostoevsky

✛ ✛
✛
✛ ✛

The Peasant Marey

✠

It was Easter Monday. The air was warm, the sky blue, the sun high, "warm" and bright, but I was plunged in gloom. I wandered aimlessly behind the barracks in the prison yard, looked at the palings of the strong prison fence, counting them mechanically, though I did not particularly want to count them, but doing it more out of habit than anything else. It was the second day of "holidays" in prison. The convicts were not taken out to work, lots of them were drunk, cursing and quarrelling broke out every minute in different corners of the prison. Disgusting, coarse songs; groups of convicts playing cards under the bunks; several convicts who had run amok and had been dealt with summarily by their own comrades, were lying half dead on the bunks, covered with sheepskins, until they should recover consciousness; the knives that had already been drawn several times—all this had so harrowing an effect on me during the two days of holidays that it made me ill. I could never bear without disgust the wild orgies of the common people, and here in this place this was specially true. On such days even the officials never looked into the prison, carried out no searches, did not look for drinks, realizing that once a year even these outcasts had to be given a chance of enjoying themselves and that otherwise things would be much worse. At last blind fury blazed up in my heart. I met the Pole, M—ski,[1] one of the political prisoners. He gave me a black look, with flashing eyes and trembling lips. *"Je hais ces brigands!"* he hissed at me in an undertone and walked past me. I went back to the barracks, although I had rushed out of them like a madman only a quarter of an hour before, when

[1] O. Miretski, who was serving a prison sentence with Dostoevsky.

six strong peasants had hurled themselves on the drunken
Tartar Gazin in an attempt to quieten him and had begun
beating him. They beat him senselessly—a camel might have
been killed by such blows. But they knew that it was not easy
to kill this Hercules, and they beat him therefore without any
qualms. Now, on my return, I noticed Gazin lying unconscious
and without any sign of life on a bunk in a corner at the
other end of the barracks; he lay covered with a sheepskin,
and they all passed by him in silence, knowing very well that
if the man was unlucky he might die from a beating like that.
I made my way to my place opposite the window with the
iron bars and lay on my back with my eyes closed and my
hands behind my head. I liked to lie like that: no one would
bother a sleeping man, and meanwhile one could dream and
think. But I found it difficult to dream: my heart was beating
uneasily and M—ski's words were still echoing in my ears:
"Je hais ces brigands!" However, why dwell on these scenes; I
sometimes even now dream of those times at night, and none
of my dreams is more agonizing. Perhaps it will be noticed
that to this day I have hardly ever spoken in print of my life
in prison; *The House of the Dead* I wrote fifteen years ago in
the person of a fictitious character who was supposed to have
killed his wife. I may add, incidentally, just as an interesting
detail, that many people have thought and have been maintain-
ing ever since the publication of that book of mine, that I was
sent to Siberia for the murder of my wife.

By and by I did forget my surroundings and became imperceptibly lost in memories. During the four years of my
imprisonment I was continually recalling my past and seemed
in my memories to live my former life all over again. These
memories cropped up by themselves; I seldom evoked them
consciously. It would begin from some point, some imper-
ceptible feature, which then grew little by little into a complete
picture, into some clear-cut and vivid impression. I used to
analyze those impressions, adding new touches to an event
that had happened long ago, and, above all, correcting it, correcting it incessantly, and that constituted my chief amusement. This time I for some reason suddenly remembered one
fleeting instant in my early childhood when I was only nine
years old—an instant that I seemed to have completely forgotten; but at that time I was particularly fond of memories of
my early childhood. I remembered an August day in our village; a dry, bright day, though rather cold and windy; summer

was drawing to a close, and we should soon have to leave for Moscow and again have to spend all winter over the boring French lessons, and I was so sorry to leave the country. I walked past the threshing floors and, going down a ravine, climbed up into the dense thicket of bushes which stretched from the other side of the ravine to the wood. I got amongst the bushes, and I could hear not very far away, about thirty yards perhaps, a peasant plowing by himself on a clearing. I knew he was plowing up the steep slope of a hill. The horse must have found it very hard going, for from time to time I heard the peasant's call from a distance: "Gee up! Gee up!" I knew almost all our peasants, but I did not know which of them was plowing now, nor did it really matter to me who it was because I was occupied with my own affairs—I too was busy, breaking off a switch from a hazel tree to strike frogs with; hazel twigs are very lovely, but they are also very brittle, much more brittle than birch twigs. I was also interested in beetles and other insects, and I was collecting them; some of them were very beautiful. I also liked the small quick red and yellow lizards with black spots, but I was afraid of snakes. However, there were many fewer snakes than lizards. There were not many mushrooms there; to get mushrooms one had to go to the birch wood, and I was about to go there. And there was nothing in the world I loved so much as the wood with its mushrooms and wild berries, its beetles and its birds, its hedgehogs and squirrels, and its damp smell of rotted leaves. And even as I write this I can smell the fragrance of our birch wood: these impressions remain with you for your whole life. Suddenly amid the dead silence I heard clearly and distinctly the shout, "Wolf! Wolf!" I uttered a shriek and, panic-stricken, screamed at the top of my voice and rushed out to the clearing straight to the plowing peasant.

It was our peasant Marey. I do not know if there is such a name, but everybody called him Marey. He was a peasant of about fifty, thick-set and over medium height, with a large, grizzled, dark brown beard. I knew him, but till that day I had scarcely ever spoken to him. When he heard my cry, he even stopped his old mare, and when, unable to stop myself I clutched at his wooden plow with one hand and at his sleeve with the other, he saw how terrified I was.

"There's a wolf there!" I cried, breathless.

He threw up his head and looked round involuntarily, for a moment almost believing me.

"Where's the wolf?"

"Someone shouted—shouted just now 'Wolf! Wolf!' " I stammered.

"There, there! There are no wolves hereabouts," he murmured, trying to calm me. "You've been dreaming, sonny. Who ever heard of wolves in these parts?"

But I was trembling all over and I was still clutching at his smock, and I suppose I must have been very pale. He looked at me with a worried smile, evidently anxious and troubled about me.

"Dear, dear, how frightened you are," he said, shaking his head. "Don't be frightened, sonny. Oh, you poor thing, you! There, there."

He stretched out his hand and suddenly stroked my cheek.

"There now! Christ be with you, cross yourself, there's a good lad!"

But I did not cross myself; the corners of my mouth were still twitching, and that seemed to strike him particularly. He quietly stretched out his thick finger with its black nail, smeared with earth, and gently touched my trembling lips.

"Dear, oh dear," he smiled at me with a slow motherly sort of smile, "Lord, how frightened he is, the poor lad!"

I realized at last that there was no wolf and that I had imagined the shout, "Wolf! Wolf!" The shout, though, was very clear and distinct, but such shouts (and not only about wolves) I had imagined once or twice before, and I knew it. (I grew out of these hallucinations a few years later.)

"Well, I'll go now," I said, looking up at him, questioningly and shyly.

"Run along, run along, son, I'll be awatching you," he said, adding, "Don't you worry, I shan't let the wolf get you!" and he smiled at me with the same motherly smile. "Well, Christ be with you. Run along, run along, sonny," and he made the sign of the cross over me, and then crossed himself too.

I walked away, looking back anxiously every few yards. While I was walking away, Marey stood still with his mare and looked after me, nodding his head at me every time I looked round. As a matter of fact, I was a little ashamed of myself for having let him see how frightened I was, but I was still very much afraid of the wolf as I was walking away till I climbed up the steep side of the ravine and came to the first threshing barn. There my terror left me completely, and our watchdog Volchok suddenly appeared out of nowhere and rushed at me. With Volchok at my side I completely recovered my spirits and turned around to Marey for the last time. I could no longer see his face clearly, but I felt that he was still nodding and smiling tenderly at me. I waved to him and he waved back to me and started his mare.

"Gee up!" I heard his call in the distance again, and the mare pulled at the wooden plow once more.

All this came back to me all at once, I don't know why, but with an amazing accuracy of detail. I suddenly came to and sat up on my bunk and, I remember, I could still feel the gentle smile of memory on my lips. For another minute I went on recalling that incident from my childhood.

When I returned home from Marey that day I did not tell anybody about my "adventure." It was not much of an adventure, anyway. And, besides, I soon forgot all about Marey. Whenever I happened to come across him now and then, I never spoke to him either about the wolf or anything else, and now twenty years later in Siberia I suddenly remembered this meeting so distinctly that not a single detail of it was lost, which means of course that it must have been hidden in my mind without my knowing it, of itself and without any effort on my part, and came back to me suddenly when it was wanted. I remembered the tender, motherly smile of that serf, the way he made the sign of the cross over me and crossed himself, the way he nodded at me. "Lord, how afeered he is, the poor lad!" And particularly that thick finger of his, smeared with earth, with which he touched my twitching lips so gently and with such shy tenderness. No doubt, anyone would have done his best to calm a child, but something quite different seemed to have happened during that solitary meeting; and if I had been his own son, he could not have looked at me with eyes shining with brighter love. And who compelled him to look like that? He was one of our serfs, a peasant who was our property, and after all I was the son of his master. No one would have known that he had been so good to me, and no one would have rewarded him for it. Did he really love little children as much as that? There are such people, no doubt. Our meeting took place in a secluded spot, in a deserted field, and only God perhaps saw from above with what profound and enlightened human feeling, and with what delicate, almost womanly, tenderness the heart of a coarse, savagely ignorant Russian serf was filled, a serf who at the time neither expected nor dreamt of his emancipation.

Tell me, was not this what Konstantin Akaskov perhaps meant when he spoke of the high degree of culture of our people?

And so when I got off the bunk and looked round, I suddenly felt I remember, that I could look at these unhappy creatures with quite different eyes, and that suddenly by some miracle all hatred and anger had vanished from my heart. I walked round the prison peering into the faces I came across. That rascal of a peasant with his shaven head and branded face, yelling his hoarse drunken song at the top of his voice— why, he, too, may be the same sort of peasant as Marey: I cannot possibly look into his heart, can I? That evening I again met M—ski. Poor man! He could have no memories about Marey or peasants like him and he could have no other opinion of these people except, *"Je hais ces brigands!"* Yes, it was much harder for those Poles than for us!

The
Crocodile

✠

A true story of how a gentleman of a certain age and of respectable appearance was swallowed alive by the crocodile in the Arcade, and of the consequences that followed.

> *Ohè Lambert! Où est Lambert?*
> *As tu vu Lambert?*

I

On the thirteenth of January of this present year, 1865, at half-past twelve in the day, Elena Ivanovna, the wife of my cultured friend Ivan Matveich, who is a colleague in the same department, and may be said to be a distant relation of mine, too, expressed the desire to see the crocodile now on view at a fixed charge in the Arcade. As Ivan Matveich had already in his pocket his ticket for a tour abroad (not so much for the sake of his health as for the improvement of his mind), and was consequently free from his official duties and had nothing whatever to do that morning, he offered no objection to his wife's irresistible fancy, but was positively aflame with curiosity himself.

"A capital idea!" he said, with the utmost satisfaction. "We'll have a look at the crocodile! On the eve of visiting Europe it is well to acquaint ourselves on the spot with its indigenous inhabitants." And with these words, taking his wife's arm, he set off with her at once for the Arcade. I joined them, as I usually do, being an intimate friend of the family. I have never seen Ivan Matveich in a more agreeable frame of mind than he was on that memorable morning—how true it is that we know not beforehand the fate that awaits us! On entering the Arcade he was at once full of admiration for the splendors of the building, and when we reached the shop in which the monster lately arrived in Petersburg was being exhibited, he volunteered to pay the quarter-ruble for me to the crocodile owner—a thing which had never happened before. Walking into a little room, we observed that besides the crocodile there were in it parrots of the species known as cockatoo, and also a group of monkeys in a special case in a recess. Near the entrance, along the left wall stood a big tin tank that looked like a bath covered with a thin iron grating, filled with water to the depth of two inches. In this shallow pool was kept a huge crocodile, which lay like a log absolutely motionless and apparently deprived of all its faculties by our damp climate, so inhospitable to foreign visitors. This monster at first aroused no special interest in any one of us.

"So this is the crocodile!" said Elena Ivanovna, with a pathetic cadence of regret. "Why, I thought it was . . . something different."

Most probably she thought it was made of diamonds. The owner of the crocodile, a German, came out and looked at us with an air of extraordinary pride.

"He has a right to be," Ivan Matveich whispered to me, "he knows he is the only man in Russia exhibiting a crocodile."

This quite nonsensical observation I ascribe also to the extremely good-humored mood which had overtaken Ivan Matveich, who was on other occasions of rather envious disposition.

"I fancy your crocodile is not alive," said Elena Ivanovna, piqued by the irresponsive stolidity of the proprietor, and addressing him with a charming smile in order to soften his churlishness—a maneuver so typically feminine.

"Oh, no, madam," the latter replied in broken Russian; and instantly moving the grating half off the tank, he poked the monster's head with a stick.

Then the treacherous monster, to show that it was alive, faintly stirred its paws and tail, raised its snout and emitted something like a prolonged snuffle.

"Come, don't be cross, Karlchen," said the German caressingly, gratified in his vanity.

"How horrid that crocodile is! I am really frightened," Elena Ivanovna twittered, still more coquettishly. "I know I shall dream of him now."

"But he won't bite you if you do dream of him," the German retorted gallantly, and was the first to laugh at his own jest, but none of us responded.

"Come, Semyon Semyonich," said Elena Ivanovna, addressing me exclusively, "let us go and look at the monkeys. I am awfully fond of monkeys; they are such darlings . . . and the crocodile is horrid."

"Oh, don't be afraid, my dear!" Ivan Matveich called after us, gallantly displaying his manly courage to his wife. "This drowsy denison of the realms of the Pharaohs will do us no harm." And he remained by the tank. What is more, he took his glove and began tickling the crocodile's nose with it, wishing, as he said afterwards, to induce him to snort. The proprietor showed his politeness to a lady by following Elena Ivanovna to the case of monkeys.

So everything was going well, and nothing could have been foreseen. Elena Ivanovna was quite skittish in her raptures over the monkeys, and seemed completely taken up with them. With shrieks of delight she was continually turning to me, as though determined not to notice the proprietor, and kept gushing with laughter at the resemblance she detected between these monkeys and her intimate friends and acquaintances. I, too, was amused, for the resemblance was unmistakable. The German did not know whether to laugh or not, and so at last was reduced to frowning. And it was at that moment that a terrible, I may say unnatural, scream set the room vibrating. Not knowing what to think, for the first moment I stood still, numb with horror, but noticing that Elena Ivanovna was screaming too, I quickly turned round—and what did I behold! I saw—oh heavens!—I saw the luckless Ivan Matveich in the terrible jaws of the crocodile, held by them round the waist, lifted horizontally in the air and desperately kicking. Then— one moment, and no trace remained of him. But I must describe it in detail, for I stood all the while motionless, and had time to watch the whole process taking place before me with an attention and interest such as I never remember to have felt before. "What," I thought at that critical moment, "what if all that had happened to me instead of Ivan Matveich —how unpleasant it would have been for me!"

But to return to my story. The crocodile began by turning the unhappy Ivan Matveich in his terrible jaws so that he could swallow his legs first; then bringing up Ivan Matveich, who kept trying to jump out and clutching at the sides of the tank, sucked him down again as far as his waist. Then bringing him up again, gulped him down, and so again and again. In this way Ivan Matveich was visibly disappearing before our eyes. At last, with a final gulp, the crocodile swallowed my cultured friend entirely, this time leaving no trace of him. From the outside of the crocodile we could see the protuberances of Ivan Matveich's figure as he passed down the inside of the monster. I was on the point of screaming again when destiny played another treacherous trick upon us. The crocodile made a tremendous effort, probably oppressed by the magnitude of the object he had swallowed, once more opened his terrible jaws, and with a final hiccup he suddenly let the head of Ivan Matveich pop out for a second, with an expression of despair on his face. In that brief instant the spectacles dropped off his nose to the bottom of the tank. It seemed as though that despairing countenance had only popped out to cast one last look on the objects around it, to take its last farewell of all earthly pleasures. But it had not time to carry out its intention; the crocodile made another effort, gave a gulp and instantly it vanished again—this time for ever. This appearance and disappearance of a still living human head was so horrible, but at the same—either from its rapidity and unexpectedness or from the dropping of the spectacles—there was something so comic about it that I suddenly quite unexpectedly exploded with laughter. But pulling myself together and realising that to laugh at such a moment was not the thing for an old family friend, I turned at once to Elena Ivanovna and said with a sympathetic air:

"Now it's all over with our friend Ivan Matveich!"

I cannot even attempt to describe how violent was the agitation of Elena Ivanovna during the whole process. After the first scream she seemed rooted to the spot, and stared at the catastrophe with apparent indifference, though her eyes looked as though they were starting out of her head; then she suddenly went off into a heart-rending wail, but I seized her hands. At this instant the proprietor, too, who had at first been also petrified by horror, suddenly clasped his hands and cried, gazing upwards:

"Oh my crocodile! *Oh mein allerliebster Karlchen! Mutter, Mutter, Mutter!*"

A door at the rear of the room opened at this cry, and the *Mutter,* a rosy-cheeked, elderly but dishevelled woman in a cap made her appearance, and rushed with a shriek to her German.

A perfect Bedlam followed. Elena Ivanovna kept shrieking out the same phrase, as though in a frenzy, "Flay him! flay him!" apparently entreating them—probably in a moment of oblivion—to flay somebody for something. The proprietor and *Mutter* took no notice whatever of either of us; they were both bellowing like calves over the crocodile.

"He did for himself! He will burst himself at once, for he did swallow a *ganz* official!" cried the proprietor.

"Unser Karlchen, unser allerliebster Karlchen wird sterben," howled his wife.

"We are bereaved and without bread!" chimed in the proprietor.

"Flay him! flay him! flay him!" clamored Elena Ivanovna, clutching at the German's coat.

"He did tease the crocodile. For what did your man tease the crocodile?" cried the German, pulling away from her. "You will if *Karlchen wird* burst, therefore pay, *das war mein Sohn, das war mein einziger Sohn.*"

I must own I was intently indignant at the sight of such egoism in the German and the cold-heartedness of his dishevelled *Mutter;* at the same time Elena Ivanovna's reiterated shriek of "Flay him! flay him!" troubled me even more and absorbed at last my whole attention, positively alarming me. I may as well say straight off that I entirely misunderstood this strange exclamation: it seemed to me that Elena Ivanovna had for the moment taken leave of her senses, but nevertheless wishing to avenge the loss of her beloved Ivan Matveich, was demanding by way of compensation that the crocodile should be severely thrashed, while she was meaning something quite different. Looking round at the door, not without embarrassment, I began to entreat Elena Ivanovna to calm herself, and above all not to use the shocking word "flay." For such a reactionary desire here, in the midst of the Arcade and of the most cultured society, not two paces from the hall where at this very minute Mr. Lavrov was perhaps delivering a public lecture, was not only impossible but unthinkable, and might at any moment bring upon us the hisses of culture and the caricatures of Mr. Stepanov. To my horror I was immediately proved to be correct in my alarmed suspicions: the curtain that divided the crocodile room from the little entry where the quarter-rubles were taken suddenly parted, and in the opening there appeared a figure with moustaches and beard, carrying a cap, with the upper part of its body bent a long way forward, though the feet were scrupulously held beyond the threshold of the crocodile room in order to avoid the necessity of paying the entrance money.

"Such a reactionary desire, madam," said the stranger, trying to avoid falling over in our direction and to remain standing outside the room, "does no credit to your development, and is conditioned by lack of phosphorus in your brain. You will be promptly held up to shame in the *Chronicle of Progress* and in our satirical prints . . ."

But he could not complete his remarks; the proprietor coming to himself, and seeing with horror that a man was talking in the crocodile room without having paid entrance money, rushed furiously at the progressive stranger and turned him out with a punch from each fist. For a moment both vanished from our sight behind a curtain, and only then I grasped that the whole uproar was about nothing. Elena Ivanovna turned out quite innocent; she had, as I have mentioned already, no idea whatever of subjecting the crocodile to a degrading corporal punishment, and had simply expressed the desire that he should be opened and her husband released from his interior.

"What! You wish that my crocodile be perished!" the proprietor yelled, running in again. "No! let your husband be perished first, before my crocodile! . . . *Mein Vater* showed crocodile, *mein Grossvater* showed crocodile, *mein Sohn* will show crocodile, and I will show crocodile! All will show crocodile! I am known to *ganz Europa*, and you are not known to *ganz Europa*, and you must pay me a *strafe!*"

"*Ja, ja,*" put in the vindictive German woman, "we shall not let you go. *Strafe,* since Karlchen is burst!"

"And, indeed, it's useless to flay the creature," I added calmly, anxious to get Elena Ivanovna away home as quickly as possible, "as our dear Ivan Matveich is by now probably soaring somewhere in the empyrean."

"My dear"—we suddenly heard, to our intense amazement, the voice of Ivan Matveich—"my dear, my advice is to apply direct to the superintendent's office, as without the assistance of the police the German will never be made to see reason."

These words, uttered with firmness and aplomb, and expressing an exceptional presence of mind, for the first minute so astounded us that we could not believe our ears. But, of course, we ran at once to the crocodile's tank, and with equal reverence and incredulity listened to the unhappy captive. His voice was muffled, thin and even squeaky, as though it came from a considerable distance. It reminded one of a jocose person who, covering his mouth with a pillow, shouts from an adjoining room, trying to mimic the sound of two peasants

calling to one another in a deserted plain or across a wide
ravine—a performance to which I once had the pleasure of
listening in a friend's house at Christmas.

"Ivan Matveich, my dear, and so you are alive!" faltered
Elena Ivanovna.

"Alive and well," answered Ivan Matveich, "and, thanks to
the Almighty, swallowed without any damage whatever. I am
only uneasy as to the view my superiors may take of the incident; for after getting a permit to go abroad I've got into
a crocodile, which seems anything but clever."

"But, my dear, don't trouble your head about being clever;
first of all we must somehow excavate you from where you
are," Elena Ivanovna interrupted.

"Excavate!" cried the proprietor. "I will not let my crocodile be excavated. Now the *publicum* will come many more,
and I will *fünfzig* kopeks ask and Karlchen will cease to
burst."

"*Gott sei dank!*" put in his wife.

"They are right," Ivan Matveich observed tranquilly; "the
principles of economics before everything."

"My dear! I will fly at once to the authorities and lodge
a complaint, for I feel that we cannot settle this mess by
ourselves."

"I think so too," observed Ivan Matveich; "but in our age
of industrial crisis it is not easy to rip open the belly of a
crocodile without economic compensation, and meanwhile the
inevitable question presents itself: What will the German take
for his crocodile? And with it another: How will it be paid?
For, as you know, I have no means . . ."

"Perhaps out of your salary . . ." I observed timidly, but
the proprietor interrupted me at once.

"I will not the crocodile sell; I will for three thousand the
crocodile sell! I will for four thousand the crocodile sell! Now
the *publicum* will come very many. I will for five thousand
the crocodile sell!"

In fact he gave himself insufferable airs. Covetousness and
a revolting greed gleamed joyfully in his eyes.

"I am going!" I cried indignantly.

"And I! I too! I shall go to Andrey Osipich himself. I will
soften him with my tears," whined Elena Ivanovna.

"Don't do that, my dear," Ivan Matveich hastened to inter-
pose. He had long been jealous of Andrey Osipich on his

wife's account, and he knew she would enjoy going to weep before a gentleman of refinement, for tears suited her.

"And I don't advise you to do so either, my friend," he added, addressing me. "It's no good plunging headlong in that slap-dash way; there's no knowing what it may lead to. You had much better go today to Timofey Semyonich, as though to pay an ordinary visit; he is an old-fashioned and by no means brilliant man, but he is trustworthy, and what matters most of all, he is straightforward. Give him my greetings and describe the circumstances of the case. And since I owe him seven rubles over our last game of cards, take the opportunity to pay him the money; that will soften the stern old man. In any case his advice may serve as a guide for us. And meanwhile take Elena Ivanovna home. . . . Calm yourself my dear," he continued, addressing her. "I am weary of these outcries and feminine squabblings, and should like a nap. It's soft and warm in here, though I have hardly had time to look round in this unexpected haven."

"Look round! Why, is it light in there?" cried Elena Ivanovna in a tone of relief.

"I am surrounded by impenetrable night," answered the poor captive; "but I can feel and, so to speak, have a look round with my hands. . . . Good-by; set your mind at rest and don't deny yourself recreation and diversion. Till tomorrow! And you, Semyon Semyonich, come to me in the evening, and as you are absent-minded and may forget it, tie a knot in your handkerchief."

I confess I was glad to get away, for I was overtired and somewhat bored. Hastening to offer my arm to the disconsolate Elena Ivanovna, whose charms were only enhanced by her agitation, I hurriedly led her out of the crocodile room.

"The charge will be another quarter-ruble in the evening," the proprietor called after us.

"Oh, dear, how greedy they are!" said Elena Ivanovna, looking at herself in every mirror on the walls of the Arcade, and evidently aware that she was looking prettier than usual.

"The principles of economics," I answered with some emotion, proud that passers-by should see the lady on my arm.

"The principles of economics," she drawled in a touching little voice. "I did not in the least understand what Ivan Matveich said about those horrid economics just now."

"I will explain to you," I answered, and began at once telling her of the beneficial effects of the introduction of for-

eign capital into our country, upon which I had read an article
in the *Petersburg News* and the *Voice* that morning.

"How strange it is," she interrupted, after listening for some
time. "But do leave off, you horrid man. What nonsense you
are talking. . . . Tell me, do I look purple?"

"You look perfect, and not purple!" I observed, seizing the
opportunity to pay her a compliment.

"Naughty man!" she said complacently. "Poor Ivan Matveich," she added a minute later, putting her little head on
one side coquettishly. "I am really sorry for him. Oh, dear!"
she cried suddenly, "how is he going to have his dinner . . .
and . . . and . . . what will he do . . . if he wants anything?"

"An unforeseen question," I answered, perplexed in my
turn. To tell the truth, it had not entered my head, so much
more practical are women than we men in the solution of the
problems of daily life!

"Poor dear! how could he have got into such a mess . . .
nothing to amuse him, and in the dark. . . . How vexing it is
that I have no photograph of him. . . . And so now I am a
sort of widow," she added, with a seductive smile, evidently
interested in her new position. "Hm! . . . I am sorry for him,
though."

It was, in short, the expression of the very natural and in-
telligible grief of a young and interesting wife for the loss of
her husband. I took her home at last, soothed her, and after
dining with her and drinking a cup of aromatic coffee, set off
at six o'clock to Timofey Semyonich, calculating that at that
hour all married people of settled habits would be sitting or
lying down at home.

Having written this first chapter in a style appropriate to
the incident recorded, I intend to proceed in a language more
natural though less elevated, and I beg to forewarn the reader
of the fact.

II

The venerable Timofey Semyonich met me rather nervously,
as though somewhat embarrassed. He led me to his tiny study
and shut the door carefully, "that the children may not hinder
us," he added with evident uneasiness. There he made me sit
down on a chair by the writing table, sat down himself in an
easy chair, wrapped round him the skirts of his old wadded

dressing gown, and assumed an official and even severe air, in readiness for anything, though he was not my chief nor Ivan Matveich's, and had hitherto been reckoned as a colleague and even a friend.

"First of all," he said, "take note that I am not a person in authority, but just such a subordinate official as you and Ivan Matveich. . . . I have nothing to do with it, and do not intend to mix myself up in the affair."

I was surprised to find that he apparently knew all about it already. In spite of that I told him the whole story over in detail. I spoke with positive excitement, for I was at that moment fulfilling the obligations of a true friend. He listened without special surprise, but with evident signs of suspicion.

"Only fancy," he said, "I always believed that this would be sure to happen to him."

"Why, Timofey Semyonich? It is a very unusual incident in itself . . ."

"I admit it. But Ivan Matveich's whole career in the service was leading up to this end. He was flighty—conceited indeed. It was always 'progress' and ideas of all sorts, and this is what progress brings people to!"

"But this is a most unusual incident and cannot possibly serve as a general rule for all progressives."

"Yes, indeed it can. You see, it's the effect of overeducation, I assure you. For overeducation leads people to poke their noses into all sorts of places, especially where they are not invited. Though perhaps you know best," he added, as though offended. "I am an old man and not of much education. I began as a soldier's son, and this year has been the jubilee of my service."

"Oh, no, Timofey Semyonich, not at all. On the contrary, Ivan Matveich is eager for your advice; he is eager for your guidance. He implores it, so to say, with tears."

"So to say, with tears! Hm! Those are crocodile's tears and one cannot quite believe in them. Tell me, what possessed him to want to go abroad? And how could he afford to go? Why, he has no private means!"

"He had saved the money from his last bonus," I answered plaintively. "He only wanted to go for three months—to Switzerland . . . to the land of William Tell."

"William Tell? Hm!"

"He wanted to meet the spring at Naples, to see the museums, the customs, the animals . . ."

"Hm! The animals! I think it was simply from pride. What animals? Animals, indeed! Haven't we animals enough? We have museums, menageries, camels. There are bears quite close to Petersburg! And here he's got inside a crocodile himself . . ."

"Oh, come, Timofey Semyonich! The man is in trouble, the man appeals to you as to a friend, as to an older relation, craves for advice—and you reproach him. Have pity at least on the unfortunate Elena Ivanovna!"

"You are speaking of his wife? A charming little lady," said Timofey Semyonich, visibly softening and taking a pinch of snuff with relish. "Particularly prepossessing. And so plump, and always putting her pretty little head on one side. . . . Very agreeable. Andrey Osipich was speaking of her only the other day."

"Speaking of her?"

"Yes, and in very flattering terms. Such a bust, he said, such eyes, such hair. . . . A sugarplum, he said, not a lady— and then he laughed. He is still a young man, of course." Timofey Semyonich blew his nose with a loud noise. "And yet, young though he is, what a career he is making for himself."

"That's quite a different thing, Timofey Semyonich."

"Of course, of course."

"Well, what do you say then, Timofey Semyonich?"

"Why, what can I do?"

"Give advice, guidance, as a man of experience, a relative! What are we to do? What steps are we to take? Go to the authorities and . . ."

"To the authorities? Certainly not," Timofey Semyonich replied hurriedly. "If you ask my advice, you had better, above all, hush the matter up and act, so to speak, as a private person. It is a suspicious incident, quite unheard of. Unheard of, above all; there is no precedent for it, and it is far from creditable. . . . And so discretion above all. . . . Let him lie there a bit. We must wait and see . . ."

"But how can we wait and see, Timofey Semyonich? What if he is stifled there?"

"Why should he be? I think you told me that he made himself fairly comfortable there?"

I told him the whole story over again. Timofey Semyonich pondered.

"Hm!" he said, twisting his snuffbox in his hands. "To my

mind it's really a good thing he should lie there a bit, instead
of going abroad. Let him reflect at his leisure. Of course he
mustn't be stifled, and so he must take measures to preserve
his health, avoiding a cough, for instance, and so on. . . .
And as for the German, it's my personal opinion he is within
his rights, and even more so than the other side, because it
was the other party who got into *his* crocodile without asking
permission, and not *he* who got into Ivan Matveich's crocodile
without asking permission, though, so far as I recollect, the
latter has no crocodile. And a crocodile is private property,
and so it is impossible to slit him open without compensation."

"For the saving of human life, Timofey Semyonich."

"Oh, well, that's a matter for the police. You must go to
them."

"But Ivan Matveich may be needed in the department. He
may be asked for."

"Ivan Matveich needed? Ha-ha! Besides, he is on leave, so
that we may ignore him—let him inspect the countries of
Europe! It will be a different matter if he doesn't turn up
when his leave is over. Then we shall ask for him and make
inquiries."

"Three months! Timofey Semyonich, for pity's sake!"

"It's his own fault. Nobody thrust him there. At this rate
we should have to get a nurse to look after him at government
expense, and that is not allowed for in the regulations. But
the chief point is that the crocodile is private property, so
that the principles of economics apply in this question. And
the principles of economics are paramount. Only the other
evening, at Luka Andreich's, Ignati Prokofyich was saying so.
Do you know Ignati Prokofyich? A capitalist, in a big way of
business, and he speaks so fluently. 'We need industrial development,' he said; 'there is very little development among us.
We must create it. We must create capital, so we must create
a middle class, the so-called bourgeoisie. And as we haven't
capital we must attract it from abroad. We must, in the first
place, give facilities to foreign companies to buy up lands in
Russia as is done now abroad. The communal holding of land
is poison, is ruin.' And, you know, he spoke with such heat;
well, that's all right for him—a wealthy man, and not in the
service. 'With the communal system,' he said, 'there will be no
improvement in industrial development or agriculture. Foreign companies,' he said, 'must as far as possible buy up the
whole of our land in big lots, and then split it up, split it up,

split it up, in the smallest parts possible'—and do you know he pronounced the words 'split it up' with such determination— 'and then sell it as private property. Or rather, not sell it, but simply let it. When,' he said, 'all the land is in the hands of foreign companies they can fix any rent they like. And so the peasant will work three times as much for his daily bread and he can be turned out at pleasure. So that he will feel it, will be submissive and industrious, and will work three times as much for the same wages. But as it is, with the commune, what does he care? He knows he won't die of hunger, so he is lazy and drunken. And meanwhile money will be attracted into Russia, capital will be created and the bourgeoisie will spring up. The English political and literary paper, *The Times,* in an article the other day on our finances stated that the reason our financial position was so unsatisfactory was that we had no middle class, no big fortunes, no accommodating proletariat.' Ignati Prokofyich speaks well. He is an orator. He wants to lay a report on the subject before the authorities, and then to get it published in the *News.* That's something very different from verses like Ivan Matveich's . . ."

"But how about Ivan Matveich?" I put in, after letting the old man babble on.

Timofey Semyonich was sometimes fond of talking and showing that he was not behind the times, but knew all about things.

"How about Ivan Matveich? Why, I am coming to that. Here we are, anxious to bring foreign capital into the country —and only consider: as soon as the capital of a foreigner, who has been attracted to Petersburg, has been doubled through Ivan Matveich, instead of protecting the foreign capitalist, we are proposing to rip open the belly of his original capital—the crocodile. Is it consistent? To my mind, Ivan Matveich, as the true son of his fatherland, ought to rejoice and to be proud that through him the value of a foreign crocodile has been doubled and possibly even trebled. That's just what is wanted to attract capital. If one man succeeds, mind you, another will come with a crocodile, and a third will bring two or three of them at once, and capital will grow up about them— there you have a bourgeoisie. It must be encouraged."

"Upon my word, Timofey Semyonich!" I cried, "you are demanding almost supernatural self-sacrifice from poor Ivan Matveich."

"I demand nothing, and I beg you, before everything—

as I have said already—to remember that I am not a person in authority and so cannot demand anything of any one. I am speaking as a son of the fatherland, that is, not as the *Son of the Fatherland,* but as a son of the fatherland. Again, what possessed him to get into the crocodile? A respectable man, a man of good grade in the service, lawfully married— and then to behave like that! Is it consistent?"

"But it was an accident."

"Who knows? And where is the money to compensate the owner to come from?"

"Perhaps out of his salary, Timofey Semyonich?"

"Would that be enough?"

"No, it wouldn't, Timofey Semyonich," I answered sadly. "The proprietor was at first alarmed that the crocodile would burst, but as soon as he was sure that it was all right, he began to bluster and was delighted to think that he could double the charge for entry."

"Treble and quadruple perhaps! The public will simply stampede the place now, and crocodile owners are smart people. Besides, it's not Lent yet, and people are keen on diversions, and so I say again, the great thing is that Ivan Matveich should preserve his incognito, don't let him be in a hurry. Let everybody know, perhaps, that he is in the crocodile, but don't let them be officially informed of it. Ivan Matveich is in particularly favorable circumstances for that, for he is reckoned to be abroad. It will be said he is in the crocodile, and we will refuse to believe it. That is how it can be managed. The great thing is that he should wait; and why should he be in a hurry?"

"Well, but if . . ."

"Don't worry, he has a good constitution . . ."

"Well, and afterwards, when he has waited?"

"Well, I won't conceal from you that the case is exceptional in the highest degree. One doesn't know what to think of it, and the worst of it is there is no precedent. If we had a precedent we might have something to go by. But as it is, what is one to say? It will certainly take time to settle it."

A happy thought flashed upon my mind.

"Cannot we arrange," I said, "that if he is destined to remain in the entrails of the monster and it is the will of Providence that he should remain alive, that he should send in a petition to be reckoned as still serving?"

"Hm! . . . Possibly as on leave and without salary . . ."

"But couldn't it be with salary?"

"On what grounds?"

"As sent on a special commission."

"What commission and where?"

"Why, into the entrails, the entrails of the crocodile. . . . So to speak, for exploration, for investigation of the facts on the spot. It would, of course, be a novelty, but that is progressive and would at the same time show zeal for enlightenment."

Timofey Semyonich thought a little.

"To send a special official," he said at last, "to the inside of a crocodile to conduct a special inquiry is, in my personal opinion, an absurdity. It is not in the regulations. And what sort of special inquiry could there be there?"

"The scientific study of nature on the spot, in the living subject. The natural sciences are all the fashion nowadays, botany. . . . He could live there and report his observations. . . . For instance, concerning digestion or simply habits. For the sake of accumulating facts."

"You mean as statistics. Well, I am no great authority on that subject, indeed I am no philosopher at all. You say 'facts'—we are overwhelmed with facts as it is, and don't know what to do with them. Besides, statistics are a danger."

"In what way?"

"They are a danger. Moreover, you will admit he will report facts, so to speak, lying like a log. And, can one do one's official duties lying like a log? That would be another novelty and a dangerous one; and again, there is no precedent for it. If we had any sort of precedent for it, then, to my thinking, he might have been given the job."

"But no live crocodiles have been brought over hitherto, Timofey Semyonich."

"Hm . . . yes," he reflected again. "Your objection is a just one, if you like, and might indeed serve as a ground for carrying the matter further; but consider again, that if with the arrival of living crocodiles government clerks begin to disappear, and then on the ground that they are warm and comfortable there, expect to receive the official sanction for their position, and then take their ease there . . . you must admit it would be a bad example. We should have every one trying to go the same way to get a salary for nothing."

"Do your best for him, Timofey Semyonich. By the way,

Ivan Matveich asked me to give you seven rubles he had lost
to you at cards."

"Ah, he lost that the other day at Nikifor Nikiforich's. I
remember. And how gay and amusing he was—and now!"

The old man was genuinely touched.

"Intercede for him, Timofey Semyonich!"

"I will do my best. I will speak in my own name, as a private person, as though I were asking for information. And
meanwhile, you find out indirectly, unofficially, how much
would the proprietor consent to take for his crocodile?"

Timofey Semyonich was visibly more friendly.

"Certainly," I answered. "And I will come back to you at
once to report."

"And his wife . . . is she alone now? Is she depressed?"

"You should call on her, Timofey Semyonich."

"I will. I thought of doing so before; it's a good opportunity.
. . . And what on earth possessed him to go and look at the
crocodile. Though, indeed, I should like to see it myself."

"Go and see the poor fellow, Timofey Semyonich."

"I will. Of course, I don't want to raise his hopes by doing
so. I shall go as a private person. . . . Well, goodbye, I am
going to Nikifor Nikiforich's again; shall you be there?"

"No, I am going to see the poor prisoner."

"Yes, now he is a prisoner! . . . Ah, that's what comes of
thoughtlessness!"

I said good-by to the old man. Ideas of all kinds were stray-
ing through my mind. A good-natured and most honest man,
Timofey Semyonich, yet, as I left him, I felt pleased at the
thought that he had celebrated his fiftieth year of service, and
that Timofey Semyonichs are now a rarity among us. I flew at
once, of course, to the Arcade to tell poor Ivan Matveich all
the news. And, indeed, I was moved by curiosity to know how
he was getting on in the crocodile and how it was possible to
live in a crocodile. And, indeed, was it possible to live in a
crocodile at all? At times it really seemed to me as though it
were all an outlandish, monstrous dream, especially as an outlandish monster was the chief figure in it.

III

And yet it was not a dream, but actual, indubitable fact.
Should I be telling the story if it were not? But to continue.

It was late, about nine o'clock, before I reached the Arcade, and I had to go into the crocodile room by the back entrance, for the German had closed the shop earlier than usual that evening. Now in the seclusion of domesticity he was walking about in a greasy old frock coat, but he seemed three times as pleased as he had been in the morning. It was evidently that he had no apprehensions now, and that the public had been coming "many more." The *Mutter* came out later, evidently to keep an eye on me. The German and the *Mutter* frequently whispered together. Although the shop was closed he charged me a quarter-ruble. What unnecessary exactitude!

"You will every time pay; the public will one ruble, and you one quarter pay; for you are the good friend of your good friend; and I a friend respect . . ."

"Are you alive, are you alive, my cultured friend?" I cried, as I approached the crocodile, expecting my words to reach Ivan Matveich from a distance and to flatter his vanity.

"Alive and well," he answered, as though from a long way off or from under the bed, though I was standing close beside him. "Alive and well; but of that later. . . . How are things going?"

As though purposely not hearing the question, I was just beginning with sympathetic haste to question him how he was, what it was like in the crocodile, and what, in fact, there was inside a crocodile. Both friendship and common civility demanded this. But with capricious annoyance he interrupted me.

"How are things going?" he shouted, in a shrill and on this occasion particularly revolting voice, addressing me peremptorily as usual.

I described to him my whole conversation with Timofey Semyonich down to the smallest detail. As I told my story I tried to show my resentment in my voice.

"The old man is right," Ivan Matveich pronounced as abruptly as usual in his conversation with me. "I like practical people, and can't endure sentimental milksops. I am ready to admit, however, that your idea about a special commission is not altogether absurd. I certainly have a great deal to report, both from a scientific and from an ethical point of view. But now all this has taken a new and unexpected aspect, and it is not worth while to trouble about mere salary. Listen attentively. Are you sitting down?"

"No, I am standing up."

"Sit down on the floor if there is nothing else, and listen attentively."

Resentfully I took a chair and put it down on the floor with a bang, in my anger.

"Listen," he began dictatorially. "The public came today in masses. There was no room left in the evening, and the police came in to keep order. At eight o'clock, that is, earlier than usual, the proprietor thought it necessary to close the shop and end the exhibition to count the money he had taken and prepare for tomorrow more conveniently. So I know there will be a regular fair tomorrow. And we may assume that all the most cultivated people in the capital, the ladies and the best society, the foreign ambassadors, the leading lawyers and so on, will all be present. What's more, people will be flowing here from the remotest provinces of our vast and interesting empire. The upshot of it is that I am the cynosure of all eyes, and though hidden to sight, I am eminent. I shall teach the idle crowd. Taught by experience, I shall be an example of greatness and resignation to fate! I shall be, so to say, a pulpit from which to instruct mankind. The mere biological details I can furnish about the monster I am inhabiting are of priceless value. And so, far from repining at what has happened, I confidently hope for the most brilliant of careers."

"You won't find it wearisome?" I asked sarcastically.

What irritated me more than anything was the extreme pomposity of his language. Nevertheless, it all rather disconcerted me. "What on earth, what, can this frivolous blockhead find to be so cocky about?" I muttered to myself. "He ought to be crying instead of being cocky."

"No!" he answered my observation sharply, "for I am full of great ideas, only now can I at leisure ponder over the amelioration of the lot of humanity. Truth and light will come forth now from the crocodile. I shall certainly develop a new economic theory of my own and I shall be proud of it—which I have hitherto been prevented from doing by my official duties and by trivial distractions. I shall refute everything and be a new Fourier. By the way, did you give Timofey Semyonich the seven rubles?"

"Yes, out of my own pocket," I answered, trying to emphasise that fact in my voice.

"We will settle it," he answered superciliously. "I confidently expect my salary to be raised, for who should get a raise if not I? I am of the utmost service now. But to business. My wife?"

"You are, I suppose, inquiring after Elena Ivanovna?"

"My wife?" he shouted, this time in a positive squeal.

There was no help for it! Meekly, though gnashing my teeth, I told him how I had left Elena Ivanovna. He did not even hear me out.

"I have special plans in regard to her," he began impatiently. "If I am celebrated *here,* I wish her to be celebrated *there.* Savants, poets, philosophers, foreign mineralogists, statesmen, after conversing in the morning with me, will visit her *salon* in the evening. From next week onwards she must have an 'At Home' every evening. With my salary doubled, we shall have the means for entertaining, and as the entertainment must not go beyond tea and hired footmen—that's settled. Both here and there they will talk of me. I have long thirsted for an opportunity for being talked about, but could not attain it, fettered by my humble position and low grade in the service. And now all this has been attained by a simple gulp on the part of the crocodile. Every word of mine will be listened to, every utterance will be thought over, repeated, printed. And I'll teach them what I am worth! They shall understand at last what abilities they have allowed to vanish in the entrails of a monster. 'This man might have been Foreign Minister or might have ruled a kingdom,' some will say. 'And that man did not rule a kingdom,' others will say. In what way am I inferior to a Garnier-Pagesishki or whatever they are called? My wife must be a worthy second—I have brains, she has beauty and charm. 'She is beautiful, and that is why she is his wife,' some will say. 'She is beautiful *because* she is his wife,' others will amend. To be ready for anything let Elena Ivanovna buy tomorrow the Encyclopedia edited by Andrey Krayevski, that she may be able to converse on any topic. Above all, let her be sure to read the political leader in the *Petersburg News,* comparing it every day with the *Voice.* I imagine that the proprietor will consent to take me sometimes with the crocodile to my wife's brilliant *salon.* I will be in a tank in the middle of the magnificent drawing room, and I will scintillate with witticisms which I will prepare in the morning. To the statesmen I will impart my projects; to the poet I will speak in rhyme; with the ladies I can be amusing and charming without impropriety, since I shall be no danger to their husbands' peace of mind. To all the rest I shall serve

as a pattern of resignation to fate and the will of Providence. I
shall make my wife a brilliant literary lady; I shall bring her
forward and explain her to the public; as my wife she must be
full of the most striking virtues; and if they are right in calling
Andrey Alexandrovich our Russian Alfred de Musset, they
will be still more right in calling her our Russian Yevgenia
Tour."

I must confess that although this wild nonsense was rather
in Ivan Matveich's habitual style, it did occur to me that he
was in a fever and delirious. It was the same, everyday Ivan
Matveich, but magnified twenty times.

"My friend," I asked him, "are you hoping for a long life?
Tell me, in fact, are you well? How do you eat, how do you
sleep, how do you breathe? I am your friend, and you must
admit that the incident is most unnatural, and consequently
my curiosity is most natural."

"Idle curiosity and nothing else," he pronounced senten-
tiously, "but you shall be satisfied. You ask how I am managing in the entrails of the monster? To begin with, the
crocodile, to my amusement, turns out to be perfectly empty.
His inside consists of a sort of huge empty sack made of
gutta-percha, like the elastic goods sold in the Gorokhovi
Street, in the Morskaya, and, if I am not mistaken, in the
Voznesenski Prospect. Otherwise, if you think of it, how could
I find room?"

"Is it possible?" I cried, in a surprise that may well be
understood. "Can the crocodile be perfectly empty?"

"Perfectly," Ivan Matveich maintained sternly and impres-
sively. "And in all probability, it is so constructed by the laws
of Nature. The crocodile possesses nothing but jaws furnished
with sharp teeth, and besides the jaws, a tail of considerable
length—that is all, properly speaking. The middle part between these two extremities is an empty space enclosed by
something of the nature of gutta-percha, probably really gutta-
percha."

"But the ribs, the stomach, the intestines, the liver, the
heart?" I interrupted quite angrily.

"There is nothing, absolutely nothing of all that, and probably there never has been. All that is the idle fancy of frivolous
travellers. As one inflates an air cushion, I am now with my
person inflating the crocodile. He is incredibly elastic. Indeed,
you might, as the friend of the family, get in with me if you
were generous and self-sacrificing enough—and even with you

here there would be room to spare. I even think that in the last
resort I might send for Elena Ivanovna. However, this void,
hollow formation of the crocodile is quite in keeping with the
teachings of natural science. If, for instance, one had to construct a new crocodile, the question would naturally present
itself. What is the fundamental characteristic of the crocodile?
The answer is clear: to swallow human beings. How is one, in
constructing the crocodile, to secure that he should swallow
people? The answer is clearer still: construct him hollow. It
was settled by physics long ago that Nature abhors a vacuum.
Hence the inside of the crocodile must be hollow so that it may
abhor the vacuum, and consequently swallow and so fill itself
with anything it can come across. And that is the sole rational cause why every crocodile swallows men. It is not the
same in the constitution of man: the emptier a man's head is,
for instance, the less he feels the thirst to fill it, and that is
the one exception to the general rule. It is all as clear as
day to me now. I have deduced it by my own observation and
experience, being, so to say, in the very bowels of Nature, in
its retort, listening to the throbbing of its pulse. Even etymol-
ogy supports me, for the very word crocodile means voracity.
Crocodile—*crocodillo*—is evidently an Italian word, dating
perhaps from the Egyptian Pharaohs, and evidently derived
from the French verb *croquer,* which means to eat, to devour,
in general to absorb nourishment. All these remarks I intend to
deliver as my first lecture in Elena Ivanovna's *salon* when they
take me there in the tank."

"My friend, oughtn't you at least to take some purgative?" I
cried involuntarily.

"He is in a fever, a fever, he is feverish!" I repeated to myself in alarm.

"Nonsense!" he answered contemptuously. "Besides, in my
present position it would be most inconvenient. I knew,
though, you would be sure to talk of taking medicine."

"But, my friend, how . . . how do you take food now?
Have you dined today?"

"No, but I am not hungry, and most likely I shall never
take food again. And that, too, is quite natural; filling the
whole interior of the crocodile I make him feel always full.
Now he need not be fed for some years. On the other hand,
nourished by me, he will naturally impart to me all the vital
juices of his body; it is the same as with some accomplished
coquettes who embed themselves and their whole persons for

the night in raw steak, and then, after their morning bath, are fresh, supple, buxom and fascinating. In that way nourishing the crocodile, I myself obtain nourishment from him, consequently we mutually nourish one another. But as it is difficult even for a crocodile to digest a man like me, he must, no doubt, be conscious of a certain weight in his stomach— an organ which he does not, however, possess—and that is why, to avoid causing the creature suffering, I do not often turn over, and although I could turn over I do not do so from humanitarian motives. This is the one drawback of my present position, and in an allegorical sense Timofey Semyonich was right in saying I was lying like a log. But I will prove that even lying like a log—nay, that only lying like a log—one can revolutionize the lot of mankind. All the great ideas and movements of our newspapers and magazines have evidently been the work of men who were lying like logs; that is why they call them divorced from the realities of life—but what does it matter, their saying that! I am constructing now a complete system of my own, and you wouldn't believe how easy it is! You have only to creep into a secluded corner or into a crocodile, to shut your eyes, and you immediately devise a perfect millennium for mankind. When you went away this afternoon I set to work at once and have already invented three systems, now I am preparing the fourth. It is true that at first one must refute everything that has gone before, but from the crocodile it is so easy to refute it; besides, it all becomes clearer, seen from the inside of the crocodile. . . . There are some drawbacks, though small ones, in my position, however; it is somewhat damp here and covered with a sort of slime; moreover, there is a smell of india rubber like the smell of my old goloshes. That is all, there are no other drawbacks."

"Ivan Matveich," I interrupted, "all this is a miracle in which I can scarcely believe. And can you, can you intend never to dine again?"

"What trivial nonsense you are troubling about, you thoughtless, frivolous creature! I talk to you about great ideas, and you . . . Understand that I am sufficiently nourished by the great ideas which light up the darkness in which I am enveloped. The good-natured proprietor has, however, after consulting the kindly *Mutter,* decided with her that they will every morning insert into the monster's jaws a bent metal tube, something like a whistle pipe, by means of which I can absorb coffee or broth with bread soaked in it. The pipe has already been requested in the neighborhood, but I think this is superfluous luxury. I hope to live at least a thousand years, if it is true that crocodiles live so long, which, by the way— good thing I thought of it—you had better look up in some natural history tomorrow and tell me, for I may have been mistaken and have mixed it up with some excavated monster. There is only one reflection rather troubles me: as I am dressed in cloth and have boots on, the crocodile can obviously not digest me. Besides, I am alive, and so am opposing the process of digestion with my whole will power; for you can understand that I do not wish to be turned into what all nourishment turns into, for that would be too humiliating for me. But there is one thing I am afraid of: in a thousand years the cloth of my coat, unfortunately of Russian make, may decay, and then, left without clothing, I might perhaps, in spite of my indignation, begin to be digested; and though by day nothing would induce me to allow it, at night, in my sleep, when a man's will deserts him, I may be overtaken by the humiliating destiny of a potato, a pancake, or veal. Such an idea reduces me to fury. This alone is an argument for the revision of the tariff and the encouragement of the importation of English cloth, which is stronger and so will withstand Nature longer when one is swallowed by a crocodile. At the first opportunity I will impart this idea to some statesman and at the same time to the political writers on our Petersburg dailies. Let them publish it abroad. I trust this will not be the only idea they will borrow from me. I foresee that every morning a regular crowd of them, provided with quarter-rubles from the editorial office, will be flocking round me to seize my ideas on the telegrams of the previous day. In brief, the future presents itself to me in the rosiest light."

"Fever, fever!" I whispered to myself.

"My friend, and freedom?" I asked, wishing to learn his views thoroughly. "You are, so to speak, in prison, while every man has a right to the enjoyment of freedom."

"You are a fool," he answered. "Savages love independence, wise men love order; and if there is no order . . ."

"Ivan Matveich, spare me, please!"

"Hold your tongue and listen!" he squealed, vexed at my interrupting him. "Never has my spirit soared as now. In my narrow refuge there is only one thing that I dread—the literary criticisms of the monthlies and the hiss of our satirical papers. I am afraid that thoughtless visitors, stupid and envious people and nihilists in general, may turn me into ridicule. But I will take measures. I am impatiently awaiting the response of the public tomorrow, and especially the opinion of the newspapers. You must tell me about the papers tomorrow."

"Very good; to-morrow I will bring a perfect pile of papers with me."

"Tomorrow it is too soon to expect reports in the newspapers, for it will take four days for it to be advertised. But from today come to me every evening by the back way through the yard. I am intending to employ you as my secretary. You shall read the newspapers and magazines to me, and I will dictate to you my ideas and give you commissions. Be particularly careful not to forget the foreign dispatches. Let all the European dispatches be here every day. But enough; most likely you are sleepy by now. Go home, and do not think of what I said just now about criticisms: I am not afraid of it, for the critics themselves are in critical position. One has only to be wise and virtuous and one will certainly get on to a pedestal. If not Socrates, then Diogenes, or perhaps both of them together—that is my future rôle among mankind."

So frivolously and boastfully did Ivan Matveich hasten to express himself before me, like feverish weak-willed women who, as we are told by the proverb, cannot keep a secret. All that he told me about the crocodile struck me as most suspicious. How was it possible that the crocodile was absolutely hollow? I don't mind betting that he was bragging from vanity and partly to humiliate me. It is true that he was an invalid and one must make allowances for invalids; but I must frankly confess, I never could endure Ivan Matveich. I have been trying all my life, from a child up, to escape from his tutelage and have not been able to; A thousand times over I have been tempted to break with him altogether, and every time I have been drawn to him again, as though I were still hoping to prove something to him or to revenge myself on him. A strange thing, this friendship! I can positively assert that nine-tenths of my friendship for him was made up of malice. On this occasion, however, we parted with genuine feeling.

"Your friend a very clever man!" the German said to me in an undertone as he moved to see me out; he had been listening all the time attentively to our conversation.

"*À propos,*" I said, "while I think of it: how much would you ask for your crocodile in case any one wanted to buy it?"

Ivan Matveich, who heard the question, was waiting with

curiosity for the answer; it was evident that he did not want the German to ask too little; anyway, he cleared his throat in a peculiar way on hearing my question.

At first the German would not listen—was positively angry. "No one will dare my own crocodile to buy!" he cried furiously, and turned as red as a boiled lobster. "Me not want to sell the crocodile! I would not for the crocodile a million thalers take. I took a hundred and thirty thalers from the public today, and I shall tomorrow ten thousand take, and then a hundred thousand every day I shall take. I will not him sell."

Ivan Matveich positively chuckled with satisfaction. Controlling myself—for I felt it was a duty to my friend— I hinted coolly and reasonably to the crazy German that his calculations were not quite correct, that if he makes a hundred thousand every day, all Petersburg will have visited him in four days, and then there will be no one left to bring him rubles, that life and death are in God's hands, that the crocodile may burst or Ivan Matveich may fall ill and die, and so on and so on.

The German grew pensive.

"I will him drops from the chemist's get," he said, after pondering, "and will save your friend that he die not."

"Drops are all very well," I answered, "but consider, too, that the thing may get into the law courts. Ivan Matveich's wife may demand the restitution of her lawful spouse. You are intending to get rich, but do you intend to give Elena Ivanovna a pension?"

"No, me not intend," said the German in stern decision.

"No, we not intend," said the *Mutter,* with positive malignancy.

"And so would it not be better for you to accept something now, at once, a secure and solid though moderate sum, than to leave things to chance? I ought to tell you that I am inquiring simply from curiosity."

The German drew the *Mutter* aside to consult with her in a corner where there stood a case with the largest and ugliest monkey of his collection.

"Well, you will see!" said Ivan Matveich.

As for me, I was at that moment burning with the desire, first, to give the German a thrashing, next, to give the *Mutter* an even sounder one, and, thirdly, to give Ivan Matveich the soundest thrashing of all for his boundless vanity. But all this paled beside the answer of the rapacious German.

After consultation with the *Mutter* he demanded for his crocodile fifty thousand rubles in bonds of the last Russian loan with lottery voucher attached, a brick house in Gorohovy Street with a chemist's shop attached, and in addition the rank of Russian colonel.

"You see!" Ivan Matveich cried triumphantly. "I told you so! Apart from this last senseless desire for the rank of a colonel, he is perfectly right, for he fully understands the present value of the monster he is exhibiting. The economic principle before everything!"

"Upon my word!" I cried furiously to the German. "But what should you be made a colonel for? What exploit have you performed? What service have you done? In what way have you gained military glory? You are really crazy!"

"Crazy!" cried the German, offended. "No, a person very sensible, but you very stupid! I have a colonel deserved for that I have a crocodile shown and in him a live *hofrath* sitting! And a Russian can a crocodile not show and a live *hofrath* in him sitting! Me extremely clever man and much wish colonel to be!"

"Well, good-by, then, Ivan Matveich!" I cried, shaking with fury, and I went out of the crocodile room almost at a run.

I felt that in another minute I could not have answered for myself. The unnatural expectations of these two block-heads were insupportable. The cold air refreshed me and somewhat moderated my indignation. At last, after spitting vigorously fifteen times on each side, I took a cab, got home, undressed and flung myself into bed. What vexed me more than anything was my having become his secretary. Now I was to die of boredom there every evening, doing the duty of a true friend! I was ready to beat myself for it, and I did, in fact, after putting out the candle and pulling up the bed-clothes, punch myself several times on the head and various parts of my body. That somewhat relieved me, and at last I fell asleep fairly soundly, in fact, for I was very tired. All night long I could dream of nothing but monkeys, but towards morning I dreamt of Elena Ivanovna.

IV

The monkeys I dreamed about, I surmise, because they were shut up in the case at the German's; but Elena Ivanovna was a different story.

I may as well say at once, I loved the lady, but I make haste
—post-haste—to make a qualification. I loved her as a father,
neither more nor less. I judge that because I often felt an
irresistible desire to kiss her little head or her rosy cheek. And
although I never carried out this inclination, I would not have
refused even to kiss her lips. And not merely her lips, but her
teeth, which always gleamed so charmingly like two rows of
pretty, well-matched pearls when she laughed. She laughed
extraordinarily often. Ivan Matveich in demonstrative moments used to call her his "darling absurdity"—a name extremely happy and appropriate. She was a perfect sugarplum,
and that was all one could say of her. Therefore I am utterly at
a loss to understand what possessed Ivan Matveich to imagine
his wife as a Russian Yevgenia Tour? Anyway, my dream, with
the exception of the monkeys, left a most pleasant impression
upon me, and going over all the incidents of the previous day
as I drank my morning cup of tea, I resolved to go and see
Elena Ivanovna at once on my way to the office—which, indeed, I was bound to do as the friend of the family.

In a tiny little room out of the bedroom—the so-called little
drawing room, though their big drawing room was little too—
Elena Ivanovna was sitting, in some half-transparent morning
wrapper, on a smart little sofa before a little tea table, drinking
coffee out of a little cup in which she was dipping a minute
biscuit. She was ravishingly pretty, but struck me as being at
the same time rather pensive.

"Ah, that's you, naughty man!" she said, greeting me with
an absent-minded smile. "Sit down, featherhead, have some
coffee. Well, what were you doing yesterday? Were you at the
masquerade?"

"Why, were you? I don't go, you know. Besides, yesterday
I was visiting our captive. . . ." I sighed and assumed a pious
expression as I took the coffee.

"Whom? . . . What captive? . . . Oh, yes! Poor fellow!
Well, how is he—bored? Do you know . . . I wanted to ask
you . . . I suppose I can ask for a divorce now?"

"A divorce!" I cried in indignation and almost spilled the
coffee. "It's that swarthy fellow," I thought to myself bitterly.

There was a certain swarthy gentleman with little moustaches who was something in the architectural line, and who
came far too often to see them, and was extremely skillful
in amusing Elena Ivanovna. I must confess I hated him and
there was no doubt that he had succeeded in seeing Elena

Ivanovna yesterday either at the masquerade or even here, and putting all sorts of nonsense into her head.

"Why," Elena Ivanovna rattled off hurriedly, as though it were a lesson she had learnt, "if he is going to stay on in the crocodile, perhaps not come back all his life, while I sit waiting for him here. A husband ought to live at home, and not in a crocodile. . . ."

"But this was an unforeseen occurrence," I was beginning, in very comprehensible agitation.

"Oh, no, don't talk to me, I won't listen, I won't listen," she cried, suddenly getting quite cross. "You are always against me, you wretch! There's no doing anything with you, you will never give me any advice! Other people tell me that I can get a divorce because Ivan Matveich will not get his salary now."

"Elena Ivanovna! is it you I hear!" I exclaimed pathetically. "What villain could have put such an idea into your head? And divorce on such a trivial ground as a salary is quite impossible. And poor Ivan Matveich, poor Ivan Matveich is, so to speak, burning with love for you even in the bowels of the monster. What's more, he is melting away with love like a lump of sugar. Yesterday while you were enjoying yourself at the masquerade, he was saying that he might in the last resort send for you as his lawful spouse to join him in the entrails of the monster, especially as it appears the crocodile is exceedingly roomy, not only able to accommodate two but even three persons. . . ."

And then I told her all that interesting part of my conversation the night before with Ivan Matveich.

"What, what!" she cried, in surprise. "You want me to get into the monster too, to be with Ivan Matveich? What an idea! And how am I to get in there, in my hat and crinoline? Heavens, what foolishness! And what should I look like while I was getting into it, and very likely there would be some one there to see me! It's absurd! And what should I have to eat there? And . . . and . . . and what should I do there when . . . Oh, my goodness, what will they think of next? . . . And what should I have to amuse me there? . . . You say there's a smell of gutta-percha? And what should I do if we quarrelled—should we have to go on staying there side by side? Foo, how horrid!"

"I agree, I agree with all those arguments, my sweet Elena Ivanovna," I interrupted, striving to express myself with that natural enthusiasm which always overtakes a man when he

feels the truth is on his side. "But one thing you have not appreciated in all this, you have not realized that he cannot live
without you if he is inviting you there; that is a proof of love,
passionate, faithful, ardent love. . . . You have thought too
little of his love, dear Elena Ivanovna!"

"I won't, I won't, I won't hear anything about it!" waving
me off with her pretty little hand with glistening pink nails that
had just been washed and polished. "Horrid man! You will
reduce me to tears! Get into it yourself, if you like the prospect. You are his friend, get in and keep him company, and
spend your life discussing some tedious science. . . ."

"You are wrong to laugh at this suggestion"—I checked
the frivolous woman with dignity—"Ivan Matveich has invited me as it is. You, of course, are summoned there by
duty; for me, it would be an act of generosity. But when Ivan
Matveich described to me last night the elasticity of the crocodile, he hinted very plainly that there would be room not only
for you two, but for me also as a friend of the family, especially if I wished to join you, and therefore . . ."

"How so, the three of us?" cried Elena Ivanovna, looking
at me in surprise. "Why, how should we . . . are we going
to be all three there together? Ha-ha-ha! How silly you both
are! Ha-ha-ha! I shall certainly pinch you all the time, you
wretch! Ha-ha-ha! Ha-ha-ha!"

And falling back on the sofa, she laughed till she cried. All
this—the tears and the laughter—were so fascinating that I
could not resist rushing eagerly to kiss her hand, which she
did not oppose, though she did pinch my ears lightly as a sign
of reconciliation.

Then we both grew very cheerful, and I described to her in
detail all Ivan Matveich's plans. The thought of her evening
receptions and her *salon* pleased her very much.

"Only I should need a great many new dresses," she observed, "and so Ivan Matveich must send me as much of his
salary as possible and as soon as possible. Only . . . only I
don't know about that," she added thoughtfully. "How can he
be brought here in the tank? That's very absurd. I don't want
my husband to be carried about in a tank. I should feel quite
ashamed for my visitors to see it. . . . I don't want that, no,
I don't."

"By the way, while I think of it, was Timofey Semyonich
here yesterday?"

"Oh, yes, he was; he came to comfort me, and do you know,

we played cards all the time. He played for sweetmeats, and if I lost he was to kiss my hands. What a wretch he is! And only fancy, he almost came to the masquerade with me, really!"

"He was carried away by his feelings!" I observed. "And who would not be with you, you charmer?"

"Oh, get along with your compliments! Stay, I'll give you a pinch as a parting present. I've learnt to pinch awfully well lately. Well, what do you say to that? By the way, you say Ivan Matveich spoke several times of me yesterday?"

"N-no, not exactly. . . . I must say he is thinking more now of the fate of humanity, and wants . . ."

"Oh, let him! You needn't go on! I am sure it's fearfully boring. I'll go and see him some time. I shall certainly go tomorrow. Only not today; I've got a headache, and besides, there will be such a lot of people there today. . . . They'll say, 'That's his wife,' and I shall feel ashamed. . . . Good-by. You will be . . . there this evening, won't you?"

"To see him, yes. He asked me to go and take him the papers."

"That's capital. Go and read to him. But don't come and see me today. I am not well, and perhaps I may go and see some one. Good-by, you naughty man."

"It's that swarthy fellow is going to see her this evening," I thought.

At the office, of course, I gave no sign of being consumed by these cares and anxieties. But soon I noticed some of the most progressive papers seemed to be passing particularly rapidly from hand to hand among my colleagues, and were being read with an extremely serious expression of face. The first one that reached me was the *News-sheet,* a paper of no particular party but humanitarian in general, for which it was regarded with contempt among us, though it was read. Not without surprise I read in it the following paragraph:

"Yesterday strange rumors were circulating among the spacious ways and sumptuous buildings of our vast metropolis. A certain well-known *bon-vivant* of the highest society, probably weary of the *cuisine* at Borel's and at the X. Club, went into the Arcade, into the place where an immense crocodile recently brought to the metropolis is being exhibited, and insisted on its being prepared for his dinner. After bargaining with the proprietor he at once set to work to devour him (that is, not the pro-

prietor, a very meek and punctilious German, but his crocodile), cutting juicy morsels with his penknife from the living
animal, and swallowing them with extraordinary rapidity. By
degrees the whole crocodile disappeared into the vast recesses
of his stomach, so that he was even on the point of attacking
an ichneumon, a constant companion of the crocodile, probably imagining that the latter would be as savoury. We are by
no means opposed to that new article of diet with which
foreign *gourmands* have long been familiar. We have, indeed,
predicted that it would come. English lords and travellers
make up regular parties for catching crocodiles in Egypt, and
consume the back of the monster cooked like beefsteak, with
mustard, onions and potatoes. The French who followed in
the train of Lesseps prefer the paws baked in hot ashes, which
they do, however, in opposition to the English, who laugh at
them. Probably both ways would be appreciated among us. For
our part, we are delighted at a new branch of industry, of
which our great and varied fatherland stands pre-eminently in
need. Probably before a year is out crocodiles will be brought
in hundreds to replace this first one, lost in the stomach of a
Petersburg *gourmand*. And why should not the crocodile be
acclimatized among us in Russia? If the water of the Neva is
too cold for these interesting strangers, there are ponds in the
capital and rivers and lakes outside it. Why not breed crocodiles at Pargolovo, for instance, or at Pavlovsk, in the
Presensky Ponds and in Samoteka in Moscow? While providing agreeable, wholesome nourishment for our fastidious
gourmands, they might at the same time entertain the ladies
who walk about these ponds and instruct the children in natural history. The crocodile skin might be used for making
jewel cases, boxes, cigar cases, pocketbooks, and possibly
more than one thousand saved up in the greasy notes that are
peculiarly beloved of merchants might be laid by in crocodile
skin. We hope to return more than once to this interesting
topic."

Though I had foreseen something of the sort, yet the reck-
less inaccuracy of the paragraph overwhelmed me. Finding no
one with whom to share my impression, I turned to Prokhor
Savitch who was sitting opposite to me, and noticed that the
latter had been watching me for some time, while in his hand
he held the *Voice* as though he were on the point of passing
it to me. Without a word he took the *News-sheet* from me,
and as he handed me the *Voice* he drew a line with his nail

against an article to which he probably wished to call my attention. This Prokhor Savitch was a very queer man; a taciturn old bachelor, he was not on intimate terms with any of us, scarcely spoke to any one in the office, always had an opinion of his own about everything, but could not bear to impart it to any one. He lived alone. Hardly any one among us had ever been in his lodging.

This was what I read in the *Voice*.

"Every one knows that we are progressive and humanitarian and want to be on a level with Europe in this respect. But in spite of all our exertions and the efforts of our paper we are still far from maturity, as may be judged from the shocking incident which took place yesterday in the Arcade and which we predicted long ago. A foreigner arrives in the capital bringing with him a crocodile which he begins exhibiting in the Arcade. We immediately hasten to welcome a new branch of useful industry such as our powerful and varied fatherland stands in great need of. Suddenly yesterday at four o'clock in the afternoon a gentleman of exceptional stoutness enters the foreigner's shop in an intoxicated condition, pays his entrance money, and immediately without any warning leaps into the jaws of the crocodile, who was forced, of course, to swallow him, if only from an instinct of self-preservation. to avoid being crushed. Tumbling into the inside of the crocodile, the stranger at once dropped asleep. Neither the shouts of the foreign proprietor, nor the lamentations of his terrified family, nor threats to send for the police made the slightest impression. Within the crocodile was heard nothing but laughter and a promise to flay him (*sic*), though the poor mammal, compelled to swallow such a mass, was vainly shedding tears. An uninvited guest is worse than a Tartar. But in spite of the proverb the insolent visitor would not leave. We do not know how to explain such barbarous incidents which prove our lack of culture and disgrace us in the eyes of foreigners. The recklessness of the Russian temperament has found a fresh outlet. It may be asked what was the object of the uninvited visitor? A warm and comfortable abode? But there are many excellent houses in the capital with very cheap and comfortable lodgings, with the Neva water laid on, and a staircase lighted by gas, frequently with a hall porter maintained by the proprietor. We would call our readers' attention to the barbarous treatment of domestic animals: it is difficult, of course, for the crocodile to digest such a mass all at once, and now he lies swollen out to the size of a mountain, awaiting death in insufferable agonies. In Europe persons guilty of inhumanity towards domestic animals have long been punished by law. But in spite of our European enlightenment, in spite of our European pavements, in spite of the European architecture of our houses, we are still far from shaking off our time-honored traditions.

'*Though the houses are new, the conventions are old.*'

"And, indeed, the houses are not new, at least the staircases in them are not. We have more than once in our paper alluded to the fact that in the Petersburg Side in the house of the merchant Lukyanov the steps of the wooden staircase have decayed, fallen away, and have long been a danger for Afimya Skapidarov, a soldier's wife who works in the house, and is often obliged to go up the stairs with water or armfuls of wood. At last our predictions have come true: yesterday evening at half-past eight Afimya Skapidarov fell down with a basin of soup and broke her leg. We do not know whether Lukyanov will mend his staircase now, Russians are often wise after the event, but the victim of Russian carelessness has by now been taken to the hospital. In the same way we shall never cease to maintain that the house-porters who clear away the mud from the wooden pavement in the Viborgsky Side ought not to spatter the legs of passersby, but should throw the mud up into heaps as is done in Europe," and so, and so on.

"What's this?" I asked in some perplexity, looking at Prokhor Savitch. "What's the meaning of it?"

"How do you mean?"

"Why, upon my word! Instead of pitying Ivan Matveich, they pity the crocodile!"

"What of it? They have pity even for a beast, a *mammal*. We must be up to Europe, mustn't we? They have a very warm feeling for crocodiles there too. He-he-he!"

Saying this, queer old Prokhor Savitch dived into his papers and would not utter another word.

I stuffed the *Voice* and the *News-sheet* into my pocket and collected as many old copies of the newspapers as I could find for Ivan Matveich's diversion in the evening, and though the evening was far off, yet on this occasion I slipped away from the office early to go to the Arcade and look, if only from a distance, at what was going on there, and to listen to the various remarks and currents of opinion. I foresaw that there would be a regular crush there, and turned up the collar of my coat to meet it. I somehow felt rather shy—so unaccustomed are we to publicity. But I feel that I have no right to report my own prosaic feelings when faced with this remarkable and original incident.

The Dream of a Ridiculous Man

✠

A Fantastic Story

I am a ridiculous man. They call me a madman now. That would be a distinct rise in my social position were it not that they still regard me as being as ridiculous as ever. But that does not make me angry any more. They are all dear to me now even while they laugh at me—yes, even then they are for some reason particularly dear to me. I shouldn't have minded laughing with them—not at myself, of course, but because I love them—had I not felt so sad as I looked at them. I feel sad because they do not know the truth, whereas I know it. Oh, how hard it is to be the only man to know the truth! But they won't understand that. No, they will not understand.

And yet in the past I used to be terribly distressed at appearing to be ridiculous. No, not appearing to be, but being. I've always cut a ridiculous figure. I suppose I must have known it from the day I was born. At any rate, I've known for certain that I was ridiculous ever since I was seven years old. Afterwards I went to school, then to the university, and—well—the more I learned, the more conscious did I become of the fact that I was ridiculous. So that for me my years of hard work at the university seem in the end to have existed for the sole purpose of demonstrating and proving to me, the more deeply engrossed I became in my studies, that I was an utterly absurd person. And as during my studies, so all my life. Every year the same consciousness that I was ridiculous in every way strengthened and intensified in my mind. They always laughed at me. But not one of them knew or suspected that if there were one man on earth who knew better than anyone else that he was ridiculous, that man was I. And this—I mean, the fact that they did not know it—was the bitterest pill for me to swallow. But there I was myself at fault. I was always so proud that I never wanted to confess it to anyone. No, I wouldn't do that for anything in the world. As the years passed, this pride increased in me so that I do believe that if ever I had by chance confessed it to any one I should have blown my brains out the same evening. Oh, how I suffered in the days of my youth from the thought that I might not myself resist the impulse to confess it to my schoolfellows. But ever since I became a man I grew for some unknown reason a little more composed in my mind, though I was more and more conscious of that awful characteristic of mine. Yes, most decidedly for some unknown reason, for to this day I have not been able to find out why that was so. Perhaps it was because I was becoming terribly disheartened owing to one circumstance which was beyond my power to control, namely, the conviction which was gaining upon me that nothing in the whole world *made any difference*. I had long felt it dawning upon me, but I was fully convinced of it only last year, and that, too, all of a sudden, as it were. I suddenly felt that it made *no* difference to me whether the world existed or whether nothing existed anywhere at all. I began to be acutely conscious that *nothing existed in my own lifetime*. At first I couldn't help feeling that at any rate in the past many things had existed; but later on I came to the conclusion that there had not been anything even in the past, but that for some reason it had merely seemed to have been. Little by little I became convinced that there would be nothing in the future, either. It was then that I suddenly ceased to be angry with people and almost stopped noticing them. This indeed disclosed itself in the smallest trifles. For instance, I would knock against people while walking in the street. And not because I was lost in thought—I had nothing to think about—I had stopped thinking about anything at that time: it made no difference to me. Not that I had found an answer to all the questions. Oh, I had not settled a single question, and there were thousands of them! But *it made no difference to me,* and all the questions disappeared.

And, well, it was only after that that I learnt the truth. I learnt the truth last November, on the third of November, to be precise, and every moment since then has been imprinted indelibly on my mind. It happened on a dismal evening, as dismal an evening as could be imagined. I was returning home at about eleven o'clock and I remember thinking all the time that there could not be a more dismal evening. Even the weather was foul. It had been pouring all day, and the rain too was the coldest and most dismal rain that ever was, a sort of menacing rain—I remember that—a rain with a distinct animosity towards people. But about eleven o'clock it had stopped suddenly, and a horrible dampness descended upon everything, and it became much damper and colder than when it had been raining. And a sort of steam was rising from everything, from every cobble in the street, and from every sidestreet if you peered closely into it from the street as far as the eye could reach. I could not help feeling that if the gaslight had been extinguished everywhere, everything would have seemed much more cheerful, and that the gaslight oppressed the heart so much just because it shed a light upon it all. I had had scarcely any dinner that day. I had been spending the whole evening with an engineer who had two more friends visiting him. I never opened my mouth, and I expect I must have got on their nerves. They were discussing some highly controversial subject, and suddenly got very excited over it. But it really did not make any difference to them. I could see that. I knew that their excitement was not genuine. So I suddenly blurted it out. "My dear fellows," I said, "you don't really care a damn about it, do you?" They were not in the least offended, but they all burst out laughing at me. That was because I had said it without meaning to rebuke them, but simply because it made no difference to me. Well, they realized that it made no difference to me, and they felt happy.

When I was thinking about the gaslight in the streets, I looked up at the sky. The sky was awfully dark, but I could clearly distinguish the torn wisps of cloud and between them fathomless dark patches. All of a sudden I became aware of a little star in one of those patches and I began looking at it intently. That was because the little star gave me an idea: I made up my mind to kill myself that night. I had made up my mind to kill myself already two months before and, poor as I am, I bought myself an excellent revolver and loaded it the same day. But two months had elapsed and it was still lying in the drawer. I was so utterly indifferent to everything that I was anxious to wait for the moment when I would not be so indifferent and then kill myself. Why—I don't know. And so every night during these two months I thought of shooting myself as I was going home. I was only waiting for the right moment. And now the little star gave me an idea, and I made up my mind then and there that it should *most certainly* be that night. But why the little star gave me the idea—I don't know.

And just as I was looking at the sky, this little girl suddenly grasped me by the elbow. The street was already deserted and there was scarcely a soul to be seen. In the distance a cabman was fast asleep on his box. The girl was about eight years old. She had a kerchief on her head, and she wore only an old, shabby little dress. She was soaked to the skin, but what stuck in my memory was her little torn wet boots. I still remember them. They caught my eye especially. She suddenly began tugging at my elbow and calling me. She was not crying, but saying something in a loud, jerky sort of voice, something that did not make sense, for she was trembling all over and her teeth were chattering from cold. She seemed to be terrified of something and she was crying desperately, "Mummy! Mummy!" I turned round to look at her, but did not utter a word and went on walking. But she ran after me and kept tugging at my clothes, and there was a sound in her voice which in very frightened children signifies despair. I know that sound. Though her words sounded as if they were choking her, I realized that her mother must be dying somewhere very near, or that something similar was happening to her, and that she had run out to call someone, to find someone who would help her mother. But I did not go with her; on the contrary, something made me drive her away. At first I told her to go and find a policeman. But she suddenly clasped her hands and, whimpering and gasping for breath, kept running at my side and would not leave me. It was then that I stamped my foot and shouted at her. She just cried, "Sir! Sir! . . ." and then she left me suddenly and rushed headlong across the road: another man appeared there and she evidently rushed from me to him.

I climbed to the fifth floor. I live apart from my landlord. We all have separate rooms as in an hotel. My room is very small and poor. My window is a semicircular skylight. I have a sofa covered with American cloth, a table with books on it, two chairs and a comfortable armchair, a very old armchair indeed, but low-seated and with a high back serving as a headrest. I sat down in the armchair, lighted the candle, and began thinking. Next door in the other room behind the partition, the usual bedlam was going on. It had been going on since the day before yesterday. A retired army captain lived there, and he had visitors—six merry gentlemen who drank vodka and played faro with an old pack of cards. Last night they had a fight and I know that two of them were for a long time pulling each other about by the hair. The landlady wanted to complain, but she is dreadfully afraid of the captain. We had only one more lodger in our rooms, a thin little lady, the wife of an army officer, on a visit to Petersburg with her three little children who had all been taken ill since their arrival at our house. She and her children were simply terrified of the captain and they lay shivering and crossing themselves all night long, and the youngest child had a sort of nervous attack from fright. This captain (I know that for a fact) sometimes stops people on Nevski Avenue and asks them for a few coppers, telling them he is very poor. He can't get a job in the Civil Service, but the strange thing is (and that's why I am telling you this) that the captain had never once during the month he had been living with us made me feel in the least irritated. From the very first, of course, I would not have anything to do with him, and he himself was bored with me the very first time we met. But however big a noise they raised behind their partition and however many of them there were in the captain's room, it makes no difference to me. I sit up all night and, I assure you, I don't hear them at all—so completely do I forget about them. You see, I stay awake all night till daybreak, and that has been going on for a whole year now. I sit up all night in the armchair at the table—doing nothing. I read books only in the daytime. At night I sit like that without even thinking about anything in particular: some thoughts wander in and out of my mind, and I let them come and go as they please. In the night the candle burns out completely.

I sat down at the table, took the gun out of the drawer, and put it down in front of me. I remember asking myself as I put it down, "Is it to be then?" and I replied with complete certainty, "It is!" That is to say, I was going to shoot myself. I knew I should shoot myself that night for certain. What I did not know was how much longer I should go on sitting at the table till I shot myself. And I should of course have shot myself, had it not been for the little girl.

II

You see, though nothing made any difference to me, I could feel pain, for instance, couldn't I? If anyone had struck me, I should have felt pain. The same was true so far as my moral perceptions were concerned. If anything happened to arouse my pity, I should have felt pity, just as I used to do at the time when things did make a difference to me. So I had felt pity that night: I should most decidedly have helped a child. Why then did I not help the little girl? Because of a thought that had occurred to me at the time: when she was pulling at me and calling me, a question suddenly arose in my mind and I could not settle it. It was an idle question, but it made me angry. What made me angry was the conclusion I drew from the reflection that if I had really decided to do away with myself that night, everything in the world should have been more indifferent to me than ever. Why then should I have suddenly felt that I was not indifferent and be sorry for the little girl? I remember that I was very sorry for her, so much so that I felt a strange pang which was quite incomprehensible in my position. I'm afraid I am unable better to convey that fleeting sensation of mine, but it persisted with me at home when I was sitting at the table, and I was very much irritated. I had not been so irritated for a long time past. One train of thought followed another. It was clear to me that so long as I was still a human being and not a meaningless cipher, and till I became a cipher, I was alive, and consequently able to suffer, be angry, and feel shame at my actions. Very well. But if, on the other hand, I were going to kill myself in, say, two hours, what did that little girl matter to me and what did I care for shame or anything else in the world? I was going to turn into a cipher, into an absolute cipher. And surely the realisation that I should soon cease to exist *altogether,* and hence everything would cease to exist, ought to have had some slight effect on my feeling of pity for the little girl or on my feeling of shame after so mean an action. Why after all did I stamp and shout so fiercely at the little girl? I did it because I thought that not only did I feel no pity, but that it wouldn't matter now if I were guilty of the most inhuman baseness, since in another two hours everything would become extinct. Do you believe me when I tell you that that was the only reason why I shouted like that? I am almost convinced of it now. It seemed clear to me that life and the world in some way or other depended on me now. It might almost be said that the world seemed to be created for me alone. If I were to shoot myself, the world would cease to exist—for me at any rate. To say nothing of the possibility that nothing would in fact exist for anyone after me and the whole world would dissolve as soon as my consciousness became extinct, would disappear in a twinkling like a phantom, like some integral part of my consciousness, and vanish without leaving a trace behind, for all this world and all these people exist perhaps only in my consciousness.

I remember that as I sat and meditated, I began to examine all these questions which thronged in my mind one after another from quite a different angle, and thought of something quite new. For instance, the strange notion occurred to me that if I had lived before on the moon or on Mars and had committed there the most shameful and dishonorable action that can be imagined, and had been so disgraced and dishonored there as can be imagined and experienced only occasionally in a dream, a nightmare, and if, finding myself afterwards on earth, I had retained the memory of what I had done on the other planet, and moreover knew that I should never in any circumstances go back there—if that were to have happened, should I or should I not have felt, as I looked from the earth upon the moon, that *it made no difference* to me? Should I or should I not have felt ashamed of that action? The questions were idle and useless, for the gun was already lying before me and there was not a shadow of doubt in my mind that *it* was going to take place for certain, but they excited and maddened me. It seemed to me that I could not die now without having settled something first. The little girl, in fact, had saved me, for by these questions I put off my own execution.

Meanwhile things had grown more quiet in the captain's room: they had finished their card game and were getting ready to turn in for the night, and now were only grumbling and swearing at each other in a half-hearted sort of way. It was at that moment that I suddenly fell asleep in my armchair at the table, a thing that had never happened to me before.

I fell asleep without being aware of it at all. Dreams, as

we all know, are very curious things: certain incidents in them are presented with quite uncanny vividness, each detail executed with the finishing touch of a jeweller, while others you leap across as though entirely unaware of, for instance, space and time. Dreams seem to be induced not by reason but by desire, not by the head but by the heart, and yet what clever tricks my reason has sometimes played on me in dreams! And furthermore what incomprehensible things happen to it in a dream. My brother, for instance, died five years ago. I sometimes dream about him: he takes a keen interest in my affairs, we are both very interested, and yet I know very well all through my dream that my brother is dead and buried. How is it that I am not surprised that, though dead, he is here beside me, doing his best to help me? Why does my reason accept all this without the slightest hesitation? But enough. Let me tell you about my dream. Yes, I dreamed that dream that night. My dream of the third of November. They are making fun of me now by saying that it was only a dream. But what does it matter whether it was a dream or not, so long as that dream revealed the Truth to me? For once you have recognized the truth and seen it, you know it is the one and only truth and that there can be no other, whether you are asleep or awake. But never mind. Let it be a dream, but remember that I had intended to cut short by suicide the life that means so much to us, and that my dream —my dream—oh, it revealed to me a new, grand, regenerated, strong life!

Listen.

III

I have said that I fell asleep imperceptibly and even while I seemed to be revolving the same thoughts again in my mind. Suddenly I dreamed that I picked up the gun and, sitting in my armchair, pointed it straight at my heart—at my heart, and not at my head. For I had firmly resolved to shoot myself through the head, through the right temple, to be precise. Having aimed the gun at my breast, I paused for a second or two, and suddenly my candle, the table and the wall began moving and swaying before me. I fired quickly.

In a dream you sometimes fall from a great height, or you are being murdered or beaten, but you never feel any pain unless you really manage somehow or other to hurt yourself in bed, when you feel pain and almost always wake up from it. So it was in my dream: I did not feel any pain, but it seemed as though with my shot everything within me was shaken and everything was suddenly extinguished, and a terrible darkness descended all around me. I seemed to have become blind and dumb. I was lying on something hard, stretched out full length on my back. I saw nothing and could not make the slightest movement. All round me people were walking and shouting. The captain was yelling in his deep bass voice, the landlady was screaming and—suddenly another hiatus, and I was being carried in a closed coffin. I could feel the coffin swaying and I was thinking about it, and for the first time the idea flashed through my mind that I was dead, dead as a doornail, that I knew it, that there was not the least doubt about it, that I could neither see nor move, and yet I could feel and reason. But I was soon reconciled to that and, as usually happens in dreams, I accepted the facts without questioning them.

And now I was buried in the earth. They all went away, and I was left alone, entirely alone. I did not move. Whenever before I imagined how I should be buried in a grave, there was only one sensation I actually associated with the grave, namely, that of damp and cold. And so it was now. I felt that I was very cold, especially in the tips of my toes, but I felt nothing else.

I lay in my grave and, strange to say, I did not expect anything, accepting the idea that a dead man had nothing to expect as an incontestable fact. But it was damp. I don't know how long a time passed, whether an hour, or several days, or many days. But suddenly a drop of water, which had seeped through the lid of the coffin, fell on my closed left eye. It was followed by another drop a minute later, then after another minute by another drop, and so on. One drop every minute. All at once deep indignation blazed up in my heart, and I suddenly felt a twinge of physical pain in it. "That's my wound," I thought. "It's the shot I fired. There's a bullet there. . . ." And drop after drop still kept falling every minute on my closed eyelid. And suddenly I called (not with my voice, for I was motionless, but with the whole of my being) upon Him who was responsible for all that was happening to me:

"Whoever Thou art, and if anything more rational exists than what is happening here, let it, I pray Thee, come to pass here too. But if Thou art revenging Thyself for my senseless act of self-destruction by the infamy and absurdity of life after death, then know that no torture that may be inflicted upon me can ever equal the contempt which I shall go on feeling in silence, though my martyrdom last for aeons upon aeons!"

I made this appeal and was silent. The dead silence went on for almost a minute, and one more drop fell on my closed eyelid, but I knew, I knew and believed infinitely and unshakably that everything would without a doubt change immediately. And then my grave was opened. I don't know, that is, whether it was opened or dug open, but I was seized by some dark and unknown being and we found ourselves in space. I suddenly regained my sight. It was a pitch-black night. Never, never had there been such darkness! We were flying through space at a terrific speed and we had already left the earth behind us. I did not question the being who was carrying me. I was proud and waited. I was telling myself that I was not afraid, and I was filled with admiration at the thought that I was not afraid. I cannot remember how long we were flying, nor can I give you an idea of the time; it all happened as it always does happen in dreams when you leap over space and time and the laws of nature and reason, and only pause at the points which are especially dear to your heart. All I remember is that I suddenly beheld a little star in the darkness.

"Is that Sirius?" I asked, feeling suddenly unable to restrain myself, for I had made up my mind not to ask any questions.

"No," answered the being who was carrying me, "that is the same star you saw between the clouds when you were coming home."

I knew that its face bore some resemblance to a human face. It is a strange fact but I did not like that being, and I even felt an intense aversion for it. I had expected complete nonexistence and that was why I had shot myself through the heart. And yet there I was in the hands of a being, not human of course, but which *was,* which existed. "So there is life beyond the grave!" I thought with the curious irrelevance of a dream, but at heart I remained essentially unchanged. "If I must *be* again," I thought, "and live again at someone's unalterable behest, I won't be defeated and humiliated!"

"You know I'm afraid of you and that's why you despise me," I said suddenly to my companion, unable to refrain from the humiliating remark with its implied admission, and feeling my own humiliation in my heart like the sharp prick of a needle.

He did not answer me, but I suddenly felt that I was not despised, that no one was laughing at me, that no one was even pitying me, and that our journey had a purpose, an unknown and mysterious purpose that concerned only me. Fear was steadily growing in my heart. Something was communicated to me from my silent companion—mutely but agonizingly—and it seemed to permeate my whole being. We were speeding through dark and unknown regions of space. I had long since lost sight of the constellations familiar to me. I knew that there were stars in the heavenly spaces whose light took thousands and millions of years to reach the earth. Possibly we were already flying through those spaces. I expected something in the terrible anguish that wrung my heart. And suddenly a strangely familiar and incredibly nostalgic feeling shook me to the very core: I suddenly caught sight of our sun! I knew that it could not possibly be *our* sun that gave birth to our earth, and that we were millions of miles away from our sun, but for some unknown reason I recognized with every fibre of my being that it was precisely the same sun as ours, its exact copy and twin. A sweet, nostalgic feeling filled my heart with rapture: the old familiar power of the same light which had given me life stirred an echo in my heart and revived it, and I felt the same life stirring within me for the first time since I had been in the grave.

"But if it is the sun, if it's exactly the same sun as ours," I cried, "then where is the earth?"

And my companion pointed to a little star twinkling in the darkness with an emerald light. We were making straight for it.

"But are such repetitions possible in the universe? Can that be nature's law? And if that is an earth there, is it the same earth as ours? Just the same poor, unhappy, but dear, dear earth, and beloved for ever and ever? Arousing like our earth the same poignant love for herself even in the most ungrateful of her children?" I kept crying, deeply moved by an uncontrollable, rapturous love for the dear old earth I had left behind.

The face of the poor little girl I had treated so badly flashed through my mind.

"You shall see it all," answered my companion, and a strange sadness sounded in his voice.

But we were rapidly approaching the planet. It was grow-ing before my eyes. I could already distinguish the ocean, the outlines of Europe, and suddenly a strange feeling of some great and sacred jealousy blazed up in my heart.

"How is such a repetition possible and why? I love, I can only love the earth I've left behind, stained with my blood when, ungrateful wretch that I am, I extinguished my life by shooting myself through the heart. But never, never have I ceased to love that earth, and even on the night I parted from it I loved it perhaps more poignantly than ever. Is there suf-fering on this new earth? On our earth we can truly love only with suffering and through suffering! We know not how to love otherwise. We know no other love. I want suffering in order to love. I want and thirst this very minute to kiss, with tears streaming down my cheeks, the one and only earth I have left behind. I don't want, I won't accept life on any other! . . ."

But my companion had already left me. Suddenly, and without as it were being aware of it myself, I stood on this other earth in the bright light of a sunny day, fair and beauti-ful as paradise. I believe I was standing on one of the islands which on our earth form the Greek archipelago, or some-where on the coast of the mainland close to this archipelago. Oh, everything was just as it is with us, except that everything seemed to be bathed in the radiance of some public festival and of some great and holy triumph attained at last. The gentle emerald sea softly lapped the shore and kissed it with manifest, visible, almost conscious love. Tall, beautiful trees stood in all the glory of their green luxuriant foliage, and their innumerable leaves (I am sure of that) welcomed me with their soft, tender rustle, and seemed to utter sweet words of love. The lush grass blazed with bright and fragrant flowers. Birds were flying in flocks through the air and, without being afraid of me, alighted on my shoulders and hands and joyfully beat against me with their sweet fluttering wings. And at last I saw and came to know the people of this blessed earth. They came to me themselves. They surrounded me. They kissed me. Children of the sun, children of their sun—oh, how beautiful they were! Never on our earth had I beheld such beauty in man. Only perhaps in our children during the very first years of their life could one have found a remote, though faint, reflection of this beauty. The eyes of these happy people shone with a bright lustre. Their faces were radiant with understanding and a serenity of mind that had reached its greatest fulfillment. Those faces were joyous; in the words and voices of these people there was a childlike gladness. Oh, at the first glance at their faces I at once understood all, all! It was an earth unstained by the Fall, inhabited by people who had not sinned and who lived in the same paradise as that in which, according to the legends of mankind, our first parents lived before they sinned, with the only difference that all the earth here was everywhere the same paradise. These people, laughing happily, thronged round me and overwhelmed me with their caresses; they took me home with them, and each of them was anxious to set my mind at peace. Oh, they asked me no questions, but seemed to know everything already (that was the impression I got), and they longed to remove every trace of suffering from my face as soon as possible.

IV

Well, you see, again let me repeat: All right, let us assume it was only a dream! But the sensation of the love of those innocent and beautiful people has remained with me for ever, and I can feel that their love is even now flowing out to me from over there. I have seen them myself. I have known them thoroughly and been convinced. I loved them and I suffered for them afterwards. Oh, I knew at once even all the time that there were many things about them I should never be able to understand. To me, a modern Russian progressive and a despicable citizen of Petersburg, it seemed inexplicable that, knowing so much, they knew nothing of our science, for instance. But I soon realized that their knowledge was derived from, and fostered by emotions other than those to which we were accustomed on earth, and that their aspirations, too, were quite different. They desired nothing. They were at peace with themselves. They did not strive to gain knowledge of life as we strive to understand it because their lives were full. But their knowledge was higher and deeper than the knowledge we derive from our science; for our science seeks to explain what life is and strives to understand it in order to teach others how to live, while they knew how to live without science. I understood that, but I couldn't understand their knowledge. They pointed out their trees to me, and I could not understand the intense love with which they looked on them; it was as though they were talking with beings like themselves. And, you know, I don't think I am exaggerating in saying that they talked with them! Yes, they had discovered their language, and I am sure the trees understood them. They looked upon all nature like that—the animals which lived peaceably with them and did not attack them, but loved them, conquered by their love for them. They pointed out the stars to me and talked to me about them in a way that I could not understand, but I am certain that in some curious way they communed with the stars in the heavens, not only in thought, but in some actual, living way. Oh, these people were not concerned whether I understood them or not; they loved me without it. But I too knew that they would never be able to understand me, and for that reason I hardly ever spoke to them about our earth. I merely kissed the earth on which they lived in their presence, and worshipped them without any words. And they saw that and let me worship them without being ashamed that I was worshipping them, for they themselves loved much. They did not suffer for me when, weeping, I sometimes kissed their feet, for in their hearts they were joyfully aware of the strong affection with which they would return my love. At times I asked myself in amazement how they had managed never to offend a person like me and not once arouse in a person like me a feeling of jealousy and envy. Many times I asked myself how I—a braggart and a liar—could refrain from telling them all I knew of science and philosophy, of which of course they had no idea? How it had never occurred to me to impress them with my store of learning, or impart my learning to them out of the love I bore them?

They were playful and high-spirited like children. They wandered about their beautiful woods and groves, they sang their beautiful songs, they lived on simple food—the fruits of their trees, the honey from their woods, and the milk of the animals that loved them. To obtain their food and clothes, they did not work very hard or long. They knew love and they begot children, but I never noticed in them those outbursts of *cruel* sensuality which overtake almost everybody on our earth, whether man or woman, and are the only source of almost every sin of our human race. They rejoiced in their newborn children as new sharers in their bliss. There were no quarrels or jealousy among them, and they did not even know what the words meant. Their children were the children of them all, for they were all one family. There was scarcely any illness among them, though there was death; but their old people died peacefully, as though falling asleep, surrounded by the people who took leave of them, blessing them and smiling at them, and themselves receiving with bright smiles the farewell wishes of their friends. I never saw grief or tears on those occasions. What I did see was love that seemed to reach the point of rapture, but it was a gentle, self-sufficient, and contemplative rapture. There was reason to believe that they communicated with the departed after death, and that their earthly union was not cut short by death. They found it almost impossible to understand me when I questioned them about life eternal, but apparently they were so convinced of it in their minds that for them it was no question at all. They had no places of worship, but they had a certain awareness of a constant, uninterrupted, and living union with the Universe at large. They had no specific religions, but instead they had a certain knowledge that when their earthly joy had reached the limits imposed upon it by nature, they—both the living and the dead—would reach a state of still closer communion with the Universe at large. They looked forward to that moment with joy, but without haste and without pining for it, as though already possessing it in the vague stirrings of their hearts, which they communicated to each other.

In the evening, before going to sleep, they were fond of gathering together and singing in melodious and harmonious choirs. In their songs they expressed all the sensations the parting day had given them. They praised it and bade it farewell. They praised nature, the earth, the sea, and the woods. They were also fond of composing songs about one another, and they praised each other like children. Their songs were very simple, but they sprang straight from the heart and they touched the heart. And not only in their songs alone, but they seemed to spend all their lives in perpetual praise of one another. It seemed to be a universal and all-embracing love for each other. Some of their songs were solemn and ecstatic, and I was scarcely able to understand them at all. While understanding the words, I could never entirely fathom their meaning. It remained somehow beyond the grasp of my reason, and yet it sank unconsciously deeper and deeper into my heart. I often told them that I had had a presentiment of it years ago and that all that joy and glory had been perceived by me while I was still on our earth as a nostalgic

yearning, bordering at times on unendurably poignant sorrow;
that I had had a presentiment of them all and of their glory
in the dreams of my heart and in the reveries of my soul; that
often on our earth I could not look at the setting sun without
tears. . . . That there always was a sharp pang of anguish in
my hatred of the men of our earth; why could I not hate them
without loving them too? why could I not forgive them? And
in my love for them, too, there was a sharp pang of anguish:
why could I not love them without hating them? They listened
to me, and I could tell that they did not know what I was
talking about. But I was not sorry to have spoken to them
of it, for I knew that they appreciated how much and how
anxiously I yearned for those I had forsaken. Oh yes, when
they looked at me with their dear eyes full of love, when I
realized that in their presence my heart, too, became as innocent and truthful as theirs, I did not regret my inability to
understand them, either. The sensation of the fullness of life
left me breathless, and I worshipped them in silence.

Oh, everyone laughs in my face now and everyone assures
me that I could not possibly have seen and felt anything so
definite, but was merely conscious of a sensation that arose
in my own feverish heart, and that I invented all those details myself when I woke up. And when I told them that they
were probably right, good Lord, what mirth that admission
of mine caused and how they laughed at me! Why, of course,
I was overpowered by the mere sensation of that dream and
it alone survived in my sorely wounded heart. But none the
less the real shapes and forms of my dream, that is, those I
actually saw at the very time of my dream, were filled with
such harmony and were so enchanting and beautiful, and so
intensely true, that on awakening I was indeed unable to
clothe them in our feeble words so that they were bound as
it were to become blurred in my mind; so is it any wonder
that perhaps unconsciously I was myself afterwards driven to
make up the details which I could not help distorting, particularly in view of my passionate desire to convey some of
them at least as quickly as I could. But that does not mean
that I have no right to believe that it all did happen. As a
matter of fact, it was quite possibly a thousand times better,
brighter, and more joyful than I describe it. What if it was
only a dream? All that couldn't possibly not have been. And
do you know, I think I'll tell you a secret: perhaps it was no
dream at all! For what happened afterwards was so awful, so

horribly true, that it couldn't possibly have been a mere coinage of my brain seen in a dream. Granted that my heart was responsible for my dream, but could my heart alone have been responsible for the awful truth of what happened to me afterwards? Surely my paltry heart and my vacillating and trivial mind could not have risen to such a revelation of truth! Oh, judge for yourselves: I have been concealing it all the time, but now I will tell you the whole truth. The fact is, I—corrupted them all!

v

Yes, yes, it ended in my corrupting them all! How it could have happened I do not know, but I remember it clearly. The dream encompassed thousands of years and left in me only a vague sensation of the whole. I only know that the cause of the Fall was I. Like a horrible trichina, like the germ of the plague infecting whole kingdoms, so did I infect with myself all that happy earth that knew no sin before me. They learnt to lie, and they grew to appreciate the beauty of a lie. Oh, perhaps, it all began *innocently,* with a jest, with a desire to show off, with amorous play, and perhaps indeed only with a germ, but this germ made its way into their hearts and they liked it. The voluptuousness was soon born, voluptuousness begot jealousy, and jealousy—cruelty. . . . Oh, I don't know, I can't remember, but soon, very soon the first blood was shed: they were shocked and horrified, and they began to separate and to shun one another. They formed alliances, but it was one against another. Recriminations began, reproaches. They came to know shame, and they made shame into a virtue. The conception of honor was born, and every alliance raised its own standard. They began torturing animals, and the animals ran away from them into the forests and became their enemies. A struggle began for separation, for isolation, for personality, for mine and thine. They began talking in different languages. They came to know sorrow, and they loved sorrow. They thirsted for suffering, and they said that Truth could only be attained through suffering. It was then that science made its appearance among them. When they became wicked, they began talking of brotherhood and humanity and understood the meaning of those ideas. When they became guilty of crimes, they invented justice, and drew up whole codes of law, and to ensure the carrying out of their laws they erected a guillotine. They only vaguely remembered what they had lost, and they would not believe that they ever were happy and innocent. They even laughed at the possibility of their former happiness and called it a dream. They could not even imagine it in any definite shape or form, but the strange and wonderful thing was that though they had lost faith in their former state of happiness and called it a fairy tale, they longed so much to be happy and innocent once more that, like children, they succumbed to the desire of their hearts, glorified this desire, built temples, and began offering up prayers to their own idea, their own "desire," and at the same time firmly believed that it could not be realized and brought about, though they still worshipped it and adored it with tears. And yet if they could have in one way or another returned to the state of happy innocence they had lost, and if someone had shown it to them again and had asked them whether they desired to go back to it, they would certainly have refused. The answer they gave me was, "What if we are dishonest, cruel, and unjust? We *know* it and we are sorry for it, and we torment ourselves for it, and inflict pain upon ourselves, and punish ourselves more perhaps than the merciful Judge who will judge us and whose name we do not know. But we have science and with its aid we shall again discover truth, though we shall accept it only when we perceive it with our reason. Knowledge is higher than feeling, and the consciousness of life is higher than life. Science will give us wisdom. Wisdom will reveal to us the laws. And the knowledge of the laws of happiness is higher than happiness." That is what they said to me, and having uttered those words, each of them began to love himself better than anyone else, and indeed they could not do otherwise. Every one of them became so jealous of his own personality that he strove with might and main to belittle and humble it in others; and therein he saw the whole purpose of his life. Slavery made its appearance, even voluntary slavery: the weak eagerly submitted themselves to the will of the strong on condition that the strong helped them to oppress those who were weaker than themselves. Saints made their appearance, saints who came to these people with tears and told them of their pride, of their loss of proportion and harmony, of their loss of shame. They were laughed to scorn and stoned to death. Their sacred blood was spilt on the threshold of the temples. But then men arose who began to wonder how they could all be united again, so that everybody should, without ceasing to love himself best of all, not interfere with everybody else and so that all of them should live together in a society which would at least seem to be founded on mutual understanding. Whole wars were fought over this idea. All the combatants at one and the same time firmly believed that science, wisdom, and the instinct of self-preservation would in the end force mankind to unite into a harmonious and intelligent society, and therefore, to hasten matters, the "very wise" did their best to exterminate as rapidly as possible the "not so wise" who did not understand their idea, so as to prevent them from interfering with its triumph. But the instinct of self-preservation began to weaken rapidly. Proud and voluptuous men appeared who frankly demanded all or nothing. In order to obtain everything they did not hesitate to resort to violence, and if it failed—to suicide. Religions were founded to propagate the cult of nonexistence and self-destruction for the sake of the everlasting peace in nothingness. At last these people grew weary of their senseless labors and suffering appeared on their faces, and these people proclaimed that suffering was beauty, for in suffering alone was there thought. They glorified suffering in their songs. I walked among them, wringing my hands and weeping over them, but I loved them perhaps more than before when there was no sign of suffering in their faces and when they were innocent and—oh, so beautiful! I loved the earth they had polluted even more than when it had been a paradise, and only because sorrow had made its appearance on it. Alas, I always loved sorrow and affliction, but only for myself, only for myself; for them I wept now, for I pitied them. I stretched out my hands to them, accusing, cursing, and despising myself. I told them that I alone was responsible for it all—I alone; that it was I who had brought them corruption, contamination, and lies! I implored them to crucify me, and I taught them how to make the cross. I could not kill myself; I had not the courage to do it; but I longed to receive martyrdom at their hands. I thirsted for martyrdom, I yearned for my blood to be shed to the last drop in torment and suffering. But they only laughed at me, and in the end they began looking upon me as a madman. They justified me. They said that they had got what they themselves wanted and that what was now could not have been otherwise. At last they told me that I was becoming dangerous to them and that they would lock me up in a lunatic asylum if I did not hold my peace. Then sorrow entered my soul with such force that my heart was wrung and I felt as though I were dying, and then—well, then I awoke.

It was morning, that is, the sun had not risen yet, but it was about six o'clock. When I came to, I found myself in the same armchair, my candle had burnt out, in the captain's room they were asleep, and silence, so rare in our house, reigned around. The first thing I did was to jump up in great amazement. Nothing like this had ever happened to me before, not even so far as the most trivial details were concerned. Never, for instance, had I fallen asleep like this in my armchair. Then, suddenly, as I was standing and coming to myself, I caught sight of my gun lying there ready and loaded. But I pushed it away from me at once! Oh, how I longed for life, life! I lifted up my hands and called upon eternal Truth—no, not called upon it, but wept. Rapture, infinite and boundless rapture intoxicated me. Yes, life and —preaching! I made up my mind to preach from that very moment and, of course, to go on preaching all my life. I am going to preach, I want to preach. What? Why, truth. For I have beheld truth, I have beheld it with mine own eyes, I have beheld it in all its glory!

And since then I have been preaching. Moreover, I love all who laugh at me more than all the rest. Why that is so, I don't know and I cannot explain, but let it be so. They say that even now I often get muddled and confused and that if I am getting muddled and confused now, what will be later on? It is perfectly true. I do get muddled and confused and it is quite possible that I shall be getting worse later. And, of course, I shall get muddled several times before I find out how to preach, that is, what words to use and what deeds to perform, for that is all very difficult! All this is even now as clear to me as daylight, but, pray, tell me who does not get muddled and confused? And yet all follow the same path, at least all strive to achieve the same thing, from the philosopher to the lowest criminal, only by different roads. It is an old truth, but this is what is new: I cannot even get very much muddled and confused. For I have beheld the Truth. I have beheld it and I know that people can be happy and beautiful without losing their ability to live on earth. I will not and I cannot believe that evil is the normal condition among men. And yet they all laugh at this faith of mine. But how can I help

believing it? I have beheld it—the Truth—it is not as though
I had invented it with my mind: I have beheld it, I have beheld it, and the *living image* of it has filled my soul for ever.
I have beheld it in all its glory and I cannot believe that it
cannot exist among men. So how can I grow muddled and
confused? I shall of course lose my way and I'm afraid that
now and again I may speak with words that are not my own,
but not for long: the living image of what I beheld will always
be with me and it will always correct me and lead me back
on to the right path. Oh, I'm in fine fettle, and I am of good
cheer. I will go on and on for a thousand years, if need be.
Do you know, at first I did not mean to tell you that I corrupted them, but that was a mistake—there you have my first
mistake! But Truth whispered to me that I was *lying,* and so
preserved me and set me on the right path. But I'm afraid I
do not know how to establish a heaven on earth, for I do not
know how to put it into words. After my dream I lost the
knack of putting things into words. At least, onto the most
necessary and most important words. But never mind, I shall
go on and I shall keep on talking, for I have indeed beheld
it with my own eyes, though I cannot describe what I saw.
It is this the scoffers do not understand. "He had a dream,"
they say, "a vision, a hallucination!" Oh dear, is this all they
have to say? Do they really think that is very clever? And
how proud they are! A dream! What is a dream? And what
about our life? Is that not a dream too? I will say more: even
—yes, even if this never comes to pass, even if there never is
a heaven on earth (that, at any rate, I can see very well!),
even then I shall go on preaching. And really how simple it
all is: in one day, *in one hour,* everything could be arranged
at once! The main thing is to love your neighbor as yourself
—that is the main thing, and that is everything, for nothing
else matters. Once you do that, you will discover at once how
everything can be arranged. And yet it is an old truth, a truth
that has been told over and over again, but in spite of that it
finds no place among men! "The consciousness of life is higher
than life, the knowledge of happiness is higher than happiness"—that is what we have to fight against! And I shall, I
shall fight against it! If only we all wanted it, everything
could be arranged immediately.

And—I did find that little girl. . . . And I shall go on! I
shall go on!

✠ ✠
✠

Leo Tolstoy

✠ ✠
✠
✠ ✠

The
Death
of
Ivan Ilyich

☩

I

Inside the great building of the Law Courts, during the
interval in the hearing of the Melvinski case, the members of
the judicial council and the public prosecutor were gathered
together in the private room of Ivan Yegorovich Shebek, and
the conversation turned upon the celebrated Krasovski case.
Fyodor Vassilyevich hotly maintained that the case was not
in the jurisdiction of the court. Yegor Ivanovich stood up
for his own view; but from the first Pyotr Ivanovich, who
had not entered into the discussion, took no interest in it,
but was looking through the newspapers which had just been
brought in.

"Gentlemen!" he said, "Ivan Ilyich is dead!"

"You don't say so!"

"Here, read it," he said to Fyodor Vassilyevich, handing
him the fresh still damp smelling paper.

Within a black margin was printed: "Praskovya Fyodorovna Golovin with heartfelt affliction informs friends and
relatives of the decease of her beloved husband, member of
the Court of Justice, Ivan Ilyich Golovin, who passed away
on the 4th of February. The funeral will take place on Thurs-
day at one o'clock."

Ivan Ilyich was a colleague of the gentlemen present, and
all liked him. It was some weeks now since he had been
taken ill; his illness had been said to be incurable. His post
had been kept open for him, but it had been thought that in
case of his death Alexeyev might receive his appointment, and

either Vinnikov or Shtabel would succeed to Alexeyev's. So that on hearing of Ivan Ilyich's death, the first thought of each of the gentlemen in the room was of the effect this death might have on the transfer or promotion of themselves or their friends.

"Now I am sure of getting Shtabel's place or Vinnikov's," thought Fyodor Vassilyevich. "It was promised me long ago, and the promotion means eight hundred rubles additional income, besides the grants for office expenses."

"Now I shall have to petition for my brother-in-law to be transferred from Kaluga," thought Pyotr Ivanovich. "My wife will be very glad. She won't be able to say now that I've never done anything for her family."

"I thought somehow that he'd never get up from his bed again," Pyotr Ivanovich said aloud. "I'm sorry!"

"But what was it exactly was wrong with him?"

"The doctors could not decide. That's to say, they did decide, but differently. When I saw him last, I thought he would get over it."

"Well, I positively haven't called there ever since the holidays. I've kept meaning to go."

"Had he any property?"

"I think there's something, very small, of his wife's. But something quite trifling."

"Yes, one will have to go and call. They live such a terribly long way off."

"A long way from you, you mean. Everything's a long way from your place."

"There, he can never forgive me for living the other side of the river," said Pyotr Ivanovich, smiling at Shebek. And they began to talk of the great distances between different parts of the town, and went back into the court.

Besides the reflections upon the changes and promotions in the service likely to ensue from this death, the very fact of the death of an intimate acquaintance excited in every one who heard of it, as such a fact always does, a feeling of relief that "it is he that is dead, and not I."

"Only think! he is dead, but here am I all right," each one thought or felt. The more intimate acquaintances, the so-called friends of Ivan Ilyich, could not help thinking too that now they had the exceedingly tiresome social duties to perform of going to the funeral service and paying the widow a visit of condolence.

The most intimately acquainted with their late colleague were Fyodor Vassilyevich and Pyotr Ivanovich.

Pyotr Ivanovich had been a comrade of his at the school of jurisprudence, and considered himself under obligations to Ivan Ilyich.

Telling his wife at dinner of the news of Ivan Ilyich's death and his reflections as to the possibility of getting her brother transferred into their circuit, Pyotr Ivanovich, without lying down for his usual nap, put on his frock coat and drove to Ivan Ilyich's.

At the entrance before Ivan Ilyich's flat stood a carriage and two hired hacks. Downstairs in the entry near the hat-stand there was leaning against the wall a coffin lid with tassels and braiding freshly rubbed up with pipe clay. Two ladies were taking off their cloaks. One of them he knew, the sister of Ivan Ilyich; the other was a lady he did not know. Pyotr Ivanovich's colleague, Shvarts, was coming down; and from the top stair, seeing who it was coming in, he stopped and winked at him, as though to say: "Ivan Ilyich has made a mess of it; it's a very different matter with you and me."

Shvarts's face, with his English whiskers and all his thin figure in his frock coat, had, as it always had, an air of elegant solemnity; and this solemnity, always such a contrast to Shvarts's playful character, had a special piquancy here. So thought Pyotr Ivanovich.

Pyotr Ivanovich let the ladies pass on in front of him, and walked slowly up the stairs after them. Shvarts had not come down, but was waiting at the top. Pyotr Ivanovich knew what for; he wanted obviously to settle with him where their game of "screw" was to be that evening. The ladies went up to the widow's room; while Shvarts, with his lips tightly and gravely shut, and amusement in his eyes, with a twitch of his eyebrows motioned Pyotr Ivanovich to the right, to the room where the dead man was.

Pyotr Ivanovich went in, as people always do on such occasions, in uncertainty as to what he would have to do there. One thing he felt sure of—that crossing oneself never comes amiss on such occasions. As to whether it was necessary to bow down while doing so, he did not feel quite sure, and so chose a middle course. On entering the room he began crossing himself, and made a slight sort of bow. So far as the movements of his hands and head permitted him, he glanced while doing so about the room. Two young men,

one a high school boy, nephews probably, were going out
of the room, crossing themselves. An old lady was standing
motionless; and a lady, with her eyebrows queerly lifted, was
saying something to her in a whisper. A deacon in a frock
coat, resolute and hearty, was reading something aloud with
an expression that precluded all possibility of contradiction.
A young peasant who used to wait at table, Gerasim, walking
with light footsteps in front of Pyotr Ivanovich, was sprin-
kling something on the floor. Seeing this, Pyotr Ivanovich
was at once aware of the faint odor of the decomposing
corpse. On his last visit to Ivan Ilyich Pyotr Ivanovich had
seen this peasant in his room; he was performing the duties
of a sicknurse, and Ivan Ilyich liked him particularly. Pyotr
Ivanovich continued crossing himself and bowing in a direction intermediate between the coffin, the deacon, and the holy
pictures on the table in the corner. Then when this action of
making the sign of the cross with his hand seemed to him to
have been unduly prolonged, he stood still and began to scruti-
nize the dead man.

The dead man lay, as dead men always do lie, in a peculiarly heavy dead way, his stiffened limbs sunk in the cushions of the coffin, and his head bent back for ever on the
pillow, and thrust up, as dead men always do, his yellow
waxen forehead with bald spots on the sunken temples, and
his nose that stood out sharply and, as it were, squeezed on
the upper lip. He was much changed, even thinner since
Pyotr Ivanovich had seen him, but his face—as always with
the dead—was more handsome, and, above all, more impressive than it had been when he was alive. On the face was
an expression what had to be done having been done, and
rightly done. Besides this, there was too in that expression
a reproach or reminder for the living. This reminder seemed
to Pyotr Ivanovich uncalled for, or, at least, to have nothing
to do with him. He felt something unpleasant; and so Pyotr
Ivanovich once more crossed himself hurriedly, and, as it
struck him, too hurriedly, not quite in accordance with the
proprieties, turned and went to the door. Shvarts was waiting
for him in the adjoining room, standing with his legs apart
and both hands behind his back playing with his top hat. A
single glance at the playful, sleek, and elegant figure of Shvarts
revived Pyotr Ivanovich. He felt that he, Shvarts, was above
it, and would not give way to depressing impressions. The
mere sight of him said plainly: the incident of the service over

the body of Ivan Ilyich cannot possibly constitute a sufficient
ground for recognizing the business of the session suspended,
—in other words, in no way can it hinder us from shuffling
and cutting a pack of cards this evening, while the footman
sets four unsanctified candles on the table for us; in fact, there
is no ground for supposing that this incident could prevent us
from spending the evening agreeably. He said as much indeed
to Pyotr Ivanovich as he came out, proposing that the party
should meet at Fyodor Vassilyevich's. But apparently it was
Pyotr Ivanovich's destiny not to play "screw" that evening.
Praskovya Fyodorovna, a short, fat woman who, in spite of all
efforts in a contrary direction, was steadily broader from her
shoulders downwards, all in black, with lace on her head and
her eyebrows as queerly arched as those of the lady standing
beside the coffin, came out of her own apartments with some
other ladies, and conducting them to the dead man's room,
said: "The service will take place immediately; come in."

Shvarts, making an indefinite bow, stood still, obviously
neither accepting or declining this invitation. Praskovya Fyodorovna, recognising Pyotr Ivanovich, sighed, went right up
to him, took his hand, and said, "I know that you were a true
friend of Ivan Ilyich's . . ." and looked at him, expecting
from him the suitable action in response to these words. Pyotr
Ivanovich knew that, just as before he had to cross himself,
now what he had to do was to press her hand, to sigh and to
say, "Ah, I was indeed!" And he did so. And as he did so, he
felt that the desired result had been attained; that he was
touched, and she was touched.

"Come, since it's not begun yet, I have something I want
to say to you," said the widow. "Give me your arm."

Pyotr Ivanovich gave her his arm, and they moved towards
the inner rooms, passing Shvarts, who winked gloomily at
Pyotr Ivanovich.

"So much for our 'screw'! Don't complain if we find another partner. You can make a fifth when you do get away,"
said his humorous glance.

Pyotr Ivanovich sighed still more deeply and despondently,
and Praskovya Fyodorovna pressed his hand gratefully. Going
into her drawing room, which was upholstered with pink
cretonne and lighted by a dismal looking lamp, they sat down
at the table, she on a sofa and Pyotr Ivanovich on a low
ottoman with deranged springs which yielded spasmodically
under his weight. Praskovya Fyodorovna was about to warn

him to sit on another seat, but felt such a recommendation out of keeping with her position, and changed her mind. Sitting down on the ottoman, Pyotr Ivanovich remembered how Ivan Ilyich had arranged this drawing room, and had consulted him about this very pink cretonne with green leaves. Seating herself on the sofa, and pushing by the table (the whole drawing room was crowded with furniture and things), the widow caught the lace of her black fichu in the carving of the table. Pyotr Ivanovich got up to disentangle it for her; and the ottoman, freed from his weight, began bobbing up spasmodically under him. The widow began unhooking her lace herself, and Pyotr Ivanovich again sat down, suppressing the mutinous ottoman springs under him. But the widow could not quite free herself, and Pyotr Ivanovich rose again, and again the ottoman became mutinous and popped up with a positive snap. When this was all over, she took out a clean cambric handkerchief and began weeping. Pyotr Ivanovich had been chilled off by the incident with the lace and the struggle with the ottoman springs, and he sat looking sullen. This awkward position was cut short by the entrance of Sokolov, Ivan Ilyich's butler, who came in to announce that the place in the cemetery fixed on by Praskovya Fyodorovna would cost two hundred rubles. She left off weeping, and with the air of a victim glancing at Pyotr Ivanovich, said in French that it was very terrible for her. Pyotr Ivanovich made a silent gesture signifying his unhesitating conviction that it must indeed be so.

"Please, smoke," she said in a magnanimous, and at the same time, crushed voice, and she began discussing with Sokolov the question of the price of the site for the grave.

Pyotr Ivanovich, lighting a cigarette, listened to her very circumstantial inquiries as to the various prices of sites and her decision as to the one to be selected. Having settled on the site for the grave, she made arrangements also about the choristers. Sokolov went away.

"I see to everything myself," she said to Pyotr Ivanovich, moving on one side the albums that lay on the table; and noticing that the table was in danger from the cigarette ash, she promptly passed an ash tray to Pyotr Ivanovich, and said: "I consider it affectation to pretend that my grief prevents me from looking after practical matters. On the contrary, if anything could—not console me . . . but distract me, it is seeing after everything for him." She took out her handkerchief again, as though preparing to weep again; and suddenly, as though struggling with herself, she shook herself, and began speaking calmly: "But I've business to talk about with you."

Pyotr Ivanovich bowed, carefully keeping in check the springs of the ottoman, which had at once begun quivering under him.

"The last few days his sufferings were awful."

"Did he suffer very much?" asked Pyotr Ivanovich.

"Oh, awfully! For the last moments, hours indeed, he never left off screaming. For three days and nights in succession he screamed incessantly. It was insufferable. I can't understand how I bore it; one could hear it through three closed doors. Ah, what I suffered!"

"And was he really conscious?" asked Pyotr Ivanovich.

"Yes," she whispered, "up to the last minute. He said good-by to us a quarter of an hour before his death, and asked Volodya to be taken away too."

The thought of the sufferings of a man he had known so intimately, at first as a light-hearted boy, a schoolboy, then grown up as a partner at whist, in spite of the unpleasant consciousness of his own and this woman's hypocrisy, suddenly horrified Pyotr Ivanovich. He saw again that forehead, the nose that seemed squeezing the lip, and he felt frightened for himself. "Three days and nights of awful suffering and death. Why, that may at once, any minute, come upon me too," he thought, and he felt for an instant terrified. But immediately, he could not himself have said how, there came to his support the customary reflection that this had happened to Ivan Ilyich and not to him, and that to him this must not and could not happen; that in thinking thus he was giving way to depression, which was not the right thing to do, as was evident from Shvarts's expression of face. And making these reflections, Pyotr Ivanovich felt reassured, and began with interest inquiring details about Ivan Ilyich's end, as though death were a mischance peculiar to Ivan Ilyich, but not at all incidental to himself.

After various observations about the details of the truly awful physical sufferings endured by Ivan Ilyich (these details Pyotr Ivanovich learned only through the effect Ivan Ilyich's agonies had had on the nerves of Praskovya Fyodorovna), the widow apparently thought it time to get to business.

"Ah, Pyotr Ivanovich, how hard it is, how awfully, awfully hard!" and she began to cry again.

Pyotr Ivanovich sighed, and waited for her to blow her

nose. When she had done so, he said, "Indeed it is," and
again she began to talk, and brought out what was evidently
the business she wished to discuss with him; that business
consisted in the inquiry as to how on the occasion of her
husband's death she was to obtain a grant from the government. She made a show of asking Pyotr Ivanovich's advice
about a pension. But he perceived that she knew already
to the minutest details, what he did not know himself indeed,
everything that could be got out of the government on the
ground of this death; but that what she wanted to find out
was, whether there were not any means of obtaining a little
more? Pyotr Ivanovich tried to imagine such means; but after
pondering a little, and out of politeness abusing the government for its stinginess, he said that he believed that it was
impossible to obtain more. Then she sighed and began unmistakably looking about for an excuse for getting rid of her
visitor. He perceived this, put out his cigarette, got up, pressed
her hand, and went out into the passage.

In the dining room, where was the bric-à-brac clock that
Ivan Ilyich had been so delighted at buying, Pyotr Ivanovich
met the priest and several people he knew who had come to
the service for the dead, and saw too Ivan Ilyich's daughter, a
handsome young lady. She was all in black. Her very slender
figure looked even slenderer than usual. She had a gloomy,
determined, almost wrathful expression. She bowed to Pyotr
Ivanovich as though he were to blame in some way. Behind
the daughter, with the same offended air on his face, stood a
rich young man, whom Pyotr Ivanovich knew, too, an examining magistrate, the young lady's *fiancé,* as he had heard. He
bowed dejectedly to him, and would have gone on into the
dead man's room, when from the staircase there appeared the
figure of the son, the high school boy, extraordinarily like Ivan
Ilyich. He was the little Ivan Ilyich over again as Pyotr Ivanovich remembered him at school. His eyes were red with crying,
and had that look often seen in unclean boys of thirteen or
fourteen. The boy, seeing Pyotr Ivanovich, scowled morosely
and bashfully. Pyotr Ivanovich nodded to him and went into
the dead man's room. The service for the dead began—candles,
groans, incense, tears, sobs. Pyotr Ivanovich stood frowning,
staring at his feet in front of him. He did not once glance
at the dead man, and right through to the end did not once
give way to depressing influences, and was one of the first to
walk out. In the hall there was no one. Gerasim, the young

peasant, darted out of the dead man's room, tossed over with his strong hand all the fur cloaks to find Pyotr Ivanovich's, and gave it him.

"Well, Gerasim, my boy?" said Pyotr Ivanovich, so as to say something. "A sad business, isn't it?"

"It's God's will. We shall come to the same," said Gerasim, showing his white, even, peasant teeth in a smile, and, like a man in a rush of extra work, he briskly opened the door, called up the coachman, saw Pyotr Ivanovich into the carriage, and darted back to the steps as though bethinking himself of what he had to do next.

Pyotr Ivanovich had a special pleasure in the fresh air after the smell of incense, of the corpse, and of carbolic acid.

"Where to?" asked the coachman.

"It's not too late. I'll still go round to Fyodor Vassilyevich's."

And Pyotr Ivanovich drove there. And he did, in fact, find them just finishing the first rubber, so that he came just at the right time to take a hand.

II

The previous history of Ivan Ilyich was the simplest, the most ordinary, and the most awful.

Ivan Ilyich died at the age of forty-five, a member of the Judicial Council. He was the son of an official, whose career in Petersburg through various ministries and departments had been such as leads people into that position in which, though it is distinctly obvious that they are unfit to perform any kind of real duty, they yet cannot, owing to their long past service and their official rank, be dismissed; and they therefore receive a specially created fictitious post, and by no means fictitious thousands—from six to ten—on which they go on living till extreme old age. Such was the privy councillor, the superfluous member of various superfluous institutions, Ilya Efimovich Golovin.

He had three sons. Ivan Ilyich was the second son. The eldest son's career was exactly like his father's, only in a different department, and he was by now close to that stage in the service in which the same sinecure would be reached. The third son was the unsuccessful one. He had in various positions always made a mess of things, and was now employed in the railway department. And his father and his

brothers, and still more their wives, did not merely dislike
meeting him, but avoided, except in extreme necessity, recol-
lecting his existence. His sister had married Baron Gref, a
Petersburg official of the same stamp as his father-in-law.
Ivan Ilyich was *le phénix de la famille,* as people said. He
was not so frigid and precise as the eldest son, nor so wild as
the youngest. He was the happy mean between them—a
shrewd, lively, pleasant, and well-bred man. He had been educated with his younger brother at the school of jurisprudence.
The younger brother had not finished the school course, but
was expelled when in the fifth class. Ivan Ilyich completed the
course successfully. At school he was just the same as he was
later on all his life—an intelligent fellow, highly good-humored
and sociable, but strict in doing what he considered to be his
duty. His duty he considered whatever was so considered by
those persons who were set in authority over him. He was not a
toady as a boy, nor later on as a grownup person; but from his
earliest years he was attracted, as a fly to the light, to persons
of good standing in the world, assimilated their manners and
their views of life, and established friendly relations with them.
All the enthusiasms of childhood and youth passed, leaving
no great traces in him; he gave way to sensuality and to vanity,
and latterly when in the higher classes at school to liberalism,
but always keeping within certain limits which were unfail-
ingly marked out for him by his instincts.

At school he had committed actions which had struck him
beforehand as great vileness, and gave him a feeling of loathing for himself at the very time he was committing them.
But later on, perceiving that such actions were committed also
by men of good position, and were not regarded by them
as base, he was able, not to regard them as good, but to forget about them completely, and was never mortified by recollections of them.

Leaving the school of jurisprudence in the tenth class, and
receiving from his father a sum of money for his outfit, Ivan
Ilyich ordered his clothes at Sharmer's, hung on his watch-
chain a medallion inscribed *respice finem,* said good-by to
the prince who was the principal of his school, had a farewell
dinner with his comrades at Donon's, and with all his new
fashionable belongings—travelling trunk, linen, suits of clothes,
shaving and toilet appurtenances, and travelling rug, all ordered and purchased at the very best shops—set off to take the
post of secretary on special commissions for the governor of

a province, a post which had been obtained for him by his father.

In the province Ivan Ilyich without loss of time made himself a position as easy and agreeable as his position had been in the school of jurisprudence. He did his work, made his career, and at the same time led a life of well-bred social gaiety. Occasionally he visited various districts on official duty, behaved with dignity both with his superiors and his inferiors; and with exactitude and an incorruptible honesty of which he could not help feeling proud, performed the duties with which he was intrusted, principally having to do with the dissenters. When engaged in official work he was, in spite of his youth and taste for frivolous amusement, exceedingly reserved, official, and even severe. But in social life he was often amusing and witty, and always good-natured, well-bred, and *bon enfant*, as was said of him by his chief and his chief's wife, with whom he was like one of the family.

In the province there was, too, a connection with one of the ladies who obtruded their charms on the stylish young lawyer. There was a dressmaker, too, and there were drinking bouts with smart officers visiting the neighborhood, and visits to a certan outlying street after supper; there was a rather cringing obsequiousness in his behaviour, too, with his chief, and even his chief's wife. But all this was accompanied with such a tone of the highest breeding, that it could not be called by harsh names; it all came under the rubric of the French saying, *Il faut que la jeunesse se passe*. Everything was done with clean hands, in clean shirts, with French phrases, and, what was of most importance, in the highest society, and consequently with the approval of people of rank.

Such was Ivan Ilyich's career for five years, and then came a change in his official life. New methods of judicial procedure were established; new men were wanted to carry them out. And Ivan Ilyich became such a new man. Ivan Ilyich was offered the post of examining magistrate, and he accepted it in spite of the fact that this post was in another province, and he would have to break off all the ties he had formed and form new ones. Ivan Ilyich's friends met together to see him off, had their photographs taken in a group, presented him with a silver cigarette case, and he set off to his new post.

As an examining magistrate, Ivan Ilyich was as *comme il faut*, as well-bred, as adroit in keeping official duties apart from private life, and as successful in gaining universal respect, as he had been as secretary of private commissions. The duties of his new office were in themselves of far greater interest and attractiveness for Ivan Ilyich. In his former post it had been pleasant to pass in his smart uniform from Sharmer's through the crowd of petitioners and officials waiting timorously and envying him, and to march with his easy swagger straight into the governor's private room, there to sit down with him to tea and cigarettes. But the persons directly subject to his authority were few. The only such persons were the district police superintendents and the dissenters, when he was serving on special commissions. And he liked treating such persons affably, almost like comrades; liked to make them feel that he, able to annihilate them, was behaving in this simple, friendly way with them. But such people were then few in number. Now as an examining magistrate Ivan Ilyich felt that every one—every one without exception—the most dignified, the most self-satisfied people, all were in his hands, and that he had but to write certain words on a sheet of paper with a printed heading, and this dignified self-satisfied person would be brought before him in the capacity of a defendant or a witness; and if he did not care to make him sit down, he would have to stand up before him and answer his questions. Ivan Ilyich never abused this authority of his; on the contrary, he tried to soften the expression of it. But the consciousness of this power and the possibility of softening its effect constituted for him the chief interest and attractiveness of his new position. In the work itself, in the preliminary inquiries, that is, Ivan Ilyich very rapidly acquired the art of setting aside every consideration irrelevant to the official aspect of the case, and of reducing every case, however complex, to that form in which it could in a purely external fashion be put on paper, completely excluding his personal view of the matter, and what was of paramount importance, observing all the necessary formalities. All this work was new. And he was one of the first men who put into practical working the reforms in judicial procedure enacted in 1864.

On settling in a new town in his position as examining magistrate, Ivan Ilyich made new acquaintances, formed new ties, took up a new line, and adopted a rather different attitude. He took up an attitude of somewhat dignified aloofness towards the provincial authorities, while he picked out the best circle among the legal gentlemen and wealthy gentry living in the town, and adopted a tone of slight dissatisfaction with the government, moderate liberalism, and lofty civic virtue. With this, while making no change in the elegance of his getup, Ivan Ilyich in his new office gave up shaving, and left his beard free to grow as it liked. Ivan Ilyich's existence in the new town proved to be very agreeable; the society which took the line of opposition to the governor was friendly and good; his income was larger, and he found a source of increased enjoyment in whist, at which he began to play at this time; and having a faculty for playing cards good-humoredly, and being rapid and exact in his calculations, he was as a rule on the winning side.

After living two years in the new town, Ivan Ilyich met his future wife. Praskovya Fyodorovna Mikhel was the most attractive, clever, and brilliant girl in the set in which Ivan Ilyich moved. Among other amusements and recreations after his labors as a magistrate, Ivan Ilyich started a light, playful flirtation with Praskovya Fyodorovna.

Ivan Ilyich when he was an assistant secretary had danced as a rule; as an examining magistrate he danced only as an exception. He danced now as it were under protest, as though to show "that though I am serving on the new reformed legal code, and am of the fifth class in official rank, still if it comes to a question of dancing, in that line, too, I can do better than others." In this spirit he danced now and then towards the end of the evening with Praskovya Fyodorovna, and it was principally during these dances that he won the heart of Praskovya Fyodorovna. She fell in love with him. Ivan Ilyich had no clearly defined intention of marrying; but when the girl fell in love with him, he put the question to himself: "After all, why not get married?"

The young lady, Praskovya Fyodorovna, was of good family, nice-looking. There was a little bit of property. Ivan Ilyich might have reckoned on a more brilliant match, but this was a good match. Ivan Ilyich had his salary; she, he hoped, would have as much of her own. It was a good family; she was a sweet, pretty, and perfectly *comme il faut* young woman. To say that Ivan Ilyich got married because he fell in love with his wife and found in her sympathy with his views of life, would be as untrue as to say that he got married because the people of his world approved of the match. Ivan Ilyich was influenced by both considerations; he was doing what was agreeable to himself in securing such a wife, and at the same time doing what persons of higher standing looked upon as the correct thing.

And Ivan Ilyich got married.

The process itself of getting married and the early period of married life, with the conjugal caresses, the new furniture, the new crockery, the new house linen, all up to the time of his wife's pregnancy, went off very well; so that Ivan Ilyich had already begun to think that so far from marriage breaking up that kind of frivolous, agreeable, light-hearted life, always decorous and always approved by society, which he regarded as the normal life, it would even increase its agreeableness. But at that point, in the early months of his wife's pregnancy, there came in a new element, unexpected, unpleasant, tiresome and unseemly, which could never have been anticipated, and from which there was no escape.

His wife, without any kind of reason, it seemed to Ivan Ilyich, *de gaité de cœur*, as he expressed it, began to disturb the agreeableness and decorum of their life. She began without any sort of justification to be jealous, exacting in her demands on his attention, squabbled over everything, and treated him to the coarsest and most unpleasant scenes.

At first Ivan Ilyich hoped to escape from the unpleasantness of this position by taking up the same frivolous and well-bred line that had served him well on other occasions of difficulty. He endeavoured to ignore his wife's ill-humor, went on living light-heartedly and agreeably as before, invited friends to play cards, tried to get away himself to the club or to his friends. But his wife began on one occasion with such energy, abusing him in such coarse language, and so obstinately persisted in her abuse of him every time he failed in carrying out her demands, obviously having made up her mind firmly to persist till he gave way, that is, stayed at home and was as dull as she was, that Ivan Ilyich took alarm. He perceived that matrimony, at least with his wife, was not invariably conducive to the pleasures and proprieties of life; but, on the contrary, often destructive of them, and that it was therefore essential to erect some barrier to protect himself from these disturbances. And Ivan Ilyich began to look about for such means of protecting himself. His official duties were the only thing that impressed Praskovya Fyodorovna, and Ivan Ilyich began to use his official position and the duties arising from it in his struggle with his wife to fence off his own independent world apart.

With the birth of the baby, the attempts at nursing it, and

the various unsuccessful experiments with foods, with the illnesses, real and imaginary, of the infant and its mother, in which Ivan Ilyich was expected to sympathize, though he never had the slightest idea about them, the need for him to fence off a world apart for himself outside his family life became still more imperative. As his wife grew more irritable and exacting, so did Ivan Ilyich more and more transfer the center of gravity of his life to his official work. He became fonder and fonder of official life, and more ambitious than he had been.

Very quickly, not more than a year after his wedding, Ivan Ilyich had become aware that conjugal life, though providing certain comforts, was in reality a very intricate and difficult business towards which one must, if one is to do one's duty, that is, lead the decorous life approved by society, work out for oneself a definite line, just as in the government service.

And such a line Ivan Ilyich did work out for himself in his married life. He expected from his home life only those comforts—of dinner at home, of housekeeper and bed which it could give him, and, above all, that perfect propriety in external observances required by public opinion. For the rest, he looked for good-humored pleasantness, and if he found it he was very thankful. If he met with antagonism and querulousness, he promptly retreated into the separate world he had shut off for himself in his official life, and there he found solace.

Ivan Ilyich was prized as a good official, and three years later he was made assistant public prosecutor. The new duties of this position, their dignity, the possibility of bringing any one to trial and putting any one in prison, the publicity of the speeches and the success Ivan Ilyich had in that part of his work,—all this made his official work still more attractive to him.

Children were born to him. His wife became steadily more querulous and ill-tempered, but the line Ivan Ilyich had taken up for himself in home life put him almost out of reach of her grumbling.

After seven years of service in the same town, Ivan Ilyich was transferred to another province with the post of public prosecutor. They moved, money was short, and his wife did not like the place they had moved to. The salary was indeed a little higher than before, but their expenses were larger. Besides, a couple of children died, and home life consequently became even less agreeable for Ivan Ilyich.

For every mischance that occurred in their new place of residence, Praskovya Fyodorovna blamed her husband. The greater number of subjects of conversation between husband and wife, especially the education of the children, led to questions which were associated with previous quarrels, and quarrels were ready to break out at every instant. There remained only those rare periods of being in love which did indeed come upon them, but never lasted long. These were the islands at which they put in for a time, but they soon set off again upon the ocean of concealed hostility, that was made manifest in their aloofness from one another. This aloofness might have distressed Ivan Ilyich if he had believed that this ought not to be so, but by now he regarded this position as perfectly normal, and it was indeed the goal towards which he worked in his home life. His aim was to make himself more and more free from the unpleasant aspects of domestic life and to render them harmless and decorous. And he attained this aim by spending less and less time with his family; and when he was forced to be at home, he endeavoured to secure his tranquillity by the presence of outsiders. The great thing for Ivan Ilyich was having his office. In the official world all the interest of life was concentrated for him. And this interest absorbed him. The sense of his own power, the consciousness of being able to ruin any one he wanted to ruin, even the external dignity of his office, when he made his entry into the court or met subordinate officials, his success in the eyes of his superiors and his subordinates, and, above all, his masterly handling of cases, of which he was conscious,—all this delighted him and, together with chats with his colleagues, dining out, and whist, filled his life. So that, on the whole, Ivan Ilyich's life still went on in the way he thought it should go—agreeably and decorously.

So he lived for another seven years. His eldest daughter was already sixteen, another child had died, and there was left only one other, a boy at the high school, a subject of dissension. Ivan Ilyich wanted to send him to the school of jurisprudence, while Praskovya Fyodorovna to spite him sent him to the high school. The daughter had been educated at home, and had turned out well; the boy too did fairly well at his lessons.

III

Such was Ivan Ilyich's life for seventeen years after his marriage. He had been by now a long while prosecutor, and had refused several appointments offered him, looking out for a more desirable post, when there occurred an unexpected incident which utterly destroyed his peace of mind. Ivan Ilyich had been expecting to be appointed presiding judge in a university town, but a certain Goppe somehow stole a march on him and secured the appointment. Ivan Ilyich took offence, began upbraiding him, and quarrelled with him and with his own superiors. A coolness was felt towards him, and on the next appointment that was made he was again passed over.

This was in the year 1880. That year was the most painful one in Ivan Ilyich's life. During that year it became evident on the one hand that his pay was insufficient for his expenses; on the other hand, that he had been forgotten by every one, and that what seemed to him the most monstrous, the cruelest injustice, appeared to other people as a quite commonplace fact. Even his father felt no obligation to assist him. He felt that every one had deserted him, and that every one regarded his position with an income of three thousand five hundred rubles as a quite normal and even fortunate one. He alone, with a sense of the injustice done him, and the everlasting nagging of his wife and the debts he had begun to accumulate, living beyond his means, knew that his position was far from being normal.

The summer of that year, to cut down his expenses, he took a holiday and went with his wife to spend the summer in the country at her brother's.

In the country, with no official duties to occupy him, Ivan Ilyich was for the first time a prey not to simple boredom, but to intolerable depression; and he made up his mind that things could not go on like that, and that it was absolutely necessary to take some decisive steps.

After a sleepless night spent by Ivan Ilyich walking up and down the terrace, he determined to go to Petersburg to take active steps and to get transferred to some other department, so as to revenge himself on *them,* the people, that is, who had not known how to appreciate him.

Next day, in spite of all the efforts of his wife and his mother-in-law to dissuade him, he set off to Petersburg.

He went with a single object before him—to obtain a post with an income of five thousand. He was ready now to be satisfied with a post in any department, of any tendency, with any kind of work. He must only have a post—a post with five thousand, in the executive department, the banks, the railways, the Empress Marya's institutions, even in the customs duties— what was essential was five thousand, and essential it was, too, to get out of the department in which they had failed to appreciate his value.

And, behold, this quest of Ivan Ilyich's was crowned with wonderful, unexpected success. At Kursk there got into the same first-class carriage F. S. Ilyin, an acquaintance, who told him of a telegram just received by the governor of Kursk, announcing a change about to take place in the ministry—Pyotr Ivanovich was to be superseded by Ivan Semyonovich.

The proposed change, apart from its significance for Russia, had special significance for Ivan Ilyich from the fact that by bringing to the front a new person, Pyotr Petrovich, and obviously, therefore, his friend Zakhar Ivanovich, it was in the highest degree propitious to Ivan Ilyich's own plans. Zakhar Ivanovich was a friend and schoolfellow of Ivan Ilyich's.

At Moscow the news was confirmed. On arriving at Petersburg, Ivan Ilyich looked up Zakhar Ivanovich, and received a positive promise of an appointment in his former department— that of justice.

A week later he telegraphed to his wife: *"Zakhar Miller's place. At first report I receive appointment."*

Thanks to these changes, Ivan Ilyich unexpectedly obtained, in the same department as before, an appointment which placed him two stages higher than his former colleagues, and gave him an income of five thousand, together with the official allowance of three thousand five hundred for travelling expenses. All his ill-humor with his former enemies and the whole department was forgotten, and Ivan Ilyich was completely happy.

Ivan Ilyich went back to the country more light-hearted and good-tempered than he had been for a very long while. Praskovya Fyodorovna was in better spirits, too, and peace was patched up between them. Ivan Ilyich described what respect every one had shown him in Petersburg; how all those who had been his enemies had been put to shame, and were cringing now before him; how envious they were of his appointment, and still more of the high favor in which he stood at Petersburg.

Praskovya Fyodorovna listened to this, and pretended to believe it, and did not contradict him in anything, but confined herself to making plans for her new arrangements in the town to which they would be moving. And Ivan Ilyich saw with delight that these plans were his plans; that they were agreed; and that his life after this disturbing hitch in its progress was about to regain its true, normal character of light-hearted agreeableness and propriety.

Ivan Ilyich had come back to the country for a short stay only. He had to enter upon the duties of his new office on the 10th of September; and besides, he needed some time to settle in a new place, to move all his belongings from the other province, to purchase and order many things in addition; in short, to arrange things as settled in his own mind, and almost exactly as settled in the heart too of Praskovya Fyodorovna.

And now when everything was so successfully arranged, and when he and his wife were agreed in their aim, and were, besides, so little together, they got on with one another as they had not got on together since the early years of their married life. Ivan Ilyich had thought of taking his family away with him at once; but his sister and his brother-in-law, who had suddenly become extremely cordial and intimate with him and his family, were so pressing in urging them to stay that he set off alone.

Ivan Ilyich started off; and the light-hearted temper produced by his success, and his good understanding with his wife, one thing backing up another, did not desert him all the time. He found a charming set of apartments, the very thing both husband and wife had dreamed of. Spacious, lofty reception rooms in the old style, a comfortable, dignified looking study for him, rooms for his wife and daughter, a schoolroom for his son, everything as though planned on purpose for them. Ivan Ilyich himself looked after the furnishing of them, chose the wallpapers, bought furniture, by preference antique furniture, which had a peculiar *comme-il-faut* style to his mind, and it all grew up and grew up, and really attained the ideal he had set before himself. When he had half finished arranging the house, his arrangement surpassed his own expectations. He saw the *comme-il-faut* character, elegant and free from vulgarity, that the whole would have when it was all ready. As he fell asleep he pictured to himself the reception room as it would be. Looking at the drawing room, not yet finished, he could see the hearth, the screen, the *étagère,* and the little chairs dotted here and there, the plates and dishes on the wall, and the bronzes as they would be when they were all put in their places. He was delighted with the thought of how he would impress Praskovya and Lizanka, who had taste too in this line. They would never expect anything like it. He was particularly successful in coming across and buying cheap old pieces of furniture, which gave a peculiarly aristocratic air to the whole. In his letters he purposely disparaged everything so as to surprise them. All this so absorbed him that the duties of his new office, though he was so fond of his official work, interested him less than he had expected. During sittings of the court he had moments of inattention; he pondered the question which sort of cornices to have on the window blinds, straight or fluted. He was so interested in this business that he often set to work with his own hands, moved a piece of furniture, or hung up curtains himself. One day he went up a ladder to show a workman, who did not understand, how he wanted some hangings draped, made a false step and slipped; but, like a strong and nimble person, he clung on, and only knocked his side against the corner of a frame. The bruised place ached, but it soon passed off. Ivan Ilyich felt all this time particularly good-humored and well. He wrote: "I feel fifteen years younger." He thought his house furnishing would be finished in September, but it dragged on to the middle of October. But then the effect was charming; not he only said so, but every one who saw it told him so too.

In reality, it was all just what is commonly seen in the houses of people who are not exactly wealthy but want to look like wealthy people, and so succeed only in being like one another—hangings, dark wood, flowers, rugs and bronzes, everything dark and highly polished, everything that all people of a certain class have so as to be like all people of a certain class. And in his case it was all so like that it made no impression at all; but it all seemed to him somehow special. When he met his family at the railway station and brought them to his newly furnished rooms, all lighted up in readiness, and a footman in a white tie opened the door into an entry decorated with flowers, and then they walked into the drawing room and the study, uttering cries of delight, he was very happy, conducted them everywhere, eagerly drinking in their praises, and beaming with satisfaction. The same evening, while they talked about various things at tea, Praskovya Fyodorovna inquired about his fall, and he laughed and showed them how he had gone flying, and how he had frightened the upholsterer.

"It's as well I'm something of an athlete. Another man might have been killed, and I got nothing worse than a blow here; when it's touched it hurts, but it's going off already; nothing but a bruise."

And they began to live in their new abode, which, as is always the case, when they had got thoroughly settled in they found to be short of just one room, and with their new income, which, as always, was only a little—some five hundred rubles —too little, and everything went very well. Things went particularly well at first, before everything was quite finally arranged, and there was still something to do to the place—something to buy, something to order, something to move, something to make to fit. Though there were indeed several disputes between husband and wife, both were so well satisfied, and there was so much to do, that it all went off without serious quarrels. When there was nothing left to arrange, it became a little dull, and something seemed to be lacking, but by then they were making acquaintances and forming habits, and life was filled up again.

Ivan Ilyich, after spending the morning in the court, returned home to dinner, and at first he was generally in a good humor, although this was apt to be upset a little, and precisely on account of the new abode. Every spot on the tablecloth, on the hangings, the string of a window blind broken, irritated him. He had devoted so much trouble to the arrangement of the rooms that any disturbance of their order distressed him. But, on the whole, the life of Ivan Ilyich ran its course as, according to his conviction, life ought to do—easily, agreeably, and decorously. He got up at nine, drank his coffee, read the newspaper, then put on his official uniform and went to the court. There the routine of the daily work was ready mapped out for him, and he stepped into it at once. People with petitions, inquiries in the office, the office itself, the sittings—public and preliminary. In all this the great thing necessary was to exclude everything with the sap of life in it, which always disturbs the regular course of official business, not to admit any sort of relations with people except the official relations; the motive of all intercourse had to be simply the official motive, and the intercourse itself to be only official. A man would come, for instance, anxious for certain information.

Ivan Ilyich, not being the functionary on duty, would have nothing whatever to do with such a man. But if this man's relation to him as a member of the court is such as can be formulated on official stamped paper—within the limits of such a relation Ivan Ilyich would do everything, postively everything he could, and in doing so would observe the semblance of human friendly relations, that is, the courtesies of social life. But where the official relation ended, there everything else stopped too. This art of keeping the official aspect of things apart from his real life, Ivan Ilyich possessed in the highest degree; and through long practice and natural aptitude, he had brought it to such a pitch of perfection that he even permitted himself at times, like a skilled specialist as it were in jest, to let the human and official relations mingle. He allowed himself this liberty just because he felt he had the power at any moment if he wished it to take up the purely official line again and to drop the human relation. This thing was not simply easy, agreeable, and decorous; in Ivan Ilyich's hands it attained a positively artistic character. In the intervals of business he smoked, drank tea, chatted a little about politics, a little about public affairs, a little about cards, but most of all about appointments in the service. And tired, but feeling like some artist who has skilfully played his part in the performance, one of the first violins in the orchestra, he returned home. At home his daughter and her mother had been paying calls somewhere, or else some one had been calling on them; the son had been at school, had been preparing his lessons with his teachers, and duly learning correctly what was taught at the high school. Everything was as it should be. After dinner, if there were no visitors, Ivan Ilyich sometimes read some book of which people were talking, and in the evening sat down to work, that is, read official papers, compared them with the laws, sorted depositions, and put them under the laws. This he found neither tiresome nor entertaining. It was tiresome when he might have been playing "screw"; but if there were no "screw" going on, it was anyway better than sitting alone or with his wife. Ivan Ilyich's pleasures were little dinners, to which he invited ladies and gentlemen of good social position, and such methods of passing the time with them as were usual with such persons, so that his drawing room might be like all other drawing rooms.

Once they even gave a party—a dance. And Ivan Ilyich en-

joyed it, and everything was very successful, except that it led
to a violent quarrel with his wife over the tarts and sweetmeats.
Praskovya Fyodorovna had her own plan; while Ivan Ilyich
insisted on getting everything from an expensive pastry cook,
and ordered a great many tarts, and the quarrel was because
these tarts were left over and the pastry cook's bill came to
forty-five rubles. The quarrel was a violent and unpleasant
one, so much so that Praskovya Fyodorovna called him, "Fool,
imbecile." And he clutched at his head, and in his anger made
some allusion to a divorce. But the party itself was enjoyable.
There were all the best people, and Ivan Ilyich danced with
Princess Trufonov, the sister of the one so well known in connection with the charitable association called, "Bear my Burden." His official pleasures lay in the gratification of his pride;
his social pleasures lay in the gratification of his vanity. But
Ivan Ilyich's most real pleasure was the pleasure of playing
"screw," the Russian equivalent for "poker." He admitted to
himself that, after all, after whatever unpleasant incidents there
had been in his life, the pleasure which burned like a candle
before all others was sitting with good players, and not noisy
partners, at "screw"; and, of course, a four-hand game (playing with five was never a success, though one pretends to like
it particularly), and with good cards, to play a shrewd, serious
game, then supper and a glass of wine. And after "screw," especially after winning some small stakes (winning large sums
was unpleasant), Ivan Ilyich went to bed in a particularly
happy frame of mind.

So they lived. They moved in the very best circle, and were
visited by people of consequence and young people.

In their views of their circle of acquaintances, the husband,
the wife, and the daughter were in complete accord; and without any expressed agreement on the subject, they all acted
alike in dropping and shaking off various friends and relations,
shabby persons who swooped down upon them in their drawing
room with Japanese plates on the walls, and pressed their
civilities on them. Soon these shabby persons ceased fluttering
about them, and none but the very best society was seen at the
Golovins. Young men began to pay attention to Lizanka; and
Petrishchev, the son of Dimitri Ivanovich Petrishchev, and the
sole heir of his fortune, an examining magistrate, began to be
so attentive to Lizanka, that Ivan Ilyich had raised the question
with his wife whether it would not be as well to arrange a

sledge drive for them, or to get up some theatricals. So they lived. And everything went on in this way without change, and everything was very nice.

IV

All were in good health. One could not use the word ill health in connection with the symptoms Ivan Ilyich sometimes complained of, namely, a queer taste in his mouth and a sort of uncomfortable feeling on the left side of the stomach.

But it came to pass that this uncomfortable feeling kept increasing, and became not exactly a pain, but a continual sense of weight in his side and irritable temper. This irritable temper continually growing and growing, began at last to mar the agreeable easiness and decorum that had reigned in the Golovin household. Quarrels between the husband and wife became more and more frequent, and soon all the easiness and amenity of life had fallen away, and mere propriety was maintained with difficulty. Scenes became again more frequent. Again there were only islands in the sea of contention—and but few of these—at which the husband and wife could meet without an outbreak. And Praskovya Fyodorovna said now, not without grounds, that her husband had a trying temper. With her characteristic exaggeration, she said he had always had this awful temper, and she had needed all her sweetness to put up with it for twenty years. It was true that it was he now who began the quarrels. His gusts of temper always broke out just before dinner, and often just as he was beginning to eat, at the soup. He would notice that some piece of the crockery had been chipped, or that the food was not nice, or that his son put his elbow on the table, or his daughter's hair was not arranged as he liked it. And whatever it was, he laid the blame of it on Praskovya Fyodorovna. Praskovya Fyodorovna had at first retorted in the same strain, and said all sorts of horrid things to him; but on two occasions, just at the beginning of dinner, he had flown into such a frenzy that she perceived that it was due to physical derangement, and was brought on by taking food, and she controlled herself; she did not reply, but simply made haste to get dinner over. Praskovya Fyodorovna took great credit to herself for this exercise of self-control. Making up her mind that her husband had a fearful temper, and made her life miserable, she began to feel sorry for herself. And the more she felt for herself, the more she hated her husband. She began to wish he were dead; yet could not wish it, because then there would be no income. And this exasperated her against him even more. She considered herself dreadfully unfortunate, precisely because even his death could not save her, and she felt irritated and concealed it, and this hidden irritation on her side increased his irritability.

After one violent scene, in which Ivan Ilyich had been particularly unjust, and after which he had said in explanation that he certainly was irritable, but that it was due to illness, she said that if he were ill he ought to take steps, and insisted on his going to see a celebrated doctor.

He went. Everything was as he had expected; everything was as it always is. The waiting and the assumption of dignity, that professional dignity he knew so well, exactly as he assumed it himself in court, and the sounding and listening and questions that called for answers that were foregone conclusions and obviously superfluous, and the significant air that seemed to insinuate—you only leave it all to us, and we will arrange everything, for us it is certain and incontestable how to arrange everything, everything in one way for every man of every sort. It was all exactly as in his court of justice. Exactly the same air as he put on in dealing with a man brought up for judgment, the doctor put on for him.

The doctor said: This and that proves that you have such-and-such a thing wrong inside you; but if that is not confirmed by analysis of this and that, then we must assume this and that. If we assume this and that, then—and so on. To Ivan Ilyich there was only one question of consequence, Was his condition dangerous or not? But the doctor ignored that irrelevant inquiry. From the doctor's point of view this was a side issue, not the subject under consideration; the only real question was the balance of probabilities between a loose kidney, chronic catarrh, and appendicitis. It was not a question of the life of Ivan Ilyich, but the question between the loose kidney and the intestinal appendix. And this question, as it seemed to Ivan Ilyich, the doctor solved in a brilliant manner in favor of the appendix, with the reservation that analysis of the water might give a fresh clue, and that then the aspect of the case would be altered. All this was point for point identical with what Ivan Ilyich had himself done in brilliant fashion a thousand times over in dealing with some man on his trial. Just as brilliantly the doctor made his summing up, and triumphantly, gaily even, glanced over his spectacles at the prisoner in the dock. From the doctor's summing up Ivan Ilyich deduced the conclusion—that things looked bad, and that he, the doctor, and most likely every one else, did not care, but that things looked bad for him. And this conclusion impressed Ivan Ilyich morbidly, arousing in him a great feeling of pity for himself, of great anger against this doctor who could be unconcerned about a matter of such importance.

But he said nothing of that. He got up, and, laying the fee on the table, he said, with a sigh, "We sick people probably often ask inconvenient questions. Tell me, is this generally a dangerous illness or not?"

The doctor glanced severely at him with one eye through his spectacles, as though to say: "Prisoner at the bar, if you will not keep within the limits of the questions allowed you, I shall be compelled to take measures for your removal from the precincts of the court." "I have told you what I thought necessary and suitable already," said the doctor; "the analysis will show anything further." And the doctor bowed him out.

Ivan Ilyich went out slowly and dejectedly, got into his sledge, and drove home. All the way home he was incessantly going over all the doctor had said, trying to translate all these complicated, obscure, scientific phrases into simple language, and to read in them an answer to the question, Is it bad—is it very bad, or nothing much as yet? And it seemed to him that the upshot of all the doctor had said was that it was very bad. Everything seemed dismal to Ivan Ilyich in the streets. The sledge drivers were dismal, the houses were dismal, the people passing, and the shops were dismal. This ache, this dull gnawing ache, that never ceased for a second, seemed, when connected with the doctor's obscure utterances, to have gained a new, more serious significance. With a new sense of misery Ivan Ilyich kept watch on it now.

He reached home and began to tell his wife about it. His wife listened; but in the middle of his account his daughter came in with her hat on, ready to go out with her mother. Reluctantly she half sat down to listen to these tedious details, but she could not stand it for long, and her mother did not hear his story to the end.

"Well, I'm very glad," said his wife; "now you must be sure and take the medicine regularly. Give me the prescription; I'll send Gerasim to the chemist's!" And she went to get ready to go out.

He had not taken breath while she was in the room, and he heaved a deep sigh when she was gone.

"Well," he said, "may be it really is nothing as yet."

He began to take the medicine, to carry out the doctor's directions, which were changed after the analysis of the water. But it was just at this point that some confusion arose, either in the analysis or in what ought to have followed from it. The doctor himself, of course, could not be blamed for it, but it turned out that things had not gone as the doctor had told him. Either he had forgotten or told a lie, or was hiding something from him.

But Ivan Ilyich still went on just as exactly carrying out the doctor's direction, and in doing so he found comfort at first.

From the time of his visit to the doctor Ivan Ilyich's principal occupation became the exact observance of the doctor's prescriptions as regards hygiene and medicine and the careful observation of his ailment in all the functions of his organism. Ivan Ilyich's principal interest came to be people's ailments and people's health. When anything was said in his presence about sick people, about deaths and recoveries, especially in the case of an illness resembling his own, he listened, trying to conceal his excitement, asked questions, and applied what he heard to his own trouble.

The ache did not grow less; but Ivan Ilyich made great efforts to force himself to believe that he was better. And he succeeded in deceiving himself so long as nothing happened to disturb him. But as soon as he had a mischance, some unpleasant words with his wife, a failure in his official work, an unlucky hand at "screw," he was at once acutely sensible of his illness. In former days he had borne with such mishaps, hoping soon to retrieve the mistake, to make a struggle, to reach success later, to have a lucky hand. But now he was cast down by every mischance and reduced to despair. He would say to himself: "Here I'm only just beginning to get better, and the medicine has begun to take effect, and now this mischance or disappointment." And he was furious against the mischance or the people who were causing him the disappointment and killing him, and he felt that this fury was killing him, but could not check it. One would have thought that it should have been clear to him that this exasperation against circumstances and people was aggravating his disease, and that therefore he ought not to pay attention to the unpleasant incidents. But his reasoning took quite the opposite direction. He said that he needed peace, and was on the watch for everything that disturbed his peace, and at the slightest disturbance of it he flew into a rage. What made his position worse was that he read medical books and consulted doctors. He got worse so gradually that he might have deceived himself, comparing one day with another, the difference was so slight. But when he consulted the doctors, then it seemed to him that he was getting worse, and very rapidly so indeed. And in spite of this, he was continually consulting the doctors.

That month he called on another celebrated doctor. The second celebrity said almost the same as the first, but put his questions differently; and the interview with this celebrity only redoubled the doubts and terrors of Ivan Ilyich. A friend of a friend of his, a very good doctor, diagnosed the disease quite differently; and in spite of the fact that he guaranteed recovery, by his questions and his suppositions he confused Ivan Ilyich even more and strengthened his suspicions. A homeopath gave yet another diagnosis of the complaint, and prescribed medicine, which Ivan Ilyich took secretly for a week; but after a week of the homeopathic medicine he felt no relief, and losing faith both in the other doctor's treatment and in this, he fell into even deeper depression. One day a lady of his acquaintance talked to him of the healing wrought by the holy pictures. Ivan Ilyich caught himself listening attentively and believing in the reality of the facts alleged. This incident alarmed him. "Can I have degenerated to such a point of intellectual feebleness?" he said to himself. "Nonsense! it's all rubbish. I must not give way to nervous fears, but fixing on one doctor, adhere strictly to his treatment. That's what I will do. Now it's settled. I won't think about it, but till next summer I will stick to the treatment, and then I shall see. Now I'll put a stop to this wavering!" It was easy to say this, but impossible to carry it out. The pain in his side was always dragging at him, seeming to grow more acute and ever more incessant; it seemed to him that the taste in his mouth was queerer, and there was a loathsome smell even from his breath, and his appetite and strength kept dwindling. There was no deceiving himself; something terrible, new, and so important that nothing more important had ever been in Ivan Ilyich's life, was taking place in him, and he alone knew of it. All about him did not or would not understand, and believed that everything in the world was going on as before. This was what tortured Ivan Ilyich more than anything. Those of his own household, most of all his wife and daughter, who were absorbed in a perfect whirl of visits, did not, he saw, comprehend it at all, and were annoyed that he was so depressed and exacting, as though he were to blame for it. Though they tried indeed to disguise it, he saw he was a nuisance to them; but that his wife had taken up a definite line of her own in regard to his illness, and stuck to it regardless of what he might say and do. This line was expressed thus: "You know," she would say to acquaintances, "Ivan Ilyich cannot, like all other simple-hearted folks, keep to the treatment prescribed him. One day he'll take his drops and eat what he's ordered, and go to bed in good time; the next day, if I don't see to it, he'll suddenly forget to take his medicine, eat sturgeon (which is forbidden by the doctors), yes, and sit up at 'screw' till past midnight."

"Why, when did I do that?" Ivan Ilyich asked in vexation one day at Pyotr Ivanovich's.

"Why, yesterday, with Shebek."

"It makes no difference. I couldn't sleep for pain."

"Well, it doesn't matter what you do it for, only you'll never get well like that, and you make us wretched."

Praskovya Fyodorovna's external attitude to her husband's illness, openly expressed to others and to himself, was that Ivan Ilyich was to blame in the matter of his illness, and that the whole illness was another injury he was doing to his wife. Ivan Ilyich felt that the expression of this dropped from her unconsciously, but that made it no easier for him.

In his official life, too, Ivan Ilyich noticed, or fancied he noticed, a strange attitude to him. At one time it seemed to him that people were looking inquisitively at him, as a man who would shortly have to vacate his position; at another time his friends would suddenly begin chaffing him in a friendly way over his nervous fears, as though that awful and horrible, unheard-of thing that was going on within him, incessantly gnawing at him, and irresistibly dragging him away somewhere, were the most agreeable subject for joking. Shvarts especially, with his jocoseness, his liveliness, and his *comme-il-faut* tone, exasperated Ivan Ilyich by reminding him of himself ten years ago.

Friends came sometimes to play cards. They sat down to the card table; they shuffled and dealt the new cards. Diamonds were led and followed by diamonds, the seven. His partner said, "Can't trump," and played the two of diamonds. What then? Why, delightful, capital, it should have been—he had a trump hand. And suddenly Ivan Ilyich feels that gnawing ache, that taste in his mouth, and it strikes him as something grotesque that with that he could be glad of a trump hand.

He looks at Mikhail Mikhaylovich, his partner, how he taps on the table with his red hand, and affably and indulgently abstains from snatching up the trick, and pushes the cards towards Ivan Ilyich so as to give him the pleasure of taking them up, without any trouble, without even stretching out his hand. "What, does he suppose that I'm so weak that I can't stretch out my hand?" thinks Ivan Ilyich, and he forgets the trumps, and trumps his partner's cards, and plays his trump hand without making three tricks; and what's the most awful thing of all is that he sees how upset Mikhail Mikhaylovich is about it, while he doesn't care a bit, and it's awful for him to think why he doesn't care.

They all see that he's in pain, and say to him, "We can stop if you're tired. You go and lie down." Lie down? No, he's not in the least tired; they will play the rubber. All are gloomy and silent. Ivan Ilyich feels that it is he who has brought this gloom upon them, and he cannot disperse it. They have supper, and the party breaks up, and Ivan Ilyich is left alone with the consciousness that his life is poisoned for him and poisons the life of others, and that this poison is not losing its force, but is continually penetrating more and more deeply into his whole existence.

And with the consciousness of this, and with the physical pain in addition, and the terror in addition to that, he must lie in his bed, often not able to sleep for pain the greater part of the night; and in the morning he must get up again, dress, go to the law court, speak, write, or, if he does not go out, stay at home for all the four-and-twenty hours of the day and night, of which each one is a torture. And he had to live thus on the edge of the precipice alone, without one man who would understand and feel for him.

v

In this way one month, then a second, passed by. Just before the New Year his brother-in-law arrived in the town on a visit to them. Ivan Ilyich was at the court when he arrived. Praskovya Fyodorovna had gone out shopping. Coming home and going into his study, he found there his brother-in-law, a healthy, florid man, engaged in unpacking his trunk. He raised his head, hearing Ivan Ilyich's step, and for a second stared at him without a word. That stare told Ivan Ilyich everything. His brother-in-law opened his mouth to utter an "Oh!" of surprise, but checked himself. That confirmed it all.

"What! have I changed?"

"Yes, there is a change."

And all Ivan Ilyich's efforts to draw him into talking of his appearance his brother-in-law met with obstinate silence. Praskovya Fyodorovna came in; the brother-in-law went to see her. Ivan Ilyich locked his door and began gazing at himself in the looking glass, first full face, then in profile. He took up his photograph, taken with his wife, and compared the portrait with what he saw in the looking glass. The change was immense. Then he bared his arm to the elbow, looked at it, pulled the sleeve down again, sat down on an ottoman and felt blacker than night.

"I mustn't, I mustn't," he said to himself, jumped up, went to the table, opened some official paper, tried to read it, but could not. He opened the door, went into the drawing room. The door into the drawing room was closed. He went up to it on tiptoe and listened.

"No, you're exaggerating," Praskovya Fyodorovna was saying.

"Exaggerating? You can't see it. Why, he's a dead man. Look at his eyes—there's no light in them. But what's wrong with him?"

"No one can tell. Nikolayev" (that was another doctor) "said something, but I don't know. Leshchetiski" (this was the celebrated doctor) "said the opposite."

Ivan Ilyich walked away, went to his own room, lay down, and fell to musing. "A kidney—a loose kidney." He remembered all the doctors had told him, how it had been detached, and how it was loose; and by an effort of imagination he tried to catch that kidney and to stop it, to strengthen it. So little was needed, he fancied. "No, I'll go again to Pyotr Ivanovich" (this was the friend who had a friend, a doctor). He rang, ordered the horse to be put in, and got ready to go out.

"Where are you off to, *Jean?*" asked his wife with a peculiarly melancholy and exceptionally kind expression.

This exceptionally kind expression exasperated him. He looked darkly at her.

"I want to see Pyotr Ivanovich."

He went to the friend who had a friend a doctor. And with him to the doctor's. He found him in, and had a long conversation with him.

Reviewing the anatomical and physiological details of what, according to the doctor's view, was taking place within him, he understood it all. It was just one thing—a little thing wrong with the intestinal appendix. It might all come right. Only strengthen one sluggish organ, and decrease the undue activity of another, and absorption would take place, and all would be set right. He was a little late for dinner. He ate his dinner, talked cheerfully, but it was a long while before he could go to his own room to work. At last he went to his study, and at once sat down to work. He read his legal documents and did his work, but the consciousness never left him of having a matter of importance very near to his heart which he had put off, but would look into later. When he had finished his work, he remembered that the matter near his heart was thinking about the intestinal appendix. But he did not give himself up to it; he went into the drawing room to tea. There were visitors; and there was talking, playing on the piano, and singing; there was the young examining magistrate, the desirable match for the daughter. Ivan Ilyich spent the evening, as Praskovya Fyodorovna observed, in better spirits than any of them; but he never forgot for an instant that he had the important matter of the intestinal appendix put off for consideration later. At eleven o'clock he said good night and went to his own room. He had slept alone since his illness in a little room adjoining his study. He went in, undressed, and took up a novel of Zola, but did not read it; he fell to thinking. And in his imagination the desired recovery of the intestinal appendix had taken place. There had been absorption, rejection, reestablishment of the regular action.

"Why, it's all simply that," he said to himself. "One only wants to assist nature." He remembered the medicine, got up, took it, lay down on his back, watching for the medicine to act beneficially and overcome the pain. "It's only to take it regularly and avoid injurious influences; why, already I feel rather better, much better." He began to feel his side; it was not painful to the touch. "Yes, I don't feel it—really, much better already." He put out the candle and lay on his side. "The appendix is getting better, absorption." Suddenly he felt the familiar, old, dull, gnawing ache, persistent, quiet, in earnest. In his mouth the same familiar loathsome taste. His heart sank, and his brain felt dim, misty. "My God, my God!" he said, "again, again, and it will never cease." And suddenly the whole thing rose before him in quite a different aspect. "Intestinal appendix! kidney!" he said to himself. "It's not a question of the appendix, not a question of the kidney, but of life and . . . death. Yes, life has been and now it's going, going away, and I cannot stop it. Yes. Why deceive myself? Isn't it obvious to every one, except me, that I'm dying, and it's only a question of weeks, of days—at once perhaps. There was light, and now there is darkness. I was here, and now I'm going! Where?" A cold chill ran over him, his breath stopped. He heard nothing but the throbbing of his heart.

"I shall be no more, then what will there be? There'll be nothing. Where then shall I be when I'm no more? Can this be dying? No; I don't want to!" He jumped up, tried to light the candle; and fumbling with trembling hands, he dropped the candle and the candlestick on the floor and fell back again on the pillow. "Why trouble? it doesn't matter," he said to himself, staring with open eyes into the darkness. "Death. Yes, death. And they—all of them—don't understand, and don't want to understand, and feel no pity. They are playing. (He caught through the closed doors the faraway cadence of a voice and the accompaniment.) They don't care, but they will die too. Fools! Me sooner and them later; but it will be the same for them. And they are merry. The beasts!" Anger stifled him. And he was agonizingly, insufferably miserable. "It cannot be that all men always have been doomed to this awful horror!" He raised himself.

"There is something wrong in it; I must be calm, I must think it all over from the beginning." And then he began to consider. "Yes, the beginning of my illness. I knocked my side, and I was just the same, that day and the days after; it ached a little, then more, then doctors, then depression, misery, and again doctors; and I've gone on getting closer and closer to the abyss. Strength growing less. Nearer and nearer. And here I am, wasting away, no light in my eyes. I think of how to cure the appendix, but this is death. Can it be death?" Again a horror came over him; gasping for breath, he bent over, began feeling for the matches, and knocked his elbow against the bedside table. It was in his way and hurt him; he felt furious with it, in his anger knocked against it more violently, and upset it. And in despair, breathless, he fell back on his spine waiting for death to come that instant.

The visitors were leaving at that time. Praskovya Fyodorovna was seeing them out. She heard something fall, and
came in.

"What is it?"

"Nothing. I dropped something by accident."

She went out, brought a candle. He was lying, breathing
hard and fast, like a man who has run a mile, and staring
with fixed eyes at her.

"What is it, *Jean?*"

"No—othing, I say. I dropped something."—"Why speak?
She won't understand," he thought.

She certainly did not understand. She picked up the candle,
lighted it for him, and went out hastily. She had to say good-
by to a departing guest. When she came back, he was lying
in the same position on his back, looking upwards.

"How are you—worse?"

"Yes."

She shook her head, sat down.

"Do you know what, *Jean?* I wonder if we hadn't better
send for Leshchetiski to see you here?"

This meant calling in the celebrated doctor, regardless of
expense. He smiled malignantly, and said no. She sat a moment longer, went up to him, and kissed him on the forehead.

He hated her with all the force of his soul when she was
kissing him, and had to make an effort not to push her away.

"Good night. Please God, you'll sleep."

"Yes."

VI

Ivan Ilyich saw that he was dying, and was in continual
despair.

At the bottom of his heart Ivan Ilyich knew that he was
dying; but so far from growing used to this idea, he simply
did not grasp it—he was utterly unable to grasp it.

The example of the syllogism that he had learned in Kise-
veter's logic—Caius is a man, men are mortal, therefore Caius
is mortal—had seemed to him all his life correct only as regards Caius, but not at all as regards himself. In that case it
was a question of Caius, a man, an abstract man, and it was
perfectly true, but he was not Caius, and was not an abstract
man; he had always been a creature quite, quite different
from all others; he had been little Vanya with a mamma and

papa, and Mitya and Volodya, with playthings and a coachman and a nurse; afterwards with Katenka, with all the joys
and griefs and ecstasies of childhood, boyhood, and youth.
What did Caius know of the smell of the leathern ball Vanya
had been so fond of? Had Caius kissed his mother's hand
like that? Caius had not heard the silk rustle of his mother's
skirts. He had not made a riot at school over the pudding. Had
Caius been in love like that? Could Caius preside over the
sittings of the court?

And Caius certainly was mortal, and it was right for him to
die; but for me, little Vanya, Ivan Ilyich, with all my feelings
and ideas—for me it's a different matter. And it cannot be
that I ought to die. That would be too awful.

That was his feeling.

"If I had to die like Caius, I should have known it was so,
some inner voice would have told me so. But there was nothing
of the sort in me. And I and all my friends, we felt that it
was not at all the same as with Caius. And now here it is!"
he said to himself. "It can't be! It can't be, but it is! How is it?
How's one to understand it?" And he could not conceive it,
and tried to drive away this idea as false, incorrect, and morbid, and to supplant it by other, correct, healthy ideas. But
this idea, not as an idea merely, but as it were an actual fact,
came back again and stood confronting him.

And to replace this thought he called up other thoughts, one
after another, in the hope of finding support in them. He tried
to get back into former trains of thought, which in old days
had screened off the thought of death. But, strange to say, all
that had in old days covered up, obliterated the sense of death,
could not now produce the same effect. Latterly, Ivan Ilyich
spent the greater part of his time in these efforts to restore his
old trains of thought which had shut off death. At one time
he would say to himself, "I'll put myself into my official work;
why, I used to live in it." And he would go to the law courts,
banishing every doubt. He would enter into conversation with
his colleagues, and would sit carelessly, as his old habit was,
scanning the crowd below dreamily, and with both his wasted
hands he would lean on the arms of the oak armchair just
as he always did; and bending over to a colleague, pass the
papers to him and whisper to him, then suddenly dropping his
eyes and sitting up straight, he would pronounce the familiar
words that opened the proceedings. But suddenly in the middle,
the pain in his side, utterly regardless of the stage he had

reached in his conduct of the case, began its work. It riveted
Ivan Ilyich's attention. He drove away the thought of it, but
it still did its work, and then *It* came and stood confronting
him and looked at him, and he felt turned to stone, and the
light died away in his eyes, and he began to ask himself again,
"Can it be that *It* is the only truth?" And his colleagues and
his subordinates saw with surprise and distress that he, the
brilliant, subtle judge, was losing the thread of his speech,
was making blunders. He shook himself, tried to regain his
self-control, and got somehow to the end of the sitting, and
went home with the painful sense that his judicial labors could
not as of old hide from him what he wanted to hide; that he
could not by means of his official work escape from *It*. And
the worst of it was that *It* drew him to itself not for him to do
anything in particular, but simply for him to look at *It* straight
in the face, to look at *It* and, doing nothing, suffer unspeak-
ably.

And to save himself from this, Ivan Ilyich sought amusements, other screens, and these screens he found, and for a
little while they did seem to save him; but soon again they
were not so much broken down as let the light through, as
though *It* pierced through everything, and there was nothing
that could shut *It* off.

Sometimes during those days he would go into the drawing
room he had furnished, that drawing room where he had
fallen, for which—how bitterly ludicrous it was for him to
think of it!—for the decoration of which he had sacrificed
his life, for he knew that it was that bruise that had started
his illness. He went in and saw that the polished table had
been scratched by something. He looked for the cause, and
found it in the bronze clasps of the album, which had been
twisted on one side. He took up the album, a costly one, which
he had himself arranged with loving care, and was vexed
at the carelessness of his daughter and her friends. Here a page
was torn, here the photographs had been shifted out of their
places. He carefully put it to rights again and bent the clasp
back.

Then the idea occurred to him to move all this *établissement*
of the albums to another corner where the flowers stood. He
called the footman; or his daughter or his wife came to help
him. They did not agree with him, contradicted him; he
argued, got angry. But all that was very well, since he did not
think of *It*; *It* was not in sight.

But then his wife would say, as he moved something himself, "Do let the servants do it, you'll hurt yourself again," and all at once *It* peeped through the screen; he caught a glimpse of *It*. He caught a glimpse of *It*, but still he hoped *It* would hide itself. Involuntarily though, he kept watch on his side; there it is just the same still, aching still, and now he cannot forget it, and *It* is staring openly at him from behind the flowers. What's the use of it all?

"And it's the fact that here, at that curtain, as if it had been storming a fort, I lost my life. Is it possible? How awful and how silly! It cannot be! It cannot be, and it is."

He went into his own room, lay down, and was again alone with *It*. Face to face with *It*, and nothing to be done with *It*. Nothing but to look at *It* and shiver.

VII

How it came to pass during the third month of Ivan Ilyich's illness, it would be impossible to say, for it happened little by little, imperceptibly, but it had come to pass that his wife and his daughter and his son and their servants and their acquaintances, and the doctors, and, most of all, he himself— all were aware that all interest in him for other people consisted now in the question how soon he would leave his place empty, free the living from the constraint of his presence, and be set free himself from his sufferings.

He slept less and less; they gave him opium, and began to inject morphine. But this did not relieve him. The dull pain he experienced in the half asleep condition at first only relieved him as a change, but then it became as bad, or even more agonizing, than the open pain. He had special things to eat prepared for him according to the doctors' prescriptions; but these dishes became more and more distasteful, more and more revolting to him.

Special arrangements, too, had to be made for his other physical needs, and this was a continual misery to him. Misery from the uncleanliness, the unseemliness, and the stench, from the feeling of another person having to assist in it.

But just from this most unpleasant side of his illness there came comfort to Ivan Ilyich. There always came into his room on these occasions to clear up for him the peasant who waited on table, Gerasim.

Gerasim was a clean, fresh, young peasant, who had grown stout and hearty on the good fare in town. Always cheerful and bright. At first the sight of this lad, always cleanly dressed in the Russian style, engaged in this revolting task, embarrassed Ivan Ilyich.

One day, getting up from the night stool, too weak to replace his clothes, he dropped on to a soft low chair and looked with horror at his bare, powerless thighs, with the muscles so sharply standing out on them.

Then there came in with light, strong steps Gerasim, in his thick boots, diffusing a pleasant smell of tar from his boots, and bringing in the freshness of the winter air. Wearing a clean hempen apron, and a clean cotton shirt, with his sleeves tucked up on his strong, bare young arms, without looking at Ivan Ilyich, obviously trying to check the radiant happiness in his face so as not to hurt the sick man, he went up to the night stool.

"Gerasim," said Ivan Ilyich faintly.

Gerasim started, clearly afraid that he had done something amiss, and with a rapid movement turned towards the sick man his fresh, good-natured, simple young face, just beginning to be downy with the first growth of beard.

"Yes, your honor."

"I'm afraid this is very disagreeable for you. You must excuse me. I can't help it."

"Why, upon my word, sir!" And Gerasim's eyes beamed, and he showed his white young teeth in a smile. "What's a little trouble? It's a case of illness with you, sir."

And with his deft, strong arms he performed his habitual task, and went out, stepping lightly. And five minutes later, treading just as lightly, he came back.

Ivan Ilyich was still sitting in the same way in the armchair.

"Gerasim," he said, when the latter had replaced the night stool all sweet and clean, "please help me; come here." Gerasim went up to him. "Lift me up. It's difficult for me alone, and I've sent Dimitri away."

Gerasim went up to him; as lightly as he stepped he put his strong arms round him, deftly and gently lifted and supported him, with the other hand pulled up his trousers, and would have set him down again. But Ivan Ilyich, asked him to carry him to the sofa. Gerasim, without effort, carefully not squeezing him, led him, almost carrying him, to the sofa, and settled him there.

"Thank you; how neatly and well . . . you do everything."

Gerasim smiled again, and would have gone away. But Ivan Ilyich felt his presence such a comfort that he was reluctant to let him go.

"Oh, move that chair near me, please. No, that one, under my legs. I feel easier when my legs are higher."

Gerasim picked up the chair, and without letting it knock, set it gently down on the ground just at the right place, and lifted Ivan Ilyich's legs on to it. It seemed to Ivan Ilyich that he was easier just at the moment when Gerasim lifted his legs higher.

"I'm better when my legs are higher," said Ivan Ilyich. "Put that cushion under me."

Gerasim did so. Again he lifted his legs to put the cushion under them. Again it seemed to Ivan Ilyich that he was easier at that moment when Gerasim held his legs raised. When he laid them down again, he felt worse.

"Gerasim," he said to him, "are you busy just now?"

"Not at all, sir," said Gerasim, who had learned among the town-bred servants how to speak to gentlefolks.

"What have you left to do?"

"Why, what I have to do? I've done everything, there's only the wood to chop for tomorrow."

"Then hold my legs up like that—can you?"

"To be sure, I can." Gerasim lifted the legs up. And it seemed to Ivan Ilyich that in that position he did not feel the pain at all.

"But how about the wood?"

"Don't you trouble about that, sir. We shall have time enough."

Ivan Ilyich made Gerasim sit and hold his legs, and began to talk to him. And, strange to say, he fancied he felt better while Gerasim had hold of his legs.

From that time forward Ivan Ilyich would sometimes call Gerasim, and get him to hold his legs on his shoulders, and he liked talking with him. Gerasim did this easily, readily, simply, and with a good nature that touched Ivan Ilyich. Health, strength, and heartiness in all other people were offensive to Ivan Ilyich; but the strength and heartiness of Gerasim did not mortify him, but soothed him.

Ivan Ilyich's great misery was due to the deception that for some reason or other every one kept up with him—that he was simply ill, and not dying, and that he need only keep quiet and follow the doctor's orders, and then some great change for the better would be the result. He knew that whatever they might do, there would be no result except more agonizing sufferings and death. And he was made miserable by this lie, made miserable at their refusing to acknowledge what they all knew and he knew, by their persisting in lying over him about his awful position, and in forcing him too to take part in this lie. Lying, lying, this lying carried on over him on the eve of his death, and destined to bring that terrible, solemn act of his death down to the level of all their visits, curtains, sturgeons for dinner . . . was a horrible agony for Ivan Ilyich. And, strange to say, many times when they had been going through the regular performance over him, he had been within a hair's-breadth of screaming at them: "Cease your lying! You know, and I know, that I'm dying; so do, at least, give over lying!" But he had never had the spirit to do this. The terrible, awful act of his dying was, he saw, by all those about him, brought down to the level of a casual, unpleasant, and to some extent indecorous, incident (somewhat as they would behave with a person who should enter a drawing room smelling unpleasant). It was brought down to this level by that very decorum to which he had been enslaved all his life. He saw that no one felt for him, because no one would even grasp his position. Gerasim was the only person who recognized the position, and felt sorry for him. And that was why Ivan Ilyich was only at ease with Gerasim. He felt comforted when Gerasim sometimes supported his legs for whole nights at a stretch, and would not go away to bed, saying, "Don't you worry yourself, Ivan Ilyich, I'll get sleep enough yet," or when suddenly dropping into the familiar peasant forms of speech, he added: "If thou weren't sick, but as 'tis, 'twould be strange if I didn't wait on thee." Gerasim alone did not lie; everything showed clearly that he alone understood what it meant, and saw no necessity to disguise it, and simply felt sorry for his sick, wasting master. He even said this once straight out, when Ivan Ilyich was sending him away.

"We shall all die. So what's a little trouble?" he said, meaning by this to express that he did not complain of the trouble just because he was taking this trouble for a dying man, and he hoped that for him too some one would be willing to take the same trouble when his time came.

Apart from this deception, or in consequence of it, what made the greatest misery for Ivan Ilyich was that no one felt for him as he would have liked them to feel for him. At certain moments, after prolonged suffering, Ivan Ilyich, ashamed as he would have been to own it, longed more than anything for some one to feel sorry for him, as for a sick child. He longed to be petted, kissed, and wept over, as children are petted and comforted. He knew that he was an important member of the law courts, that he had a beard turning grey, and that therefore it was impossible. But still he longed for it. And in his relations with Gerasim there was something approaching to that. And that was why being with Gerasim was a comfort to him. Ivan Ilyich longs to weep, longs to be petted and wept over, and then there comes in a colleague, Shebek; and instead of weeping and being petted, Ivan Ilyich puts on his serious, severe, earnest face, and from mere inertia gives his views on the effect of the last decision in the Court of Appeal, and obstinately insists upon them. This falsity around him and within him did more than anything to poison Ivan Ilyich's last days.

VIII

It was morning. All that made it morning for Ivan Ilyich was that Gerasim had gone away, and Pyotr the footman had come in; he had put out the candles, opened one of the curtains, and begun surreptitiously setting the room to rights. Whether it were morning or evening, Friday or Sunday, it all made no difference; it was always just the same thing. Gnawing, agonizing pain never ceasing for an instant; the hopeless sense of life always ebbing away, but still not yet gone; always swooping down on him that fearful, hated death, which was the only reality, and always the same falsity. What were days, or weeks, or hours of the day to him?

"Will you have tea, sir?"

"He wants things done in their regular order. In the morning the family should have tea," he thought, and only said—

"No."

"Would you care to move on to the sofa?"

"He wants to make the room tidy, and I'm in his way. I'm uncleanness, disorder," he thought, and only said—

"No, leave me alone."

The servant still moved busily about his work. Ivan Ilyich stretched out his hand. Pyotr went up to offer his services.

"What can I get you?"

"My watch."

Pyotr got out the watch, which lay just under his hand, and gave it to him.

"Half-past eight. Are they up?"

"Not yet, sir. Vladimir Ivanovich" (that was his son) "has gone to the high school, and Praskovya Fyodorovna gave orders that she was to be waked if you asked for her. Shall I send word?"

"No, no need. Should I try some tea?" he thought.

"Yes, tea . . . bring it."

Pyotr was on his way out. Ivan Ilyich felt frightened of being left alone. "How keep him? Oh, the medicine. Pyotr, give me my medicine. Oh well, may be, medicine may still be some good." He took the spoon, drank it. "No, it does no good. It's all rubbish, deception," he decided, as soon as he tasted the familiar, mawkish, hopeless taste. "No, I can't believe it now. But the pain, why this pain; if it would only cease for a minute." And he groaned. Pyotr turned round. "No, go on. Bring the tea."

Pyotr went away. Ivan Ilyich, left alone, moaned, not so much from the pain, awful as it was, as from misery. Always the same thing again and again, all these endless days and nights. If it would only be quicker. Quicker to what? Death, darkness. No, no. Anything better than death!

When Pyotr came in with the tea on a tray, Ivan Ilyich stared for some time absent-mindedly at him, not grasping who he was and what he wanted. Pyotr was disconcerted by this stare. And when he showed he was disconcerted, Ivan Ilyich came to himself.

"Oh yes," he said, "tea, good, set it down. Only help me to wash and put on a clean shirt."

And Ivan Ilyich began his washing. He washed his hands slowly, and then his face, cleaned his teeth, combed his hair, and looked in the looking glass. He felt frightened at what he saw, especially at the way his hair clung limply to his pale forehead. When his shirt was being changed, he knew he would be still more terrified if he glanced at his body, and he avoided looking at himself. But at last it was all over. He put on his dressing gown, covered himself with a rug, and sat in the armchair to drink his tea. For one moment he felt refreshed; but as soon as he began to drink the tea, again there was the same taste, the same pain. He forced himself to finish it, and lay down, stretched out his legs. He lay down and dismissed Pyotr.

Always the same. A gleam of hope flashes for a moment, then again the sea of despair roars about him again, and always pain, always pain, always heartache, and always the same thing. Alone it is awfully dreary; he longs to call some one, but he knows beforehand that with others present it will be worse. "Morphine again—only to forget again. I'll tell him, the doctor, that he must think of something else. It can't go on; it can't go on like this."

One hour, two hours pass like this. Then there is a ring at the front door. The doctor, perhaps. Yes, it is the doctor, fresh, hearty, fat, and cheerful, wearing that expression that seems to say, "You there are in a panic about something, but we'll soon set things right for you." The doctor is aware that this expression is hardly fitting here, but he has put it on once and for all, and can't take it off, like a man who has put on a frock coat to pay a round of calls.

In a hearty, reassuring manner the doctor rubs his hands.

"I'm cold. It's a sharp frost. Just let me warm myself," he says with an expression, as though it's only a matter of waiting a little till he's warm, and as soon as he's warm he'll set everything to rights.

"Well, now, how are you?"

Ivan Ilyich feels that the doctor would like to say, "How's the little trouble?" but that he feels that he can't talk like that, and says, "How did you pass the night?"

Ivan Ilyich looks at the doctor with an expression that asks—

"Is it possible you're never ashamed of lying?"

But the doctor does not care to understand this look.

And Ivan Ilyich says—

"It's always just as awful. The pain never leaves me, never ceases. If only there were something!"

"Ah, you're all like that, all sick people say that. Come, now I do believe I'm thawed; even Praskovya Fyodorovna, who's so particular, could find no fault with my temperature. Well, now I can say good morning." And the doctor shakes hands.

And dropping his former levity, the doctor, with a serious face, proceeds to examine the patient, feeling his pulse, to take his temperature, and then the tappings and soundings begin.

Ivan Ilyich knows positively and indubitably that it's all

nonsense and empty deception; but when the doctor, kneeling down, stretches over him, putting his ear first higher, then lower, and goes through various gymnastic evolutions over him with a serious face, Ivan Ilyich is affected by this, as he used sometimes to be affected by the speeches of the lawyers in court, though he was perfectly well aware that they were telling lies all the while and why they were telling lies.

The doctor, kneeling on the sofa, was still sounding him, when there was the rustle of Praskovya Fyodorovna's silk dress in the doorway, and she was heard scolding Pyotr for not having let her know that the doctor had come.

She comes in, kisses her husband, and at once begins to explain that she has been up a long while, and that it was only through a misunderstanding that she was not there when the doctor came.

Ivan Ilyich looks at her, scans her all over, and sets down against her her whiteness and plumpness, and the cleanness of her hands and neck, and the glossiness of her hair, and the gleam full of life in her eyes. With all the force of his soul he hates her. And when she touches him it makes him suffer from the thrill of hatred he feels for her.

Her attitude to him and his illness is still the same. Just as the doctor had taken up a certain line with the patient which he was not now able to drop, so she too had taken up a line with him—that he was not doing something he ought to do, and was himself to blame, and she was lovingly reproaching him for his neglect, and she could not now get out of this attitude.

"Why, you know, he won't listen to me; he doesn't take his medicine at the right times. And what's worse still, he insists on lying in a position that surely must be bad for him —with his legs in the air."

She described how he made Gerasim hold his legs up.

The doctor smiled with kindly condescension that said, "Oh well, it can't be helped, these sick people do take up such foolish fancies; but we must forgive them."

When the examination was over, the doctor looked at his watch, and then Praskovya Fyodorovna informed Ivan Ilyich that it must, of course, be as he liked, but she had sent today for a celebrated doctor, and that he would examine him, and have a consultation with Mikhail Danilovich (that was the name of their regular doctor).

"Don't oppose it now, please. This I'm doing entirely for

my own sake," she said ironically, meaning it to be understood that she was doing it all for his sake, and was only saying this to give him no right to refuse her request. He lay silent, knitting his brows. He felt that he was hemmed in by such a tangle of falsity that it was hard to disentangle anything from it.

Everything she did for him was entirely for her own sake, and she told him she was doing for her own sake what she actually was doing for her own sake as something so incredible that he would take it as meaning the opposite.

At half-past eleven the celebrated doctor came. Again came the sounding, and then grave conversation in his presence and in the other room about the kidney and the appendix, and questions and answers, with such an air of significance, that again, instead of the real question of life and death, which was now the only one that confronted him, the question that came uppermost was of the kidney and the appendix, which were doing something not as they ought to do, and were for that reason being attacked by Mikhail Danilovich and the celebrated doctor, and forced to mend their ways.

The celebrated doctor took leave of him with a serious, but not a hopeless face. And to the timid question that Ivan Ilyich addressed to him while he lifted his eyes, shining with terror and hope, up towards him, Was there a chance of recovery? he answered that he could not answer for it, but that there was a chance. The look of hope with which Ivan Ilyich watched the doctor out was so piteous that, seeing it, Praskovya Fyodorovna positively burst into tears, as she went out of the door to hand the celebrated doctor his fee in the next room.

The gleam of hope kindled by the doctor's assurance did not last long. Again the same room, the same pictures, the curtains, the wallpaper, the medicine-bottles, and ever the same, his aching suffering body. And Ivan Ilyich began to moan; they gave him injections, and he sank into oblivion. When he waked up it was getting dark; they brought him his dinner. He forced himself to eat some broth; and again everything the same, and again the coming night.

After dinner at seven o'clock, Praskovya Fyodorovna came into his room, dressed as though to go to a *soirée*, with her full bosom laced in tight, and traces of powder on her face. She had in the morning mentioned to him that they were going to the theatre. Sarah Bernhardt was visiting the town, and they had a box, which he had insisted on their taking

By now he had forgotten about it, and her smart attire was an offence to him. But he concealed this feeling when he recollected that he had himself insisted on their taking a box and going, because it was an aesthetic pleasure, beneficial and instructive for the children.

Praskovya Fyodorovna came in satisfied with herself, but yet with something of a guilty air. She sat down, asked how he was, as he saw, simply for the sake of asking, and not for the sake of learning anything, knowing indeed that there was nothing to learn, and began telling him how absolutely necessary it was; how she would not have gone for anything, but the box had been taken, and Ellen, their daughter, and Petrishchev (the examining lawyer, the daughter's suitor) were going, and that it was out of the question to let them go alone. But that she would have liked much better to stay with him. If only he would be sure to follow the doctor's prescription while she was away.

"Oh, and Fyodor Dmitryevich" (the suitor) "would like to come in. May he? And Liza?"

"Yes, let them come in."

The daughter came in, in full dress, her fresh young body bare, while his body made him suffer so. But she made a show of it; she was strong, healthy, obviously in love, and impatient of the illness, suffering, and death that hindered her happiness.

Fyodor Dmitryevich came in too in evening dress, his hair curled *à la Capoul*, with his long sinewy neck tightly fenced round by a white collar, with his vast expanse of white chest and strong thighs displayed in narrow black trousers, with one white glove in his hand and a crush opera hat.

Behind him crept in unnoticed the little high school boy in his new uniform, poor fellow, in gloves, and with that awful blue ring under his eyes that Ivan Ilyich knew the meaning of.

He always felt sorry for his son. And pitiable indeed was his scared face of sympathetic suffering. Except Gerasim, Ivan Ilyich fancied that Volodya was the only one that understood and was sorry.

They all sat down; again they asked how he was. A silence followed. Liza asked her mother about the opera glass. An altercation ensued between the mother and daughter as to who had taken it, and where it had been put. It turned into an unpleasant squabble.

Fyodor Dmitryevich asked Ivan Ilyich whether he had seen

Sarah Bernhardt? Ivan Illyich could not at first catch the question that was asked him, but then he said, "No, have you seen her before?"

"Yes, in *Adrienne Lecouvreur*."

Praskovya Fyodorovna observed that she was particularly good in that part. The daughter made some reply. A conversation sprang up about the art and naturalness of her acting, that conversation that is continually repeated and always the same.

In the middle of the conversation Fyodor Dmitryevich glanced at Ivan Ilyich and relapsed into silence. The others looked at him and became mute, too. Ivan Ilyich was staring with glittering eyes straight before him, obviously furious with them. This had to be set right, but it could not anyhow be set right. This silence had somehow to be broken. No one would venture on breaking it, and all began to feel alarmed that the decorous deception was somehow breaking down, and the facts would be exposed to all. Liza was the first to pluck up courage. She broke the silence. She tried to cover up what they were all feeling, but inadvertently she gave it utterance.

"*If we are going,* though, it's time to start," she said, glancing at her watch, a gift from her father; and with a scarcely perceptible meaning smile to the young man, referring to something only known to themselves, she got up with a rustle of her skirts.

They all got up, said good-by, and went away. When they were gone, Ivan Ilyich fancied he was easier; there was no falsity—that had gone away with them, but the pain remained. That continual pain, that continual terror, made nothing harder, nothing easier. It was always worse.

Again came minute after minute, hour after hour, still the same and still no end, and ever more terrible the inevitable end.

"Yes, send Gerasim," he said in answer to Pyotr's question.

IX

Late at night his wife came back. She came in on tiptoe, but he heard her, opened his eyes, and made haste to close them again. She wanted to send away Gerasim and sit up with him herself instead. He opened his eyes and said, "No, go away."

"Are you in great pain?"

"Always the same."

"Take some opium."

He agreed, and drank it. She went away.

Till three o'clock he slept a miserable sleep. It seemed to him that he and his pain were being thrust somewhere into a narrow, deep, black sack, and they kept pushing him further and further in, and still could not thrust him to the bottom. And this operation was awful to him, and was accompanied with agony. And he was afraid, and yet wanted to fall into it, and struggled and yet tried to get into it. And all of a sudden he slipped and fell and woke up. Gerasim, still the same, is sitting at the foot of the bed half dozing peacefully, patient. And he is lying with his wasted legs clad in stockings, raised on Gerasim's shoulders, the same candle burning in the alcove, and the same interminable pain.

"Go away, Gerasim," he whispered.

"It's all right, sir. I'll stay a bit longer."

"No, go away."

He took his legs down, lay sideways on his arm, and he felt very sorry for himself. He only waited till Gerasim had gone away into the next room; he could restrain himself no longer, and cried like a child. He cried at his own helplessness, at his awful loneliness, at the cruelty of people, at the cruelty of God, at the absence of God.

"Why hast Thou done all this? What brought me to this? Why, why torture me so horribly?"

He did not expect an answer, and wept indeed that there was and could be no answer. The pain grew more acute again, but he did not stir, did not call.

He said to himself, "Come, more then; come, strike me! But what for? What have I done to Thee? what for?"

Then he was still, ceased weeping, held his breath, and was all attention; he listened, as it were, not to a voice uttering sounds, but to the voice of his soul, to the current of thoughts that rose up within him.

"What is it you want?" was the first clear idea able to be put into words that he grasped.

"What? Not to suffer, to live," he answered.

And again he was utterly plunged into attention so intense that even the pain did not distract him.

"To live? Live how?" the voice of his soul was asking.

"Why, live as I used to live before—happily and pleasantly."

"As you used to live before—happily and pleasantly?"

queried the voice. And he began going over in his imagination the best moments of his pleasant life. But strange to say, all these best moments of his pleasant life seemed now not at all what they had seemed then. All—except the first memories of childhood—there, in his childhood there had been something really pleasant in which one could have lived if it had come back. But the creature who had this pleasant experience was no more; it was like a memory of some one else.

As soon as he reached the beginning of what had resulted in him as he was now, Ivan Ilyich, all that had seemed joys to him then now melted away before his eyes and were transformed into something trivial, and often disgusting.

And the further he went from childhood, the nearer to the actual present, the more worthless and uncertain were the joys. It began with life at the school of jurisprudence. Then there had still been something genuinely good; then there had been gaiety; then there had been friendship; then there had been hopes. But in the higher classes these good moments were already becoming rarer. Later on, during the first period of his official life, at the governor's, good moments appeared; but it was all mixed, and less and less of it was good. And further on even less was good, and the further he went the less good there was.

His marriage . . . as gratuitous as the disillusion of it and the smell of his wife's breath and the sensuality, the hypocrisy! And that deadly official life, and anxiety about money, and so for one year, and two, and ten, and twenty, and always the same thing. And the further he went, the more deadly it became. "As though I had been going steadily downhill, imagining that I was going uphill. So it was in fact. In public opinion I was going uphill, and steadily as I got up it life was ebbing away from me. . . . And now the work's done, there's only to die.

"But what is this? What for? It cannot be! It cannot be that life has been so senseless, so loathsome? And if it really was so loathsome and senseless, then why die, and die in agony? There's something wrong.

"Can it be I have not lived as one ought?" suddenly came into his head. "But how not so, when I've done everything as it should be done?" he said, and at once dismissed this only solution of all the enigma of life and death as something utterly out of the question.

"What do you want now? To live? Live how? Live as you

live at the courts when the usher booms out: 'The Judge is coming!' . . . The judge is coming, the judge is coming," he repeated to himself. "Here he is, the judge! But I'm not to blame!" he shrieked in fury. "What's it for?" And he left off crying, and turning with his face to the wall, fell to pondering always on the same question, "What for, why all this horror?"

But however much he pondered, he could not find an answer. And whenever the idea struck him, as it often did, that it all came of his never having lived as he ought, he thought of all the correctness of his life and dismissed the strange idea.

X

Another fortnight had passed. Ivan Ilyich could not now get up from the sofa. He did not like lying in bed, and lay on the sofa. And lying almost all the time facing the wall, in loneliness he suffered all the inexplicable agonies, and in loneliness pondered always that inexplicable question, "What is it? Can it be true that it's death?" And an inner voice answered, "Yes, it is true." "Why these agonies?" and a voice answered, "For no reason." Beyond and besides this there was nothing.

From the very beginning of his illness, ever since Ivan Ilyich first went to the doctor's, his life had been split up into two contradictory moods, which were continually alternating—one was despair and the anticipation of an uncomprehended and awful death; the other was hope and an absorbed watching over the actual condition of his body. First there was nothing confronting him but a kidney or intestine which had temporarily declined to perform their duties, then there was nothing but unknown awful death, which there was no escaping.

These two moods had alternated from the very beginning of the illness; but the further the illness progressed, the more doubtful and fantastic became the conception of the kidney, and the more real the sense of approaching death.

He had but to reflect on what he had been three months before and what he was now, to reflect how steadily he had been going downhill, for every possibility of hope to be shattered.

Of late, in the loneliness in which he found himself, lying with his face to the back of the sofa, a loneliness in the middle of a populous town and of his numerous acquaintances and his family, a loneliness than which none more complete could be found anywhere—not at the bottom of the sea, not deep down in the earth;—of late in this fearful loneliness Ivan Ilyich had lived only in imagination in the past. One by one the pictures of his past rose up before him. It always began from what was nearest in time and went back to the most remote, to childhood, and rested there. If Ivan Ilyich thought of the stewed prunes that had been offered him for dinner that day, his mind went back to the damp, wrinkled French plum of his childhood, of its peculiar taste and the flow of saliva when the stone was sucked; and along with this memory of a taste there rose up a whole series of memories of that period—his nurse, his brother, his playthings. "I mustn't . . . it's too painful," Ivan Ilyich said to himself, and he brought himself back to the present. The button on the back of the sofa and the creases in the morocco. "Morocco's dear, and doesn't wear well; there was a quarrel over it. But the morocco was different, and different too the quarrel when we tore father's portfolio and were punished, and mamma bought us the tarts." And again his mind rested on his childhood, and again it was painful, and he tried to drive it away and think of something else.

And again at that point, together with that chain of associations, quite another chain of memories came into his heart, of how his illness had grown up and become more acute. It was the same there, the further back the more life there had been. There had been both more that was good in life and more of life itself. And the two began to melt into one. "Just as the pain goes on getting worse and worse, so has my whole life gone on getting worse and worse," he thought. One light spot was there at the back, at the beginning of life, and then it kept getting blacker and blacker, and going faster and faster. "In inverse ratio to the square of the distance from death," thought Ivan Ilyich. And the image of a stone falling downwards with increasing velocity sank into his soul. Life, a series of increasing sufferings, falls more and more swiftly to the end, the most fearful sufferings. "I am falling." He shuddered, shifted himself, would have resisted, but he knew beforehand that he could not resist; and again, with eyes weary with gazing at it, but unable not to gaze at what was before him, he stared at the back of the sofa and waited, waited expecting that fearful fall and shock and dissolution.

"Resistance is impossible," he said to himself. "But if one could at least comprehend what it's for? Even that's impossible. It could be explained if one were to say that I hadn't lived as I ought. But that can't be alleged," he said to himself, thinking of all the regularity, correctness, and propriety of his life. "That really can't be admitted," he said to himself, his lips smiling ironically as though some one could see his smile and be deceived by it. "No explanation! Agony, death. . . . What for?"

XI

So passed a fortnight. During that fortnight an event occurred that had been desired by Ivan Ilyich and his wife. Petrishchev made a formal proposal. This took place in the evening. Next day Praskovya Fyodorovna went in to her husband, resolving in her mind how to inform him of Fyodor Dmitryevich's proposal, but that night there had been a change for the worse in Ivan Ilyich. Praskovya Fyodorovna found him on the same sofa, but in a different position. He was lying on his face, groaning, and staring straight before him with a fixed gaze.

She began talking of remedies. He turned his stare on her. She did not finish what she had begun saying; such hatred of her in particular was expressed in that stare.

"For Christ's sake, let me die in peace," he said.

She would have gone away, but at that moment the daughter came in and went up to say good morning to him. He looked at his daughter just as at his wife, and to her inquiries how he was, he told her drily that they would soon all be rid of him. Both were silent, sat a little while, and went out.

"How are we to blame?" said Liza to her mother. "As though we had done it! I'm sorry for papa, but why punish us?"

At the usual hour the doctor came. Ivan Ilyich answered, "Yes, no," never taking his exasperated stare from him, and towards the end he said, "Why, you know that you can do nothing, so let me be."

"We can relieve your suffering," said the doctor.

"Even that you can't do; let me be."

The doctor went into the drawing room and told Praskovya Fyodorovna that it was very serious, and that the only re-source left them was opium to relieve his sufferings, which must be terrible. The doctor said his physical sufferings were terrible, and that was true; but even more terrible than his physical sufferings were his mental sufferings, and in that lay his chief misery.

His moral sufferings were due to the fact that during that night, as he looked at the sleepy, good-natured, broad-cheeked face of Gerasim, the thought had suddenly come into his head, "What if in reality all my life, my conscious life, has been not the right thing?" The thought struck him that what he had regarded before as an utter impossibility, that he had spent his life not as he ought, might be the truth. It struck him that those scarcely detected impulses of struggle within him against what was considered good by persons of higher position, scarcely detected impulses which he had dismissed, that they might be the real thing, and everything else might be not the right thing. And his official work, and his ordering of his daily life and of his family, and these social and official interests,—all that might be not the right thing. He tried to defend it all to himself. And suddenly he felt all the weakness of what he was defending. And it was useless to defend it.

"But if it's so," he said to himself, "and I am leaving life with the consciousness that I have lost all that was given me, and there's no correcting it, then what?" He lay on his back and began going over his whole life entirely anew. When he saw the footman in the morning, then his wife, then his daughter, then the doctor, every movement they made, every word they uttered, confirmed for him the terrible truth that had been revealed to him in the night. In them he saw himself, saw all in which he had lived, and saw distinctly that it was all not the right thing; it was a horrible, vast deception that concealed both life and death. This consciousness intensified his physical agonies, multiplied them tenfold. He groaned and tossed from side to side and pulled at the covering over him. It seemed to him that it was stifling him and weighing him down. And for that he hated them.

They gave him a big dose of opium; he sank into unconsciousness; but at dinner time the same thing began again. He drove them all away, and tossed from side to side.

His wife came to him and said, "*Jean*, darling, do this for my sake" (for my sake?). "It can't do harm, and it often does good. Why, it's nothing. And often in health people——"

He opened his eyes wide.

"What? Take the sacrament? What for? No. Besides . . ."

She began to cry.

"Yes, my dear. I'll send for our priest, he's so nice."

"All right, very well," he said.

When the priest came and confessed him he was softened, felt as it were a relief from his doubts, and consequently from his sufferings, and there came a moment of hope. He began once more thinking of the intestinal appendix and the possibility of curing it. He took the sacrament with tears in his eyes.

When they laid him down again after the sacrament for a minute, he felt comfortable, and again the hope of life sprang up. He began to think about the operation which had been suggested to him. "To live, I want to live," he said to himself. His wife came in to congratulate him; she uttered the customary words and added—

"It's quite true, isn't it, that you're better?"

Without looking at her, he said, "Yes."

Her dress, her figure, the expression of her face, the tone of her voice,—all told him the same: "Not the right thing. All that in which you lived and are living is lying, deceit, hiding life and death away from you." And as soon as he had formed that thought, hatred sprang up in him, and with that hatred agonizing physical sufferings, and with these sufferings the sense of inevitable, approaching ruin. Something new was happening; there were screwing and shooting pains, and a tightness in his breathing.

The expression of his face as he uttered that "Yes" was terrible. After uttering that "Yes," looking her straight in the face, he turned on to his face, with a rapidity extraordinary in his weakness, and shrieked—

"Go away, go away, let me be!"

XII

From that moment there began the scream that never ceased for three days, and was so awful that through two closed doors one could not hear it without horror. At the moment when he answered his wife he grasped that he had fallen, that there was no return, that the end had come, quite the end, while doubt was still as unsolved, still remained doubt.

"Oo! Oo—o! Oo!" he screamed in varying intonations. He had begun screaming, "I don't want to!" and so had gone on screaming on the same vowel sound—oo!

All those three days, during which time did not exist for him, he was struggling in that black sack into which he was being thrust by an unseen resistless force. He struggled as the man condemned to death struggles in the hands of the executioner, knowing that he cannot save himself. And every moment he felt that in spite of all his efforts to struggle against it, he was getting nearer and nearer to what terrified him. He felt that his agony was due both to his being thrust into this black hole and still more to his not being able to get right into it. What hindered him from getting into it was the claim that his life had been good. That justification of his life held him fast and would not let him get forward, and it caused him more agony than all.

All at once some force struck him in the chest, in the side, and stifled his breathing more than ever; he rolled forward into the hole, and there at the end there was some sort of light. It had happened with him, as it had sometimes happened to him in a railway carriage, when he had thought he was going forward while he was going back, and all of a sudden recognized his real direction.

"Yes, it has all been not the right thing," he said to himself, "but that's no matter." He could, he could do the right thing. "What is the right thing?" he asked himself, and suddenly he became quiet.

This was at the end of the third day, two hours before his death. At that very moment the schoolboy had stealthily crept into his father's room and gone up to his bedside. The dying man was screaming and waving his arms. His hand fell on the schoolboy's head. The boy snatched it, pressed it to his lips, and burst into tears.

At that very moment Ivan Ilyich had rolled into the hole, and caught sight of the light, and it was revealed to him that his life had not been what it ought to have been, but that that could still be set right. He asked himself, "What is the right thing?"—and became quiet, listening. Then he felt some one was kissing his hand. He opened his eyes and glanced at his son. He felt sorry for him. His wife went up to him. He glanced at her. She was gazing at him with open mouth, the tears unwiped streaming over her nose and cheeks, a look of despair on her face. He felt sorry for her.

"Yes, I'm making them miserable," he thought. "They're sorry, but it will be better for them when I die." He would have said this, but had not the strength to utter it. "Besides,

why speak, I must act," he thought. With a glance to his wife
he pointed to his son and said—

"Take away . . . sorry for him. . . . And you too . . ."
He tried to say "forgive," but said "forgo" . . . and too weak
to correct himself, shook his hand, knowing that He would
understand Whose understanding mattered.

And all at once it became clear to him that what had tortured him and would not leave him was suddenly dropping
away all at once on both sides and on ten sides and on all
sides. He was sorry for them, must act so that they might not
suffer. Set them free and be free himself of those agonies.
"How right and how simple!" he thought. "And the pain?" he
asked himself. "Where's it gone? Eh, where are you, pain?"

He began to watch for it.

"Yes, here it is. Well, what of it, let the pain be.

"And death. Where is it?"

He looked for his old accustomed terror of death, and did
not find it. "Where is it? What death?" There was no terror,
because death was not either.

In the place of death there was light.

"So this is it!" he suddenly exclaimed aloud.

"What joy!"

To him all this passed in a single instant, and the meaning
of that instant suffered no change after. For those present his
agony lasted another two hours. There was a rattle in his
throat, a twitching in his wasted body. Then the rattle and
the gasping came at longer and longer intervals.

"It is over!" some one said over him.

He caught those words and repeated them in his soul.

"Death is over," he said to himself. "It's no more."

He drew in a breath, stopped midway in the breath, stretched
and died.

March 25, 1886.

✠ ✠

Anton Chekhov

✠ ✠
✠
✠ ✠

Vanka

✠

Nine-year-old Vanka Zhukov, who had been apprentice to the shoemaker Aliakhin for three months, did not go to bed the night before Christmas. He waited till the master and mistress and the assistants had gone out to an early church service, to procure from his employer's cupboard a small vial of ink and a penholder with a rusty nib; then, spreading a crumpled sheet of paper in front of him, he began to write.

Before, however, deciding to make the first letter, he looked furtively at the door and at the window, glanced several times at the somber ikon, on either side of which stretched shelves full of lasts, and heaved a heart-rending sigh. The sheet of paper was spread on a bench, and he himself was on his knees in front of it.

"Dear Grandfather Konstantin Makarich," he wrote, "I am writing you a letter. I wish you a Happy Christmas and all God's holy best. I have no mamma or papa, you are all I have."

Vanka gave a look towards the window in which shone the reflection of his candle, and vividly pictured to himself his grandfather, Konstantin Makarich, who was night watchman at Messrs. Zhivarev. He was a small, lean, unusually lively and active old man of sixty-five, always smiling and blear-eyed. All day he slept in the servants' kitchen or trifled with the cooks. At night, enveloped in an ample sheepskin coat, he strayed round the domain tapping with his cudgel. Behind him, each hanging its head, walked the old bitch Kashtanka, and the dog Viun, so named because of his black coat and long body and his resemblance to a loach. Viun was an unusually civil and friendly dog, looking as kindly at a stranger as at his masters, but he was not to be trusted. Beneath his deference and humbleness was hid the most inquisitorial maliciousness. No one knew better than he how to sneak up and take a bite at a leg, or slip into the larder or steal a muzhik's chicken. More than once they had nearly broken his hind legs, twice he had been hung up, every week he was nearly flogged to death, but he always recovered.

At this moment, for certain, Vanka's grandfather must be standing at the gate, blinking his eyes at the bright red windows of the village church, stamping his feet in their high felt boots, and jesting with the people in the yard; his cudgel will be hanging from his belt, he will be hugging himself with cold, giving a little dry, old man's cough, and at times pinching a servant girl or a cook.

"Won't we take some snuff?" he asks, holding out his snuffbox to the women. The women take a pinch of snuff, and sneeze.

The old man goes into indescribable ecstasies, breaks into loud laughter, and cries:

"Off with it, it will freeze to your nose!"

He gives his snuff to the dogs, too. Kashtanka sneezes, twitches her nose, and walks away offended. Viun deferentially refuses to sniff and wags his tail. It is glorious weather, not a breath of wind, clear, and frosty; it is a dark night, but the whole village, its white roofs and streaks of smoke from the chimneys, the trees silvered with hoarfrost, and the snow-drifts, you can see it all. The sky scintillates with bright twinkling stars, and the Milky Way stands out so clearly that it looks as if it had been polished and rubbed over with snow for the holidays. . . .

Vanka sighs, dips his pen in the ink, and continues to write:

"Last night I got a thrashing, my master dragged me by my hair into the yard, and belabored me with a shoemaker's stirrup, because, while I was rocking his brat in its cradle, I unfortunately fell asleep. And during the week, my mistress told me to clean a herring, and I began by its tail, so she took the herring and stuck its snout into my face. The assistants tease me, send me to the tavern for vodka, make me steal the master's cucumbers, and the master beats me with whatever is handy. Food there is none; in the morning it's bread, at dinner, gruel, and in the evening bread again. As for tea or sour-cabbage soup, the master and the mistress themselves guzzle that. They make me sleep in the vestibule, and when their brat cries, I don't sleep at all, but have to rock the cradle. Dear Grandpapa, for Heaven's sake, take me away from here, home to our village, I can't bear this any more. . . . I bow to the ground to you, and will pray to God for ever and ever, take me from here or I shall die. . . ."

The corners of Vanka's mouth went down, he rubbed his eyes with his dirty fist, and sobbed.

"I'll grate your tobacco for you," he continued, "I'll pray to God for you, and if there is anything wrong, then flog me like the grey goat. And if you really think I shan't find work, then I'll ask the manager, for Christ's sake, to let me clean the boots, or I'll go instead of Fedya as underherdsman. Dear Grandpapa, I can't bear this any more, it'll kill me. . . . I wanted to run away to our village, but I have no boots, and I was afraid of the frost, and when I grow up I'll look after you, no one shall harm you, and when you die I'll pray for the repose of your soul, just like I do for mamma Pelageya.

"As for Moscow, it is a large town, there are all gentlemen's houses, lots of horses, no sheep, and the dogs are not vicious. The children don't come round at Christmas with a star, no one is allowed to sing in the choir, and once I saw in a shop window hooks on a line and fishing rods, all for sale, and for every kind of fish, awfully convenient. And there was one hook which would catch a sheat-fish weighing a pound. And there are shops with guns, like the master's, and I am sure they must cost 100 rubles each. And in the meat-shops there are woodcocks, partridges, and hares, but who shot them or where they come from, the shopman won't say.

"Dear Grandpa, and when the masters give a Christmas tree, take a golden walnut and hide it in my green box. Ask the young lady, Olga Ignatyevna, for it, say it's for Vanka."

Vanka sighed convulsively, and again stared at the window. He remembered that his grandfather always went to the forest for the Christmas tree, and took his grandson with him. What happy times! The frost crackled, his grandfather crackled, and as they both did, Vanka did the same. Then before cutting down the Christmas tree his grandfather smoked his pipe, took a long pinch of snuff, and made fun of poor frozen little Vanka. . . . The young fir trees, wrapt in hoar-frost, stood motionless, waiting for which of them would die. Suddenly a hare springing from somewhere would dart over the snowdrift. . . . His grandfather could not help shouting:

"Catch it, catch it, catch it! Ah, short-tailed devil!"

When the tree was down, his grandfather dragged it to the master's house, and there they set about decorating it. The young lady, Olga Ignatyevna, Vanka's great friend, busied herself most about it. When little Vanka's mother, Pelageya, was still alive, and was servant woman in the house, Olga Ignatyevna used to stuff him with sugar candy, and, having nothing to do, taught him to read, write, count up to one hundred, and even to dance the quadrille. When Pelageya died, they placed the orphan Vanka in the kitchen with his grandfather, and from the kitchen he was sent to Moscow to Aliakhin, the shoemaker.

"Come quick, dear Grandpapa," continued Vanka, "I beseech you for Christ's sake take me from here. Have pity on a poor orphan, for here they beat me, and I am frightfully hungry, and so sad that I can't tell you, I cry all the time. The other day the master hit me on the head with a last; I fell to the ground, and only just returned to life. My life is a misfortune, worse than any dog's. . . . I send greetings to Alyona, to one-eyed Yegor, and the coachman, and don't let any one have my mouth organ. I remain, your grandson, Ivan Zhukov, dear Grandpapa, do come."

Vanka folded his sheet of paper in four, and put it into an envelope purchased the night before for a kopek. He thought a little, dipped the pen into the ink, and wrote the address:

"The village, to my grandfather." He then scratched his head, thought again, and added: "Konstantin Makarich." Pleased at not having been interfered with in his writing, he put on his cap, and, without putting on his sheepskin coat, ran out in his shirtsleeves into the street.

The shopman at the poulterer's, from whom he had inquired the night before, had told him that letters were to be put into postboxes, and from there they were conveyed over the whole earth in mail troikas by drunken postboys and to the sound of bells. Vanka ran to the first postbox and slipped his precious letter into the slit.

An hour afterwards, lulled by hope, he was sleeping soundly. In his dreams he saw a stove, by the stove his grandfather sitting with his legs dangling down, barefooted, and reading a letter to the cooks, and Viun walking round the stove wagging his tail.

The
Kiss

✠

On the evening of the twentieth of May, at eight o'clock, all six batteries of the N Artillery Brigade on their way to camp arrived at the village of Miestechki with the intention of spending the night.

The confusion was at its worst—some officers fussed about the guns, others in the church square arranged with the quartermaster—when from behind the church rode a civilian upon a most remarkable mount. The small, short-tailed bay with well-shaped neck progressed with a wobbly motion, all the time making dancelike movements with its legs as if some one were switching its hoofs. When he had drawn rein level with the officers the rider doffed his cap and said ceremoniously—

"His Excellency, General von Rabbek, whose house is close by, requests the honor of the officers' company at tea. . . ."

The horse shook its head, danced, and wobbled to the rear; its rider again took off his cap, and, turning his strange steed, disappeared behind the church.

"The devil take it!" was the general exclamation as the officers dispersed to their quarters. "We can hardly keep our eyes open, yet along comes this von Rabbek with his tea! I know that tea!"

The officers of the six batteries had lively memories of a past invitation. During recent maneuvers they had been asked, together with their Cossack comrades, to tea at the house of a local country gentleman, an officer in retirement, by title a Count; and this hearty, hospitable Count overwhelmed them with attentions, fed them to satiety, poured vodka down their throats, and made them stay the night. All this, of course, they enjoyed. The trouble was that the old soldier entertained his guests too well. He kept them up till daybreak while he poured forth tales of past adventures; he dragged them from room to room to point out valuable paintings, old engravings, and rare arms; he read them holograph letters from celebrated men. And the weary officers, bored to death, listened, gaped, yearned for their beds, and yawned cautiously in their sleeves, until at last when their host released them it was too late for sleep.

Was von Rabbek another old Count? It might easily be. But there was no neglecting his invitation. The officers washed and dressed, and set out for von Rabbek's house. At the church square they learnt that they must descend the hill to the river, and follow the bank till they reached the general's gardens, where they would find a path direct to the house. Or, if they chose to go up hill, they would reach the general's barns half a verst from Miestechki. It was this route they chose.

"But who is this von Rabbek?" asked one. "The man who commanded the N Cavalry Division at Plevna?"

"No, that was not von Rabbek, but simply Rabbe—without the von."

"What glorious weather!"

At the first barn they came to, two roads diverged; one ran straight forward and faded in the dusk; the other turning to the right led to the general's house. As the officers drew near they talked less loudly. To right and left stretched rows of red-roofed brick barns, in aspect heavy and morose as the barracks of provincial towns. In front gleamed the lighted windows of von Rabbek's house.

"A good omen, gentlemen!" cried a young officer. "Our setter runs in advance. There is game ahead!"

On the face of Lieutenant Lobitko, the tall stout officer referred to, there was not one trace of hair though he was twenty-five years old. He was famed among comrades for the instinct which told him of the presence of women in the neighborhood. On hearing his comrade's remark, he turned his head and said—

"Yes. There are women there. My instinct tells me."

A handsome, well-preserved man of sixty, in mufti, came to the hall door to greet his guests. It was von Rabbek. As he pressed their hands, he explained that though he was delighted to see them, he must beg pardon for not asking them to spend the night; as guests he already had his two sisters, their children, his brother, and several neighbors—in fact, he had not one spare room. And though he shook their hands and apologized and smiled, it was plain that he was not half as glad to see them as was last year's Count, and that he had invited them merely because good manners demanded it. The officers climbing the soft-carpeted steps and listening to their host understood this perfectly well; and realized that they carried into the house an atmosphere of intrusion and alarm. Would any man—they asked themselves—who had gathered his two sisters and their children, his brother and his neighbors, to celebrate, no doubt, some family festival, find pleasure in the invasion of nineteen officers whom he had never seen before?

A tall, elderly lady, with a good figure, and a long face with black eyebrows, who resembled closely the ex-Empress Eugenie, greeted them at the drawing room door. Smiling courteously and with dignity, she affirmed that she was delighted to see the officers, and only regretted that she could not ask them to stay the night. But the courteous, dignified smile disappeared when she turned away, and it was quite plain that she had seen many officers in her day, that they caused not the slightest interest, and that she had invited them merely because an invitation was dictated by good breeding and by her position in the world.

In a big dining room seated at a big table sat ten men and women, drinking tea. Behind them, veiled in cigar smoke, stood several young men, among them one, red-whiskered and extremely thin, who spoke English loudly with a lisp. Through an open door the officers saw into a brightly lighted room with blue wallpaper.

"You are too many to introduce singly, gentlemen!" said the general loudly, with affected joviality. "Make one another's acquaintance, please—without formalities!"

The visitors, some with serious, even severe faces, some smiling constrainedly, all with a feeling of awkwardness, bowed, and took their seats at the table. Most awkward of all felt Staff Captain Ryabovich, a short, round-shouldered, spectacled officer, whiskered like a lynx. While his brother officers looked serious or smiled constrainedly, his face, his lynx whiskers, and his spectacles seemed to explain: "I am the most timid, modest, undistinguished officer in the whole brigade." For some time after he took his seat at the table he could not fix his attention on any single thing. Faces, dresses, the cut glass cognac bottles, the steaming tumblers, the moulded cornices—all merged in a single, overwhelming sentiment which caused him intense fright and made him wish to hide his head. Like an inexperienced lecturer he saw everything before him, but could distinguish nothing, and was in fact the victim of what men of science diagnose as "psychical blindness."

But slowly conquering his diffidence, Ryabovich began to distinguish and observe. As became a man both timid and unsocial, he remarked first of all the amazing temerity of his new friends. Von Rabbek, his wife, two elderly ladies, a girl in lilac, and the red-whiskered youth who, it appeared, was a young von Rabbek, sat down among the officers as unconcernedly as if they had held rehearsals, and at once plunged into various heated arguments in which they soon involved their guests. That artillerists have a much better time than cavalrymen or infantrymen was proved conclusively by the lilac girl, while von Rabbek and the elderly ladies affirmed the converse. The conversation became desultory. Ryabovich listened to the lilac girl fiercely debating themes she knew nothing about and took no interest in, and watched the insincere smiles which appeared on and disappeared from her face.

While the von Rabbek family with amazing strategy inveigled their guests into the dispute, they kept their eyes on every glass and mouth. Had every one tea, was it sweet enough, why didn't one eat biscuits, was another fond of cognac? And the longer Ryabovich listened and looked, the more pleased he was with this disingenuous, disciplined family.

After tea the guests repaired to the drawing room. Instinct had not cheated Lobitko. The room was packed with young women and girls, and ere a minute had passed the setter lieutenant stood beside a very young, fair-haired girl in black, and, bending down as if resting on an invisible sword, shrugged his shoulders coquettishly. He was uttering, no doubt, most unentertaining nonsense, for the fair girl looked indulgently at his sated face, and exclaimed indifferently, "Indeed!" And this indifferent "Indeed!" might have quickly convinced the setter that he was on a wrong scent.

Music began. As the notes of a mournful valse throbbed out of the open window, through the heads of all flashed the feeling that outside that window it was springtime, a night of May. The air was odorous of young poplar leaves, of roses and lilacs—and the valse and the spring was sincere. Ryabovich, with valse and cognac mingling tipsily in his head, gazed at the window with a smile; then began to follow the movements of the women; and it seemed that the smell of roses, poplars, and lilacs came not from the gardens outside, but from the women's faces and dresses.

They began to dance. Young von Rabbek valsed twice

round the room with a very thin girl; and Lobitko, slipping on the parqueted floor, went up to the girl in lilac, and was granted a dance. But Ryabovich stood near the door with the wallflowers, and looked silently on. Amazed at the daring of men who in sight of a crowd could take unknown women by the waist, he tried in vain to picture himself doing the same. A time had been when he envied his comrades their courage and dash, suffered from painful heartsearchings, and was hurt by the knowledge that he was timid, round-shouldered, and undistinguished, that he had lynx whiskers, and that his waist was much too long. But with years he had grown reconciled to his own insignificance, and now looking at the dancers and loud talkers, he felt no envy, but only mournful emotions.

At the first quadrille von Rabbek junior approached and invited two nondancing officers to a game of billiards. The three left the room; and Ryabovich who stood idle, and felt impelled to join in the general movement, followed. They passed the dining room, traversed a narrow glazed corridor, and a room where three sleepy footmen jumped from a sofa with a start; and after walking, it seemed, through a whole houseful of rooms, entered a small billiard room.

Von Rabbek and the two officers began their game. Ryabovich, whose only game was cards, stood near the table and looked indifferently on, as the players, with unbuttoned coats, wielded their cues, moved about, joked, and shouted obscure technical terms. Ryabovich was ignored, save when one of the players jostled him or caught his cue, and turning towards him said briefly, "Pardon!" so that before the game was over he was thoroughly bored, and impressed by a sense of his superfluity, resolved to return to the drawing room, and turned away.

It was on the way back that his adventure took place. Before he had gone far he saw that he had missed the way. He remembered distinctly the room with the three sleepy footmen; and after passing through five or six rooms entirely vacant, he saw his mistake. Retracing his steps, he turned to the left, and found himself in an almost dark room which he had not seen before; and after hesitating a minute, he boldly opened the first door he saw, and found himself in complete darkness. Through a chink of the door in front peered a bright light; from afar throbbed the dulled music of a mournful mazurka. Here, as in the drawing room, the windows were open wide, and the smell of poplars, lilacs, and roses flooded the air.

Ryabovich paused in irresolution. For a moment all was still. Then came the sound of hasty footsteps; then, without any warning of what was to come, a dress rustled, a woman's breathless voice whispered "At last!" and two soft, scented, unmistakably womanly arms met round his neck, a warm cheek impinged on his, and he received a sounding kiss. But hardly had the kiss echoed through the silence when the unknown shrieked loudly, and fled away—as it seemed to Ryabovich—in disgust. Ryabovich himself nearly screamed, and rushed headlong towards the bright beam in the door-chink.

As he entered the drawing room his heart beat violently, and his hands trembled so perceptibly that he clasped them behind his back. His first emotion was shame, as if every one in the room already knew that he had just been embraced and kissed. He retired into his shell, and looked fearfully around. But finding that hosts and guests were calmly dancing or talking, he regained courage, and surrendered himself to sensations experienced for the first time in life. The unexampled had happened. His neck, fresh from the embrace of two soft, scented arms, seemed anointed with oil; near his left mustache, where the kiss had fallen, trembled a slight, delightful chill, as from peppermint drops; and from head to foot he was soaked in new and extraordinary sensations, which continued to grow and grow.

He felt that he must dance, talk, run into the garden, laugh unrestrainedly. He forgot altogether that he was round-shouldered, undistinguished, lynx-whiskered, that he had an "indefinite exterior"—a description from the lips of a woman he had happened to overhear. As Madame von Rabbek passed him he smiled so broadly and graciously that she came up and looked at him questioningly.

"What a charming house you have!" he said, straightening his spectacles.

And Madame von Rabbek smiled back, said that the house still belonged to her father, and asked were his parents alive, how long he had been in the Army, and why he was so thin. After hearing his answers she departed. But though the conversation was over, he continued to smile benevolently, and think what charming people were his new acquaintances.

At supper Ryabovich ate and drank mechanically what was put before him, heard not a word of the conversation, and devoted all his powers to the unraveling of his mysterious, romantic adventure. What was the explanation? It was plain that one of the girls, he reasoned, had arranged a meeting in the dark room, and after waiting some time in vain had, in her nervous tension, mistaken Ryabovich for her hero. The mistake was likely enough, for on entering the dark room Ryabovich had stopped irresolutely as if he, too, were waiting for some one. So far the mystery was explained.

"But which of them was it?" he asked, searching the women's faces. She certainly was young, for old women do not indulge in such romances. Secondly, she was not a servant. That was proved unmistakably by the rustle of her dress, the scent, the voice . . .

When at first he looked at the girl in lilac she pleased him; she had pretty shoulders and arms, a clever face, a charming voice. Ryabovich piously prayed that it was she. But, smiling insincerely, she wrinkled her long nose, and that at once gave her an elderly air. So Ryabovich turned his eyes on the blonde in black. The blonde was younger, simpler, sincerer; she had charming kiss curls, and drank from her tumbler with inexpressible grace. Ryabovich hoped it was she—but soon he noticed that her face was flat, and bent his eyes on her neighbor.

"It is a hopeless puzzle," he reflected. "If you take the arms and shoulders of the lilac girl, add the blonde's curls, and the eyes of the girl on Lobitko's left, then——"

He composed a portrait of all these charms, and had a clear vision of the girl who had kissed him. But she was nowhere to be seen.

Supper over, the visitors, sated and tipsy, bade their entertainers good-by. Both host and hostess again apologized for not asking them to spend the night.

"I am very glad, very glad, gentlemen!" said the general, and this time seemed to speak sincerely, no doubt because speeding the parting guest is a kindlier office than welcoming him unwelcomed. "I am very glad indeed! I hope you will visit me on your way back. Without ceremony, please! Which way will you go? Up the hill? No, go down the hill and through the garden. That way is shorter."

The officers took his advice. After the noise and glaring illumination within doors, the garden seemed dark and still. Until they reached the wicket gate all kept silence. Merry, half tipsy, and content, as they were, the night's obscurity and stillness inspired pensive thoughts. Through their brains, as through Ryabovich's, sped probably the same question: "Will the time ever come when I, like von Rabbek, shall have a big house, a family, a garden, the chance of being gracious—even insincerely—to others, of making them sated, tipsy, and content?"

But once the garden lay behind them, all spoke at once, and burst into causeless laughter. The path they followed led straight to the river, and then ran beside it, winding around bushes, ravines, and overhanging willow trees. The track was barely visible; the other bank was lost entirely in gloom. Sometimes the black water imaged stars, and this was the only indication of the river's speed. From beyond it sighed a drowsy snipe, and beside them in a bush, heedless of the crowd, a nightingale chanted loudly. The officers gathered in a group, and swayed the bush, but the nightingale continued his song.

"I like his cheek!" they echoed admiringly. "He doesn't care a kopek! The old rogue!"

Near their journey's end the path turned up the hill, and joined the road not far from the church enclosure; and there the officers, breathless from climbing, sat on the grass and smoked. Across the river gleamed a dull red light, and for want of a subject they argued the problem, whether it was a bonfire, a window light, or something else. Ryabovich looked also at the light, and felt that it smiled and winked at him as if it knew about the kiss.

On reaching home, he undressed without delay, and lay upon his bed. He shared the cabin with Lobitko and a Lieutenant Merzlyakov, a staid, silent little man, by repute highly cultivated, who took with him everywhere *The Messenger of Europe,* and read it eternally. Lobitko undressed, tramped impatiently from corner to corner, and sent his servant for beer. Merzlyakov lay down, balanced the candle on his pillow, and hid his head behind *The Messenger of Europe*.

"Where is she now?" muttered Ryabovich, looking at the soot-blacked ceiling.

His neck still seemed anointed with oil, near his mouth still trembled the speck of peppermint chill. Through his brain twinkled successively the shoulders and arms of the lilac girl, the kiss curls and honest eyes of the girl in black, the waists, dresses, brooches. But though he tried his best to fix these vagrant images, they glimmered, winked, and dissolved; and as they faded finally into the vast black curtain which hangs before the closed eyes of all men, he began to hear hurried footsteps, the rustle of petticoats, the sound of a kiss. A strong, causeless joy possessed him. But as he surrendered himself to this joy, Lobitko's servant returned with the news that no beer was obtainable. The lieutenant resumed his impatient march up and down the room.

"The fellow's an idiot," he exclaimed, stopping first near Ryabovich and then near Merzlyakov. "Only the worst numbskull and blockhead can't get beer! *Canaille!*"

"Every one knows there's no beer here," said Merzlyakov, without lifting his eyes from *The Messenger of Europe*.

"You believe that!" exclaimed Lobitko. "Lord in heaven, drop me on the moon, and in five minutes I'll find both beer and women! I will find them myself! Call me a rascal if I don't!"

He dressed slowly, silently lighted a cigarette, and went out.

"Rabbek, Grabbek, Labbek," he muttered, stopping in the hall. "I won't go alone, devil take me! Ryabovich, come for a walk! What?"

As he got no answer, he returned, undressed slowly, and lay down. Merzlyakov sighed, dropped *The Messenger of Europe,* and put out the light. "Well?" muttered Lobitko, puffing his cigarette in the dark.

Ryabovich pulled the bedclothes up to his chin, curled himself into a roll, and strained his imagination to join the twinkling images into one coherent whole. But the vision fled him. He soon fell asleep, and his last impression was that he had been caressed and gladdened, that into his life had crept something strange, and indeed ridiculous, but uncommonly good and radiant. And this thought did not forsake him even in his dreams.

When he awoke the feeling of anointment and peppermint chill were gone. But joy, as on the night before, filled every vein. He looked entranced at the window panes gilded by the rising sun, and listened to the noises outside. Some one spoke loudly under the very window. It was Lebedetzki, commander of his battery, who had just overtaken the brigade. He was talking to the sergeant major, loudly, owing to lack of practice in soft speech.

"And what next?" he roared.

"During yesterday's shoeing, your honor, *Golubchik* was pricked. The *feldscher* ordered clay and vinegar. And last night, your honor, mechanic Artemiev was drunk, and the lieutenant ordered him to be put on the limber of the reserve gun carriage."

The sergeant major added that Karpov had forgotten the tent pegs and the new lanyards for the friction tubes, and that the officers had spent the evening at General von Rabbek's. But here at the window appeared Lebedetzki's red-bearded face. He blinked his short-sighted eyes at the drowsy men in bed, and greeted them.

"Is everything all right?"

"The saddle wheeler galled his withers with the new yoke," answered Lobitko.

The commander sighed, mused a moment, and shouted—
"I am thinking of calling on Alexandra Yevgrofovna. I want to see her. Good-by! I will catch you up before night."

Fifteen minutes later the brigade resumed its march. As he passed von Rabbek's barns Ryabovich turned his head and looked at the house. The Venetian blinds were down; evidently all still slept. And among them slept she—she who had kissed him but a few hours before. He tried to visualize her asleep. He projected the bedroom window opened wide with green branches peering in, the freshness of the morning air, the smell of poplars, lilacs, and roses, the bed, a chair, the dress which rustled last night, a pair of tiny slippers, a ticking watch on the table—all these came to him clearly with every detail. But the features, the kind, sleepy smile—all, in short, that was essential and characteristic—fled his imagination as quicksilver flees the hand. When he had covered half a verst he again turned back. The yellow church, the house, gardens, and river were bathed in light. Imagining an azure sky, the green-banked river specked with silver sunshine flakes was inexpressibly fair; and, looking at Miestechki for the last time, Ryabovich felt sad, as if parting for ever wtih something very near and dear.

By the road before him stretched familiar, uninteresting scenes; to the right and left, fields of young rye and buckwheat with hopping rooks; in front, dust and the napes of human necks; behind, the same dust and faces. Ahead of the column marched four soldiers with swords—that was the advance guard. Next came the bandsmen. Advance guard and bandsmen, like mutes in a funeral procession, ignored the regulation intervals and marched too far ahead. Ryabovich, with the first gun of Battery No. 5, could see four batteries ahead.

To a layman, the long, lumbering march of an artillery brigade is novel, interesting, inexplicable. It is hard to under-

stand why a single gun needs so many men; why so many,
such strangely harnessed horses are needed to drag it. But to
Ryabovich, a master of all these things, it was profoundly dull.
He had learned years ago why a solid sergeant major rides
beside the officer in front of each battery, why the sergeant
major is called the *unosni,* and why the drivers of leaders and
wheelers ride behind him. Ryabovich knew why the near horses
are called saddle horses, and why the off horses are called led
horses—and all of this was interesting beyond words. On one
of the wheelers rode a soldier still covered with yesterday's
dust, and with a cumbersome, ridiculous guard on his right
leg. But Ryabovich, knowing the use of this leg guard, found
it in no way ridiculous. The drivers, mechanically and with
occasional cries, flourished their whips. The guns in themselves
were impressive. The limbers were packed with tarpaulin-
covered sacks of oats; and the guns themselves, hung around
with teapots and satchels, looked like harmless animals,
guarded for some obscure reason by men and horses. In the
lee of the gun tramped six gunners, swinging their arms; and
behind each gun came more *unosniye,* leaders, wheelers; and
yet more guns, each as ugly and uninspiring as the one in
front. And as every one of the six batteries in the brigade had
four guns, the procession stretched along the road at least half
a verst. It ended with a wagon train, with which, its head bent
in thought, walked the donkey Magar, brought from Turkey
by a battery commander.

Dead to his surroundings, Ryabovich marched onward, looking at the napes ahead or at the faces behind. Had it not been
for last night's event, he would have been half asleep. But now
he was absorbed in novel, entrancing thoughts. When the
brigade set out that morning he had tried to argue that the kiss
had no significance save as a trivial though mysterious adventure; that it was without real import; and that to think of it
seriously was to behave himself absurdly. But logic soon flew
away and surrendered him to his vivid imaginings. At times he
saw himself in von Rabbek's dining room, *tête-à-tête* with a
composite being, formed of the girl in lilac and the blonde in
black. At times he closed his eyes, and pictured himself with
a different, this time quite an unknown, girl of cloudy feature;
he spoke to her, caressed her, bent over her shoulder; he imagined war and parting . . . then reunion, the first supper together, children. . . .

"To the brakes!" rang the command as they topped the brow of each hill.

Ryabovich also cried "To the brakes!" and each time dread that the cry would break the magic spell, and recall him to realities.

They passed a big country house. Ryabovich looked across the fence into the garden, and saw a long path, straight as a ruler, carpeted with yellow sand, and shaded by young birches. In an ecstasy of enchantment, he pictured little feminine feet treading the yellow sand; and, in a flash, imagination restored the woman who had kissed him, the woman he had visualized after supper the night before. The image settled in his brain and never afterwards forsook him.

The spell reigned until midday, when a loud command came from the rear of the column.

"Attention! Eyes right! Officers!"

In a *calèche* drawn by a pair of white horses appeared the general of brigade. He stopped at the second battery, and called out something which no one understood. Up galloped several officers, among them Ryabovich.

"Well, how goes it?" The general blinked his red eyes, and continued, "Are there any sick?"

Hearing the answer, the little skinny general mused a moment, turned to an officer, and said—

"The driver of your third gun wheeler has taken off his leg guard and hung it on the limber. *Canaille!* Punish him!"

Then raising his eyes to Ryabovich, he added—

"And in your battery, I think, the harness is too loose."

Having made several other equally tiresome remarks, he looked at Lobitko, and laughed.

"Why do you look so downcast, Lieutenant Lobitko? You are sighing for Madame Lopukhova, eh? Gentlemen, he is pining for Madame Lopukhova!"

Madame Lopukhova was a tall, stout lady, long past forty. Being partial to big women, regardless of age, the general ascribed the same taste to his subordinates. The officers smiled respectfully; and the general, pleased that he had said something caustic and laughable, touched the coachman's back and saluted. The *calèche* whirled away.

"All this, though it seems to me impossible and unearthly, is in reality very commonplace," thought Ryabovich, watching the clouds of dust raised by the general's carriage. "It is an everyday event, and within every one's experience. . . .

This old general, for instance, must have loved in his day; he is married now, and has children. Captain Vakhter is also married, and his wife loves him, though he has an ugly red neck and no waist. . . . Salmanov is coarse, and a typical Tartar, but he has had a romance ending in marriage. . . . I, like the rest, must go through it all sooner or later."

And the thought that he was an ordinary man, and that his life was ordinary, rejoiced and consoled him. He boldly visualized *her* and his happiness, and let his imagination run mad.

Towards evening the brigade ended its march. While the other officers sprawled in their tents, Ryabovich, Merzlyakov, and Lobitko sat around a packing case and supped. Merzlyakov ate slowly, and, resting *The Messenger of Europe* on his knees, read on steadily. Lobitko, chattering without cease, poured beer into his glass. But Ryabovich, whose head was dizzy from uninterrupted daydreams, ate in silence. When he had drunk three glasses he felt tipsy and weak; and an overmastering impulse forced him to relate his adventure to his comrades.

"A most extraordinary thing happened to me at von Rabbek's," he began, doing his best to speak in an indifferent, ironical tone. "I was on my way, you understand, from the billiard room . . ."

And he attempted to give a very detailed history of the kiss. But in a minute he had told the whole story. In that minute he had exhausted every detail; and it seemed to him terrible that the story required such a short time. It ought, he felt, to have lasted all the night. As he finished, Lobitko, who as a liar himself believed in no one, laughed incredulously. Merzlyakov frowned, and, with his eyes still glued to *The Messenger of Europe,* said indifferently—

"God knows who it was! She threw herself on your neck, you say, and didn't cry out! Some lunatic, I expect!"

"It must have been a lunatic," agreed Ryabovich.

"I, too, have had adventures of that kind," began Lobitko, making a frightful face. "I was on my way to Kovno. I travelled second class. The carriage was packed, and I couldn't sleep. So I gave the guard a ruble, and he took my bag, and put me in a *coupé.* I lay down, and pulled my rug over me. It was pitch dark, you understand. Suddenly I felt some one tapping my shoulder and breathing in my face. I stretched out my hand and felt an elbow. Then I opened my eyes. Imagine!

A woman! Coal black eyes, lips red as good coral, nostrils breathing passion, breasts—buffers!"

"Draw it mild!" interrupted Merzlyakov in his quiet voice. "I can believe about the breasts, but if it was pitch dark how could you see the lips?"

By laughing at Merzlyakov's lack of understanding, Lobitko tried to shuffle out of the dilemma. The story annoyed Ryabovich. He rose from the box, lay on his bed, and swore that he would never again take any one into his confidence.

Life in camp passed without event. The days flew by, each like the one before. But on every one of these days Ryabovich felt, thought, and acted as a man in love. When at daybreak his servant brought him cold water, and poured it over his head, it flashed at once into his half-awakened brain that something good and warm and caressing had crept into his life.

At night when his comrades talked of love and of women, he drew in his chair, and his face was the face of an old soldier who talks of battles in which he has taken part. And when the rowdy officers, led by setter Lobitko, made Don Juanesque raids upon the neighboring "suburb," Ryabovich, though he accompanied them, was morose and conscience-struck, and mentally asked *her* forgiveness. In free hours and sleepless nights, when his brain was obsessed by memories of childhood, of his father, his mother, of everything akin and dear, he remembered always Miestechki, the dancing horse, von Rabbek, von Rabbek's wife, so like the ex-Empress Eugenie, the dark room, the chink in the door.

On the thirty-first of August he left camp, this time not with the whole brigade but with only two batteries. As an exile returning to his native land, he was agitated and enthralled by daydreams. He longed passionately for the queer-looking horse, the church, the insincere von Rabbeks, the dark room; and that internal voice which cheats so often the lovelorn whispered an assurance that he should see *her* again. But doubt tortured him. How should he meet her? What must he say? Would she have forgotten the kiss? If it came to the worst—he consoled himself—if he never saw her again, he might walk once more through the dark room, and remember. . . .

Towards evening the white barns and well-known church rose on the horizon. Ryabovich's heart beat wildly. He ignored the remark of an officer who rode by, he forgot the whole world, and he gazed greedily at the river glimmering afar, at the green roofs, at the dovecote, over which fluttered birds, dyed golden by the setting sun.

As he rode towards the church, and heard again the quarter-master's raucous voice, he expected every second a horseman to appear from behind the fence and invite the officers to tea. . . . But the quartermaster ended his harangue, the officers hastened to the village, and no horseman appeared.

"When Rabbek hears from the peasants that we are back he will send for us," thought Ryabovich. And so assured was he of this, that when he entered the hut he failed to understand why his comrades had lighted a candle, and why the servants were preparing the samovar.

A painful agitation oppressed him. He lay on his bed. A moment later he rose to look for the horseman. But no horseman was in sight. Again he lay down; again he rose; and this time, impelled by restlessness, went into the street, and walked towards the church. The square was dark and deserted. On the hill stood three silent soldiers. When they saw Ryabovich they started and saluted, and he, returning their salute, began to descend the well-remembered path.

Beyond the stream, in a sky stained with purple, the moon slowly rose. Two chattering peasant women walked in a kitchen garden and pulled cabbage leaves; behind them their log cabins stood out black against the sky. The river bank was as it had been in May; the bushes were the same; things differed only in that the nightingale no longer sang, that it smelt no longer of poplars and young grass.

When he reached von Rabbek's garden Ryabovich peered through the wicket gate. Silence and darkness reigned. Save only the white birch trunks and patches of pathway, the whole garden merged in a black, impenetrable shade. Ryabovich listened greedily, and gazed intent. For a quarter of an hour he loitered; then hearing no sound, and seeing no light, he walked wearily towards home.

He went down to the river. In front rose the general's bathing box; and white towels hung on the rail of the bridge. He climbed on to the bridge and stood still; then, for no reason whatever, touched a towel. It was clammy and cold. He looked down at the river which sped past swiftly, murmuring almost inaudibly against the bathing box piles. Near the left bank glowed the moon's ruddy reflection, overrun by ripples which stretched it, tore it in two, and, it seemed, would sweep it away as twigs and shavings are swept.

"How stupid! How stupid!" thought Ryabovich, watching the hurrying ripples. "How stupid everything is!"

Now that hope was dead, the history of the kiss, his impatience, his ardor, his vague aspirations and disillusion appeared in a clear light. It no longer seemed strange that the general's horseman had not come, and that he would never again see *her* who had kissed him by accident instead of another. On the contrary, he felt, it would be strange if he did ever see her again. . . .

The water flew past him, whither and why no one knew. It had flown past in May; it had sped a stream into a great river; a river, into the sea; it had floated on high in mist and fallen again in rain; it might be, the water of May was again speeding past under Ryabovich's eyes. For what purpose? Why?

And the whole world—life itself seemed to Ryabovich an inscrutable, aimless mystification. . . . Raising his eyes from the stream and gazing at the sky, he recalled how Fate in the shape of an unknown woman had once caressed him; he recalled his summer fantasies and images—and his whole life seemed to him unnaturally thin and colorless and wretched. . . .

When he reached the cabin his comrades had disappeared. His servant informed him that all had set out to visit "General Fonrabbkin," who had sent a horseman to bring them. . . . For a moment Ryabovich's heart thrilled with joy. But that joy he extinguished. He cast himself upon his bed, and wroth with his evil fate, as if he wished to spite it, ignored the invitation.

Gooseberries

✠

The sky had been overcast since early morning; it was a still day, not hot, but tedious, as it usually is when the weather is gray and dull, when clouds have been hanging over the fields for a long time, and you wait for the rain that does not come. Ivan Ivanich, a veterinary, and Burkin, a high school teacher, were already tired with walking, and the plain seemed endless to them. Far ahead were the scarcely visible windmills of the village of Mironositskoe; to the right lay a range of hills that disappeared in the distance beyond the village, and both of them knew that over there were the river, and fields, green willows, homesteads, and if you stood on one of the hills, you could see from there another vast plain, telegraph poles, and a train that from afar looked like a caterpillar crawling, and in clear weather you could even see the town. Now, when it was still and when nature seemed mild and pensive, Ivan Ivanich and Burkin were filled with love for this plain, and both of them thought what a beautiful land it was.

"Last time when we were in Elder Prokofi's barn," said Burkin, "you were going to tell me a story."

"Yes; I wanted to tell you about my brother."

Ivan Ivanich heaved a slow sigh and lit his pipe before beginning his story, but just then it began to rain. And five minutes later there was a downpour, and it was hard to tell when it would be over. The two men halted, at a loss; the dogs, already wet, stood with their tails between their legs and looked at them feelingly.

"We must find shelter somewhere," said Burkin. "Let's go to Alyokhin's; it's quite near."

"Let's."

They turned aside and walked across a mown meadow, now going straight ahead, now bearing to the right, until they reached the road. Soon poplars came into view, a garden, then the red roofs of barns; the river gleamed, and the view opened on a broad expanse of water with a mill and a white bathing cabin. That was Sofyino, Alyokhin's place.

The mill was going, drowning out the sound of the rain; the dam was shaking. Wet horses stood near the carts, their heads drooping, and men were walking about, their heads covered with sacks. It was damp, muddy, dreary; and the water looked cold and unkind. Ivan Ivanich and Burkin felt cold and messy and uncomfortable through and through; their feet were heavy with mud and when, having crossed the dam, they climbed up to the barns, they were silent as though they were cross with each other.

The noise of a winnowing machine came from one of the barns, the door was open, and clouds of dust were pouring from within. On the threshold stood Alyokhin himself, a man of forty, tall and rotund, with long hair, looking more like a professor or an artist than a gentleman farmer. He was wearing a white blouse, badly in need of washing, that was belted with a rope, and drawers, and his high boots were plastered with mud and straw. His eyes and nose were black with dust. He recognized Ivan Ivanich and Burkin and was apparently very glad to see them.

"Please go up to the house, gentlemen," he said, smiling; "I'll be there directly, in a moment."

It was a large structure of two stories. Alyokhin lived downstairs in what was formerly the stewards' quarters: two rooms that had arched ceilings and small windows; the furniture was plain, and the place smelled of rye bread, cheap vodka, and harness. He went into the showy rooms upstairs only rarely, when he had guests. Once in the house, the two visitors were met by a chambermaid, a young woman so beautiful that both of them stood still at the same moment and glanced at each other.

"You can't imagine how glad I am to see you, gentlemen," said Alyokhin, joining them in the hall. "What a surprise! Pelageya," he said, turning to the chambermaid, "give the guests a change of clothes. And, come to think of it, I will change, too. But I must go and bathe first, I don't think I've had a wash since spring. Don't you want to go into the bathing cabin? In the meanwhile things will be got ready here."

The beautiful Pelageya, with her soft, delicate air, brought them bath towels and soap, and Alyokhin went to the bathing cabin with his guests.

"Yes, it's a long time since I've bathed," he said, as he undressed. "I've an excellent bathing cabin, as you see—it was put up by my father—but somehow I never find time to use it." He sat down on the steps and lathered his long hair and neck, and the water around him turned brown.

"I say—" observed Ivan Ivanich significantly, looking at his head.

"I haven't had a good wash for a long time," repeated Alyokhin, embarrassed, and soaped himself once more; the water about him turned dark blue, the color of ink.

Ivan Ivanich came out of the cabin, plunged into the water with a splash and swam in the rain, thrusting his arms out wide; he raised waves on which white lilies swayed. He swam out to the middle of the river and dived and a minute later came up in another spot and swam on and kept diving, trying to touch bottom. "By God!" he kept repeating delightedly, "by God!" He swam to the mill, spoke to the peasants there, and turned back and in the middle of the river lay floating, exposing his face to the rain. Burkin and Alyokhin were already dressed and ready to leave, but he kept on swimming and diving. "By God!" he kept exclaiming. "Lord, have mercy on me."

"You've had enough!" Burkin shouted to him.

They returned to the house. And only when the lamp was lit in the big drawing room upstairs, and the two guests, in silk dressing gowns and warm slippers, were lounging in arm-chairs, and Alyokhin himself, washed and combed, wearing a new jacket, was walking about the room, evidently savoring the warmth, the cleanliness, the dry clothes and light footwear, and when pretty Pelageya, stepping noiselessly across the carpet and smiling softly, brought in a tray with tea and jam, only then did Ivan Ivanich begin his story, and it was as though not only Burkin and Alyokhin were listening, but also the ladies, old and young, and the military men who looked down upon them, calmly and severely, from their gold frames.

"We are two brothers," he began, "I, Ivan Ivanich, and my brother, Nikolay Ivanich, who is two years my junior. I went in for a learned profession and became a veterinary; Nikolay at nineteen began to clerk in a provincial branch of the Treasury. Our father was a *kantonist*,[1] but he rose to be an officer and so a nobleman, a rank that he bequeathed to us together with a small estate. After his death there was a lawsuit and we lost the estate to creditors, but be that as it may, we spent our childhood in the country. Just like peasant children we

[1] The son of a private, registered at birth in the army and trained in a military school.

passed days and nights in the fields and the woods, herded horses, stripped bast from the trees, fished, and so on. And, you know, whoever even once in his life has caught a perch or seen thrushes migrate in the autumn, when on clear, cool days they sweep in flocks over the village, will never really be a townsman and to the day of his death will have a longing for the open. My brother was unhappy in the government office. Years passed, but he went on warming the same seat, scratching away at the same papers, and thinking of one and the same thing: how to get away to the country. And little by little this vague longing turned into a definite desire, into a dream of buying a little property somewhere on the banks of a river or a lake.

"He was a kind and gentle soul and I loved him, but I never sympathized with his desire to shut himself up for the rest of his life on a little property of his own. It is a common saying that a man needs only six feet of earth. But six feet is what a corpse needs, not a man. It is also asserted that if our educated class is drawn to the land and seeks to settle on farms, that's a good thing. But these farms amount to the same six feet of earth. To retire from the city, from the struggle, from the hub-bub, to go off and hide on one's own farm—that's not life, it is selfishness, sloth, it is a kind of monasticism, but monasti-cism without works. Man needs not six feet of earth, not a farm, but the whole globe, all of Nature, where unhindered he can display all the capacities and peculiarities of his free spirit.

"My brother Nikolay, sitting in his office, dreamed of eating his own *shchi,* which would fill the whole farmyard with a delicious aroma, of picnicking on the green grass, of sleeping in the sun, of sitting for hours on the seat by the gate gazing at field and forest. Books on agriculture and the farming items in almanacs were his joy, the delight of his soul. He liked news-papers too, but the only things he read in them were adver-tisements of land for sale, so many acres of tillable land and pasture, with house, garden, river, mill, and millpond. And he pictured to himself garden paths, flowers, fruit, birdhouses with starlings in them, crucians in the pond, and all that sort of thing, you know. These imaginary pictures varied with the ad-vertisements he came upon, but somehow gooseberry bushes figured in every one of them. He could not picture to himself a single countryhouse, a single rustic nook, without gooseber-ries.

" 'Country life has its advantages,' he used to say. 'You sit on the veranda having tea, and your ducks swim in the pond, and everything smells delicious and—the gooseberries are ripening.'

"He would draw a plan of his estate and invariably it would contain the following features: a) the master's house; b) servants' quarters; c) kitchen garden; d) a gooseberry patch. He lived meagerly: he deprived himself of food and drink; he dressed God knows how, like a beggar, but he kept on saving and salting money away in the bank. He was terribly stingy. It was painful for me to see it, and I used to give him small sums and send him something on holidays, but he would put that away too. Once a man is possessed by an idea, there is no doing anything with him.

"Years passed. He was transferred to another province, he was already past forty, yet he was still reading newspaper advertisements and saving up money. Then I heard that he was married. Still for the sake of buying a property with a gooseberry patch he married an elderly, homely widow, without a trace of affection for her, but simply because she had money. After marrying her, he went on living parsimoniously, keeping her half-starved, and he put her money in the bank in his own name. She had previously been the wife of a postmaster, who had got her used to pies and cordials. This second husband did not even give her enough black bread. She began to sicken, and some three years later gave up the ghost. And, of course, it never for a moment occurred to my brother that he was to blame for her death. Money, like vodka, can do queer things to a man. Once in our town a merchant lay on his deathbed; before he died, he ordered a plateful of honey and he ate up all his money and lottery tickets with the honey, so that no one should get it. One day when I was inspecting a drove of cattle at a railway station, a cattle dealer fell under a locomotive and it sliced off his leg. We carried him in to the infirmary, the blood was gushing from the wound—a terrible business, but he kept begging us to find his leg and was very anxious about it: he had twenty rubles in the boot that was on that leg, and he was afraid they would be lost."

"That's a tune from another opera," said Burkin.

Ivan Ivanich paused a moment and then continued:

"After his wife's death, my brother began to look around for a property. Of course, you may scout about for five years and in the end make a mistake, and buy something quite different from what you have been dreaming of. Through an agent

my brother bought a mortgaged estate of three hundred acres
with a house, servants' quarters, a park, but with no orchard,
no gooseberry patch, no duck pond. There was a stream, but
the water in it was the color of coffee, for on one of its banks
there was a brickyard and on the other a glue factory. But my
brother was not at all disconcerted: he ordered a score of
gooseberry bushes, planted them, and settled down to the life
of a country gentleman.

"Last year I paid him a visit. I thought I would go and see
how things were with him. In his letter to me my brother called
his estate 'Chumbaroklov Waste, or Gimalayskoe' (our surname was Chimsha-Gimalaysky). I reached the place in the
afternoon. It was hot. Everywhere there were ditches, fences,
hedges, rows of fir trees, and I was at a loss as to how to get
to the yard and where to leave my horse. I made my way to
the house and was met by a fat dog with reddish hair that
looked like a pig. It wanted to bark, but was too lazy. The
cook, a fat, barelegged woman, who also looked like a pig,
came out of the kitchen and said that the master was resting
after dinner. I went in to see my brother, and found him sitting
up in bed, with a quilt over his knees. He had grown older,
stouter, flabby; his cheeks, his nose, his lips jutted out: it
looked as though he might grunt into the quilt at any moment.

"We embraced and dropped tears of joy and also of sadness
at the thought that the two of us had once been young, but
were now gray and nearing death. He got dressed and took me
out to show me his estate.

" 'Well, how are you getting on here?' I asked.

" 'Oh, all right, thank God. I am doing very well.'

"He was no longer the poor, timid clerk he used to be but
a real landowner, a gentleman. He had already grown used to
his new manner of living and developed a taste for it. He ate
a great deal, steamed himself in the bathhouse, was growing
stout, was already having a lawsuit with the village commune
and the two factories and was very much offended when the
peasants failed to address him as 'Your Honor.' And he concerned himself with his soul's welfare too in a substantial,
upperclass manner, and performed good deeds not simply, but
pompously. And what good works! He dosed the peasants with
bicarbonate and castor oil for all their ailments and on his
name day he had a thanksgiving service celebrated in the center
of the village, and then treated the villagers to a gallon of
vodka, which he thought was the thing to do. Oh, those hor-

rible gallons of vodka! One day a fat landowner hauls the peasants up before the rural police officer for trespassing, and the next, to mark a feast day, treats them to a gallon of vodka, and they drink and shout 'Hurrah' and when they are drunk bow down at his feet. A higher standard of living, overeating and idleness develop the most insolent self-conceit in a Russian. Nikolay Ivanich, who when he was a petty official was afraid to have opinions of his own even if he kept them to himself, now uttered nothing but incontrovertible truths and did so in the tone of a minister of state: 'Education is necessary, but the masses are not ready for it; corporal punishment is generally harmful, but in some cases it is useful and nothing else will serve.'

" 'I know the common people, and I know how to deal with them,' he would say. 'They love me. I only have to raise my little finger, and they will do anything I want.'

"And all this, mark you, would be said with a smile that bespoke kindness and intelligence. Twenty times over he repeated: 'We, of the gentry,' 'I, as a member of the gentry.' Apparently he no longer remembered that our grandfather had been a peasant and our father just a private. Even our surname, 'Chimsha-Gimalaysky,' which in reality is grotesque, seemed to him sonorous, distinguished, and delightful.

"But I am concerned now not with him, but with me. I want to tell you about the change that took place in me during the few hours that I spent on his estate. In the evening when we were having tea, the cook served a plateful of gooseberries. They were not bought, they were his own gooseberries, the first ones picked since the bushes were planted. My brother gave a laugh and for a minute looked at the gooseberries in silence, with tears in his eyes—he could not speak for excitement. Then he put one berry in his mouth, glanced at me with the triumph of a child who has at last been given a toy he was longing for and said: 'How tasty!' And he ate the gooseberries greedily, and kept repeating: 'Ah, how delicious! Do taste them!'

"They were hard and sour, but as Pushkin has it,
The falsehood that exalts we cherish more
Than meaner truths that are a thousand strong.

I saw a happy man, one whose cherished dream had so obviously come true, who had attained his goal in life, who had got what he wanted, who was satisfied with his lot and with himself. For some reason an element of sadness had always mingled with my thoughts of human happiness, and now at the sight of a happy man I was assailed by an oppressive feeling bordering on despair. It weighed on me particularly at night. A bed was made up for me in a room next to my brother's bedroom, and I could hear that he was wakeful, and that he would get up again and again, go to the plate of gooseberries and eat one after another. I said to myself: how many contented, happy people there really are! What an overwhelming force they are! Look at life: the insolence and idleness of the strong, the ignorance and brutishness of the weak, horrible poverty everywhere, overcrowding, degeneration, drunkenness, hypocrisy, lying— Yet in all the houses and on all the streets there is peace and quiet; of the fifty thousand people who live in our town there is not one who would cry out, who would vent his indignation aloud. We see the people who go to market, eat by day, sleep by night, who babble nonsense, marry, grow old, good-naturedly drag their dead to the cemetery, but we do not see or hear those who suffer, and what is terrible in life goes on somewhere behind the scenes. Everything is peaceful and quiet and only mute statistics protest: so many people gone out of their minds, so many gallons of vodka drunk, so many children dead from malnutrition— And such a state of things is evidently necessary; obviously the happy man is at ease only because the unhappy ones bear their burdens in silence, and if there were not this silence, happiness would be impossible. It is a general hypnosis. Behind the door of every contented, happy man there ought to be someone standing with a little hammer and continually reminding him with a knock that there are unhappy people, that however happy he may be, life will sooner or later show him its claws, and trouble will come to him—illness, poverty, losses, and then no one will see or hear him, just as now he neither sees nor hears others. But there is no man with a hammer. The happy man lives at his ease, faintly fluttered by small daily cares, like an aspen in the wind—and all is well."

"That night I came to understand that I too had been contented and happy," Ivan Ivanich continued, getting up. "I too over the dinner table or out hunting would hold forth on how to live, what to believe, the right way to govern the people. I too would say that learning was the enemy of darkness, that education was necessary but that for the common people the three R's were sufficient for the time being. Freedom is a boon,

I used to say, it is as essential as air, but we must wait awhile. Yes, that's what I used to say, and now I ask: Why must we wait?" said Ivan Ivanich, looking wrathfully at Burkin. "Why must we wait, I ask you? For what reason? I am told that nothing can be done all at once, that every idea is realized gradually, in its own time. But who is it that says so? Where is the proof that it is just? You cite the natural order of things, the law governing all phenomena, but is there law, is there order in the fact that I, a living, thinking man, stand beside a ditch and wait for it to close up of itself or fill up with silt, when I could jump over it or throw a bridge across it? And again, why must we wait? Wait, until we have no strength to live, and yet we have to live and are eager to live!

"I left my brother's place early in the morning, and ever since then it has become intolerable for me to stay in town. I am oppressed by the peace and the quiet, I am afraid to look at the windows, for there is nothing that pains me more than the spectacle of a happy family sitting at table having tea. I am an old man now and unfit for combat, I am not even capable of hating. I can only grieve inwardly, get irritated, worked up, and at night my head is ablaze with the rush of ideas and I cannot sleep. Oh, if I were young!"

Ivan Ivanich paced up and down the room excitedly and repeated, "If I were young!"

He suddenly walked up to Alyokhin and began to press now one of his hands, now the other.

"Pavel Konstantinich," he said imploringly, "don't quiet down, don't let yourself be lulled to sleep! As long as you are young, strong, alert, do not cease to do good! There is no happiness and there should be none, and if life has a meaning and a purpose, that meaning and purpose is not our happiness but something greater and more rational. Do good!"

All this Ivan Ivanich said with a pitiful, imploring smile, as though he were asking a personal favor.

Afterwards all three of them sat in armchairs in different corners of the drawing room and were silent. Ivan Ivanich's story satisfied neither Burkin nor Alyokhin. With the ladies and generals looking down from the golden frames, seeming alive in the dim light, it was tedious to listen to the story of the poor devil of a clerk who ate gooseberries. One felt like talking about elegant people, about women. And the fact that they were sitting in a drawing room where everything—the chandelier under its cover, the armchairs, the carpets underfoot—testified that the very people who were now looking down from the frames had once moved about here, sat and had tea, and the fact that lovely Pelageya was noiselessly moving about—that was better than any story.

Alyokhin was very sleepy; he had gotten up early, before three o'clock in the morning, to get some work done, and now he could hardly keep his eyes open, but he was afraid his visitors might tell an interesting story in his absence, and he would not leave. He did not trouble to ask himself if what Ivan Ivanich had just said was intelligent or right. The guests were not talking about groats, or hay, or tar, but about something that had no direct bearing on his life, and he was glad of it and wanted them to go on.

"However, it's bedtime," said Burkin, rising. "Allow me to wish you good night."

Alyokhin took leave of his guests and went downstairs to his own quarters, while they remained upstairs. They were installed for the night in a big room in which stood two old wooden beds decorated with carvings and in the corner was an ivory crucifix. The wide cool beds which had been made by the lovely Pelageya gave off a pleasant smell of clean linen.

Ivan Ivanich undressed silently and got into bed.

"Lord forgive us sinners!" he murmured, and drew the bedclothes over his head.

His pipe, which lay on the table, smelled strongly of burnt tobacco, and Burkin, who could not sleep for a long time, kept wondering where the unpleasant odor came from.

The rain beat against the window panes all night.

✠ ✠
✠

Leonid Andreyev

✠ ✠
✠
✠ ✠

Lazarus

✠

When Lazarus rose from the grave, after three days and nights in the mysterious thraldom of death, and returned alive to his home, it was a long time before anyone noticed the evil peculiarities in him that were later to make his very name terrible. His friends and relatives were jubilant that he had come back to life. They surrounded him with tenderness, they were lavish of their eager attentions, spending the greatest care upon his food and drink and the new garments they made for him. They clad him gorgeously in the glowing colors of hope and laughter, and when, arrayed like a bridegroom, he sat at the table with them again, ate again, and drank again, they wept fondly and summoned the neighbors to look upon the man miraculously raised from the dead.

The neighbors came and were moved with joy. Strangers arrived from distant cities and villages to worship the miracle. They burst into stormy exclamations, and buzzed around the house of Mary and Martha, like so many bees.

That which was new in Lazarus' face and gestures they explained naturally, as the traces of his severe illness and the shock he had passed through. It was evident that the disintegration of the body had been halted by a miraculous power, but that the restoration had not been complete; that death had left upon his face and body the effect of an artist's unfinished sketch seen through a thin glass. On his temples, under his eyes, and in the hollow of his cheek lay a thick, earthy blue. His fingers were blue, too, and, under his nails, which had grown long in the grave, the blue had turned livid. Here and there on his lips and body, the skin, blistered in the grave, had burst open and left reddish glistening cracks, as if covered with a thin, glassy slime. And he had grown exceedingly stout. His body was horribly bloated and suggested the fetid, damp smell of putrefaction. But the cadaverous, heavy odor that

clung to his burial garments, and, as it seemed, to his very
body, soon wore off, and after some time the blue of his hands
and face softened, and the reddish cracks of his skin smoothed
out, though they never disappeared completely. Such was the
aspect of Lazarus in his second life. It looked natural only to
those who had seen him buried.

Not merely Lazarus' face, but his very character, it seemed,
had changed; though it astonished no one and did not attract
the attention it deserved. Before his death Lazarus had been
cheerful and careless, a lover of laughter and harmless jest. It
was because of his good humor, pleasant and equable, his freedom from meanness and gloom, that he had been so beloved
by the Master. Now he was grave and silent; neither he himself jested nor did he laugh at the jests of others; and the words
he occasionally spoke were simple, ordinary and necessary
words—words as much devoid of sense and depth as are the
sounds with which an animal expresses pain and pleasure, thirst
and hunger. Such words a man may speak all his life, and no
one would ever know the sorrows and joys that dwelt within
him.

Thus it was that Lazarus sat at the festive table among his
friends and relatives—his face the face of a corpse over which,
for three days, death had reigned in darkness; his garments
gorgeous and festive, glittering with gold, bloody red and
purple; his mien heavy and silent. He was horribly changed
and strange, but as yet undiscovered. In high waves, now mild,
now stormy, the festivities went on around him. Warm glances
of love caressed his face, still cold with the touch of the grave;
and a friend's warm hand patted his bluish, heavy hand. And
the music played joyous tunes mingled of the sounds of the
tympanum, the pipe, the zither and the dulcimer. It was as if
bees were humming, locusts buzzing and birds singing over the
happy home of Mary and Martha.

II

Someone recklessly lifted the veil. By one breath of an uttered
word he destroyed the serene charm, and uncovered the truth
in its ugly nakedness. No thought was clearly defined in his
mind when he smilingly asked, "Why don't you tell us, Lazarus, what was There?" And all became silent, struck with the
question. Only now did it seem to occur to them that for three

days Lazarus had been dead; and they looked with curiosity, awaiting an answer. But Lazarus remained silent.

"You won't tell us?" the inquirer wondered. "Is it so terrible There?" Again his thought lagged behind his words. Had it preceded them, he would not have asked the question, for, at the very moment he uttered it, his heart sank with a dread fear.

All grew restless; they awaited the words of Lazarus anxiously. But he was silent, cold and severe, and his eyes were cast down. And now, as if for the first time, they perceived the horrible bluishness of his face and the loathsome corpulence of his body. On the table, as if forgotten by Lazarus, lay his livid blue hand, and all eyes were riveted upon it, as though expecting the desired answer from that hand. The musicians still played; then silence fell upon them, too, and the gay sounds died down, as scattered coals are extinguished by water. The pipe became mute, and the ringing tympanum and the murmuring dulcimer; and as though a chord were broken, as though song itself were dying, the zither echoed a trembling, broken sound. Then all was quiet.

"You won't?" the inquirer repeated, unable to restrain his babbling tongue. Silence reigned, and the livid blue hand lay motionless. It moved slightly, and the company sighed with relief and raised their eyes. Lazarus, risen from the dead, was looking straight at them, embracing all with one glance, heavy and terrible.

This was on the third day after Lazarus had arisen from the grave. Since then, many had felt that his gaze was the gaze of destruction, but neither those who had been forever crushed by it, nor those who in the prime of life (mysterious even as death) had found the will to resist his glance, could ever explain the terror that lay immovable in the depths of his black pupils. He looked quiet and simple. One felt that he had no intention to hide anything, but also no intention to tell anything. His look was cold, as of one who is entirely indifferent to all that is alive. And many careless people who pressed around him, and did not notice him, later learned with wonder and fear the name of this stout, quiet man who brushed against them with his sumptuous, gaudy garments. The sun did not stop shining when he looked, neither did the fountain cease playing, and the eastern sky remained cloudless and blue as always; but the man who fell under his inscrutable gaze could no longer feel the sun, nor hear the fountain, nor recognize his native sky. Sometimes he would cry bitterly, sometimes tear his hair in despair and madly call for help; but generally it happened that the men thus stricken by the gaze of Lazarus began to fade away listlessly and quietly and pass into a slow death lasting many long years. They died in the presence of everybody, colorless, haggard and gloomy, like trees withering on rocky ground. Those who screamed in madness sometimes came back to life; but the others, never.

"So you won't tell us, Lazarus, what you saw There?" the inquirer repeated for the third time. But now his voice was dull, and a dead, gray weariness had appeared in his eyes. The faces of all present were also covered by the same dead, gray weariness, like a mist. The guests stared at one another stupidly, not knowing why they had come together or why they sat around this rich table. They stopped talking, and vaguely felt it was time to leave; but they could not overcome the lassitude that spread through their muscles. So they continued to sit there, each one isolated, like little dim lights scattered in the darkness of night.

The musicians were paid to play, and they again took up the instruments, and again played gay or mournful airs. But it was music made to order, always the same tunes, and the guests listened wonderingly. Why was this music necessary, they thought, why was it necessary and what good did it do for people to pull at strings and blow their cheeks into thin pipes, and produce varied and strange-sounding noises?

"How badly they play!" someone said.

The musicians were insulted and left. Then the guests departed one by one, for it was nearing night. And when the quiet darkness enveloped them, and it became easier to breathe, the image of Lazarus suddenly arose in stern splendor before each one. There he stood, with the blue face of a corpse and the raiment of a bridegroom, sumptuous and resplendent, in his eyes that cold stare in the depths of which lurked *The Horrible!* They stood still as if turned into stone. The darkness surrounded them, and in the midst of this darkness flamed up the horrible apparition, the supernatural vision, of the one who for three days had lain under the measureless power of death. Three days he had been dead. Thrice had the sun risen and set—and he had lain dead. The children had played, the water had murmured as it streamed over the rocks, the hot dust had clouded the highway—and he had been dead. And now he was among them again, touched them, looked at them—*looked at them!* And through the black rings of his pupils, as through dark glasses, the unfathomable *There* gazed upon humanity.

III

No one took care of Lazarus, and no friends or kindred remained with him. Only the great desert, enfolding the Holy City, came close to the threshold of his abode. It entered his home, and lay down on his couch like a spouse, and put out all the fires. No one cared for Lazarus. One after the other went away, even his sisters, Mary and Martha. For a long while Martha did not want to leave him, for she did not know who would nurse him or take care of him; and she cried and prayed. But one night, when the wind was roaming about the desert, and the rustling cypress trees were bending over the roof, she dressed herself quietly, and quietly went away. Lazarus probably heard how the door was slammed—it had not shut properly, and the wind kept knocking it continually against the post—but he did not rise, did not go out, did not try to find out the reason. And the whole night until the morning the cypress trees hissed over his head, and the door swung to and fro, allowing the cold, greedily prowling desert to enter his dwelling. Everybody shunned him as though he were a leper. They wanted to put a bell on his neck to avoid meeting him. But someone, turning pale, remarked it would be terrible if at night, under the windows, one should happen to hear Lazarus' bell, and all grew pale and assented.

Since he did nothing for himself, he would probably have starved had not his neighbors, in trepidation, saved some food for him. Children brought it to him. They did not fear him, neither did they laugh at him in the innocent cruelty in which children often laugh at unfortunates. They were indifferent to him, and Lazarus showed the same indifference to them. He showed no desire to thank them for their services; he did not try to pat the dark hands and look into the simple, shining, little eyes. Abandoned to the ravages of time and the desert, his house was falling to ruins, and his hungry, bleating goats had long been scattered among his neighbors. His wedding garments had grown old. He wore them without changing them, as he had donned them on that happy day when the musicians played. He did not see the difference between old and new, between torn and whole. The brilliant colors were burnt and faded; the vicious dogs of the city and the sharp thorns of the desert had rent the fine clothes to shreds.

During the day, when the sun beat down mercilessly upon all living things, and even the scorpions, convulsed with a mad desire to sting, hid under the stones, he sat motionless in the burning rays, lifting high his blue face and shaggy, wild beard.

While yet the people were unafraid to speak to him, some-one had asked him, "Poor Lazarus! Do you find it pleasant to sit so, and look at the sun?" And he answered, "Yes, it is pleasant."

The thought suggested itself to people that the cold of the three days in the grave had been so intense, its darkness so deep, that there was not in all the earth enough heat or light to warm Lazarus and lighten the gloom of his eyes; and in-quirers turned away with a sigh.

And when the setting sun, flat and purple red, descended to earth, Lazarus went into the desert and walked straight towards it, as though intending to reach it. Always he walked directly towards the sun, and those who tried to follow him and find out what he did at night in the desert had indelibly imprinted upon their mind's vision the black silhouette of a tall, stout man against the red background of an immense disk. The hor-rors of the night drove them away, and so they never found out what Lazarus did in the desert; but the image of the black form against the red was burned forever into their brains. Like an animal with a cinder in its eye, which furiously rubs its muzzle against its paws, they foolishly rubbed their eyes; but the impression left by Lazarus was ineffaceable, forgotten only in death.

There were people living far away who never saw Lazarus and only heard of him. With an audacious curiosity which is stronger than fear and feeds on fear, with a secret sneer in their hearts, some of them came to him one day as he basked in the sun, and entered into conversation with him. At that time his appearance had changed for the better and was not so frightful. At first the visitors snapped their fingers and thought disapprovingly of the foolish inhabitants of the Holy City. But when the short talk came to an end and they went home, their expression was such that the inhabitants of the Holy City at once knew their errand and said, "Here go some more madmen at whom Lazarus has looked." The speakers raised their hands in silent pity.

Other visitors came, among them brave warriors in clinking

armor, who knew not fear, and happy youths, who made merry with laughter and song. Busy merchants, jingling their coins, ran in for a while, and proud attendants at the Temple placed their staffs at Lazarus' door. But no one returned the same as he came. A frightful shadow fell upon their souls, and gave a new appearance to the old, familiar world.

Those who felt any desire to speak, after they had been stricken by the gaze of Lazarus, described the change that had come over them somewhat like this:

All objects seen by the eye and palpable to the hand became empty, light and transparent, as though they were light shadows in the darkness; and this darkness enveloped the whole universe. It was dispelled neither by the sun, nor by the moon, nor by the stars, but embraced the earth like a mother, and clothed it in a boundless, black veil.

Into all bodies it penetrated, even into iron and stone; and the particles of the body lost their unity and became lonely. Even to the heart of the particles it penetrated, and the particles of the particles became lonely.

The vast emptiness which surrounds the universe was not filled with things seen, with sun or moon or stars; it stretched boundless, penetrating everywhere, disuniting everything, body from body, particle from particle.

In emptiness the trees spread their roots, themselves empty; in emptiness rose phantom temples; palaces and houses—all empty; and in the emptiness moved restless Man, himself empty and light, like a shadow.

There was no more a sense of time; the beginning of all things and their end merged into one. In the very moment when a building was being erected and one could hear the builders striking with their hammers, one seemed already to see its ruins, and then emptiness where the ruins were.

A man was just born, and funeral candles were already lighted at his head, and then were extinguished; and soon there was emptiness where before had been the man and the candles.

And surrounded by Darkness and Empty Waste, Man trembled hopelessly before the dread of the Infinite.

So spoke those who had a desire to speak. But much more could probably have been told by those who did not want to talk, and who died in silence.

IV

At that time there lived in Rome a celebrated sculptor by the
name of Aurelius. Out of clay, marble and bronze he created
forms of gods and men of such beauty that this beauty was
proclaimed immortal. But he himself was not satisfied, and said
there was a supreme beauty that he had never succeeded in
expressing in marble or bronze. "I have not yet gathered the
radiance of the moon," he said; "I have not yet caught the
glare of the sun. There is no soul in my marble, there is no
life in my beautiful bronze." And when by moonlight he would
slowly wander along the roads, crossing the black shadows of
the cypress trees, his white tunic flashing in the moonlight,
those he met used to laugh good-naturedly and say, "Is it
moonlight that you're gathering, Aurelius? Why didn't you
bring some baskets along?"

And he, too, would laugh and point to his eyes and say,
"Here are the baskets in which I gather the light of the moon
and the radiance of the sun."

And that was the truth. In his eyes shone moon and sun.
But he could not transmit the radiance to marble. Therein lay
the greatest tragedy of his life. He was a descendant of an
ancient race of patricians, had a good wife and children, and
except in this one respect, lacked nothing.

When the dark rumor about Lazarus reached him, he consulted his wife and friends and decided to make the long voyage to Judea, in order that he might look upon the man miraculously raised from the dead. He felt lonely in those days
and hoped on the way to renew his jaded energies. What they
told him about Lazarus did not frighten him. He had meditated much upon death. He did not like it, nor did he like
those who tried to harmonize it with life. On this side, beautiful life; on the other, mysterious death, he reasoned, and no
better lot could befall a man than to live—to enjoy life and
the beauty of living. And he already had conceived a desire to
convince Lazarus of the truth of this view and to return his
soul to life even as his body had been returned. This task did
not appear impossible, for the reports about Lazarus, fearsome
and strange as they were, did not tell the whole truth about
him, but only carried a vague warning against something awful.

Lazarus was getting up from a stone to follow in the path
of the setting sun on the evening when the rich Roman, ac-

companied by an armed slave, approached him, and in a ringing voice called to him: "Lazarus!"

Lazarus saw a proud and beautiful face, made radiant by fame, and white garments and precious jewels shining in the sunlight. The ruddy rays of the sun lent to the head and face a likeness to dimly shining bronze—that was what Lazarus saw. He sank back to his seat obediently, and wearily lowered his eyes.

"It is true you are not beautiful, my poor Lazarus," the Roman said quietly, playing with his gold chain. "You are even frightful, my poor friend; and death was not lazy the day when you so carelessly fell into its arms. But you are as fat as a barrel, and 'Fat people are not bad,' as the great Cæsar said. I do not understand why people are so afraid of you. You will permit me to stay with you overnight? It is already late, and I have no abode."

Nobody had ever asked Lazarus to be allowed to pass the night with him.

"I have no bed," he said.

"I am somewhat of a warrior and can sleep sitting," the Roman replied. "We shall make a light."

"I have no light."

"Then we shall converse in the darkness, like two friends. I suppose you have some wine?"

"I have no wine."

The Roman laughed. "Now I understand why you are so gloomy and why you do not like your second life. No wine? Well, we shall do without. You know there are words that go to one's head even as Falernian wine."

With a motion of his head he dismissed the slave, and they were alone. And again the sculptor spoke, but it seemed as though the sinking sun had penetrated into his words. They faded, pale and empty, as if trembling on weak feet, as if slipping and falling, drunk with the wine of anguish and despair. And black chasms appeared between the two men—like remote hints of vast emptiness and vast darkness.

"Now I am your guest and you will not ill-treat me, Lazarus!" said the Roman. "Hospitality is binding even upon those who have been three days dead. Three days, I am told, you were in the grave. It must have been cold there . . . and it is from there that you have brought this bad habit of doing without light and wine. I like a light. It gets dark so quickly here. Your eyebrows and forehead have an interesting line:

even as the ruins of castles covered with the ashes of an earth-
quake. But why in such strange, ugly clothes? I have seen the
bridegrooms of your country, they wear clothes like that—such
ridiculous clothes—such awful garments. . . . Are you a
bridegroom?"

Already the sun had disappeared. A gigantic black shadow
was approaching fast from the west, as if prodigious bare feet
were rustling over the sand. And the chill breezes stole up
behind.

"In the darkness you seem even bigger, Lazarus, as though
you had grown stouter in these few minutes. Do you feed on
darkness, perchance? . . . And I would like a light . . . just
a small light . . . just a small light. And I am cold. The nights
here are so barbarously cold. . . . If it were not so dark, I
should say you were looking at me, Lazarus. Yes, it seems, you
are looking. You are looking. *You are looking at me!* . . . I
feel it . . . now you are smiling."

The night had come, and a heavy blackness filled the air.

"How good it will be when the sun rises again tomorrow.
. . . You know, I am a great sculptor . . . so my friends call
me. I create, yes, they say I create, but for that daylight is
necessary. I give life to cold marble. I melt the ringing bronze
in the fire, in a bright, hot fire. Why did you touch me with
your hand?"

"Come," Lazarus said, "you are my guest." And they went
into the house. And the shadows of the long evening fell on
the earth. . . .

The slave at last grew tired waiting for his master, and when
the sun stood high he came to the house. And he saw, directly
under its burning rays, Lazarus and his master sitting close
together. They looked straight up and were silent.

The slave wept and cried aloud, "Master, what ails you,
Master!"

The same day Aurelius left for Rome. The whole way he
was thoughtful and silent, attentively examining everything, the
people, the ship, and the sea, as though endeavoring to recall
something. On the sea a great storm overtook them, and all
the while Aurelius remained on deck and gazed eagerly at the
approaching and falling waves. When he reached home his
family were shocked at the terrible change in his demeanor,
but he calmed them with the words, "I have found it!"

In the dusty clothes which he had worn during the entire
journey and had not changed, he began his work, and the mar-

ble ringingly responded to the resounding blows of the hammer. Long and eagerly he worked, admitting no one. At last, one morning, he announced that the work was ready, and gave instructions that all his friends, and the severe critics and judges of art, be called together. Then he donned gorgeous garments, shining with gold, glowing with the purple of the byssin.

"Here is what I have created," he said thoughtfully.

His friends looked, and immediately the shadow of deep sorrow covered their faces. It was a thing monstrous, possessing none of the forms familiar to the eye, yet not devoid of a hint of some new unknown form. On a thin, tortuous little branch, or rather an ugly likeness of one, lay crooked, strange, unsightly, shapeless heaps of something turned outside in, or something turned inside out—wild fragments which seemed to be feebly trying to get away from themselves. And, accidentally, they noticed under one of the wild projections a wonderfully sculptured butterfly, with transparent wings, trembling as though with a weak longing to fly.

"Why that wonderful butterfly, Aurelius?" someone timidly asked.

"I do not know," the sculptor answered.

The truth had to be told, and one of his friends, the one who loved Aurelius best, said, "This is ugly, my poor friend. It must be destroyed. Give me the hammer." And with two blows he destroyed the monstrous mass, leaving only the wonderfully sculptured butterfly.

After that, Aurelius created nothing. He looked with absolute indifference at marble and at bronze and at his own divine creations, in which dwelt immortal beauty. In the hope of breathing into him once again the old flame of inspiration, with the idea of awakening his dead soul, his friends led him to see the beautiful creations of others, but he remained indifferent and no smile warmed his closed lips. And only after they spoke to him much and long of beauty, he would reply wearily, "But all this is—a lie."

And in the daytime, when the sun was shining, he would go into his rich and beautifully laid out garden, and finding a place where there was no shadow, would expose his bare head and his dull eyes to the glitter and burning heat of the sun. Red and white butterflies fluttered around; down into the marble cistern ran splashing water from the crooked mouth of a blissfully drunken Satyr; but he sat motionless, like a pale shadow of that other one who, in a far land, at the very gates of the stony desert, also sat motionless under the fiery sun.

V

And it came about finally that Lazarus was summoned to Rome by the great Augustus.

They dressed him in gorgeous garments as though it had been ordained that he was to remain a bridegroom to an unknown bride until the very day of his death. It was as if an old coffin, rotten and falling apart, were regilded over and over, and gay tassels were hung on it. And solemnly they conducted him in gala attire, as though in truth it were a bridal procession, the runners loudly sounding the trumpet that the way be made for the ambassadors of the Emperor. But the roads along which he passed were deserted. His entire native land cursed the execrable name of Lazarus, the man miraculously brought to life, and the people scattered at the mere report of his horrible approach. The trumpeters blew lonely blasts, and only the desert answered with a dying echo.

Then they carried him across the sea on the saddest and most gorgeous ship that was ever mirrored in the azure waves of the Mediterranean. There were many people aboard, but the ship was silent and still as a coffin, and the water seemed to moan as it parted before the short, curved prow. Lazarus sat lonely, baring his head to the sun and listening in silence to the splashing of the waters. Further away the seamen and the ambassadors gathered like a crowd of distressed shadows. If a thunderstorm had happened to burst upon them at that time, or the wind had overwhelmed the red sails, the ship would probably have perished, for none of those who were on her had strength or desire enough to fight for life. With supreme effort some went to the side of the ship and eagerly gazed at the blue, transparent abyss. Perhaps they imagined they saw a naiad flashing a pink shoulder through the waves, or an insanely joyous and drunken centaur galloping by, splashing up the water with his hoofs. But the sea was deserted and mute, and so was the watery abyss.

Listlessly Lazarus set foot on the streets of the Eternal City, as though all its riches, all the majesty of its gigantic edifices, all the luster and beauty and music of refined life, were simply the echo of the wind in the desert, or the misty images of hot, running sand. Chariots whirled by; the crowd of strong, beautiful, haughty men passed on, builders of the Eternal City and proud partakers of its life; songs rang out; fountains laughed; pearly laughter of women filled the air, while the drunkard philosophized and the sober ones smilingly listened; horseshoes rattled on the pavement. And surrounded on all sides by glad sounds, a fat, heavy man moved like a cold spot of silence through the center of the city, sowing in his path grief, anger and vague, carking distress. Who dared to be sad in Rome? frowning citizens indignantly demanded; and in two days the swift-tongued Rome knew of Lazarus, the man miraculously raised from the grave, and timidly evaded him.

There were many brave men ready to try their strength, and at their senseless call Lazarus came obediently. The Emperor was so engrossed with state affairs that he delayed receiving the visitor, and for seven days Lazarus moved among the people.

A jovial drunkard met him, with a smile on his red lips. "Drink, Lazarus, drink!" he cried. "Wouldn't Augustus laugh to see you drink!" And naked, besotted women laughed, and decked the blue hands of Lazarus with rose leaves. But the drunkard looked into the eyes of Lazarus—and his joy ended forever. Thereafter he was always drunk. He drank no more, but was drunk all the time, shadowed by fearful dreams, instead of the joyous reveries that wine gives. Fearful dreams became the food of his broken spirit. Fearful dreams held him day and night in the mists of monstrous fantasy, and death itself was no more fearful than the apparition of its fierce precursor.

Lazarus came to a youth and his lass who loved each other and were beautiful in their love. Proudly and strongly holding in his arms his beloved one, the youth said, with gentle pity, "Look at us, Lazarus, and rejoice with us. Is there anything stronger than love?"

And Lazarus looked at them. And their whole life they continued to love one another, but their love became mournful and gloomy, even as those cypress trees over the tombs that feed their roots on the putrescence of the grave and strive in vain in the quiet evening hour to touch the sky with their pointed tops. Hurled by fathomless life forces into each other's arms, they mingled their kisses with tears, their joy with pain, and only succeeded in realizing the more vividly a sense of their slavery to the silent Nothing. Forever united, forever parted, they flashed like sparks, and, like sparks, went out in boundless darkness.

Lazarus came to a proud sage, and the sage said to him, "I already know all the horrors that you may tell me, Lazarus. With what else can you terrify me?"

Only a few moments passed, before the sage realized that the knowledge of the horrible is not the horrible, and that the sight of death is not death. And he felt that in the eyes of the Infinite, wisdom and folly are the same, for the Infinite knows them not. And the boundaries between knowledge and ignorance, between truth and falsehood, between top and bottom, faded, and his shapeless thought was suspended in emptiness. Then he grasped his gray head in his hands and cried out insanely, "I can't think! I can't think!"

Thus it was that under the cool gaze of Lazarus, the man miraculously raised from the dead, all that serves to arm life, its sense and its joys, perished. And people began to say it was dangerous to allow him to see the Emperor; that it would be better to kill him and bury him secretly, and swear he had disappeared. Swords were sharpened, and youths devoted to the welfare of the people announced their readiness to become assassins, when Augustus upset the cruel plans by demanding that Lazarus appear before him.

Even though Lazarus could not be kept away, it was felt that the heavy impression conveyed by his face might be somewhat softened. With that end in view, expert painters, barbers and artists were secured, and they worked on Lazarus' head the whole night. His beard was trimmed and curled. The disagreeable and deadly bluishness of his hands and face was covered up with paint; his hands were whitened, his cheeks rouged. The disgusting wrinkles of suffering that ridged his old face were patched up and painted, and on the smooth surface, wrinkles of good nature and laughter, and of pleasant, good-humored cheeriness, were laid on artistically with fine brushes.

Lazarus submitted indifferently to all they did with him, and soon was transformed into a stout, nice-looking old man, for all the world a quiet and good-humored grandfather of numerous grandchildren. He looked as though the smile with which he told funny stories had not left his lips, as though a quiet tenderness still lay hidden in the corner of his eyes. But the wedding dress they did not dare to take off; and they could not change his eyes—the dark, terrible eyes from out of which stared the incomprehensible *There*.

VI

Lazarus was untouched by the magnificence of the imperial apartments. He remained stolidly indifferent, as though he saw no contrast between his ruined house at the edge of the desert and the solid, beautiful palace of stone. Under his feet the hard marble of the floor took on the semblance of the moving sands of the desert, and to his eyes the throngs of gaily dressed, haughty men were as unreal as the emptiness of the air. They looked not into his face as he passed by, fearing to come under the awful bane of his eyes; but when the sound of his heavy steps announced that he had passed, heads were lifted, and eyes examined with timid curiosity the figure of the corpulent, tall, slightly stooping old man, as he slowly passed into the heart of the imperial palace. If death itself had appeared, men would not have feared it so much; for hitherto death had been known to the dead only, and life to the living only, and between these two there had been no bridge. But this strange being knew death, and that knowledge of his was felt to be mysterious and cursed. "He will kill our great, divine Augustus," men cried with horror, and they hurled curses after him. Slowly and stolidly he passed by them, penetrating even deeper into the palace.

Cæsar knew already who Lazarus was, and was prepared to meet him. He was a courageous man; he felt his power was invincible, and in the fateful encounter with the man "wonderfully raised from the dead" he refused to lean on other men's weak help. Man to man, face to face, he met Lazarus.

"Do not fix your gaze on me, Lazarus," he commanded. "I have heard that your head is like the head of Medusa, and turns into stone all upon whom you look. But I should like to have a close look at you, and to talk to you before I turn into stone," he added in a spirit of playfulness that concealed his real misgivings.

Approaching him, he examined closely Lazarus' face and his strange festive clothes. Though his eyes were sharp and keen, he was deceived by the skillful counterfeit.

"Well, your appearance is not terrible, venerable sir. But

all the worse for men, when the terrible takes on such a venerable and pleasant appearance. Now let us talk."

Augustus sat down, and as much by glance as by words began the discussion. "Why did you not salute me when you entered?"

Lazarus answered indifferently, "I did not know it was necessary."

"You are a Christian?"

"No."

Augustus nodded approvingly. "That is good. I do not like the Christians. They shake the tree of life, forbidding it to bear fruit, and they scatter to the wind its fragrant blossoms. But who are you?"

With some effort Lazarus answered, "I was dead."

"I heard about that. But who are you now?"

Lazarus' answer came slowly. Finally he said again, listlessly and indistinctly, "I was dead."

"Listen to me, stranger," said the Emperor sharply, giving expression to what had been in his mind before. "My empire is an empire of the living; my people are a people of the living and not of the dead. You are superfluous here. I do not know who you are, I do not know what you have seen There, but if you lie, I hate your lies, and if you tell the truth, I hate your truth. In my heart I feel the pulse of life; in my hands I feel power, and my proud thoughts, like eagles, fly through space. Behind my back, under the protection of my authority, under the shadow of the laws I have created, men live and labor and rejoice. Do you hear this divine harmony of life? Do you hear the war cry that men hurl into the face of the future, challenging it to strife?"

Augustus extended his arms reverently and solemnly cried out, "Blessed art thou, Great Divine Life!"

But Lazarus was silent, and the Emperor continued more severely: "You are not wanted here. Pitiful remnant, half devoured of death, you fill men with distress and aversion to life. Like a caterpillar on the fields, you are gnawing away at the full seed of joy, exuding the slime of despair and sorrow. Your truth is like a rusted sword in the hands of a night assassin, and I shall condemn you to death as an assassin. But first I want to look into your eyes. Mayhap only cowards fear them, and brave men are spurred on to struggle and victory. Then will you merit not death but a reward. Look at me, Lazarus."

At first it seemed to divine Augustus as if a friend were

looking at him, so soft, so alluringly, so gently fascinating was the gaze of Lazarus. It promised not horror but quiet rest, and the Infinite dwelt there as a fond mistress, a compassionate sister, a mother. And ever stronger grew its gentle embrace, until he felt, as it were, the breath of a mouth hungry for kisses. . . . Then it seemed as if iron bones protruded in a ravenous grip and closed upon him in an iron band; and cold nails touched his heart, and slowly, slowly sank into it.

"It pains me," said divine Augustus, growing pale; "but look, Lazarus, look!"

Ponderous gates, shutting off eternity, appeared to be slowly swinging open, and through the growing aperture poured in, coldly and calmly, the awful horror of the Infinite. Boundless Emptiness and Boundless Gloom entered like two shadows, extinguishing the sun, removing the ground from under the feet and the cover from over the head. And the pain in his icy heart ceased.

"Look at me, look at me, Lazarus!" commanded Augustus, staggering. . . .

Time ceased and the beginning of things came perilously near to the end. The throne of Augustus, so recently erected, fell to pieces, and emptiness took the place of the throne and of Augustus. Rome fell silently into ruins. A new city rose in its place, and it too was erased by emptiness. Like phantom giants, cities, kingdoms and countries swiftly fell and disappeared into emptiness—swallowed up in the black maw of the Infinite. . . .

"Cease," commanded the Emperor. Already the accent of indifference was in his voice. His arms hung powerless and his eagle eyes flashed and were dimmed again, struggling against overwhelming darkness. "You have killed me, Lazarus," he said drowsily.

These words of despair saved him. He thought of the people, whose shield he was destined to be, and a sharp, redeeming pang pierced his dull heart. He thought of them doomed to perish, and he was filled with anguish. First they seemed bright shadows in the gloom of the Infinite. How terrible! Then they appeared as fragile vessels with life-agitated blood, and hearts that knew both sorrow and great joy. And he thought of them with tenderness.

And so thinking and feeling, inclining the scales now to the side of life, now to the side of death, he slowly returned to life, to find in its suffering and joy a refuge from the gloom, emptiness and fear of the Infinite.

"No, you did not kill me, Lazarus," he said firmly. "But I will kill you. Go!"

Evening came, and divine Augustus partook of food and drink with great joy. But there were moments when his raised arm would remain suspended in the air, and the light of his shining, eager eyes was dimmed. It seemed as if an icy wave of horror washed against his feet. He was vanquished but not killed, and coldly awaited his doom, like a black shadow. His nights were haunted by horror, but the bright days still brought him the joys, as well as the sorrows, of life.

Next day, by order of the Emperor, they burned out Lazarus' eyes with hot irons and sent him home. Even Augustus dared not kill him.

Lazarus returned to the desert, and the desert received him with the breath of the hissing wind and the ardor of the glowing sun. Again, with matted beard uplifted, he sat on the stone; and two black holes, where the eyes had once been, looked dull and horrible at the sky. In the distance the Holy City surged and roared restlessly, but near him all was deserted and still. No one approached the place where Lazarus, miraculously raised from the dead, passed his last days, for his neighbors had long since abandoned their homes. His cursed knowledge, driven by the hot irons from his eyes deep into the brain, lay there in ambush; as if from ambush it might spring out upon men with a thousand unseen eyes. No one dared to look at Lazarus.

And in the evening, when the sun, swollen crimson and growing larger, bent its way towards the west, blind Lazarus slowly groped after it. He stumbled against stones and fell; corpulent and feeble, he rose heavily and walked on; and against the red curtain of sunset his dark form and outstretched arms gave him the semblance of a cross.

It happened once that he went and never returned. Thus ended the second life of Lazarus, who for three days had been in the mysterious thraldom of death and then was miraculously raised from the dead.

Ben Tobit

✠

On the dread day of that monstrous injustice, when Jesus Christ was crucified among the thieves on Golgotha—on that day, Ben Tobit, a merchant in Jerusalem, had been suffering from an unbearable toothache since the early hours of the morning. It had started the night before; his right jaw had begun to hurt, and one tooth, the one in front of the wisdom tooth, seemed to have risen a little and it hurt when he touched his tongue to it. But after supper the pain disappeared, and Ben Tobit promptly forgot all about it. In fact, he had that very day traded his old donkey advantageously for a young, strong one, and so he was in rather high spirits and totally unconcerned about the ominous symptom.

That night he slept very well and very soundly, but just before dawn something began to bother him, as if someone were calling him on matters of great importance, and when Ben Tobit awakened with annoyance, he found that the toothache had returned, a direct and racking one that assailed him with the full force of sharp, stabbing pain. But now he could not tell whether it was the same tooth that had hurt him the night before, or whether other teeth were involved as well; his mouth and his head were filled with excruciating pain, as if he were being forced to chew a thousand sharp, red-hot nails. He filled his mouth with cool water from an earthen jug, and the fury of the pain subsided for a moment; his mouth began to twitch and throb, and this sensation was almost pleasant compared to the previous one. Ben Tobit lay back on his bed. He thought about his new donkey and he thought of how fortunate he would be if it were not for his teeth.

He tried to fall asleep again, but the water became warm, and in five minutes the pain was back, more savage than before. Ben Tobit sat up in his bed, and soon his body swayed back and forth like a pendulum. His whole face was pulled together and puckered about a big nose, and on that nose, turned white with agony, a drop of cold sweat gathered. Thus

267

it was that, swaying back and forth and moaning in pain, he
beheld the first rays of the sun that was destined to see Golgotha with its three crosses and to grow dim with horror and
sorrow.

Ben Tobit was a kind and good man who disliked injustice,
but when his wife awakened, he had barely opened his mouth
before he began to say a great many unpleasant things to her,
complaining repeatedly that he was left alone, like a jackal, to
howl and to writhe in agony. His wife listened patiently to the
undeserved reproaches, for she knew it was not a mean heart
that made him say such things, and she brought him many fine
remedies: cleansed dung of rats to be applied to the cheek, a
strong tincture obtained from a scorpion, and an authentic
sliver of the stone tablets that had been smashed to bits by
Moses. The rat dung helped a little, but not for long, as did
also the tincture and the sliver, but each respite was followed
by a violent onslaught of even greater pain. During the brief
periods of relief, Ben Tobit comforted himself by thinking of
his little donkey and day-dreaming about him; but when he
felt worse, he moaned, scolded his wife, and threatened to
dash his head against a rock if the pain did not subside. And
he kept pacing all the time from one corner of the flat roof of
his house to the other, ashamed to get too close to its outer
edge because the kerchief he had tied around his head made
him look like a woman.

Several times children came running to him to tell him
hastily about Jesus of Nazareth. Ben Tobit would stop for
a moment to listen to them; then he would contract his face
and, stamping his foot angrily, would send them on their way.
He was a kind man and fond of children, but now it irritated
him to be pestered with all sorts of silly things.

He was also irritated because many people in the street
and on neighboring roofs seemed to have nothing better to
do than to stare in curiosity at him with his head wrapped
in a kerchief like a woman's. He was just about to go downstairs when his wife called to him:

"Look, there are the thieves! This might interest you!"

"Leave me alone, please. Don't you see how I'm suffering?"
Ben Tobit answered angrily.

But his wife's words gave him a slight feeling that his toothache might be lessening. So he reluctantly went to the edge
of the roof. With his head tilted to one side, one eye closed,

his cheek in the palm of a hand, his face peevish and tearful, he looked down.

A huge, turbulently milling crowd, shrouded in dust, incessantly shouting, was moving up the steep, narrow street. Surrounded by the crowd, the criminals moved along with bodies bent low under the heavy burdens of the crosses, the whips of the Roman soldiers writhing like black snakes above them. One of them—the one who had long, fair hair and who was wearing a torn, blood-stained robe—stumbled on a stone someone had thrown at his feet and fell. The shouting grew louder and the crowd, like a many-colored sea, seemed to close over the fallen man. Ben Tobit suddenly winced with pain, as if someone had stabbed a red-hot needle into his tooth and twisted it there. He moaned, "Oh—oh—oh," and walked away from the edge of the roof, petulantly preoccupied and full of resentment.

"How they yell!" he said enviously, visualizing wide-open mouths with strong, never-aching teeth and thinking how he himself would be shouting if he were well. This mental image brought on another savage attack of pain. He kept shaking his kerchief-wrapped head, lowing, "M—moo—oo . . ."

"They say he healed the blind," said his wife, who had remained at the edge of the roof and had thrown a small stone at the place where Jesus, brought to his feet by the whips, moved along slowly.

"Yes, of course! Let him heal my toothache!" Ben Tobit retorted mockingly. "What a dust they kick up! Like a herd! They ought to be dispersed with a cane!" he added peevishly, in bitterness. "Help me down, Sarah!"

His wife was right; the spectacle did somewhat divert Ben Tobit, or perhaps it was the rat dung that helped him at last, and he managed to fall asleep. When he awakened, the pain was almost gone; there was only a small swelling on his right jaw, so small it was hardly noticeable. His wife said it was completely unnoticeable, but Ben Tobit smiled knowingly: he knew well what a good wife he had and how much she loved to say pleasant things. His neighbor Samuel, the tanner, came to visit, and Ben Tobit took him to see his little donkey; he listened with pride while Samuel praised him and the animal enthusiastically.

Then, to satisfy Sarah's insistent curiosity, the three of them went to see the men crucified on Golgotha. On the way, Ben Tobit told Samuel the whole story from the beginning, how he had felt an ache in his right jaw the previous evening and how he was wakened by an excruciating pain during the night. For greater effect, he put on the air of a martyr, closed his eyes, shook his head and groaned, while the gray-bearded Samuel nodded sympathetically and said, "Oh, oh, oh—how painful!"

Ben Tobit enjoyed the sympathy and repeated the story, going back to the remote past when he had first had a tooth go bad, down on the left side. So it was, in animated conversation, that they came to Golgotha. The sun that was destined to shine upon the world on this dread day had already set behind the far hills, and in the West a crimson strip like a bloody mark, stretched across the sky. Against this background the crosses stood dark and indistinct, while white-clad figures knelt at the foot of the middle cross.

The crowd had dispersed long before; it was growing cold, and, with a brief glance at the crucified men, Ben Tobit took Samuel's arm and gently turned him homeward. He felt particularly eloquent; he wanted to say more about the toothache. And so they walked away, Ben Tobit resuming the air of a martyr, shaking his head and groaning artfully, while Samuel nodded and exclaimed sympathetically. Black night was rising from the dark, deep gorges and from the distant, burned plains —as though it were trying to hide the enormous misdeed of the earth from the eyes of heaven.

Maxim Gorky

Twenty-six
Men
and a
Girl

✠

There were twenty-six of us—twenty-six living machines in a damp, underground cellar, where from morning till night we kneaded dough and rolled it into kringels.[1] Opposite the underground window of our cellar was a bricked area, green and moldy with moisture. The window was protected from outside with a close iron grating, and the light of the sun could not pierce through the window panes, covered as they were with flour dust.

Our employer had bars placed in front of the windows, so that we should not be able to give a bit of his bread to passing beggars, or to any of our fellows who were out of work and hungry. Our employer called us rogues, and gave us half rotten tripe to eat for our midday meal, instead of meat. It was swelteringly close for us cooped up in that stone underground chamber, under the low, heavy, soot-blackened, cobwebby ceiling. Dreary and sickening was our life between its thick, dirty, moldy walls.

Unrefreshed, and with a feeling of not having had our sleep out, we used to get up at five o'clock in the morning; and before six, we were already seated, worn out and apathetic, at the table, rolling out the dough which our mates had already prepared while we slept. The whole day, from ten in the early morning until ten at night, some of us sat round that table, working up in our hands the yielding paste, rolling it to and fro so that it should not get stiff; while the others kneaded the swelling mass of dough. And the whole day the simmering

[1] A kind of sweet roll.

water in the kettle, where the kringels were being cooked, sang low and sadly; and the baker's shovel scraped harshly over the oven floor, as he threw the slippery bits of dough out of the kettle on the heated bricks.

From morning till evening wood was burning in the oven, and the red glow of the fire gleamed and flickered over the walls of the bakeshop, as if silently mocking us. The giant oven was like the misshapen head of a monster in a fairy tale; it thrust itself up out of the floor, opened wide jaws, full of glowing fire, and blew hot breath upon us; it seemed to be ever watching out of its black air holes our interminable work. Those two deep holes were like eyes—the cold, pitiless eyes of a monster. They watched us always with the same darkened glance, as if they were weary of seeing before them such eternal slaves, from whom they could expect nothing human, and therefore scorned them with the cold scorn of wisdom.

In meal dust, in the mud which we brought in from the yard on our boots, in the hot, sticky atmosphere, day in, day out, we rolled the dough into kringels, which we moistened with our own sweat. And we hated our work with a glowing hatred; we never ate what had passed through our hands, and preferred black bread to kringels. Sitting opposite each other, at a long table—nine facing nine—we moved our hands and fingers mechanically during endlessly long hours, till we were so accustomed to our monotonous work that we ceased to pay any attention to it.

We had all studied each other so constantly, that each of us knew every wrinkle of his mates' faces. It was not long also before we had exhausted almost every topic of conversation; that is why we were most of the time silent, unless we were chaffing each other; but one cannot always find something about which to chaff another man, especially when that man is one's mate. Neither were we much given to finding fault with one another; how, indeed, could one of us poor devils be in a position to find fault with another, when we were all of us half dead and, as it were, turned to stone? For the heavy drudgery seemed to crush all feeling out of us. But silence is only terrible and fearful for those who have said everything and have nothing more to say to each other; for men, on the contrary, who have never begun to communicate with one another, it is easy and simple.

Sometimes, too, we sang; and this is how it happened that

we began to sing: one of us would sigh deeply in the midst of our toil, like an overdriven horse, and then we would begin one of those songs whose gentle swaying melody seems always to ease the burden on the singer's heart.

At first one sang by himself, and we others sat in silence listening to his solitary song, which, under the heavy vaulted roof of the cellar, died gradually away, and became extinguished, like a little fire in the steppes, on a wet autumn night, when the gray heaven hangs like a heavy mass over the earth. Then another would join in with the singer, and now two soft, sad voices would break into song in our narrow, dull hole of a cellar. Suddenly others would join in, and the song would roll forward like a wave, would grow louder and swell upward, till it would seem as if the damp, foul walls of our stone prison were widening out and opening. Then, all twenty-six of us would be singing; our loud, harmonious song would fill the whole cellar, our voices would travel outside and beyond, striking, as it were, against the walls in moaning sobs and sighs, moving our hearts with soft, tantalizing ache, tearing open old wounds, and awakening longings.

The singers would sigh deeply and heavily; suddenly one would become silent and listen to the others singing, then let his voice flow once more in the common tide. Another would exclaim in a stifled voice, "Ah!" and would shut his eyes, while the deep, full sound waves would show him, as it were, a road, in front of him—a sunlit, broad road in the distance, which he himself, in thought, wandered along.

But the flame flickers once more in the huge oven, the baker scrapes incessantly with his shovel, the water simmers in the kettle, and the flicker of the fire on the wall dances as before in silent mockery. While in other men's words we sing out our dumb grief, the weary burden of live men robbed of the sunlight, the burden of slaves.

So we lived, we six-and-twenty, in the vaultlike cellar of a great stone house, and we suffered each one of us, as if we had to bear on our shoulders the whole three stories of that house.

But we had something else good, besides the singing—something we loved, that perhaps took the place of the sunshine.

In the second story of our house there was established a gold embroiderer's shop, and there, living among the other embroidery girls, was Tanya, a little maidservant of sixteen. Every morning there peeped in through the glass door a rosy little face, with merry blue eyes; while a ringing, tender voice called out to us:

"Little prisoners! Have you any kringels, please, for me?"

At that clear sound, we knew so well, we all used to turn round, gazing with simple-hearted joy at the pure girlish face which smiled at us so sweetly. The sight of the small nose pressed against the windowpane, and of the white teeth gleaming between the half open lips, had become for us a daily pleasure. Tumbling over each other we used to jump up to open the door, and she would step in, bright and cheerful, holding out her apron, with her head thrown on one side, and a smile on her lips. Her thick, long chestnut hair fell over her shoulder and across her breast. But we, ugly, dirty and misshapen as we were, looked up at her—the threshold door was four steps above the floor—looked up at her with heads thrown back, wishing her good morning, and speaking strange, unaccustomed words, which we kept for her only. Our voices became softer when we spoke to her, our jests were lighter. For her—everything was different with us. The baker took from his oven a shovel of the best and the brownest kringels, and threw them deftly into Tanya's apron.

"Be off with you now, or the boss will catch you!" we warned her each time. She laughed roguishly, called out cheerfully: "Good-by, poor prisoners!" and slipped away as quick as a mouse.

That was all. But long after she had gone we talked about her to one another with pleasure. It was always the same thing as we had said yesterday and the day before, because everything about us, including ourselves and her, remained the same—as yesterday—and as always.

Painful and terrible it is when a man goes on living, while nothing changes around him; and when such an existence does not finally kill his soul, then the monotony becomes with time, even more and more painful. Generally we spoke about women in such a way, that sometimes it was loathsome to us ourselves to hear our rude, shameless talk. The women whom we knew deserved perhaps nothing better. But about Tanya we never let fall an evil word; none of us ever ventured so much as to lay a hand on her, even too free a jest she never heard from us. Maybe this was so because she never remained for long with us; she flashed on our eyes like a star falling from the sky, and vanished; and maybe because she was little and very beautiful, and everything beautiful calls forth respect, even in coarse people. And besides—though our life of penal labor had made us dull beasts, oxen, we were still men, and, like all men, could not live without worshipping something or other. Better than her we had none, and none but her took any notice of us, living in the cellar—no one, though there were dozens of people in the house. And then, too—most likely, this was the chief thing—we all regarded her as something of our own, something existing as it were only by virtue of our kringels. We took on ourselves in turns the duty of providing her with hot kringels, and this became for us like a daily sacrifice to our idol, it became almost a sacred rite, and every day it bound us more closely to her. Besides kringels, we gave Tanya a great deal of advice—to wear warmer clothes, not to run upstairs too quickly, not to carry heavy bundles of wood. She listened to all our counsels with a smile, answered them by a laugh, and never took our advice, but we were not offended at that; all we wanted was to show how much care we bestowed upon her.

Often she would apply to us with different requests, she asked us, for instance, to open the heavy door into the store-cellar, and to chop wood: with delight and a sort of pride, we did this for her, and everything else she wanted.

But when one of us asked her to mend his solitary shirt for him, she said, with a laugh of contempt:

"What next! A likely idea!"

We made great fun of the queer fellow who could entertain such an idea, and—never asked her to do anything else. We loved her—all is said in that. Man always wants to lay his love on someone, though sometimes he crushes, sometimes he sullies, with it; he may poison another life because he loves without respecting the beloved. We were bound to love Tanya, for we had no one else to love.

At times one of us would suddenly begin to reason like this:

"And why do we make so much of the wench? What is there in her? eh? What a to-do we make about her!"

The man who dared to utter such words we promptly and coarsely cut short—we wanted something to love: we had found it and loved it, and what we twenty-six loved must be for each of us unalterable, as a holy thing, and anyone who acted against us in this was our enemy. We loved, maybe, not what was really good, but you see there were twenty-six of us, and so we always wanted to see what was precious to us held sacred by the rest.

Our love is not less burdensome than hate, and maybe that is just why some proud souls maintain that our hate is more flattering than our love. But why do they not run away from us, if it is so?

Besides our department, our employer had also a bread bakery; it was in the same house, separated from our hole only by a wall; but the bakers—there were four of them—held aloof from us, considering their work superior to ours, and therefore themselves better than us; they never used to come into our workroom, and laughed contemptuously at us when they met us in the yard. We, too, did not go to see them; this was forbidden by our employer, from fear that we should steal the fancy bread. We did not like the bakers, because we envied them; their work was lighter than ours, they were paid more, and were better fed; they had a light, spacious workroom, and they were all so clean and healthy—and that made them hateful to us. We all looked gray and yellow; three of us had syphilis, several suffered from skin diseases, one was completely crippled by rheumatism. On holidays and in their leisure time the bakers wore pea jackets and creaking boots, two of them had accordions, and they all used to go for strolls in the town gardens—we wore filthy rags and leather clogs or plaited shoes on our feet, the police would not let us into the town gardens—could we possibly like the bakers?

And one day we learned that their chief baker had been drunk, the master had sacked him and had already taken on another, and that this other was a soldier, wore a satin waistcoat and a watch and gold chain. We were inquisitive to get a sight of such a dandy, and in the hope of catching a glimpse of him we kept running one after another out into the yard.

But he came of his own accord into our room. Kicking at the door, he pushed it open, and leaving it ajar, stood in the doorway smiling, and said to us:

"God help the work! Good morning, mates!"

The ice cold air, which streamed in through the open door, curled in streaks of vapor round his feet. He stood on the threshold, looked us up and down, and under his fair, twisted mustache gleamed big yellow teeth. His waistcoat was really something quite out of the common, blue-flowered, brilliant with shining little buttons of red stones. He also wore a watch chain.

He was a fine fellow, this soldier; tall, healthy, rosy-cheeked, and his big, clear eyes had a friendly, cheerful glance. He wore on his head a white starched cap, and from under his spot-lessly clean apron peeped the pointed toes of fashionable, well-blacked boots.

Our baker asked him politely to shut the door. The soldier did so without hurrying himself, and began to question us about the master. We explained to him, all speaking together, that our employer was a thorough-going brute, a rogue, a knave, and a slave driver; in a word, we repeated to him all that can and must be said about an employer, but cannot be repeated here. The soldier listened to us, twisted his mustache, and watched us with a friendly, open-hearted look.

"But haven't you got a lot of girls here?" he asked suddenly.

Some of us began to laugh deferentially, others put on a meaning expression, and one of us explained to the soldier that there were nine girls here.

"You make the most of them?" asked the soldier, with a wink.

We laughed, but not so loudly, and with some embarrass-ment. Many of us would have liked to have shown the soldier that we also were tremendous fellows with the girls, but not one of us could do so; and one of our number confessed as much, when he said in a low voice:

"That sort of thing is not in our line."

"Well, no; it wouldn't quite do for you," said the soldier with conviction, after having looked us over. "There is some-thing wanting about you all. You don't look the right sort. You've no sort of appearance; and the women, you see, they like a bold appearance, they will have a well setup body. Everything has to be tiptop for them. That's why they respect strength. They want an arm like that!"

The soldier drew his right hand, with its turned up shirt sleeve, out of his pocket, and showed us his bare arm. It was white and strong, and covered with shining yellow hairs.

"Leg and chest, all must be strong. And then a man must be dressed in the latest fashion, so as to show off his looks to ad-vantage. Yes, all the women take to me. Whether I call to them, or whether I beckon them, they with one accord, five at a time, throw themselves at my head."

He sat down on a flour sack, and told at length all about the way women loved him, and how bold he was with them. Then he left, and after the door had creaked to behind him, we sat for a long time silent, and thought about him and his talk. Then we all suddenly broke silence together, and it became apparent that we were all equally pleased with him. He was such a nice, openhearted fellow; he came to see us without any standoffishness, sat down and chatted. No one else came to us like that, and no one else talked to us in that friendly sort of way. And we continued to talk of him and his coming triumph among the embroidery girls, who passed us by with contemptuous sniffs when they saw us in the yard, or who looked straight through us as if we had been air. But we admired them always when we met them outside, or when they walked past our windows; in winter, in fur jackets and toques to match; in summer, in hats trimmed with flowers, and with colored parasols in their hands. We talked, however, about these girls in a way that would have made them mad with shame and rage, if they could have heard us.

"If only he does not get hold of little Tanya!" said the baker, suddenly, in an anxious tone of voice.

We were silent, for these words troubled us. Tanya had quite gone out of our minds, supplanted, put on one side by the strong, fine figure of the soldier.

Then began a lively discussion; some of us maintained that Tanya would never lower herself so; others thought she would not be able to resist him, and the third group proposed to give him a thrashing if he should try to annoy Tanya. And, finally, we all decided to watch the soldier and Tanya, and to warn the girl against him. This brought the discussion to an end.

Four weeks had passed by since then; during this time the soldier baked white bread, walked about with the gold embroidery girls, visited us often, but did not talk any more about his conquests; only twisted his mustache, and licked his lips lasciviously.

Tanya called in as usual every morning for "little kringels," and was as gay and as nice and friendly with us as ever. We certainly tried once or twice to talk to her about the soldier, but she called him a "goggle-eyed calf," and made fun of him all round, and that set our minds at rest. We saw how the gold embroidery girls carried on with the soldier, and we were proud of our girl; Tanya's behavior reflected honor on us all; we imitated her, and began in our talks to treat the soldier with small consideration. She became dearer to us, and we greeted her with more friendliness and kindliness every morning.

One day the soldier came to see us, a bit drunk, and sat

down and began to laugh. When we asked him what he was
laughing about, he explained to us:

"Why two of them—that Lidka girl and Grushka—have
been clawing each other on my account. You should have
seen the way they went for each other! Ha! ha! One got hold
of the other one by the hair, threw her down on the floor
of the passage, and sat on her! Ha! ha! ha! They scratched
and tore each others' faces. It was enough to make one die
with laughter! Why is it women can't fight fair? Why do they
always scratch one another, eh?"

He sat on the bench, healthy, fresh and jolly; he sat there
and went on laughing. We were silent. This time he made an
unpleasant impression on us.

"Well, it's a funny thing what luck I have with the women-
folk! Eh? I've laughed till I'm ill! One wink, and it's all over
with them! It's the d-devil!"

He raised his white hairy hands, and slapped them down
on his knees. And his eyes seemed to reflect such frank astonishment, as if he were himself quite surprised at his good
luck with women. His fat, red face glistened with delight and
self satisfaction, and he licked his lips more than ever.

Our baker scraped the shovel violently and angrily along
the oven floor, and all at once he said sarcastically:

"There's no great strength needed to pull up fir saplings,
but try a real pine tree."

"Why—what do you mean by saying that to me?" asked the
soldier.

"Oh, well . . ."

"What is it?"

"Nothing—it slipped out!"

"No, wait a minute! What's the point? What pine tree?"

Our baker did not answer, working rapidly away with the
shovel at the oven; flinging into it the half-cooked kringels,
taking out those that were done, and noisily throwing them
on the floor to the boys who were stringing them on bast. He
seemed to have forgotten the soldier and his conversation with
him. But the soldier had all at once dropped into a sort of
uneasiness. He got up on to his feet, and went to the oven, at
the risk of knocking against the handle of the shovel, which
was waving spasmodically in the air.

"No, tell me, do—who is it? You've insulted me. I? There's
not one could withstand me, n-no! And you say such insulting
things to me?"

He really seemed genuinely hurt. He must have had nothing else to pride himself on except his gift for seducing women;
maybe, except for that, there was nothing living in him, and
it was only that by which he could feel himself a living man.

There are men to whom the most precious and best thing
in their lives appears to be some disease of their soul or body.
They spend their whole life in relation to it, and only living
by it, suffering from it, they sustain themselves on it, they
complain of it to others, and so draw the attention of their
fellows to themselves. For that they extract sympathy from
people, and apart from it they have nothing at all. Take from
them that disease, cure them, and they will be miserable,
because they have lost their one resource in life—they are
left empty then. Sometimes a man's life is so poor, that he
is driven instinctively to prize his vice and to live by it; one
may say for a fact that often men are vicious from boredom.

The soldier was offended, he went up to our baker and
roared:

"No, tell me do—who?"

"Tell you?" the baker turned suddenly to him.

"Well?"

"You know Tanya?"

"Well?"

"Well, there then! Only try."

"I?"

"You!"

"Her? Why that's nothing to me—pooh!"

"We shall see!"

"You will see! Ha! ha!"

"She'll——"

"Give me a month!"

"What a braggart you are, soldier!"

"A fortnight! I'll prove it! Who is it? Tanya! Pooh!"

"Well, get out. You're in my way!"

"A fortnight—and it's done! Ah, you——"

"Get out, I say!"

Our baker, all at once, flew into a rage and brandished
his shovel. The soldier staggered away from him in amazement, looked at us, paused, and softly, malignantly said, "Oh,
all right, then!" and went away.

During the dispute we had all sat silent, absorbed in it. But
when the soldier had gone, eager, loud talk and noise arose
among us.

Some one shouted to the baker: "It's a bad job that you've started, Pavel!"

"Do your work!" answered the baker savagely.

We felt that the soldier had been deeply aggrieved, and that danger threatened Tanya. We felt this, and at the same time we were all possessed by a burning curiosity, most agreeable to us. What would happen? Would Tanya hold out against the soldier? And almost all cried confidently: "Tanya? She'll hold out! You won't catch her with your bare arms!"

We longed terribly to test the strength of our idol; we forcibly proved to each other that our divinity was a strong divinity and would come victorious out of this ordeal. We began at last to fancy that we had not worked enough on the soldier, that he would forget the dispute, and that we ought to pique his vanity more keenly. From that day we began to live a different life, a life of nervous tension, such as we had never known before. We spent whole days in arguing together; we all grew, as it were, sharper; and got to talk more and better. It seemed to us that we were playing some sort of game with the devil, and the stake on our side was Tanya. And when we learned from the bakers that the soldier had begun "running after our Tanya," we felt a sort of delighted terror, and life was so interesting that we did not even notice that our employer had taken advantage of our preoccupation to increase our work by fourteen pounds of dough a day. We seemed, indeed, not even tired by our work. Tanya's name was on our lips all day long. And every day we looked for her with a certain special impatience. Sometimes we pictured to ourselves that she would come to us, and it would not be the same Tanya as of old, but somehow different. We said nothing to her, however, of the dispute regarding her. We asked her no questions, and behaved as well and affectionately to her as ever. But even in this a new element crept in, alien to our old feeling for Tanya—and that new element was keen curiosity, keen and cold as a steel knife.

"Mates! Today the time's up!" our baker said to us one morning, as he set to work.

We were well aware of it without his reminder; but still we were thrilled.

"Look at her. She'll be here directly," suggested the baker.

One of us cried out in a troubled voice, "Why! as though one could notice anything!"

And again an eager, noisy discussion sprang up among us.

Today we were about to prove how pure and spotless was the vessel into which we had poured all that was best in us. This morning, for the first time, it became clear to us, that we really were playing a great game; that we might, indeed, through the exaction of this proof of purity, lose our divinity altogether.

During the whole of the intervening fortnight we had heard that Tanya was persistently followed by the soldier, but not one of us had thought of asking her how she had behaved toward him. And she came every morning to fetch her kringels, and was the same toward us as ever.

This morning, too, we heard her voice outside: "You poor prisoners! Here I am!"

We opened the door, and when she came in we all remained, contrary to our usual custom, silent. Our eyes fixed on her, we did not know how to speak to her, what to ask her. And there we stood in front of her, a gloomy, silent crowd. She seemed to be surprised at this unusual reception; and suddenly we saw her turn white and become uneasy, then she asked, in a choking voice:

"Why are you—like this?"

"And you?" the baker flung at her grimly, never taking his eyes off her.

"What am I?"

"N—nothing."

"Well, then, give me quickly the little kringels."

Never before had she bidden us hurry.

"There's plenty of time," said the baker, not stirring, and not removing his eyes from her face.

Then, suddenly, she turned round and disappeared through the door.

The baker took his shovel and said, calmly turning away toward the oven:

"Well, that settles it! But a soldier! a common beast like that—a low cur!"

Like a flock of sheep we all pressed round the table, sat down silently, and began listlessly to work. Soon, however, one of us remarked:

"Perhaps, after all——"

"Shut up!" shouted the baker.

We were all convinced that he was a man of judgment, a man who knew more than we did about things. And at the sound of his voice we were convinced of the soldier's victory, and our spirits became sad and downcast.

At twelve o'clock—while we were eating our dinners—the soldier came in. He was as clean and as smart as ever, and looked at us—as usual—straight in the eyes. But we were all awkward in looking at him.

"Now then, honored sirs, would you like me to show you a soldier's quality?" he said, chuckling proudly.

"Go out into the passage, and look through the crack—do you understand?"

We went into the passage, and stood all pushing against one another, squeezed up to the cracks of the wooden partition of the passage that looked into the yard. We had not to wait long. Very soon Tanya, with hurried footsteps and a careworn face, walked across the yard, jumping over the puddles of melting snow and mud: she disappeared into the store cellar. Then whistling, and not hurrying himself, the soldier followed in the same direction. His hands were thrust in his pockets; his mustaches were quivering.

Rain was falling, and we saw how its drops fell into the puddles, and the puddles were wrinkled by them. The day was damp and gray—a very dreary day. Snow still lay on the roofs, but on the ground dark patches of mud had begun to appear. And the snow on the roofs too was covered by a layer of brownish dirt. The rain fell slowly with a depressing sound. It was cold and disagreeable for us waiting.

The first to come out of the store cellar was the soldier; he walked slowly across the yard, his mustaches twitching, his hands in his pockets—the same as always.

Then—Tanya, too, came out. Her eyes—her eyes were radiant with joy and happiness, and her lips—were smiling. And she walked as though in a dream, staggering, with unsteady steps.

We could not bear this quietly. All of us at once rushed to the door, dashed out into the yard and—hissed at her, reviled her viciously, loudly, wildly.

She started at seeing us, and stood as though rooted in the mud under her feet. We formed a ring round her! and malignantly, without restraint, abused her with vile words, said shameful things to her.

We did this not loudly, not hurriedly, seeing that she could not get away, that she was hemmed in by us, and we could deride her to our hearts' content. I don't know why, but we did not beat her. She stood in the midst of us, and turned her head this way and that, as she heard our insults. And we—

more and more violently flung at her the filth and venom of our words.

The color had left her face. Her blue eyes, so happy a moment before, opened wide, her bosom heaved, and her lips quivered.

We in a ring round her avenged ourselves on her as though she had robbed us. She belonged to us, we had lavished on her our best, and though that best was a beggar's crumb, still we were twenty-six, she was one, and so there was no pain we could give her equal to her guilt! How we insulted her! She was still mute, still gazed at us with wild eyes, and a shiver ran all over her.

We laughed, roared, yelled. Other people ran up from somewhere and joined us. One of us pulled Tanya by the sleeve of her blouse.

Suddenly her eyes flashed; deliberately she raised her hands to her head and straightening her hair she said loudly but calmly, straight in our faces:

"Ah, you miserable prisoners!"

And she walked straight at us, walked as directly as though we had not been before her, as though we were not blocking her way.

And hence it was that no one did actually prevent her passing.

Walking out of our ring, without turning round, she said loudly and with indescribable contempt:

"Ah, you scum—brutes."

And—was gone.

We were left in the middle of the yard, in the rain, under the gray sky without the sun.

Then we went mutely away to our damp stone cellar. As before—the sun never peeped in at our windows, and Tanya came no more!

✠ ✠
✠

Ivan Bunin

✠ ✠
✠
✠ ✠

The
Gentleman
from
San Francisco

✠

Alas, alas, that great city Babylon, that mighty city!
THE APOCALYPSE

The gentleman from San Francisco—neither at Naples nor at Capri had anyone remembered his name—was journeying to the Old World for two full years, with wife and daughter, wholly for recreation.

He felt firmly assured that he had every right to take a rest, pleasure, in a prolonged and comfortable journey, and other things besides. For such an assurance he had the good reason, that, in the first place, he was rich, and that, in the second, in spite of his fifty-eight years, he was only just taking his first plunge into life. Before this he had not lived but merely existed—to be sure, not so badly, but none the less putting all his hopes in the future. He had laboured diligently—the coolies, whom he had employed by the thousands, knew well what this meant!—and at last he saw that much had been achieved, that he was now equal to those he had at one time appointed as his models, and he decided to give himself a well-earned rest. It was a custom among his kind of people to begin the enjoyment of life with a journey to Europe, to India, to Egypt. He proposed to follow their example. Before all, of course, he desired to reward himself for his years of hard toil; nevertheless, he was happy also for his wife's and daughter's sakes. His wife had never been distinguished for any particular susceptibility to fresh impressions, but then all elderly American women are ardent travellers. As for his daughter, a girl no longer young

and somewhat ailing, the journey would do her positive good:
to say nothing of the benefits her health would derive, was
there not always the likelihood of happy encounters during
journeys? While travelling one may indeed, at times, sit at
the same table with a multimillionaire, or enjoy looking at
frescoes in his company.

The itinerary planned by the gentleman from San Francisco
was an extensive one. In December and January he hoped to
enjoy the sun of Southern Italy, the monuments of antiquity,
the *tarantella,* the serenades of strolling singers, and another
thing for which men of his age have a peculiar relish: the love
of young Neapolitan women, conferred—let us admit—not
with wholly disinterested motives; he planned to spend the
Carnival in Nice, in Monte Carlo, toward which the most
select society gravitated at this season—that society upon
which all the blessings of civilization depend: not alone the
cut of the smoking jacket, but also the stability of thrones, and
the declaration of wars, and the welfare of hotels—where
some devote themselves with ardor to automobile and sail
races, others to roulette, while a third group engages in what
is called flirting; a fourth in shooting pigeons which, emerging
from their shelters, gracefully soar upward above emerald green
lawns, against the background of a sea of the colour of forget-
me-nots, only in the next instant to strike the ground as
crumpled little shapes of white. The beginning of March he
wanted to devote to Florence; on the eve of the Passion of
Our Lord to arrive at Rome, in order to hear the *Miserere*
there; his plans also included Venice, and Paris, and bullfights
in Seville, and sea bathing in the British Isles, and Athens, and
Constantinople, and Palestine, and Egypt, and even Japan—
naturally, on the return journey . . . And everything went
splendidly at first.

It was the end of November; almost to Gibraltar itself the
ship proceeded now through an icy mist, now through a storm
with wet snow; but it sailed on unperturbed and even without
rolling; the passengers on the steamer were many, and all of
them persons of consequence; the ship—the famous *Atlantis*
—resembled the most expensive of European hotels, with all
conveniences; an all night bar, Turkish baths, a newspaper of
its own,—and life upon it flowed in accordance with a splendid
system of regulations: the passengers rose early, to the sound
of bugles, sharply reverberating through the passages at the
yet dark hour when day was so slowly and reluctantly dawning

above the gray green watery desert, ponderously restless in the mist. They put on their flannel pyjamas, drank coffee, chocolate, cocoa; then they reclined in marble bathtubs, performed exercises, awakening an appetite and a sense of well-being, attended to their daily toilet and went to breakfast. Until eleven they were supposed to promenade the decks lustily, breathing in the cool freshness of the ocean, or to play at shuffleboard and other games for a renewed stimulation of the appetite; and at eleven, to seek refreshment in bouillon and sandwiches; after which they read their newspaper with pleasure and calmly awaited lunch, a meal even more nourishing and varied than the breakfast; the following two hours were dedicated to repose; all the decks were then arranged with *chaises longues,* upon which the travellers reclined, covered up with plaid rugs, contemplating the cloudy sky and the foaming billows flashing by beyond the rail, or else gently drowsing. At five o'clock, enlivened and refreshed, they were served with strong fragrant tea and pastries; at seven, the bugle call announced dinner, consisting of nine courses. . . . At this point the gentleman from San Francisco, greatly cheered, would hurry to his magnificent *cabin de luxe,* to dress.

In the evening the tiers of the *Atlantis* gaped through the dusk as with fiery, countless eyes, and a great multitude of servants worked with especial feverishness in the kitchens, sculleries, and wine vaults. The ocean, heaving on the other side of the walls, was terrifying, but none gave it a thought, firmly believing it under the sway of the captain,—a red-haired man of monstrous bulk and ponderousness, always seeming sleepy, resembling, in his uniform frock coat, with its golden chevrons, an enormous idol; it was only very rarely that he left his mysterious quarters to appear in public. A siren on the forecastle howled ceaselessly in hellish sullenness and whined in frenzied malice, but not many of the diners heard the siren,—it was drowned by the strains of a splendid stringed orchestra, playing exquisitely and without pause in the two-tiered hall, decorated with marble, its floors covered with velvet rugs; festively flooded with the lights of crystal lustres and gilded *girandoles,* filled to capacity with diamond-bedecked ladies in *décolleté* and men in smoking jackets, graceful waiters and deferential *maîtres d'hôtel,*— among whom one, who took orders for wines exclusively, even walked about with a chain around his neck, like a lord mayor. A smoking jacket and perfect linen made the gentle-

man from San Francisco appear very much younger. Spare,
not tall, awkwardly but strongly built, groomed until he shone
and moderately animated, he sat in the aureate pearly reful-
gence of this palatial room, at a table with a bottle of amber
Johannesberg, with countless goblets, small and large, of the
thinnest glass, with a fragrant bouquet of curly hyacinths.
There was something Mongolian about his yellowish face with
clipped silvery moustache; his large teeth gleamed with gold
fillings; his stalwart, bald head glistened like old ivory. Rich,
yet in keeping with her years, was the attire of his wife,—a
big, broad, calm woman; elaborate, yet light and diaphanous,
with an innocent frankness, was that of his daughter,—a girl
innocently frank, tall, slender, with magnificent hair, exquisitely
dressed, with breath aromatic from violet cachous and with
the tenderest of tiny moles about her lips and between her
shoulder blades, slightly powdered. . . .

The dinner went on for two whole hours; after dinner there
was dancing in the ballroom, during which the men,—the
gentleman from San Francisco among their number, of course,
—with their feet cocked up, decided, upon the basis of the
latest political and stock exchange news, the destinies of na-
tions, smoking Havana cigars and drinking *liqueurs* until their
faces were flushed, while seated in the bar, where the waiters
were Negroes in red jackets, the whites of their eyes resembling peeled, hard-boiled eggs. The ocean, with a dull roar,
was moving in black mountains on the other side of the wall;
the snow gale whistled fiercely through the soaked rigging; the
whole ship quivered as it mastered both the gale and the mountains, sundering to either side, as though with a plough, their
shifting masses, which again and again boiled up and flung
themselves high, with tails of foam; the siren, stifled by the
fog, was moaning with a deathly anguish; the lookouts up in
their crow's nest froze with the cold and grew dazed from
straining their attention beyond their strength. Akin to the
grim sultry depths of the infernal regions, akin to their ulti-
mate, their ninth circle, was the womb of the steamer, below
the water line,—that womb where dully gurgled the gigantic
furnaces, devouring with their fiery maws mountains of hard
coal, cast into them by men stripped to the waist, purple from
the flames, and with smarting, filthy sweat pouring over them;
while here, in the bar, men threw their legs over the arms
of their chairs with never a care, sipping cognac and *liqueurs,*
and were wafted among clouds of spicy smoke as they indulged

in refined conversation; in the ballroom everything was radiant with light and warmth and joy; couples were now whirling in waltzes, now swaying in the tango,—and the music insistently, in some delectably shameless melancholy, supplicated always of one, always of the same thing. . . . There was an ambassador among this brilliant throng,—a lean, modest little old man; there was a rich man,—clean-shaven, lanky, of indeterminate years, and with the appearance of a prelate, in an old-fashioned frock coat; there was a well-known Spanish writer; there was a world-celebrated beauty, already just the very least trifle faded and of an unenviable morality; there was an exquisite couple in love with each other, whom all watched with curiosity and whose happiness was unconcealed: *he* danced only with *her;* sang—and with great ability—only to *her* accompaniment; everything they did was carried out so charmingly; and only the captain knew that this pair was hired by Lloyd's to play at love for good money, and that they had been sailing for a long time, now on one ship, now on another.

At Gibraltar everybody was gladdened by the sun,—it seemed like early spring; a new passenger, whose person aroused the general interest, made his appearance on board the *Atlantis,*—he was the hereditary prince of a certain Asiatic kingdom, travelling incognito; a little man who somehow seemed to be all made of wood, even though he was agile in his movements; broad of face, with narrow eyes, in gold-rimmed spectacles; a trifle unpleasant owing to the fact that his skin showed through his coarse black mustache like that of a corpse; on the whole, however, he was charming, simple, and modest. On the Mediterranean Sea there was a whiff of winter again; the billows ran high, were as multicolored as the tail of a peacock, and had snowy white crests, due, in spite of the sparklingly bright sun and perfectly clear sky, to a *tramontana,* a chill northern wind from beyond the mountains, that was joyously and madly rushing to meet the ship. . . . Then, on the second day, the sky began to pale, the horizon became covered with mist, land was nearing; Ischia, Capri appeared; through the binoculars, Naples—lumps of sugar strewn at the foot of some dove colored mass—could be seen; while over it and this dove colored object were visible the ridges of distant mountains, vaguely glimmering with the dead whiteness of snow. There was a great number of people on deck; many of the ladies and gentlemen had already put on short, light fur coats, with the fur outside; Chinese boys, patient and always speaking in a whisper, bow-legged striplings with pitch-black queues reaching to their heels and with eyelashes as long and thick as those of young girls, were already dragging, little by little, sundry plaids, canes, and portmanteaux and grips of alligator hide toward the companionways. . . . The daughter of the gentleman from San Francisco was standing beside the prince, who had been, by a happy chance, presented to her yesterday evening, and she pretended to be looking intently into the distance, in a direction he was pointing out to her, telling, explaining something or other to her, hurriedly and quietly. On account of his height he seemed a boy by contrast with others,—he was odd and not at all prepossessing of person, with his spectacles, his bowler, his English great coat, while his scanty mustache looked just as if it were of horsehair, and the swarthy, thin skin seemed to be drawn tightly over his face, and somehow had the appearance of being lacquered,—but the young girl was listening to him, without understanding, in her perturbation, what he was saying; her heart was thumping from an incomprehensible rapture in his presence and from pride that he was speaking with her, and not some one else; everything about him that was different from others,—his lean hands, his clear skin, under which flowed the ancient blood of kings, even his wholly unpretentious, yet somehow singularly neat, European dress,—everything held a secret, inexplicable charm, evoked a feeling of amorousness. As for the gentleman from San Francisco himself,—he, in a high silk hat, in gray spats over patent leather shoes, kept on glancing at the famous beauty, who was standing beside him,—a tall blonde of striking figure, with eyes painted in the latest Parisian fashion; she was holding a diminutive, hunched-up, mangy lap dog on a silver chain and was chattering to it without pause. And the daughter, in some vague embarrassment, tried not to notice her father.

Like all Americans of means, he was very generous while travelling, and, like all of them, believed in the full sincerity and good will of those who brought him food and drink with such solicitude, who served him from morn till night, anticipating his slightest wish; of those who guarded his cleanliness and rest, lugged his things around, summoned porters for him, delivered his trunks to hotels. Thus had it been everywhere, thus had it been on the ship, and thus it had to be in Naples as well. Naples grew, and drew nearer; the musicians, the brass of their instruments flashing, had already clustered upon the deck, and suddenly deafened everybody with the triumphant strains of a march; the gigantic captain, in his full dress uniform, appeared upon his stage, and, like a gracious pagan god, waved his hand amiably to the passengers,—and to the gentleman from San Francisco it seemed that it was for him alone that the march so beloved by proud America was thundering, that it was he whom the captain was felicitating upon a safe arrival. And every other passenger felt similarly about himself—or herself. And when the *Atlantis* finally entered the harbor, heaved to at the wharf with her many-tiered mass, black with people, and the gangplanks clattered down,—what a multitude of porters and their helpers in caps with gold braid, what a multitude of different *commissionaires,* whistling gamins, and strapping ragamuffins with packets of colored postal cards in their hands, made a rush toward the gentleman from San Francisco, with offers of their services! And he smiled, with a kindly con-temptuousness, at these ragamuffins, as he went toward the automobile of precisely that hotel where there was a likelihood of the prince's stopping. He drawled through his teeth, now in English, now in Italian:

"Go away! *Via!*"

Life at Naples at once assumed its wonted, ordered routine: in the early morning, breakfast in the gloomy dining room with its damp draft from windows opening on some sort of a stony little garden. The sky was overcast, holding out little promise, and there was the usual crowd of guides at the door of the vestibule; then came the first smiles of a warm, rosy sun. From the high hanging balcony Vesuvius came into view, en-veloped to its foot by radiant morning mists, and the silver and pearl eddies on the surface of the Bay, and the delicate contour of Capri against the horizon. One could see tiny bur-ros, harnessed in twos to little carts, running down below over the quay, sticky with mire, and detachments of diminutive soldiers, marching somewhere to lively and exhilarating music. Next came the procession to the waiting automobile and the slow progress through populous, narrow, and damp corridors of streets, between tall, many-windowed houses; the inspection of lifelessly clean museums, evenly and pleasantly, yet bleakly, lighted, seemingly illuminated by snow; or of cool churches, smelling of wax, which everywhere and always contain the same things; a majestic portal, screened by a heavy curtain of leather, and inside,—empty vastness, silence, quiescent tiny

flames of a seven-branched candle-stick glowing redly in the
distant depths, on an altar bedecked with laces; a solitary old
woman among the dark wooden pews; slippery tombstones
underfoot; and someone's "Descent from the Cross,"—it goes
without saying, a celebrated one. At one o'clock there was
luncheon upon the mountain of San Martino, where, toward
noon, not a few people of the very first quality gathered, and
where the daughter of the gentleman from San Francisco had
once almost fainted away for joy, because she thought she saw
the prince sitting in the hall, although she already knew through
the newspapers that he had left for a temporary stay at Rome.
At five came tea at the hotel, in the showy salon, so cozy with
its rugs and flaming fireplaces; and after that it was already
time to prepare for dinner,—and once more came the mighty
clamor of the gong reverberating through the hotel; once more
the moving queues of ladies in *décolleté*, rustling in their silks
upon the staircases and reflected in all the mirrors; once more
the palatial dining room, widely and hospitably opened, and
the red jackets of the musicians upon their platform, and the
black cluster of waiters about the *maître d'hôtel,* who, with
inordinate skill, was ladling some sort of thick, reddish soup
into plates. . . . The dinners, as everywhere else, were the
crowning glory of each day; the guests dressed for them as
for a party, and these dinners were so abundant in edibles, and
wines, and mineral waters, and sweets, and fruits, that toward
eleven o'clock at night the chambermaids were distributing
through all the rooms rubber bags with hot water to warm the
stomachs.

As it happened, the December of that year proved to be not
a wholly successful one for Naples; the porters grew confused
when one talked with them of the weather, and merely
shrugged their shoulders guiltily, muttering that they could not
recall such a year,—although it was not the first year that they
had been forced to mutter this, and to base their statement on
that "something terrible is happening everywhere"; there were
unheard of storms and torrents of rain on the Riviera; there
was snow in Athens; Etna was also all snowed over and was
aglow at night; tourists were fleeing from Palermo in all directions, to escape from the cold. The morning sun deceived
the Neapolitans every day that winter: toward noon the sky
became gray and a fine rain began falling, but grew heavier and
colder all the time; then the palms near the entrance of the
hotel glistened as though they were of tin, the town seemed

especially dirty and cramped, the museums curiously alike; the cigar stumps of the corpulent cabmen, whose rubber coats flapped in the wind like wings, seemed to have an insufferable stench, while the energetic snapping of their whips over their scrawny-necked nags was patently false; the footgear of the *signori* sweeping the rails of the tramways seemed horrible; the women, splashing through the mud, their black-haired heads bared to the rain, appeared hideously short-legged; as for the dampness, and the stench of putrid fish from the sea foaming at the quay,—there was nothing to be said. The gentleman and the lady from San Francisco began quarreling in the morning; their daughter either walked about pale, with a headache, or, coming to life again, went into raptures over everything, and was, at times both charming and beautiful: beautiful were those tender and complex emotions which had been awakened within her by meeting that unsightly man through whose veins flowed uncommon blood; for, after all is said and done, perhaps it is of no actual importance just what it is, precisely, that awakens a maiden's soul,—whether it be money, or fame, or illustrious ancestry. . . . Everybody asserted that things were quite different in Sorrento, in Capri,—there it was both warmer and sunnier, and the lemons were in blossom, and the customs were more honest, and the wine was better. And so the family from San Francisco resolved to set out with all its trunks to Capri, and, after seeing it all, after treading the stones where the palace of Tiberius had once stood, after visiting the fairylike caverns of the Blue Grotto, and hearing the bagpipers of Abruzzi, who for a whole month preceding Christmas wander over the island and sing the praises of the Virgin Mary, they meant to settle in Sorrento.

On the day of departure,—a most memorable one for the family from San Francisco!—there was no early morning sun. A heavy fog hid Vesuvius to the very base; this gray fog spread low over the leaden swell of the sea that was lost to the eye at a distance of a half a mile. Capri was quite invisible,—as if there had never been such an island in the world. And the tiny steamer that set out for it was so tossed from side to side that the family from San Francisco was laid prostrate upon the divans in the sorry general cabin of this tiny steamer, their feet wrapped up in plaid rugs, and their eyes closed. The mother suffered,—so she thought,—more than anybody; she was overcome by seasickness several times; it seemed to her that she was dying, while the stewardess, who always ran up to her

with a small basin,—she had been, for many years, day in and
day out, rolling on these waves, in sultry weather and in cold,
and yet was still tireless and kind to everybody,—merely
laughed. The daughter was dreadfully pale and held a slice of
lemon between her teeth; now she could not have been comforted even by the hope of a chance meeting with the prince
at Sorrento, where he intended to be about Christmas. The
father, who was lying on his back, in roomy overcoat and
large cap, never opened his jaws all the way over; his face had
grown darker and his mustache whiter, and his head ached
dreadfully: during the last days, thanks to the bad weather, he
had been drinking too heavily of evenings, and had too much
admired the "living pictures" in the haunts of manufactured
libertinage. But the rain kept on lashing against the jarring
windows, the water from them running down on the divans;
the wind, howling, bent the masts, and at times, aided by the
onslaught of a wave, careened the little steamer entirely to
one side, and then something in the hold would roll with a
rumble. During the stops at Castellamare, at Sorrento, things
were a trifle more bearable, but even then the rocking was
fearful,—the shore, with all its cliffs, gardens, pine groves, its
pink and white hotels and hazy mountains clad in wavy green-
ery, swayed up and down as if on a swing; boats bumped up
against the sides of the ship; sailors and steerage passengers
were shouting fiercely; somewhere, as if it had been crushed, a
baby was wailing and smothering; a raw wind was blowing in
at the door; and, from a swaying boat with the flag of the
Hotel Royal, a lisping gamin was screaming, luring travellers:
"Kgoya-al! Hôtel Kgoya-al! . . ." And the gentleman from
San Francisco, feeling himself to be incredibly old,—which
was as it should be,—was already thinking with sadness and
loathing of all these Royals, Splendids, Excelsiors, and of these
greedy, insignificant little men, reeking of garlic, called Italians.
Once, having opened his eyes and raised himself from the
divan, he saw, underneath the craggy barrier on the shore, a
cluster of stone hovels mouldy through and through, stuck one
on top of another near the very edge of the water, near boats,
near all sorts of rags, tins, and brown nets,—hovels so
wretched, that, at the recollection this was the very Italy he
had come here to enjoy, he felt despair. . . . Finally, at twi-
light, the dark mass of the island began to draw near, seemingly bored through and through by little red lights near its
base; the wind became softer, warmer, more fragrant; over the

abating waves, as opalescent as black oil, golden serpents flowed from the lanterns on the wharf. . . . Then came the sudden rumble of the anchor, and it fell with a splash into the water; the savage shouts of the boatmen, vying with one another, floated in from all quarters,—and at once the heart grew lighter, the lamps in the general cabin shone more brightly, a desire arose to eat, to drink, to smoke, to be stirring. . . . Ten minutes later the family from San Francisco had descended into a large boat; within fifteen minutes it had set foot upon the stones of the wharf, and had then got into a bright little railway car and to its buzzing started the ascent of the slope, amid the stakes of the vineyards, half-crumbled stone enclosures, and wet, gnarled orange trees, some of them under coverings of straw,—trees with thick, glossy foliage, aglimmer with the orange fruits; all these objects were sliding downward, past the open windows of the little car, toward the base of the mountain. . . . Sweetly smells the earth of Italy after rain, and her every island has its own, its especial aroma!

On this evening the island of Capri was damp and dark. But now for an instant it came into life; lights sprang up here and there, as always on the steamer's arrival. At the top of the mountain, where stood the station of the *funicular*, there was another throng of those whose duty it was to receive fittingly the gentleman from San Francisco. There were other arrivals, but they merited no attention,—several Russians, who had settled in Capri,—absent-minded because of their bookish meditations, unkempt, bearded, spectacled, the collars of their old frayed overcoats turned up; and a group of long-legged, long-necked, round-headed German youths in Tyrolean costumes, with canvas knapsacks slung over their shoulders; these stood in no need of anybody's services, feeling themselves at home everywhere, and knowing how to practice the strictest economies. The gentleman from San Francisco, on the other hand, who was calmly keeping aloof from both the one group and the other, was immediately observed. He and his ladies were promptly helped out, some men running ahead of him to show him the way. Again he was surrounded by urchins, and by those stalwart Caprian wives who bear on their heads the portmanteaux and trunks of respectable travellers. The wooden pattens of these women clattered over a little square, which seemed to belong to some opera, an electric globe swaying above it in the damp wind. The rabble of urchins burst into sharp, birdlike whistles,—and, as if on a stage, the gentleman

from San Francisco proceeded in their midst toward some
medieval arch underneath houses that had become merged into
one mass, beyond which a little echoing street,—with the tuft
of a palm above flat roofs on its left, and with blue stars in
the black sky overhead,—led slopingly to the now visible grand
entrance of the hotel, all agleam with light. . . . And again
it seemed that it was in honor of the guests from San Francisco
that this damp little town of stone on a craggy little island of
the Mediterranean Sea had come to life, that it was they who
had made the proprietor of the hotel so happy and affable, that
it was only for them that the Chinese gong began to sound
the summons to dinner through all the stories of the hotel, the
instant they had set foot in the vestibule.

The proprietor, a young man of courtly elegance, who had
met them with a polite and exquisite bow, for a minute dumb-
founded the gentleman from San Francisco. After a glance at
him, the gentleman from San Francisco suddenly remembered
that just the night before, among the confusion of numerous
images which had beset him in his sleep, he had seen precisely
this gentleman,—just like him, down to the least detail: in the
same sort of frock with rounded skirts, and with the same
pomaded and painstakingly combed head. Startled, he almost
paused. But since, from long, long before, there was not even
a mustard seed of any sort of so-called mystical emotions left
in his soul, his astonishment was dimmed the same instant; as
he proceeded through a corridor of the hotel, he spoke jest-
ingly to his wife and daughter of this strange coincidence of
dream and reality. And only his daughter glanced at him with
alarm at that moment: her heart suddenly contracted from
sadness, from a feeling of their loneliness upon this dark alien
island,—a feeling so strong that she almost burst into tears.
Nevertheless, she said nothing of her feelings to her father,—
as always.

An exalted personage—Rais XVII—who had been visiting
Capri, had just taken his departure. And now the guests from
San Francisco were conducted to the same apartments that
he had occupied. To them was assigned the ablest and hand-
somest chambermaid, a Belgian, whose waist was slenderly
and firmly corseted, and whose tiny starched cap looked like
a scalloped crown; also, the best-looking and most dignified
of flunkies, a fiery-eyed Sicilian, black as coal; and the nim-
blest of bellboys, the short and stout Luigi,—a fellow who
was very fond of a joke, and who had served many masters

in his time. And a minute later there was a slight tap at the door of the room of the gentleman from San Francisco,—the French *maître d'hôtel* had come to find out if the newly arrived guests would dine, and, in event of an answer in the affirmative,—of which, of course, there was no doubt,—to inform them that the *carte de jour* consisted of crawfish, roast beef, asparagus, pheasants, and so forth. The floor was still rocking under the gentleman from San Francisco,—so badly had the atrocious little Italian steamer tossed him about,— but, without hurrying, with his own hands, although somewhat awkwardly from being unaccustomed to such things, he shut a window that had banged when the *maître d'hôtel* had entered and had let in the odors of the distant kitchen and of the wet flowers in the garden, and with a lingering deliberateness replied that they would dine, that their table must be placed as far as possible from the door, at the other end of the dining room, that they would drink local wine and champagne,— moderately dry and only slightly chilled. The *maître d'hôtel* approved every word of his, in most varied intonations, having, in any case, but one significance,—that there was never a doubt, nor could there possibly be any, about the correctness of the wishes of the gentleman from San Francisco, and that everything would be carried out with precision. In conclusion he inclined his head, and asked deferentially:

"Will that be all, sir?"

And, having received in answer a leisurely "Yes," he added that the *tarantella* would be danced in the vestibule tonight,— the dancers would be Carmella and Giuseppe, known to all Italy, and to "the entire world of tourists."

"I have seen her on post cards," said the gentleman from San Francisco in a wholly inexpressive voice. "As for this Giuseppe,—is he her husband?"

"Her cousin, sir," answered the *maître d'hôtel*.

And, after a brief pause, during which he appeared to be considering something, the gentleman from San Francisco dismissed him with a nod.

And then he once more began his preparations, as if for a wedding ceremony: he turned on all the electric lights, filling all the mirrors with reflections of light and glitter, of furniture and opened trunks; he began shaving and washing, ringing the bell every minute, while other impatient rings from his wife's and daughter's rooms sounded through the entire corridor and interrupted his. And Luigi, in his red apron, was rushing for-

ward to answer the bell, with an agility peculiar to many stout
men, not omitting grimaces of horror that made the chambermaids, running by with glazed porcelain pails in their hands,
laugh till they cried. He knocked on the door with his knuckles,
and asked with an assumed timidity, with a deference which
verged on idiocy:

"Ha sonato, signore?"

And from the other side of the door came an unhurried
grating voice, humiliatingly polite:

"Yes, come in. . . ."

What were the thoughts, what were the emotions of the
gentleman from San Francisco on this evening, that was to be
of such significance to him? He felt nothing exceptional,—for
the trouble in this world is just that everything is apparently
all too simple! And even if he had sensed within his soul that
something was impending, he would, nevertheless, have thought
that this thing would not occur for some time to come,—in
any case, not immediately. Besides that, like everyone who has
experienced the rocking of a ship, he wanted very much to
eat, was looking forward to the first spoonful of soup, the first
mouthful of wine, and performed the usual routine of dressing, even with a certain degree of exhilaration that left no
time for reflections.

After shaving and washing himself, after inserting several
artificial teeth properly, he remained standing before a mirror,
while he wetted the remnants of his thick, pearly-gray hair and
plastered it down around his swarthy yellow skull, with brushes
set in silver; drew a suit of cream-colored silk underwear over
his strong old body, beginning to be full at the waist from
excesses in food, and put on silk socks and dancing slippers
on his shrivelled, splayed feet; sitting down, he put in order
his black trousers, drawn high by black silk braces, as well as
his snowy white shirt, with the bosom bulging out; put the
links through the glossy cuffs, and began the agonizing manipu-
lation of the collar button underneath the stiffly starched collar. The floor was still swaying beneath him, the tips of his
fingers pained him greatly, the collar button at times nipped
hard the flabby skin in the hollow under his Adam's apple, but
he was persistent and at last, his eyes glittering from the exer-
tion, his face all livid from the collar that was choking his
throat,—a collar far too tight,—he did succeed in accomplish-
ing his task, and sat down in exhaustion in front of the pier

glass. He was reflected in it from head to foot, a reflection that was repeated in all the other mirrors.

"Oh, this is dreadful!" he muttered, lowering his strong bald head, and without trying to understand, without considering, just what, precisely, was dreadful; then, with an accustomed and attentive glance, he inspected his stubby fingers, with gouty hardenings at the joints, and his convex nails of an almond color, and repeated, with conviction: "This is dreadful. . . ."

At this point the second gong, sonorously, as in some pagan temple, dinned through the entire house. And, getting up quickly from his seat, the gentleman from San Francisco drew his collar still tighter with the necktie and his stomach by means of the low-cut vest, put on his smoking jacket, arranged his cuffs, surveyed himself once more in the mirror. . . . This Carmella, swarthy, with eyes which she knew well how to use tellingly, resembling a mulatto woman, clad in a dress of many colors, with the color of orange predominant, must dance exceptionally, he imagined. And, stepping briskly out of his room and walking over the carpet to the next one,— his wife's—he asked loudly, if they would be ready soon.

"In five minutes, Dad!" a girl's voice, ringing and by now gay, responded from the other side of the door.

"Very well," said the gentleman from San Francisco.

And, leisurely, he walked through red-carpeted corridors and down staircases, in quest of the reading room. The servants he met stood aside and hugged the wall to let him pass, but he kept on his way as though he had never even noticed them. An old woman who was late for dinner, already stooping, with milky hair but *décolleté* in a light gray gown of silk, was hurrying with all her might, but drolly, in a henlike manner, and he easily outstripped her. Near the glass doors of the dining room, where all the guests had already assembled, and were beginning their dinner, he stopped before a little table piled with boxes of cigars and Egyptian cigarettes, took a large Manila cigar, and flung three *lire* upon the little table. Walking on the terrace, he glanced, in passing, through the open window; out of the darkness he felt a breath of the balmy air upon him, thought he saw the tip of an ancient palm. Its gigantic fronds seemed to reach out across the stars. He heard the distant, measured din of the sea. . . . In the reading room,—snug, quiet, and illuminated only above the tables, some gray-haired German was standing, rustling the news-

papers,—unkempt, resembling Ibsen, in round silver spectacles
and with mad, astonished eyes. After scrutinizing him coldly,
the gentleman from San Francisco sat down in a deep leather
chair in a corner near a green-shaded lamp, put on his *pince
nez*, twitching his head because his collar was choking him,
and hid himself completely behind the newspaper. He rapidly
ran through the headlines of certain items, read a few lines
about the never-ceasing Balkan war, with an accustomed gesture turned the newspaper over,—when suddenly the lines
flared up before him with a glassy glare, his neck became taut,
his eyes bulged out, the *pince nez* flew off his nose. . . . He
lunged forward, tried to swallow some air,—and made a wild
hoarse sound; his lower jaw sank, lighting up his entire mouth
with the reflection of the gold fillings; his head dropped back
on his shoulder and began to sway; the bosom of his shirt
bulged out like a basket,—and his whole body, squirming, his
heels catching the carpet, slid downward to the floor, desperately struggling with someone.

Had the German not been in the reading room, the hotel
attendants would have managed, quickly and adroitly, to hush
up this dreadful occurrence; instantly, through back passages,
seizing him by the head and feet, they would have rushed off
the gentleman from San Francisco as far away as possible,—
and not a soul among the guests would have found out what
he had been up to. But the German had dashed out of the
reading room with a scream,—he had aroused the entire house,
the entire dining room. And many jumped up from their
meal, overturning their chairs; many, paling, ran toward the
reading room. "What—what has happened?" was heard in all
languages,—and no one gave a sensible answer, no one com-
prehended anything, since even to this day men are amazed
most of all by death, and will not, in any circumstances, believe in it. The proprietor dashed from one guest to another,
trying to detain those who were running away and to pacify
them with hasty assurances that this was just a trifling occurrence, a slight fainting spell of a certain gentleman from San
Francisco. . . . No one listened to him; many had seen the
flunkeys and corridor attendants tearing the necktie, the vest,
and the rumpled smoking jacket off this gentleman, and even,
for some reason or other, the dancing slippers off his splayed
feet, clad in black silk. He was still struggling. He was still
obdurately wrestling with death; he absolutely refused to yield
to her, who had so unexpectedly and inconsiderately fallen

upon him. His head was swaying, he rattled hoarsely, like one
with his throat cut; his eyes had rolled up, like a drunkard's.
. . . When he was hurriedly carried in and laid upon a bed in
room Number Forty-three,—the smallest, the poorest, the
dampest and the coldest, situated at the end of the bottom
corridor,—his daughter ran in, with her hair down, in a little
dressing gown that had flown open, her bosom, raised up by
the corset, uncovered; then his wife, big and ponderous, already dressed for dinner,—her mouth rounded in terror. . . .
But by now he had ceased even wagging his head.

A quarter of an hour later everything in the hotel had assumed a semblance of order. Nevertheless, the evening was
irreparably spoiled. Some guests, returning to the dining room,
finished their dinner, but in silence, with aggrieved faces, while
the proprietor would approach now one group, now another,
shrugging his shoulders in polite yet impotent irritation, feeling
himself guilty without guilt, assuring everybody that he understood very well "how unpleasant all this was," and pledging
his word that he would take "all measures within his power" to
remove this unpleasantness. The *tarantella* had to be called
off, all superfluous electric lights were extinguished, the ma-
jority of the guests withdrew into the bar, and it became so
quiet that one heard distinctly the ticking of the clock in the
vestibule, whose sole occupant was a parrot, dully muttering
something, fussing in his cage before going to sleep, contriving
to doze off at last with one claw ludicrously stretched up to
the upper perch. . . . The gentleman from San Francisco was
lying upon a cheap iron bed, under coarse woolen blankets,
upon which the dull light of a single bulb beat down from
the ceiling. An ice bag was askew on his moist and cold
forehead. The livid face, already dead, was gradually growing
cold; the hoarse rattling, expelled from the open mouth, illuminated by the reflection of gold, was growing fainter. This
was no longer the gentleman from San Francisco rattling,—he
no longer existed,—but some other. His wife, his daughter, the
doctor and the servants were standing, gazing at him dully.
Suddenly, that which they awaited and feared was consum-
mated,—the rattling ceased abruptly. And slowly, slowly, before the eyes of all, a pallor suffused the face of the man who
had died, and his features seemed to grow finer, to become
irradiated with a beauty which had been rightfully his in the
long ago. . . .

The proprietor entered. *"Già è morto,"* said the doctor to

him in a whisper. The proprietor, with dispassionate face, shrugged his shoulders. The wife, down whose cheeks the tears were quietly coursing, walked up to him and timidly said that the deceased ought now to be carried to his own room.

"Oh, no, madam," hastily, correctly, but now without any amiability and not in English, but in French, retorted the proprietor, who was not at all interested now in such trifling sums as the arrivals from San Francisco might leave in his coffers. "That is absolutely impossible, madam," he said, and added in explanation that he valued the apartments occupied by them very much; that, were he to carry out her wishes, everybody in Capri would know it and the tourists would shun those apartments.

The young woman, who had been all this time gazing at him strangely, sat down on a chair, and, pressing a handkerchief to her mouth, burst into sobs. The wife dried her tears immediately, her face flaring up. She adopted a louder tone, making demands in her own language, and still incredulous of the fact that all respect for them had been completely lost. The proprietor, with polite dignity, cut her short: if madam was not pleased with the customs of the hotel, he would not venture to detain her; and he firmly announced that the body must be gotten away this very day, at dawn, that the police had already been notified, and one of the police officers would be here very soon and would carry out all the necessary formalities. Was it possible to secure even a common coffin in Capri?—madam asked. Regrettably, no,—it was beyond possibility, and no one would be able to make one in time. It would be necessary to have recourse to something else. . . . He had a suggstion.—English soda water came in large and long boxes. . . . It was possible to knock the partitions out of such a box. . . .

At night the whole hotel slept. The window in room Number Forty-three was opened,—it gave out upon a corner of the garden where, near a high stone wall with broken glass upon its crest, a consumptive banana tree was growing; the electric light was switched off; the key was turned in the door, and everybody went away. The dead man remained in the darkness,—the blue stars looked down upon him from the sky, a cricket with a pensive insouciance began his song in the wall. . . . In the dimly lit corridor two chambermaids were seated on a window sill, at some darning. Luigi, in slippers, entered with a pile of clothing in his arms.

"*Pronto?*" he asked solicitously, in an audible whisper, indicating with his eyes the fearsome door at the end of the corridor. And, he waved his hand airily in that direction. . . .
"*Partenza!*" he called out in a whisper, as though he were speeding a train, the usual phrase used in Italian depots at the departure of trains,—and the chambermaids, choking with silent laughter, let their heads sink on each other's shoulder.

Thereupon, hopping softly, he ran up to the very door, gave it the merest tap, and, inclining his head to one side, in a low voice, asked with the utmost deference:

"*Ha sonato, signore?*"

And, squeezing his throat, thrusting out his lower jaw, in a grating voice, slowly and sadly, he answered his own question, in English, as though from the other side of the door:

"Yes, come in. . . ."

And at dawn, when it had become light beyond the window of room Number Forty-three, and a humid wind had begun to rustle the tattered leaves of the banana tree; when the blue sky of morning had lifted and spread out over the Island of Capri, and the pure and clear-cut summit of Monte Solaro had grown golden against the sun that was rising beyond the distant blue mountains of Italy; when the stone masons, who were repairing the tourists' paths on the island, had set out to work,—a long box that had formerly been used for soda water was brought to room Number Forty-three. Soon it became very heavy, and was pressing hard against the knees of the junior porter, who bore it off briskly on a one horse cab over the white paved highway that was sinuously winding over the slopes of Capri, among the stone walls and the vineyards, ever downwards, to the sea itself. The cabby, a puny little man with reddened eyes, in an old jacket with short sleeves and in much-worn shoes, was suffering the after effects of drink,—he had spent the whole night long in playing with dice in a *tratoria,* and kept on lashing his sturdy little horse, rigged out in Sicilian fashion, with all sorts of little bells livelily jingling upon the bridle with its tufts of colored wool, and upon the brass points of its high pad; with a yard long feather stuck in its cropped forelock,—a feather that shook as the horse ran. The cabby kept silent; he was oppressed by his shiftlessness, his vices,—by the circumstance that he had, that night, lost to the last mite all those coppers with which his pockets had been filled. But the morning was fresh; in air such as this, with the sea all around, under the morning sky, the after effects of drink quickly evaporate, and a man is soon restored to a carefree mood, and the cabby was furthermore consoled by that unexpected windfall, conferred upon him by some gentleman from San Francisco, whose lifeless head was bobbing from side to side in the box at his back. . . . The little steamer,—a beetle lying far down below, against the tender and vivid deep blue with which the Bay of Naples is so densely and highly flooded,—was already blowing its final whistles, that reverberated loudly all over the island, whose every bend, every ridge, every stone, was as distinctly visible from every point as if there were absolutely no such thing as atmosphere. Near the wharf the junior porter was joined by the senior, who was speeding with the daughter and wife of the gentleman from San Francisco in his automobile,—they were pale, with eyes hollow from tears and a sleepless night. And ten minutes later the little steamer was again noisily making its way through the water, again running toward Sorrento, toward Castellamare, carrying away from Capri, for all time, the family from San Francisco. . . . And again peace and quiet reigned upon the island.

Upon this island, two thousand years ago, had lived a man who had become completely enmeshed in his cruel and foul deeds, who had for some reason seized the power over millions of people in his hands, and who, having himself lost his head at the senselessness of this power and from the fear of death by assassination by some one, lurking round the corner, had committed cruelties beyond all measure,—and humankind has remembered him for all time; and those who, in their collusion, just as incomprehensively and, in substance, just as cruelly as he, reign at present in power over this world, gather from all over the earth to gaze upon the ruins of that stone villa where he had dwelt on one of the steepest ascents of the island. On this marvellous morning all those who had come to Capri for just this purpose were still sleeping in the hotels, although, toward the entrances, were already being led little mouse gray burros with red saddles, upon which, after awaking and sating themselves with food, Americans and Germans, men and women, young and old, would again ponderously clamber up the steep paths this day, and after whom would again run the old Caprian beggar women, with sticks in their gnarled hands,—would run over stony paths, and always uphill, up to the very summit of Mount Tiberio. Comforted by the knowledge that the dead old man from San Francisco, who had likewise been planning to go with them but instead of that had only frightened them with a reminder of death, had already been shipped off to Naples, the travellers slept on heavily, and the quiet of the island was still undisturbed, the shops in the town were still shut. The market place in the little square alone was carrying on traffic,—in fish and greens; and the people there were all simple folk, among whom, without anything to do, as always, was standing Lorenzo the boatman, famous all over Italy,—a tall old man, a carefree rake and a handsome fellow, who had served more than once as a model to many artists; he had brought, and had already sold for a trifle, two lobsters that he had caught that night and which were already rustling in the apron of the cook of that very hotel where the family from San Francisco had passed the night, and now he could afford to stand in calm idleness even until the evening, looking about him with a kingly bearing, consciously and flauntingly picturesque with his tatters, clay pipe, and a red woolen *beretta* drooping over one ear.

And, along the precipices of Monte Solaro, upon the ancient Phœnician road, hewn out of the crags, down its stone steps, two mountaineers of Abruzzi were descending from Anacapri. One had bagpipes under his leathern mantle,—a large bag made from the skin of a she-goat, with two pipes; the other had something in the nature of wooden Pan's-reeds. They went on, —and all the land, joyous, lovely, sun-swept, spread out below them: the stony humps of the island, which was lying almost in its entirety at their feet; and that fairylike deep-blue in which it was afloat; and the shining morning vapors over the sea, toward the east, under the blinding sun, that was now beating down hotly, rising ever higher and higher; and, still in their morning vagueness, the mistily blue massive outlines of Italy, of her mountains near and far, whose beauty human speech is impotent to express. . . . Half way down the pipers slackened their pace: over the path, within a grotto in the craggy side of Monte Solaro, all bright in the sun, all bathed in its warmth and glow, in snow white raiment of gypsum, and in a royal crown, golden-rusty from inclement weathers, stood the Mother of God, meek and gracious, her orbs lifted up to heaven, to the eternal and happy abodes of Her thrice-blessed Son. The pipers bared their heads, put their reeds to their lips,—and there poured forth their naïve and humbly jubilant praises to the sun, to the morning, to Her, the Immaculate Intercessor for all those who suffer in this evil and beautiful world, and to Him Who had been born of Her womb in a cavern at Bethlehem, in a poor shepherd's shelter in the distant land of Judæa. . . .

Meanwhile, the body of the dead old man from San Francisco was returning to its home, to a grave on the shores of the New World. Having gone through many humiliations, through much human neglect, having wandered for a week from one port warehouse to another, it had finally gotten once more on board that same famous ship upon which but lately, with so much deference, he had been borne to the Old World. But now he was already being concealed from the quick,—he was lowered in his tarred coffin deep into the black hold. And once more the ship was sailing on and on upon its long sea voyage. By night it sailed past the Island of Capri, and, to one watching them from the island, there was something sad about the ship's lights, slowly disappearing over the dark sea. But, upon the ship itself, in its brilliant *salons* resplendent with lustres and marble, there was, as usual, a crowded ball that night.

There was a ball on the second night, and also on the third,—again in the midst of a raging snow gale, whirling over an ocean booming like a burial mass, and rolling in mountains arrayed in mourning by the silvery foam. The innumerable fiery eyes of the ship were barely visible, because of the snow, to the Devil watching from the crags of Gibraltar, from the stony gateway of two worlds, the ship receding into the night and the snow gale. The Devil was as enormous as a cliff, but even more enormous was the ship, many-tiered, many-funnelled, created by the pride of the New Man with an ancient heart. The snow gale smote upon its rigging and wide-throated funnels, white from the snow, but the ship was steadfast, firm, majestic—and terrifying. Upon its topmost deck were reared, in their solitude among the snowy whirlwinds, those snug, dimly lighted chambers where, plunged in a light and uneasy slumber, was its ponderous guide who resembled a pagan idol, reigning over the whole ship. He heard the pained howlings and the ferocious squealings of the storm-stifled siren, but comforted himself by the proximity of that which, in the final summing up, was incomprehensible even to himself, that which was on the other side of his wall; that large cabin, which had the appearance of being armored, and was being constantly filled by the mysterious rumbling, quivering, and crisp sputtering of blue flames, flaring up and exploding around the pale-faced operator with a metal half hoop upon his head. In the very depths, in the submerged womb of the *Atlantis,* were the thirty thousand pound masses of boilers and of all sorts of other machinery—dully glittering with steel, hissing out steam and exuding oil and boiling water,—of that kitchen, made red hot from infernal furnaces underneath, wherein was brewing the motion of the ship. Forces, fearful in their concentration, were bubbling, were being transmitted to its very keel, into an endlessly long dungeon, into a tunnel, illuminated by electricity, wherein slowly, with an inexorableness that was crushing to the human soul, was revolving within its oily couch the gigantic shaft, exactly like a living monster that had stretched itself out in this tunnel.

Meanwhile, amidship the *Atlantis,* its warm and luxurious cabins, its dining halls and ballrooms, poured forth radiance and joyousness, were humming with the voices of a well-dressed gathering, were fragrant with fresh flowers, and the strains of the stringed orchestra were their song. And again excruciatingly coiled and at intervals feverishly came together among this throng, among this glitter of lights, silks, diamonds and bared feminine shoulders, the pliant pair of hired lovers: the sinfully modest, very pretty young woman, with eyelashes cast down, with a chaste coiffure, and the well-built young man, with black hair that seemed to be pasted on, with his face pale from powder, shod in the most elegant of patent leather footgear, clad in a tight fitting dress coat with long tails,—a handsome man who resembled a huge leech. And one knew that, already for a long time, this pair had grown weary of languishing dissemblingly in their blissful torment to the sounds of the shamelessly sad music,—nor that far, far below, at the bottom of the black hold, stood a tarred coffin, neighboring on the gloomy, sultry depths of the ship that was ponderously overcoming the darkness, the ocean, the gale. . . .

1915.

A free catalogue of VINTAGE BOOKS *will be sent at your request. Write to* Vintage Books, 457 Madison Avenue, New York, New York 10022.

VINTAGE HISTORY EUROPEAN

A free catalogue of VINTAGE BOOKS *will be sent at your request. Write to* Vintage Books, 457 Madison Avenue, New York, New York 10022.